Summer Heat

Also by Defne Suman

The Silence of Scheherazade
At the Breakfast Table

Summer Heat

Defne Suman

Translated by

Betsy Göksel

HEAD
of ZEUS

An Apollo Book

First published as *Yaz Sıcağı* in Turkey in 2017 by Doğan Kitap

First published in the UK in 2024 by Head of Zeus Ltd
This paperback edition first published in 2025 by Head of Zeus Ltd,
part of Bloomsbury Publishing Plc

9 7 5 3 1 2 4 6 8

A catalogue record for this book is available from the British Library.

ISBN (PB): 9781035902323
ISBN (eBook): 9781035902316

Cover design: Matt Bray | Head of Zeus

Printed and bound in Great Britain by
CPI Group (UK) Ltd, Croydon CR0 4YY

Bloomsbury Publishing Plc
50 Bedford Square, London, WC1B 3DP, UK
Bloomsbury Publishing Ireland Limited,
29 Earlsfort Terrace, Dublin 2, D02 AY28, Ireland

HEAD OF ZEUS LTD
5–8 Hardwick Street
London EC1R 4RG

To find out more about our authors and books
visit www.headofzeus.com
For product safety related questions contact productsafety@bloomsbury.com

In memory of my father... of course

PART ONE

1

Bloody Church

Petro and I met for the first time at the Bloody Church.

It was his idea. I thought it was a coincidence. I agreed immediately, excited by the location and the old memories it would evoke: many years earlier, my grandmother Safinaz had lived in a three-storey stone house directly across from the church. My father and I used to visit her every Saturday, and when I pulled back her curtains and peeped out, I could see its red dome. The entrance was almost impossible to locate, concealed within a high wall beneath a tangle of honeysuckle vines. The door was kept locked most of the time; you had to find Pavli, the caretaker, to open it.

But nothing about our meeting was coincidental.

It was a hot summer's evening, so hot that even the leaves were parched, their edges curled. Out on Buyukada Island, where I was staying for the summer, the pine forests were on fire, the flames racing across the dark green hills and turning them to desert in the space of an hour. It was stifling in the centre of Istanbul. I sweated my way up the slope to the Bloody Church, stopping to catch my breath under the fig trees of my childhood. In the years since I'd last been in that neighbourhood the trees had grown quite a bit, their thick, dry branches contorted into strange shapes as they reached for the sun along the walls, the steps and the tin roofs. I was annoyed with myself for having taken this job in the middle of summer, as if I were a penniless university student excited to be paid for showing a tourist around the city. What was I thinking, exchanging my cool, breezy house on Buyukada, where my husband would happily make me a glass of ice-cold mint lemonade, for this sweaty trip to the city in the heat?

Petro Paraskos, the man I was due to meet in front of the Bloody Church, was a documentary film producer. He wanted to explore some Byzantine churches for a new project he had in mind and had come across my name when searching online for an art historian to accompany him. Would I be his guide? It was a strange proposal; I should have been suspicious from the start. Even though I'd written my master's thesis on churches of the late Byzantium era, I wasn't a well-known art historian – I had no articles published in international journals – so it was odd that my name had even come up. Perhaps I should also have queried his tone throughout our correspondence – was it too insistent, too assertive, even pushy? For example, he'd guessed that it would be tiring for me to come into the city from Buyukada Island every day, so suggested booking a space for me in the hotel where he was staying. Time was short and his budget was generous enough to cover an extra room. This sort of arrangement had worked well on previous assignments, he said. If it was convenient for me, we could meet on July 19th at 7 p.m. in front of the Bloody Church.

Ah, Melike, you disregarded all the signs! You ignored the voice inside your head, which whispered that your meeting with this stranger would alter the course of your fate, and jumped on a ferry to the city for the possibility of some momentary pleasure.

A woman must nourish her soul, keep her spirit fresh with little adventures, right? One man is never enough. (Who had said that? Was it grandma Safinaz?). But that was not what I was thinking as I traipsed up to my grandma's old neighbourhood to meet Petro that evening. I wasn't going to cheat on Sinan ever again. I had made that decision. I was tired, worn out. It wasn't just the keeping of secrets, being clandestine about everything and planning my moves several steps ahead in these delicate games of chess. Even more exhausting was having to deal with the offended hurt of men who would, initially, declare that they had 'no expectations', only to persist in pursuing me once we'd slept together. Where such affairs were meant to be a liberation, an escape from daily life, they had instead become just another burden. I had neither the desire nor the energy for new loves. Also, love, I had realized, as with many other pleasures, lost its flavour with repetition; in the end, it was always the same. If I was looking for novelty, I needed to shift my attention inwards, closer to home. I would be turning forty in a month. In this new phase of my life, I would discover not how many conquests I could have, but how to enjoy fidelity.

So, just that morning, instead of slipping out of the house before Sinan woke up and hurrying to Uncle Niko's bakery, where I usually had my morning tea and pastry and played sudoku, I waited under the white mosquito netting for my husband to stir. Uncle Niko, who was familiar with my grumpy morning state, always set down my breakfast on my table beside the window without greeting me, then returned to his portable radio behind the till. Sinan, on the other hand, was very talkative in the morning. He woke up with a hundred worldly and otherworldly ideas, rattling them off like machinegun fire before he even lifted his head from the pillow. From now on, though, I was going to listen to my husband's brilliant early-morning schemes with patience and smiles.

Leaving him was the last thing on my mind.

As was finding my father.

At no stage in my life had I wanted to find my father. Not during the tearful nights of my childhood when I used to secretly mourn his absence, nor in my adolescence when I might momentarily catch his aftershave on the skin of a lover I was kissing on a rickety jetty over the dark waters of the Bosphorus. When I smelled that scent, a wave would swell inside me like a tide rising in the moonlight, but even that didn't make me want to track him down to learn why – and for what new life – he had abandoned us. Why would I feel that need now? Twenty-nine years had passed since then. That morning on Buyukada, listening to Sinan's breathing, my father was not among the thoughts passing through my mind. I had closed the Orhan Kutsi chapter of my life a long time ago.

The first thing I saw were Petro's lips. He was standing in front of the red church, shielding his eyes from the glare of the sun, trying to figure out if the person coming round the corner was me. His lips were a dark pink beneath the orange sky. Too dark, too pink for a man. The word '*palikari*' came into my head. How did I know that evocative Greek word for 'a young man in his prime', I wondered? Surely those lips, the colour of unplucked cherries, indicated that he was hot-blooded.

Recognizing me, he smiled. No, it wasn't a smile – he laughed. Sunlight glinted and then faded in his huge, honey-coloured eyes. When I held out my hand for him to shake, he drew me in and hugged me. We embraced like two friends who hadn't seen each other in years. He was a tall, broad-shouldered mountain of a man. My head barely came up to his chest. Why did I always expect men who were younger than me to be small? (Yes, when I'd looked for Petro's photo online, I'd also checked his date of birth.) Was it because I couldn't quite accept my own age?

When we came out of our hug, Petro put his hands on my shoulders and stared into my eyes. There was something searching about his gaze. My heart raced.

'Shall we start right away? I have tons of things to ask you.'

His tone was hurried, but he spoke in a crisp British accent. What a surprise! During our email exchange I'd given him a voice with a Greek accent (a man with a name like Petro Paraskos had to be of Greek origin, surely!), emphasizing the 'h's and struggling with the 'sh's and 'ch's.

Luckily for us, the door into the church complex was open. This surprised me. The old caretaker Pavli would never in his life have left it unlocked. The honeysuckle vine that used to obscure the entrance was long gone as well. Petro and I filed into the neglected courtyard. Cool air licked our faces, as if the sun that had scorched every living thing beyond the walls hadn't visited the place all summer long. There was an old tricycle lying in a shadowy corner, beside a dry well with a moss-encrusted lid. Mosquitoes perched on a sagging, discoloured washing line which had been strung across the yard.

Petro didn't waste time on the courtyard, but pushed open

the glass-panelled door and went into the church. I followed him. Light from the chandelier spread a strange glow across the red carpet. Thin swirls of incense smoke rose from the iconostasis; two tall yellow candles were burning in front of the altar. Since services were no longer held here, I wondered who had lit the lamp, the candles, the incense, and for what reason. Petro approached the altar table. Pressing the tips of the first three fingers of his right hand together, he made the sign of the cross, then bent forward and kissed the picture of the Virgin Mary on the gilded white cloth.

We stood side by side on the faded red carpet under the companionable gaze of the saints. He leant towards me and whispered, 'I want to know everything...'

I lifted my head and looked at him. In contrast to his huge body and strong chin, his face was like that of a curious child. When he smiled, he revealed an orderly row of white teeth.

'... about the church, of course.' A mischievous gleam shone in his eyes.

Suddenly I felt like a student who'd not done her homework, for I really had not prepared for this tour. It had been more than ten years since I'd defended my master's thesis, and I found myself scrambling for any knowledge to share with Petro. I could easily talk about the symbols which adorned the edges of the silver icons on the walls, the reasons for the specific order in which the pictures of the saints had been organized, the mystical geometry of particular architectural features that only religious scholars could interpret. But I couldn't remember what was unique about the Bloody Church. I knew that it had been founded by the illegitimate daughter of a Byzantine emperor who came to be known as St Mary of the Mongols – hence the church's official name. She had been sent to Persia to marry the Mongol ruler Hulagu

Khan, but Hulagu had died before she even got there, so she'd married his stepson. When he also died, she returned to Constantinople and withdrew into a life of solitude, turning the church into a nunnery. From then on she was known as Panagia Mouchliotissa, St Mary of the Mongols.

I knew too that the church had great significance for Istanbul's Orthodox community. During the Ottoman conquest of Constantinople in 1453, hundreds of women and children took refuge within its walls, only to be slaughtered there by Ottoman soldiers. Sultan Mehmet II was so incensed by his own men having done this that he issued an edict declaring that thenceforth St Mary of the Mongols must remain a Christian church for eternity and should never be converted into a mosque. It was the only Byzantine church to be so designated. The name 'Bloody Church' refers to that massacre, and Mehmet's edict still hangs on its wall.

But these were basic facts that any Christian interested in spiritual matters would know. Petro could have gleaned as much from an encyclopaedia. He must have been expecting more from me. I hurriedly tried to remember something more original, but my mind had gone blank.

The pendulum clock behind the altar struck seven. All at once I felt dizzy, from the heat or the incense. I stepped away from Petro and sank into one of the dusty wooden pews lining the side walls. There must have been clocks in other corners of the church that we couldn't see, for the chiming in my brain wouldn't stop. They reminded me of my grandma Safinaz's beloved clocks, which had behaved just like this, striking the hour all together in chorus. I undid my hairclip and released my uncontrollable hair; it fell across my face, hiding me behind a curly black curtain.

Petro made his way over quietly and sat down beside

me. Rather than telling him about the church, should I tell him about the clocks in my grandma's house? Should I say, 'Petro, there were clocks everywhere in her house. I'm not exaggerating. On every floor of that stone house – in the living room, the hall, the kitchen, the pantry. There was even one hanging on the wall of the forgotten back garden, in the shade of some dried-up old fig trees. And, would you believe it, every single one of them – even the one in the backyard – worked perfectly, striking the top of the hour with only a few seconds' difference, if that, and causing all three storeys of the house to shake.'

Don't be ridiculous, Melike! Why would the man care about the clocks in your crazy grandma's house? Focus. Concentrate on the church. There's an important mosaic on the eastern side. Point that out now. Be professional. There's another mosaic depicting Mary of the Mongols asking Jesus for mercy in the name of humanity. That's not here. Where is it? Think, Melike, think. You're here in the city to do a job, don't forget that.

I sat up straight, tossed my hair behind me. I felt Petro's eyes on me, a sensation that gave me both pleasure and discomfort. Why did it feel as if I'd known this man for a long time? Did he look familiar? The closeness I'd felt when, instead of shaking my hand, he'd pulled me to him and hugged me, and I'd rested my head on his vast chest, was a different feeling from the excitement I got when embracing a strange man for the first time.

Mary of the Mongols was looking at us from within a gold-plated frame on the opposite wall. Keeping my eyes fixed on her mournful gaze, I spoke.

'Rumour has it that there were passageways under this church that opened out into tunnels. When I say tunnels, I mean labyrinths that went all the way to Hagia Sofia, and even beyond, to the sea. Should Istanbul have been blockaded, people could have escaped from here.'

Petro turned towards me, his eyes lingering shamelessly on my face. His stare made me uneasy. 'How do you know that?'

Quite so. Where had all that come from? With so much factual detail about the church to explain, why had I begun my tour-guide duties with a rumour? And why were we whispering? There was no one in the church except us. Or was there? What about the tricycle I'd seen in the garden, the mossy well lid and the dirty washing line? And Pavli the caretaker, popping into my head suddenly after so many years. Where had all these memories – the clocks, Safinaz – come from? They were like ghosts risen from the dead.

I leant my head against the wall behind me and murmured, 'I came to this church a very long time ago. The caretaker told me then.'

Petro nodded. He didn't ask any more questions. I closed my eyes. We sat there silently on the wooden pew in the cool of the church for a long time, like monks deep in meditation.

2

Red Square

It was dusk on a snowy, gloomy March day. Safinaz and I had walked into the Bloody Church hand in hand. I was eight years old.

We lit a candle each and then Safinaz sat down in one of the back rows and closed her eyes. As I wandered off among the icons, Pavli told me about the tunnels that began in the crypt and extended all the way to the sea. He whispered in my ear that my grandmother was a woman with magical powers.

As it turned out, that would be the last evening I'd spend with my grandma. But I didn't know that then.

Except maybe for the snow, that Saturday was just an ordinary Saturday. We'd got home from school at noon and my mother, my brother Cem, my father and I had eaten lunch in the brightly lit kitchen of our apartment in Galata. Then Mum took Cem to her parents' apartment in Harbiye and Dad and I set off on foot for Safinaz's house, where I would stay the night. This had been the Saturday routine for as long as I could remember. School until midday, then the boy to the maternal grandmother and the girl to the paternal grandmother for the night, leaving Mum and Dad to go out to bars and restaurants with their childless friends.

It was really cold. With my icy fingers in Dad's palm and clouds of steam coming out of our mouths, we walked along our neatly cobbled street to the little square with the famous Galata Tower, and from there down to the shore on the marble steps that were squished between some old buildings. When we climbed into one of the rowing boats that glided calmly back and forth across the steely waters of the Golden Horn, I slid my gloveless hands into the pocket of Dad's overcoat.

The opposite shore, where the elderly, grey-eyed boatman was taking us, always seemed to me like another world, a magical country where foreign languages echoed on the streets. As soon as we landed, I felt as if I was in a different time, as if I had stepped through a gauze curtain. Dad's hand, reaching out for mine, was playful, and there was a smile on his face that even his moustache couldn't mask. He was always like this on Saturdays when we went to visit his mother.

Hand in hand, we walked to the marketplace. As we passed the coffeehouse, the uncles playing backgammon knocked on the steamed-up window – tik, tik.

'Hey, Orhan, where've you been, boy?'

'Leave the *koritsaki* and come and play a game of *tavli*.'

I knew those old men. Whenever Safinaz and I went down to the market together, they would tip their hats to her in silent greeting. My grandma had been an art teacher at the school at the top of the hill. She taught in both the girls' and the boys' schools and was highly respected in the neighbourhood. Some of the old men would come out of the coffeehouse to chat with her when she passed. With their hats in their hands, they'd stand there, full of troubles. They'd look at me with sad faces and sigh.

When they said '*koritsaki*' – 'little girl' in Greek – they meant me. They were always happy to see Dad though. That day, the pastry-baker Uncle Ilias came to the door with a tray in his hand and tried to invite us inside.

'Ooh, Orhan, my boy. Welcome! You have brought joy. Little lady, you want biscotto? If your *baba sou* permits, there is lemonade. But it's cold. There is cake just out of the oven – let me bring you a plateful.'

Dad was in a hurry that day. He muttered something to Uncle Ilias and pushed me on towards the steep flight of steps. The old women sitting out in front of their houses in spite of the cold mumbled some things from their toothless mouths that I couldn't understand. The dresses hanging on washing lines strung between the narrow, bay-windowed houses were all old, all black. I wanted to ask Dad why, but he was walking so fast, I got all out of breath on the steps, trying to keep up with his long strides. The cold air was stinging my cheeks like a whip and the smell of burning coal caught in my throat. Suddenly I realized why he was rushing. He wanted to hurry up and hand me over to his mother so he could get back to Galata as soon as possible. My heart tightened. Why wouldn't he stay with us? I knew he wasn't going out with my mother that night – I'd heard them say so.

As soon as I saw her – my grandma with magical powers – at the top of the hill, I forgot all of my worries. Safinaz was waiting for us beside the school wall, wearing her grey coat with the fur collar. She was wearing her old-fashioned hat, the one that was soft like a swimming cap and the colour of milk chocolate, with flowers embroidered on the sides. She was like a statue from another era – tall and slender, with pure white skin. Safinaz Kutsi, this enchanting grandmother of mine.

Dad was annoyed. I could tell from the way he was breathing. White steam came out of his mouth as he spoke.

'You shouldn't have come out in this weather, Mother. You'll catch cold. How long have you been waiting for us?'

Safinaz didn't answer. She never talked unnecessarily.

Dad leant down, kissed my cheeks and whispered, 'Your grandmother is in your care now, Melike, my angel. Keep an eye on her and don't let her do anything silly.'

Black clouds descended over the rooftops. All of a sudden it had become really dark.

'Mother, the child's cheeks are ice cold. Go straight home. Come on, let me kiss you too. I'm worried about you, all alone in that house with nothing but a woodstove. Have you thought any more about moving to an apartment? They're building some in Gayrettepe – modern, brand-new, with central heating. Madam Piraye's friends from high school have all bought flats there. You could live above each other, all together.'

Safinaz raised her thin eyebrows but said nothing. Knowing how stubborn she was, Dad laughed, his teeth strikingly white under his black moustache. I laughed too, then ran and hid my hands in Safinaz's black leather gloves so that Dad wouldn't realize how cold I was. They were so soft.

From the top of the hill, the city below us was disappearing behind a veil of mist. Soon, our hill would be all that remained of the world, and we would be stuck like the animals on Noah's Ark atop Mount Ararat in that little square. When I say 'square', I mean the little area made up of the Greek High School for Girls, the glass frontage of an abandoned building, and the Bloody Church. I called it the Red Square. Right behind the church, the Greek Orthodox College for Boys rose like a chateau. That was red too.

Red Square belonged to another era. It wasn't just Safinaz's house, beating like a pulse with the ticking of all those clocks; her whole neighbourhood was magical.

I turned and looked at the stone steps that ran all the way down the side of the girls' school. The steps were disappearing from the earth, one by one. In fear, I shouted, 'Daddy, don't go!'

'I have to go, my beautiful daughter. You go on into the house with your grandmother. Off you go! Light the stove, roast some chestnuts, play with Mavri.'

He stood at the top of the stairs, shoved his hands into the pockets of his navy blue corduroy overcoat, and prepared to head down them. My eyes filled with tears. Safinaz would never roast chestnuts! And Mavri was a bad-tempered cat who never left the windowsill by the sewing basket. If Dad went down those steps, the mist would eat him up. I stamped my foot on the ground, even though I knew my father didn't like me doing that. He frowned.

'Mother, come on, please. Look, can't you see what's happening?'

I tried to swallow my tears. My nose was running. My voice was shaking. 'What work do you have, Dad? Are you going to play *tavli* in the marketplace?'

'No, Melike, my angel. I have business this evening. And the word for backgammon is *tavla*, not *tavli*.'

'Stay here with us!'

Mum and Dad were not getting together with their friends that evening. I'd heard Mum talking to her mother about it on the phone at midday when we got home from school.

'Orhan will leave Melike with his mum. Cem and I will come to you, Mother, and I'll stay over.'

Since Mum was staying with my brother, why couldn't Dad stay with us?

'What's the matter, Melike, darling? You're always so excited to come to your grandmother's. You even packed your bag all by yourself as soon as you got home from school.'

Dad didn't stoop down, just bent over to look at my face. I swallowed. The teardrops on my eyelashes were cold.

'The child is right, Orhan. Stay with us tonight, son. It's not safe out there.'

I raised my head and studied my grandma with interest. A wrinkle had formed between her thin eyebrows. Her behatted head was perched on her tall frame like a precious vase. Dad was raking his fingers through his curly hair, like he did when he was upset. He had come out without his beret, even though it was he who was always telling us how important it was to cover our heads to avoid catching cold; he said a person's body heat mostly escaped from their ears, which was why all through the winter he sent us off to school in hats with earflaps.

'Don't you start, Mother. The boatmen will have stopped work for the day by now and I'll have to run to make the bus as it is.'

Two snowflakes fell on his head, becoming stars, then melted into his black curls. I forgot my troubles. I withdrew my red hands from Safinaz's gloves, where I'd been hiding them from Dad, and raised them in the air.

'It's snowing! Grandma, Dad, it's snowing! Look!'

They stopped talking and turned to me.

I giggled. 'Will they close the schools on Monday?'

'If it settles, they will.'

'Let it settle, God, please. Let it settle, I beg you, God!'

'Where does this child learn such expressions, sending up prayers to God and all? I don't understand it, when no one mentions religion in our house.'

I immediately stopped talking, took two steps back and leant against the wall of the school.

Safinaz raised her sharp chin. Narrow blue veins were showing beneath the translucent skin of her neck where it protruded from the fur collar of her coat. Snowflakes were sticking to the tufts of short hair escaping from her cap.

'Look at me, Orhan. You need to be careful at the moment, do you hear me?'

'It's okay, Mother. Don't worry.'

'Listen to me. You're mixed up in something. Where is your wife tonight?'

'Mother, we're all freezing here, I swear. If you're not bothered for my sake, at least think about Melike.'

'Melike is a healthy child. A couple of snowflakes won't hurt her. You look at me. What's this business about? Where is Gulbahar tonight?'

I was catching snowflakes with my tongue in front of the school wall so that they would think I wasn't listening to them. The mist had blanked out not only the city but also its sounds. The only noise I could hear was the guk-guk-guk of the red-beaked rooster in the garden of the old pink mansion, where the chickens had taken refuge from the snow in the coop. When Safinaz asked one more time, I couldn't stop myself, and called out from the edge of the wall. 'Mum is staying with Grandmother Piraye and Grandfather tonight at their house in Harbiye. She and Cem are both staying there.'

When Safinaz raised her left eyebrow, my confidence dissolved. Dad looked angry. I was a bad girl. My eyes filled with tears again. I shouldn't have said anything. I wished I'd gone with Cem to Grandmother Piraye's house. Right now they'd be sitting around the table in that huge, bright apartment, eating crispy roast chicken and rice, and drinking apple cider. And we were here, about to be eaten up by the mist. Should I ask Dad to take me to Harbiye? No, I couldn't. It would break Safinaz's heart. Cem was Grandmother Piraye's grandchild; I was Safinaz's. That's how it had been ever since we were little. Helplessness filled my lungs like smoke. I choked back my sobs with difficulty.

Dad turned around abruptly. 'Goodbye, you two. I'll come and get Melike tomorrow afternoon. If you need anything, call me and I'll bring it over. I didn't have that phone installed in your house for nothing.'

He pivoted round again before we had time to answer, and with his hands in his pockets he hurried down the steps. The mist gobbled him up at the end of the school wall. Dad vanishing like that opened a huge void in my stomach. Safinaz took my hand and we turned and walked to the middle of the little patch of Red Square which the mist had left to us. Snowflakes were hitting my face, getting into my eyes, sticking to my eyelashes. The void in my stomach hurt, so I tried to distract myself with daydreams. If the schools were closed on Monday, maybe Cem and I could come back here again and slide down the steep hill with bits of cardboard under our bottoms.

Everywhere was so empty, so silent, that the crunch of Safinaz's boots as she walked echoed off the walls of the old houses. Even the cats were hiding somewhere, and the birds had gone quiet. The cobblestones under our feet – rough and uneven but still lovely – shone as if polished. When a boy of about my age disappeared from behind his window, I believed for a moment that nobody was left in the world but Safinaz and me. The world was like my glass globe that snowed when you shook it. A world made up of one little square. And at its centre, the two of us: Safinaz and Melike Kutsi.

Safinaz stopped at the door of the Bloody Church. All by itself, a hidden door opened in the vine-covered wall. Hand in hand, we walked into a universe that smelled of incense.

The void inside me was filled by flickering candle flames.

3

A Slip of the Tongue

As we left the church, Petro said, 'Come on, take me to your favourite restaurant. Not one of those touristy places – a neighbourhood restaurant that only you know about.'

The sun had set a long time ago, but the air hadn't cooled at all. The cobblestones that had soaked up the sun all day were now releasing their heat beneath our feet. We wandered into the winding streets surrounding the church, myself in front, Petro following. When Petro saw the Red School, he stopped, clearly excited.

'Hey, that's the Greek Orthodox College, isn't it? The famous "Great School of the Nation" – the Patriarchal Academy of Constantinople? Wow. It really is "great" – extraordinary. Is it still open? Does it still have students?'

I nodded. He whistled as he gazed up at the building's intricately decorated towers.

'Amazing! Look at that detail, all that magnificence. The architect obviously couldn't resist decorating the school like a birthday cake.'

'Yes. At the time this school was built, foreign schools were popping up like mushrooms on the other side of the Golden

Horn, in Pera. Wanting to prove the superiority of Hellenistic education, the Patriarch—'

'Come on, let's go inside!' he said, cutting me off in midsentence.

I opened and shut my mouth, not knowing what to say.

'Okay, Melike? Shall we go in?'

'I thought you were hungry.'

I was annoyed at being interrupted, but looking into his eyes, I couldn't help smiling. This Petro was just a child; a honey-eyed child with long lashes.

'Come on, Melike. *Ela, ela.* Come on.'

My hand, my little hand that Sinan loved to kiss, that Sinan called his henna-coloured dove, reached out all on its own and slipped into Petro's palm. We circled the high walls of the school, searching for a way in. His skin was as soft as dough and slightly damp. This was a hand that had never done any manual work, had never held a hammer or a screwdriver nor even carried a suitcase. Did it know how to make love?

'Look over here, Melike. Do you see what I see?'

At first I couldn't make out what he was pointing at. The street was in shadow by then. He let go of my hand and with two strides of his long legs was at the wall. Then I saw it. A ladder was leaning against the streetlight.

'What do you say?' Petro yelled joyously. 'God is on our side, right? What is this ladder if not a blessing from St Mary of the Mongols?'

Twenty years earlier, when some friends and I had been refused entry into one of the first nightclubs that had opened on the Bosphorus because we were underage, we'd climbed over the wall of the next-door parking lot and jumped down three metres to so we could enter the forbidden, perfume-scented world. I was wearing a cotton miniskirt. By the end of it my knees were bloody, my hair all messed up – the look I'd spent hours creating destroyed in an instant.

Staring down at the Red School's courtyard from the top of the wall, I had the same mix of fear and excitement as I'd felt all those years ago. But I didn't have to jump three metres this time. Mountain-man Petro was waiting for me at the bottom. Taking a deep breath, I let myself go. Whatever would be would be.

But Petro was not there. Without even checking to see if I'd landed safely, he'd wandered over to the basketball court in the middle of the schoolyard. I looked at him in surprise – I wasn't used to men leaving me high and dry. A flock of seagulls tore across the darkening sky above us. In the distance a dog was barking intermittently. I walked into the middle of the schoolyard feeling like I was inside my old snow globe. Petro was leaning against the basketball fence, lighting a cigarette.

'Want one?' I looked at the rollup he was proffering. 'There's no tobacco in it. It's pure weed.'

Okay, that's enough, Petro. You said, 'Let's break into the school,' and I said, 'Sure,' so you wouldn't think I was a grumpy middle-aged woman. I jumped off the wall like a seventeen-year-old girl. But I am not going to smoke marijuana on the school grounds. Besides, where do you think we are? Do you think this is Amsterdam, where you can just take some weed out of your pocket, roll a joint and light up in public?

He held the joint to my lips between his two fingers. Well, okay, one little puff. I was entitled to a little bit of relaxation too. I took a long, slow drag. The red glow at the end of the joint came to life, danced. I took another big drag before giving it back. Petro laughed. My chest expanded, my stomach contracted, to make way for the sweet green smoke.

Exhaling, I sat down on the ground, not caring about my light blue dress. The day's heat transferred gently from the concrete into my skin. Petro was standing up. I'm not sure how long we stayed there, silent. Five minutes? Half an hour? The weed was already doing its stuff, playing havoc with my sense of time. Sometime later I realized Petro was sitting on the ground beside me.

'My great-uncle went to this school, you know.'

'What do you mean? Is your family from Istanbul?' My voice sounded strange.

'No. Only my great-uncle was sent here. He was a boarder.'

My head was spinning pleasantly. It was a very strong joint that Petro had rolled, not like the weed in Sinan's stash.

One more puff?

Then another one.

'Why did they send only him?'

'Who?'

Really, who were we talking about? Clearly both of us had forgotten. We began to laugh. His uncle! We were talking about his maternal uncle. We said '*dayi*' in Turkish. Or maybe he was talking about his paternal uncle, in which case he would have been an '*amca*'. English was quite ridiculous, not distinguishing between the two. Though I didn't have either a *dayi* or an *amca*, so how could I comment?

'Was this uncle your grandmother's brother or your grandfather's?'

'Ha! We're talking about my Uncle Thanasis. My great-grandmother's brother. My mother's great-uncle, actually.'

'Oh, I see. Your *dayi*.'

'No he's not a *dayi* at all. He is – I mean he *was* – a gentleman. That's what I was told, anyway. Not a bully at all. No, not a *dayi*.'

'Oh no, I didn't mean that. I guess the same word in Turkish means something else in Greek. Lost in translation!'

I began to laugh. Petro joined in. I raised my head and looked up at the stars in the moonless sky. It was a brilliant summer's evening. There were the Pleiades, that cluster of tiny stars right above us. The seven sisters whose faces were covered with blue veils. What were their names? They were deities, very beautiful. One was called Elektra. And the others? One night, many years ago, Dad had taught us what they were all called, but now their names escaped me.

'He was the only boy, that's why. The girls stayed in the village. This uncle was quite brilliant. His primary school teachers persuaded my great-great-grandfather to send him. They got him a scholarship too.'

What? Who? Oh, the uncle. Uncle Thanasis. Where were his people from? He must have told me. I knew he lived in Athens now, but where was this village he was talking about? Were they one of the families who'd migrated to mainland Greece from Asia Minor? I would check his emails when I got back to the island. We'd written to each other extensively, but I obviously hadn't paid attention. Shame on me! I got serious and resumed my role.

'When was this? The date, I mean.'

'During the war, I think. Or right after. When Istanbul was in the hands of the English.'

'The period of occupation. *Mutareke yillari.*'

'What?'

I had spoken in Turkish without realizing it.

'I said, "during the occupation years". That's what we call the period between the First World War and the founding of the Turkish Republic.'

'Say something else.'

'What?'

'Speak in Turkish a little.'

'Where did you learn to boss women around like that?' I said in Turkish.

He smiled as if I'd been reciting poetry. He took a tiny drag of the last of his joint, realized there was nothing left but the cardboard filter, and stubbed it out on the cement.

'More! More Turkish.'

'Surely you're not going to leave that butt in the schoolyard?' I said in Turkish.

'Yeah, yeah,' he said, as if he understood. A warm jolt of electricity passed between his leg and mine.

'Come on, let me show you inside, Petro.'

As if he'd been waiting for this invitation, he jumped to his feet and held out his hand to help me up.

'Let's go!'

It was sweet of him not to query how I intended to show him. If it had been Sinan, there would have been a hundred questions. Sinan always needed to look at something from every angle before making a decision. To tell the truth, I had only just come up with the idea of going into the school. Was there a chance that the secret entrance that led down to the coal cellar, which Caretaker Pavli had shown me thirty years ago, would still be there, forgotten, under weeds?

'Whenever our people construct a building,' Pavli had said, 'the first thing they do, my child, before anything else, is find a hiding place, an escape hatch. Every school, every building, has a secret exit. Come. *Ela.* I will show you, but don't tell anyone. Should the need arise, you hide here. *Endaksi?* Okay?'

I led Petro around the basketball court to the front garden. I recognized the corner where the secret entrance was located when the nettles started to sting my legs. Pushing aside the weeds, I uncovered the lid. Petro got out his lighter and held out the flame. There it was! Rusty, dusty and black, insofar as I could see it in the trembling light, but there it was, with the padlock that years ago Pavli had shown me how to open and close. Okay, but what about the key? Was it in the tin box behind the fountain? I straightened up excitedly, causing us to bump into each other. Unsure, wary, we drew apart quickly.

'There should be a fountain over there. The key may be in a box behind it.' Where was that fountain?

I hurried off into the darkness. In the place where the fountain used to be, there now stood a cylindrical metal water tank and a small cabin, newly constructed. Nothing else. While I was looking around, I heard a noise from where Petro was standing and, following that, laughter.

'*Ela vre*, Melike, *pame*! Come on, let's go.'

With a single touch, Petro had opened the old padlock that had endured years of rain, sun and dirt. We followed each other down the narrow steps, Petro illuminating the route with his lighter. Once we were in the coal cellar, I would know the way. Pavli used to take me around the classrooms while my grandma was teaching the boys there; he showed me all the hidden entrances and exits of the school.

I led us along dark, humid corridors that smelled of mould and up to the main floor. I wanted to show Petro the physics laboratory in the tower, with its astronomical instruments from the nineteenth century; pictures of astral bodies and oil paintings depicting the phases of the moon. There was even a scale model of the solar system; when you plugged it in, the planets orbited the sun. And there was a prism that refracted light to produce the seven colours of the rainbow. Grabbing Petro's hand, I pulled him towards the wide marble steps whose treads were worn from years of ups and downs. He didn't come. He had stopped in the spacious main hall and was staring at the multicoloured stained glass lit by the dim light of a streetlamp.

'Petro, come on. I want to take you up to—'

He reached out and held on to my shoulder. I was struck by the strength of his grip. In the darkness, only the whites of his eyes were visible.

'Take me to your favourite restaurant.'

'What? But...'

But we'd made such an effort to get into the school! Okay, I could pass on the miraculous solar system, the wonder of my childhood, but didn't he want to see the dormitory where his great-uncle had slept, the high-ceilinged classrooms where my grandma gave her lessons, the names which had a century ago been chiselled into desks, the sad-eyed alumni in the black-and-white photos in the corridors? Didn't he want to take in the souls of the books in the south tower library, the ones that had absorbed a century's worth of dust?

'Right now, I swear, I'm as hungry as a wolf. I can't think about anything else. That's how I get when I smoke pot. My blood sugar level falls and I get "the munchies", as they say.'

I sighed. 'You're the boss.'

He took my hand. 'You know, you're really sexy when you speak Turkish. Say something else.'

I opened my mouth to say, 'You're stoned now, so leave it,' but by a slip of the tongue, I said instead, in Turkish, 'You're just like my father, Petro.'

'Ha, ha.' He laughed, as if he'd understood what I'd said.

1

Pasha's Cadillac

That snowy March night when I stayed at my grandma's house for the last time, Pasha came to visit Safinaz. Although I only saw him that once, that last night, Pasha permeated every day and night of my childhood like a ghost whose story was whispered from ear to ear. I didn't know his real name. He was always just 'Pasha' in my family, which means 'Admiral' in old Turkish. I didn't know where his Pasha-ness originated, or how he had come into Safinaz's life. I never asked. In our family certain things were not discussed, remained unvoiced. He was simply 'Pasha'; Safinaz's special friend, 'Pasha'. That was it.

Late that night he knocked at our door.

Safinaz and I were both in the big room on the first floor. I was stretched out on the bird-patterned Milas rug and Safinaz was sitting in the beige wingback chair beside the window, knitting. Mavri had settled on the arm of the chair like a sphinx, watching my grandma's hands flash back and forth with the needles. Safinaz's fingers counted the knots and looped the yarn, producing orderly row after orderly row on one needle and then the other. As the ball of wool in the basket on the floor got smaller, so the knitted wool hanging off the needles expanded. The arms of my new sweater were materializing out of nothing.

The bright ceiling light above the table where we ate our meals had been turned off, leaving only the table lamp by the wingback chair to illuminate the room. The radio was tuned to a Turkish classical music programme, a station we never listened to at home. The ticking of the clocks harmonizing with the violin music had put me in a melancholy mood. Everything about Safinaz and her home belonged to another era – the music, her possessions, even the finger waves of her hairstyle. On a different day, the musty smells would have bewitched me, sent chills down my spine, but that night I was bored. Cem would be watching television with my other grandparents now. I was jealous. I was also angry with my dad. I was feeling terribly sorry for myself.

I opened the door of the stove and stirred the fire with the poker, releasing a pungent smell of wood smoke mingled with rose oil. According to my grandma, rose oil was as precious as gold; the oil she used was extracted by hand from Isparta roses. Still holding her knitting needles, Safinaz closed her eyes and breathed in the scent wafting from the stove.

'They send this oil to Paris, you know, Melike. A former student of mine got into the rose-oil business and sends me two bottles every year. Come, let me rub a little on your wrist. Not much, one drop is enough. I pour just one drop onto the firewood – see what a delicious scent it gives off? In ancient Egypt, do you know what they placed beside their pharaohs when they buried them? Not gold, not diamonds, but pure rose oil. Why? Because you can only find the way to heaven by following the scent of rose oil.'

Reluctantly, I held out my arm. Safinaz rubbed a drop

from the glass bottle on the windowsill onto the inside of my wrist. Tomorrow, Mum would catch a whiff of that single drop and make a fuss. You smell like the Mosque, Melike darling, she'd say. Why can't your grandmother just keep the rose oil for herself! Orhan, someone's given your mother that oil again.

'The snow is definitely settling,' Safinaz said, gesturing at the dark night with her long, narrow chin.

Lifting my head from the rug, I looked out of the window. Thick white flakes were twirling through the air, falling into the garden and getting caught on the leaves. The fig tree was already covered with a thin layer.

'Ugur! Ugur will freeze, Grandma!'

'Tortoises don't freeze, my girl. Don't worry. He's asleep now. A tortoise's blood runs so slowly that the cold doesn't bother them. And anyway, the door of his house is closed and the floor is covered with cardboard.'

'Let's bring him inside, Grandma, and have him sleep in our house – in my room, beside my bed, by the stove.'

'Impossible, my child. If he comes into the heat, he'll wake up and then he'll be all out of kilter.'

'How do you know that?'

'I know, Melike, dear. How many years have I had Ugur?'

'How many?'

I stretched out on my stomach on the rug to hear the story I knew so well, crossing my legs in their red woolly tights in the air. The fire in the stove warmed my cheeks.

'I don't remember the year now, but when I found him he was just this big,' she said, holding up her index finger with the wool wrapped around it to show Ugur's size back then. 'He was walking beside the railway track. So tiny. I went to the restaurant at the train station and asked for a matchbox.

Then I knelt down beside the rails and picked him up. I put him in the matchbox and carried him, hidden in my bosom, all the way to Istanbul.'

I giggled. 'In the matchbox?'

'Yes, in the matchbox. I was travelling in a women's compartment and I kept worrying that your father's head would hit my chest and smash the little creature. Your father was a baby then. As the train rattled along, he just slept and slept.'

Curious, I sat up cross-legged on the rug. In all the times Safinaz had told me the story of finding Ugur, she'd never mentioned my father.

'Dad? Dad was on the train too?'

Safinaz didn't reply.

'Grandma? Where were you coming from? Why were you on a train?'

'Come over here and let me measure this sleeve. I wonder how much longer I need to make it.'

Mavri was watching me with suspicious eyes. When I reached out my arm to Safinaz, she hissed, exposing the black mark in the middle of her pink palate.

'Where was that station with a restaurant? Did you get on the train all by yourself? Was Aunt Zeyno there too?'

'Oof, my girl, have your arms got longer? I started the cuff of the other sleeve right here, but now it's too short. I suppose I'll have to unravel it. You're growing up so fast, my child.'

I was so ashamed of growing fast that I forgot what I'd been saying. Safinaz took the other sleeve from the basket at her feet and started unravelling it, muttering all the while. I felt bad for giving her extra work.

Mavri hissed again.

'That cat has been in a bad mood ever since Irini left,'

Safinaz murmured, her eyes still on her needles. 'Animals don't forget. They miss people more than we do. That's why she's so grumpy. Forgive her.'

Safinaz, who never apologized to anyone, was now making excuses for her cat's crotchety mood.

'When Mavri lived next door, you should have seen how gentle she was. She would wind around your legs to get you to pet her, nuzzle her head into your palm... Ah, dear Irini. When she left, she said, "Take good care of Mavri and water the geraniums. Let's get everything sorted out and then, God willing, I'll come back for them." And where is she? She still hasn't come back. How far can a person go with only one suitcase? Permission will be granted, she said, and we'll come back. But things are still tense. Even the cat yearns for her. What can we do? She'll come back, my Mavri; your mama will come. There's no way they'll take her house from her, my child; that house is legally hers. I tell you, they left carrying only one suitcase, so how can they not return? Alas, March has come around again. Add it up. How many years is that? It was the winter of '64.'

I hurriedly did the sums. It was 1971 now, which meant...

'Seven. It's been seven years.'

I expected my grandma to praise me for doing the difficult calculation so quickly. Dad said I had an aptitude for maths. When I grew up, I was going to study astronomy and discover stars. But it didn't seem like Safinaz was impressed with my mental arithmetic. Instead, she seemed withdrawn all of a sudden. She released the knitting into her lap and stared out at the snowflakes falling onto the fig leaves. I redid the calculation in my head. Yes, the answer was seven. I hadn't got it wrong.

I lay back down on the rug and gazed up at the high ceiling, which had been decorated to look like lace. Irini had been my grandma's neighbour. When I was still a baby, she was sent away to a distant place. Since then her house had stood empty. The furniture was still there, but its owner was not. Sometimes Safinaz and I would go to Irini's house together. It was right next door. The sofas and armchairs were covered with white sheets, like in Safinaz's living room. When you walked across the wooden floor, the glass-panelled sideboard shook and the crystal glassware inside rattled, which scared me to death. I didn't like Irini's house. It was because of that house that Dad and Aunt Zeyno got so angry with each other. My aunt had wanted to sell the house, but Dad wouldn't let her. They'd had a big argument on New Year's Eve and my aunt had upped and left without seeing the belly dancers on television or even eating any turkey.

Safinaz dropped the knitting needles into the basket and lit one of her skinny clove-flavoured cigarettes.

'Grandma, there's somebody in my head that talks. Talks nonstop. Is there somebody in your head too?'

'Of course, my child. That's your inner voice.'

'Does it ever stop talking?'

'Why do you want it to stop?'

'Sometimes I get so tired of hearing it.'

The voice made me sad too, but I couldn't tell her that. When I'd played dress-up, wrapping myself in a length of gauzy tulle and trying on the gold-striped shoes I'd found in the walnut trunk upstairs, I'd stared into the mirror up there and the voice had said, 'Look at yourself! You're not exactly Cinderella, are you? Cinderella is tall and slim and elegant, like your mum, but you are chubby and as dark as a gypsy. Just as those friends of your parents who are always in the house say, your father must have got you from the gypsies.

'Children who hear their inner voice are sensitive and artistic. They have gentle souls.'

'But—'

There was a sudden knock at the door. Mavri jumped beside me, then raced down the wooden staircase with an agility you wouldn't have expected from such a fat-bellied creature. The floor shook under me. There was no bell on Safinaz's door; you had to bang it with the black iron doorknocker.

Bang, bang, bang.

I sprang up from the floor.

'Grandma!'

'Don't be afraid, my girl. It must be Pavli, bringing firewood. Just wait. We're in luck, hopefully.'

Safinaz's knees cracked when she stood up, just like Dad's. She took off her glasses, put on her cardigan, and slowly walked around the table – was she limping a little? – to the window at the end of the room that looked out onto the street. Clove-scented smoke trailed behind her. I ran and grabbed onto her purple velvet skirt. At home she always wore long silk or velvet dresses with white-lace collars and cuffs. And high-heeled patent-leather mules on her feet. With the radio turned off (who had turned it off, and when?), the beating of my heart drowned out even the ticking of the clocks.

'Who is it?'

From the other side of the open window there came flurries of snow and the sound of coughing. I went nearer so I could look out. With a nervousness I found strange, Safinaz put her hands to her hair, took off her glasses chain from around her neck, gathered up her skirt, and followed Mavri downstairs.

The window was still open. I saw Pasha's car before I saw him. It was a Cadillac! I recognized it immediately. Cem and I had seen pictures in magazines, but this was the first time I'd seen a real one. Ah! Tomorrow, when I told my brother, he'd be so jealous. While he was watching television in Harbiye with our other grandparents, I had seen at a Cadillac. I might even go down and get in it. Pasha had parked in front of the Girls' High School instead of on our hill. If it had been daytime, the neighbourhood children would never have let this opportunity pass. They would have run behind the car, yelling and screaming, pestering the black swan sliding gently along the road. But everyone was inside now and the streets were empty.

I tried to memorize every last detail so I could tell Cem. Under the streetlight the shiny black long-tailed car looked as if it belonged to a different world. It was probably magic. Even the snowflakes swirling in the light of the streetlamp didn't touch it. From where I was standing, at the window on the first floor, I could see that all the red buildings had turned white, but Pasha's Cadillac remained proudly black.

I walked down the squeaky stairs on my tiptoes.

Pasha was very tall. Even when he took off his hat, he was just as tall. He dusted the snow off his shoulders with huge bony hands. His hair was white, but his eyebrows were jet black and his moustache was grey. I covered my mouth to stifle my giggles. Even in the dim light of the doorway, I could see he had a deep crease between his eyebrows.

Safinaz spoke in a tone of voice I'd never heard her use before.

'Come inside. You must be cold. Go upstairs and sit by the woodstove. I'll make tea.'

She had forgotten me.

Pasha came inside and closed the door. He must have been about the same age as my Grandfather Nafiz, but he didn't look like a grandfather. His posture and the smile under his grey moustache were different. I slipped into the kitchen behind Safinaz. Mavri followed me. My grandma was emptying the old tea she'd brewed after supper into the bin. Then she rinsed out the porcelain teapot with cracks like spider webs all over it. She almost dropped and broke it in the sink. She cut a slice of lemon, decided she'd cut it too thick, threw it in the sink, cut another slice. She never let me cut an orange or a lemon or a grapefruit with that knife, saying it would turn it black. Wrapping my sweater around me, I squatted down beside the door. The kitchen was icy cold.

'I'll have to get the tin of biscuits from the pantry. There should be some breadsticks in the bread box. Is there any cake left, I wonder? A plate here... Cognac, cognac.'

Grandma was talking to herself. Then, instead of the sugar pot, she put the salt cellar on the tray. I didn't say anything. I followed her up to the first floor, and then, holding on to the bannisters but staying a little way away from them, I raised my voice.

'Grandma, the stove in my room has gone out. I'll sleep here, on the couch.'

Pasha looked at me and smiled. Without letting go of the bannisters, I smiled back. He was sitting in the wingback chair, his legs crossed. Safinaz made everyone who came into the house take off their shoes, even Pavli, but she hadn't said anything to Pasha about that. His boots were just like his Cadillac, black and so shiny that the snow didn't stick to them.

'If the stove up there has gone out, call me. I'll come and relight it.'

When Pasha spoke, even the clocks fell silent.

I glanced uncertainly at Safinaz, but she avoided my gaze. Putting her hand on my shoulder, she pushed me up the stairs.

Up I went, dragging my heels. She had forgotten my milk. The stove in the little room upstairs that Dad used to sleep in was burning away. I didn't know when she'd gone up and tended to it. Anyway, she had magical powers. You could expect anything from my grandma. A sweet, smoky smell was coming out through the half-open door of the stove. I put on my nightdress. Safinaz drew the blue satin quilt up to my chin, leant down and kissed my forehead. My nostrils filled with the scent of rose oil. I needed to pee, but I didn't say anything. She hadn't reminded me to brush my teeth either.

'Grandma, there's a dwarf in the cupboard in the hall. Please stay with me until I fall asleep.'

'Do not be afraid, Melike, my little one. I'll open the cupboard door on my way downstairs now and look for the dwarf. If he happens to be there, he'll take fright and run away from me. I'll leave your door open a crack. See how the light from the stove has painted the wall and the ceiling orange – how beautiful that is. And anyway, nothing bad can happen to us while your Uncle Pasha is here. If you wake up, call out for me and I'll come straight away.'

'Are you going to open up the living room for him?'

Safinaz opened up her living room only for guests. The rest of the time, the sofas were covered with white sheets and the shutters were locked, just like at Irini's house.

'No, my child. Why would I open up the living room in this cold weather? We'll be just downstairs in the room on the first floor.'

Was it the firelight, turning the room into a huge orange, that made my grandma's face look so young that night? Was there a spark in her black eyes that I had never seen before? Maybe it was coming into the warmth from the cold kitchen that had turned her pink cheeks red. Even the hair around her ears curled more softly. Though she knew that an unexpected midnight visit from Pasha could be ominous, she couldn't stop love's absent-minded smile from spreading across her face. l was a child. I saw everything not with my eyes but with my heart. Weary, I smiled.

When I no longer heard the tapping of her high-heeled mules on the wooden stairs, I got up and pulled my wool cardigan over my nightdress. Trying not to look at the cupboard where the dwarf hid, I leant on the bannisters. There was whispering from downstairs, and the clink of a spoon stirring a tea glass. I wondered whether Pasha realized he had put salt instead of sugar in his tea. I pressed my hand against my mouth to keep from laughing and sat down on the top step, drawing my knees up to my stomach under my white flannel nightdress. Mavri was sitting at the bottom of the stairs, staring suspiciously at my bare feet. I waved her away. 'Go away! Git! Go away, you ugly cat!'

'I have to go back tonight, but there's no great hurry. Do not worry, I beg you. Come over to me.'

No matter how hard Pasha tried to whisper, it was impossible to quieten that booming voice. I stood up and peered over the bannisters. Pasha was sitting where I had left him, in the beige wingback chair. He had stretched out his long legs and the boots that snow wouldn't stick to towards the stove. Safinaz was sitting beside the chair on the rug I'd lain on a while ago, leaning her head on the arm of the chair. The finger waves of her white hair appeared and disappeared between Pasha's enormous fingers.

'Play the oud a bit. It's been so long since you've done that.'

I immediately sat down again and made myself as small as possible. The oud was on the same floor as my room. It was hanging on the wall next to Safinaz's bed. A rattling sound came from the dwarf's cupboard. Fearfully, I turned my eyes to Mavri. She too was looking up at the cupboard. I lowered my head and pressed my eyes into my knees beneath my white nightdress.

Safinaz mumbled something like 'the child' and 'sleep' and 'it isn't tuned anyway'.

The dwarf was moving around in the cupboard, getting ready to come out. I had to stop myself from falling asleep. If I didn't go to sleep, he wouldn't come out. I should listen to the clocks, the clocks... tick, tock, tick, tock. The ticking of the giant grandfather clock in the entrance hall carried all the way up to my floor. The cuckoo clock was right above my head. In a little while the bird would pop out with his song and the dwarf would run away. My feet were like ice blocks. Should I go back to bed? Get under my warm quilt that smelled of rose oil? I couldn't hold my pee much longer. But I couldn't stand up.

Suddenly I heard Safinaz's voice. She'd forgotten to whisper. 'How serious is it?'

Now it was Pasha who lowered his voice.

'Quite serious. I inquired about your son. There are no criminal charges against him, but the newspaper he works for is extremely questionable, and his home appears to be frequented by some undesirable types. It's true that he has a solid support network, and his wife's family have friends in high places. But in these difficult times he should be a lot more careful about the people he chooses to mix with.'

I'd been focusing all my attention on Pasha's words, so I didn't hear the cupboard door open. All of a sudden the dwarf came out. As always, his eyes were closed, his hands were extended, and his bald head rolled from side to side. He was chanting that same unintelligible rhyme. He was getting nearer and nearer, about to climb onto my chest. I screamed. No sound came out. I tried to move my legs, but they were frozen. I couldn't breathe. A warm wetness spread under me, soaking my nightdress. I began to sob.

Then I was in Safinaz's arms. She was rocking me like a baby, murmuring words in a language I recognized but didn't know. Mavri was at my feet and Pasha had gone.

The next morning, most probably Safinaz and I ate breakfast as usual at the kitchen table with its blue-flowered plastic cloth. She must have toasted some bread and set down three different colours of olive in front of me. I probably couldn't drink the black tea she served me. Resting her clove-flavoured cigarette on the edge of the ashtray, she must have separated the white of an egg for me, eaten the yolk herself. Then when Dad came to get me, she must have taken him aside and told him, this time in a different tone of voice, that he had to immediately break off all contact with his anarchist friends.

Most probably all of these things happened, but I don't remember them.

After that day, I never saw Safinaz again. Safinaz, my magical, beautiful grandma. After her death, Aunt Zeyno gave me my favourite clock, the one with the moon and the stars. She sold my grandmother's house with all the furniture, along with the deeds to Irini's house, which she had found in a drawer. She gave half of the money to my mother.

Dad had already gone by that point.

He would never come back.

The abiding memory I have of Safinaz is that soft smile, that childlike innocence on her face as she stood in the doorway of my room, which had turned into a giant orange in the firelight.

5

Farewell Telegram

Petro attacked his food with gusto, like a boy who'd been playing football all day. Even the waiters at the small, very local restaurant were in awe of the relish with which he ordered lamb stew with peas, courgette dolma, mashed potato, and mushrooms sautéed in garlic and thyme. On our way back to our table from the ordering counter, his eyes fell on the glass case displaying compote. He requested, I ordered: one portion of sour-cherry compote.

This seemed to alarm Zeki Bey, the elderly restaurant owner. 'Professor Melike,' he called out from behind the till, 'you know best, of course, but do be careful that your friend doesn't make himself ill. Our food, as you know, is freshly prepared every day, but too much of it might result in an upset stomach, especially in this hot weather and so late in the evening.'

Petro had already settled himself at the Formica table beside the mirrored wall and was gazing greedily at the plates the waiters were placing in front of him. At that late hour there were no other customers. I gestured to Zeki Bey as if to say, 'Don't worry about it.' Compared with the array of plates set out in ceremonial splendour in front of Petro, my olive-oil dishes looked pathetic.

Petro was slurping up the compote.

'What a great idea! Why don't we Greeks have a compote custom like this, I wonder?' he murmured. 'It cleans the palate between mouthfuls, so that each new bite is as intriguing as the first. A great idea. Bravo to you all. *Politiki kouzina* – or, should I say, Istanbul cuisine – is quite distinctive, of course. Delicious!'

I nodded knowingly. He should come to Buyukada one day and taste Sinan's mutton stew with leek fritters and pureed eggplant – that would give him a proper introduction to *politiki kouzina*. My husband was an expert cook. He'd taught me so many delicious dishes. I was sure that at that very moment on the island, my mother and her carer Mina were sitting down to a feast.

As if he was reading my mind, Petro said, 'You live on Prinkipo Island, right? What's the name of the island in Turkish?'

'Buyukada. I don't really live on the island. I spend my summers there.'

Yes, Melike, why not excise the word 'we' from your vocabulary and see if you can't ignore the real world for a while.

Petro caught on right away. 'Not on your own, I imagine?'

'No, not on my own. As a family. With my husband and my mother. And there's also Mina, who looks after my mother.'

'Does your mother need a carer?'

The genuine curiosity in his eyes surprised me. No, it wasn't curiosity; there was something else there – concern. Petro hadn't dwelt on the 'we' part. Instead, he had shown concern for my mother. How was it possible that he could be invested in someone he didn't know at all?

'Her nerves are a bit fragile, so it's good to have someone with her. In the winter she lives by herself in Istanbul, in a huge apartment. Mina does the housework, and she's also a companion. She's been with us for years – since I was a child. She's like a daughter to my mother now.'

Petro tossed the meat on his fork into his mouth and chewed carefully, as if tasting my words, then ate a few spoonfuls of peas. His strong jawbone moved like a sharp knife under his dark skin.

'Since you were a child, huh? Interesting. Aren't you jealous?'

'Of whom?'

'You just said Mina and your mother are like mother and daughter. Aren't you jealous of their closeness?'

'Not at all. My mother and I don't have a very warm relationship.'

He laid his fork down and looked at me with an expression I couldn't quite put my finger on. Why was I telling him all this – a man I'd only just met?

To gain some time, I continued to chew the artichoke in my mouth. Sinan would have been pleased to see that. He didn't like me wolfing down his food in a single swallow. He said one should take the time to experience the way food tasted in different parts of the mouth – on the tongue, the palate—

'If I've offended you, please tell me.'

'No, I'm not offended. It's just, um… you think you know all there is to know about the people you live with. Inevitably. I always think of my mother as a reserved old woman whose nerves are on edge, someone who needs to be protected from things. I've been tiptoeing around her for years, keeping quiet about anything that might upset her. But now I'm wondering if she's really that fragile. As I was telling you about her just now, I suddenly had my doubts. To be honest, I really don't know her that well, even though we live under the same roof for three months of the year.'

'In the house on Buyukada?'

I appreciated his attempt to say the island's name in Turkish.

'Yes, there. It's not really a house actually, more of a mansion – old, and built in the traditional style, from wood. It's falling apart from neglect now, but in my grandparents' time it was very elegant, and the garden was full of fruit trees, roses, jasmine, arbours. It belongs to my mother's family. Or rather it belonged to them, and now it's my mother's, because she was the only heir. We spend our summers with her.'

I bit my tongue. The 'we' had slipped out again, reminding him once again that I had a husband We: Sinan and Melike. I'd been married for fifteen years. *We'd* been married. I still couldn't get used to this 'we' business. Even when it came out of my own mouth, it startled me. Petro didn't look as if he cared. He dipped his forkful of mushrooms into the olive oil, garlic and thyme mix, then mumbled something with his mouth full. After he'd swallowed it down, he tried again.

'You were describing your relationship with your mother.'

I sighed. The food had cleared the effects of the weed, leaving a sweet looseness in my head. I would have loved a glass of red wine, but this was a simple restaurant. It was also right next to one of the most religious districts in Istanbul.

'There's nothing much to tell. We keep our distance from each other, make small talk, and that's about it. She has her soap operas on television, which she's glued to all day. She thinks about the girls in those programmes, worries about them more than she does about me. They're like her substitute family.'

Petro nodded. He was polishing off the dishes in front of him, one by one. I pushed away my plate of mixed vegetables in olive oil, from which I'd eaten only the single piece of artichoke. I'd lost my appetite. Gulbahar had her Mina and her soap operas. But what about me: what did I have? My husband, my secret lovers, and the university classes I taught by rote?

Now wasn't the time to be thinking about such things. Soon the inevitable question would come: 'And what about your father?' I spoke up before he could ask.

'My mother and father divorced when I was eleven. Then my mother got married again, to a wealthy widower, Dr Chetin – a surgeon with a waterfront villa on the Bosphorus, at Kirecburnu: that sort of wealth. He died prematurely. He was actually a very courteous and dignified gentleman – quiet, calm and extremely clean. You should have seen his hands! He had long, slender fingers, the nails always manicured.' I laughed.

Petro didn't say anything. I'd talked too much, probably to avoid having to discuss my father. I'd changed direction, steered the conversation away from him. If I hadn't done that, I'd have crashed on the rocks and been shipwrecked, right? I'd have had to go back to the day I fell onto my brother's chest like a hound from hell, and maybe in this rare talkative mood I was in, I'd have told Petro about my father's telegram. Why were all these memories flooding in all of a sudden? Dad's farewell telegram, the basement apartment in the house on the island (what they called 'the maids' quarters' back then), that day I pushed Cem to the floor and jumped on his head...

My poor older brother was stick-thin. He'd found me in the maids' quarters, jumping over a length of knicker elastic that I'd tied around the legs of two chairs. With trembling fingers, he handed me a piece of paper on which words had been typed very small. Some of the ink was blurry and a few letters had been obliterated. It stated: 'I will stay here, Gulbahar. I've given my lawyer power of attorney. Farewell, Orhan.'

As soon as I read it, I turned on my brother. He was lying! Trying to trick me into believing a made-up piece of paper was a telegram from our dad! Although I was three years younger than him, I was stronger, and he probably wasn't expecting to be attacked. So when I shoved him in the chest with both hands, he fell to the floor. He was trying to fool me with a piece of paper. I was going make him swallow the piece of paper. I jumped on top of him and squeezed his ribs between my knees as if I was riding a horse. He couldn't breathe. The blood drained from his pale cheeks.

As I bent over him, my Medusa hair fell into his face, making a tent around his head. The maids' quarters smelt strongly of lavender. Our faces were close under my shroud of hair, close enough for me to see the tears in his blue eyes. As I pressed down on his heaving chest, I screamed, 'You're lying! You're a liar! You made it all up!'

'It's not a lie, Melike,' he gasped. 'He's not coming back. You've seen the telegram. They're going to get a divorce. I heard them with my own ears.'

'Take that back or I'll strangle you!' I was frantic. My voice was hoarse from all the shouting. 'Stop lying!'

Someone grabbed my collar. It was Arab Fati, my mother's faithful old nanny, who still lived in the mansion. She was trying to pull me off my brother, at the same time screeching in a shrill voice which you wouldn't have been expected from such a large physique.

'Help! She's going to strangle the boy! Help! Madam Piraye, daughter Gulbahar, come quickly!'

The memory of how our tall, strong nanny had flapped around in the maids' quarters made me laugh.

'What are you thinking about?' Petro brought me out of my daze. While I'd been daydreaming he had polished off every single plate, including my olive-oil dishes, and was drinking the tea Zeki Bey had set in front of him.

'Oh, I'm sorry. I'm in such a state today.'

Oh my God. We'd only just met, and, as if my use of 'we' wasn't enough, now I was talking like those women who said, 'I'm not normally like this, but when I'm with you, I—'

'What kind of state?'

That childlike curiosity was shining in his eyes again. I wanted to reach out my napkin and wipe the olive oil from the corners of his mouth.

'For some reason, I'm getting a lot of flashbacks from my childhood tonight. Out of the blue I remembered something that happened in our house on the island. And… that hilltop where we met earlier, where the Bloody Church is, my grandmother used to live there. Maybe that's why. Istanbul has changed so much, but up there, that hilltop, the school, the church, my grandma's house, they're all exactly as they were thirty years ago. I'm probably imagining this, but I even wondered if that tricycle we saw in the churchyard was there when I was a child.'

I couldn't bring myself to say that I suspected the two yellow candles burning in the church were the candles Safinaz and I had lit thirty years ago, too. I didn't want him to think I was one of those spiritualist, New Age women.

So what did I want him to think of me, then? Who was I, even? Just as I didn't really know my mother, in truth I wasn't that good at knowing myself either, was I?

'I need to tell you something, Melike.'

Petro's face had taken on a seriousness I hadn't seen before. I felt like giggling: this new gravity didn't fit.

'I'm serious.'

'Okay. I'm listening.'

But I wasn't listening. I was thinking about other things. About my mother. After my father's farewell telegram, she withdrew from life entirely, as if we were plants that could be left to grow by themselves. I remember her, always with a novel in her hand, her blue eyes gazing vacantly at the mulberry tree in the garden. Yes, she would later go on to marry Dr Chetin, but even after we'd moved to his waterfront villa in Kirecburnu, that blank expression in her eyes remained. As for me and Cem, she moved us to the mansion on the island and abandoned us like kittens. We were just pot plants that grew a bit taller, stuck in a corner, our voices never heard. Then... then, on that first day of summer, did she not prove how easily she could discard us?

Did she not?

Was this mother's story?

I had a sudden urge to return to the island right away and sit beside my mother's bed. It was as if I had to go immediately, that night, or she would die and I would never hear her real story, left instead with only my childish understanding of her situation. I felt a mixture of remorse and anxiety.

'Forget it,' said Petro. I stared at him as if I'd just woken from a dream. Had he said something I'd missed?

He drank the last of his tea and wiped his mouth. 'Now isn't the time. Today has been tiring for both of us. Let's get back to the hotel. Tomorrow morning I'd like to finish off all the churches in this district, then go to Kumkapi in the afternoon. Which one should we begin with?' Again, I felt like a student who hadn't done her homework.

Without waiting for an answer, Petro stood up with his hand on his back pocket and walked over to Zeki Bey, who was standing at the till. I wondered if he was upset that I hadn't paid attention to what he was about to tell me. Well, what could I do? He was the one who'd had me smoke that weed. He was responsible for the state I was in. I'd listen to his story tomorrow. And when we got to the hotel, I'd call the island and talk to Mum – Sinan too, if he was still awake.

Petro had gone outside and was waiting for me in front of the restaurant. He hadn't held the door open for me. It was quiet out, the streets were empty. As soon as we left, the staff turned off the lights and locked the door.

At a table in the coffeehouse across the street, four men were playing a serious round of the tile game *okey*. They were sat beneath a television set that no one was watching. From the open windows of the houses came the smell of frying food, the clatter of knives and forks, the chatter of television speakers relaying the weather forecast. The summer of 2003 was going down on record as the driest in ten years. Water rationing would continue, there was a heatwave in Africa, a strong southerly wind, above average temperatures...

As we walked down the hill, I took Petro's arm and leant into him. Maybe that would help win his favour back. The atmosphere between us had become distant, silent, a little strained. Was he annoyed with me? He had cleverly got me to share a lot of things about my past without telling me anything about himself. I still didn't even know where he was from. Maybe he was right to be upset.

The moon had risen. Arm in arm, but without saying a word, we made our way down the narrow backstreets, to our historic-looking hotel beside the ancient Byzantine city walls.

6

On the Road

A week after that snowy night when Pasha came to see Safinaz, the generals took over the government.

I should have been happy. Schools were closed indefinitely, there was a curfew after midnight, and those friends of Mum and Dad's who'd filled our living room with endless political discussions and great clouds of cigarette smoke had melted away. But I wasn't happy. I was scared, and I didn't know why.

Dad had forbidden me from going near the windows after dark. One night, as military marching songs blared out from the radio, he caught me at my bedroom window trying to shine a torch onto our too-deserted, too-quiet street. He grabbed the torch from my hand so angrily and swiftly that I fell onto my bed.

Another night, we woke to the sound of our doorbell ringing. Someone had got into the building and had made it as far as the door to our apartment. I jumped out of bed and ran into the hallway. Mum, in her ankle-length silk nightdress, slipped into Cem's room, switched off the bedside lamp and motioned for me to come to her. Trying to avoid the wooden floorboards that squeaked, I tiptoed to the end of the hall and into the lavender-scented arms of my mother, who was sitting on the edge of my brother's narrow bed. Cem's eyes were wide with fear. Bringing his finger to his lips, he indicated that I should be quiet, even though I wasn't saying anything. At the other end of the hall, Dad had pressed his ear to the door and was waiting. He was in a white vest and had pulled some trousers on over his pyjamas. His hands were empty. We didn't own a gun.

The doorbell didn't ring for a second time. Dad stood guard in the hall for a long time. I thought I wouldn't be able to get to sleep, but with the three of us lying together on my brother's bed, the familiar smell of my mum's skin comforted me and I drifted off.

Towards morning, when I was returning to my room, I heard Mum and Dad's voices in the living room. I sneaked up and peered in. A purplish light from the courtyard filled the room. Dad was sitting on the rug between the armchair and the couch. His head was resting on Mum's slender legs, which were covered by her silk nightdress. His voice was hoarse. Mum had lowered her blond head and was running her graceful white fingers through Dad's curls, twirling, untwirling, twirling again. She spoke softly, trying to soothe him.

'It was probably someone staying with the Italians across the hall, Orhan. They must have got the apartments confused and rung the wrong bell by mistake. The police aren't after us.'

'Let's get away from here, Gulbahar. I'm nervous.'

'The children have school, Orhan. And where would we go? You must be mad!'

'They're watching everyone, Gulbahar. Last Saturday – I

didn't say anything to you at the time – Pasha came over specially to warn my mother. She was very upset.'

'Pay no attention to your mother, Orhan. What have we done? We are a family with children. We have no direct links to any political party or leftist organization. They're not going to throw us in prison because of our visitors, are they? Your mother's just old, and she's worried for no reason. If the situation were serious, they'd have dissolved parliament. The generals have taken control, that's all.'

'I don't know. Things could turn nasty, and then they'll declare martial law. Let's move somewhere else, darling. I know of a wonderful village near Antalya that's only accessible by boat. No cars, no buses, no trams, no stench of coal. Tangerine orchards. Imagine that! There are Greek houses lying empty that the villagers haven't been interested in for fifty years. They've even still got wine in the cellars. We'll catch fish, grow tomatoes.'

'And what about the newspaper? You were about to become head of the Istanbul News Service, remember?'

'Forget about the newspaper, Gulbahar. I'll get involved in encyclopaedia work instead. I spoke with Omer. I can freelance for the newspaper's Sunday piece – write articles on literature instead of politics. Maybe you can do some translations. We'll work together. And if they don't shut down the newspaper, I can write editorials.'

'We'd have to rent out this place, otherwise we couldn't get by.'

'Don't worry about that now, sugar. How much money will we need, anyway? I'll go fishing every morning; we'll plant vegetables, bake our own bread. The kids can go to the village school. All we need is enough to eat and a sweater to keep us warm. We'll create our own revolution, a real one

– enough to impress the folks back here, for all their big ideas. Let's bring up our children in nature's bosom. Let's get out of here. If it doesn't work out, we'll come back once everything's calmed down.'

Maybe it was that final line that had finally convinced my mother.

In reality, no one was out to get Dad. His entire revolutionary activity consisted of going on a janitors' protest march, which he'd done to support Veli, the man who looked after our messy old apartment building. The truth was, Dad was an adventurer who believed that moving house would make him happier. He was fed up with living in an apartment that belonged to his wealthy father-in-law. He was a little boy at heart, who wanted to prove how manly he was by going hunting and fishing.

Four days later, we left our apartment in Galata, just as we always did on a Saturday. But instead of our usual routine – Mum and Cem setting out for Harbiye, and Dad and I going in the other direction, taking a rowing boat to get to Safinaz's house – the four of us walked together to the lot where our car was parked. It was a tan-coloured Renault 12, and for some reason Mum and Dad had given it a name – 'Kurtcebe'.

My brother had his schoolbag, a New Year's gift, on his back, which that day was packed not with schoolbooks but with pyjamas, slippers, socks and two sweaters. I was carrying only my lunchbox, which was full of the thick chicken sandwiches Mum had made for us all, and a flask of orange juice. Walking ahead with our old leather suitcase in his hand, Dad was subdued. Usually on Saturdays, when the four of us left the house, he'd be merrily telling us the same old story he'd told us countless times before. 'You know, kids,' he'd begin, 'if the Number 12 still ran, we'd be able to get on the same tram, from the same stop, but going in opposite directions. When we were young, the same tram line went both to your mother's house and to mine.' Cem and I, and even Mum, would roll our eyes and mutter, 'Yeah, Dad, we know,' but he'd pay no attention, continuing undaunted. 'When your mother was at university, we'd end up sitting at the tram stop for hours. Do you remember, Gulbahar? One of us would say, "It's okay, I'll get the next one." And then, "Okay, I've missed that one. So what?" Many hours would pass. Those were the days! The Number 12 tram – what can I say? They stole our Fatih–Harbiye line.'

No, my father didn't have time to waste on Number 12 tram nostalgia on that freezing cold March morning. He was striding down the hill at a rapid pace. From time to time, without releasing the suitcase that was pulling down his right shoulder, he'd turn his head and nervously glance back at my mother, who was negotiating the icy incline more slowly, trying not to slip. Then he'd walk even faster.

We were going to a village! The most beautiful village in the world. A village full of tangerine orchards. We would catch fish and grow tomatoes. From now on we were going to live as a nuclear family. Our old weekend arrangements had come to an end, never to be resumed.

'Let's make lots of stops along the way, Gulbahar. Please. Let's pretend we're on holiday.'

'Who takes a holiday in the middle of March, Orhan?'

'We don't know when the schools will open again. We can act as if we're a regular bourgeois family, taking advantage of their closure.'

'We are a regular bourgeois family, Orhan.'

With his hands on the steering wheel, Dad turned to Cem and me, sitting in the back seat. 'Melike, Cem, what do you say to a two-year holiday – like in that book, *Deux Ans de Vacances*?'

'Keep your eyes on the road, Orhan, please!'

'Mum, did we bring my Jules Verne books?'

'No, Cem, darling, we could only bring one suitcase on our two-year holiday's Turkish version.'

'But, Mum…'

Whenever my brother got sad, excited or frightened, his face would turn red.

'Speak to your father, Cem.'

'Dad, is there a bookshop where we're going?'

'Son, the place we're going to is so beautiful, you won't have time to read. You and I will go fishing every morning. We'll bring the fish we catch back to your mum and Melike and they'll clean them and cook them. And there are ancient burial sites up in the mountains on the cliffs – the tombs of kings. We'll climb up and explore them.'

'But, Mum, I want my books. *Mum?*'

I clambered up onto the small leather suitcase between Cem and me so that I could see Dad's eyes in the rearview mirror. I would have gone fishing with him and climbed up to see the kings' tombs, but I knew it was with Cem, not me, that he wanted to have adventures. We were all quiet. Cem had turned his face towards the window and was counting the electricity poles to keep from crying. We'd got off the car ferry and were now on a road packed with trucks and buses. Kurtcebe felt very small among all those grumbly, huffing and puffing monsters.

Finally, from the front seat, Mum said, 'When we get settled, we'll call your grandmother and give her our new address so she can pack up your books and post them to us. Will that be okay, son?'

Cem sniffed in reply.

The wrinkles on Dad's forehead, which I could see in the rearview mirror, had deepened. 'Get down off that suitcase, daughter, and sit properly,' he said coldly, as if everything was my fault. 'If there was an accident, God forbid, you'd go right through the windscreen.'

I sulked. I hated it when Dad called me 'daughter'.

That evening, we came to a city set in a bowl between snow-capped mountains. With his eyes on the piece of paper in his hand, Dad navigated the backstreets until we reached a house at the top of a dead-end street.

Narrowing her eyes, Mum glanced around. It was dark now. 'Is this a guesthouse? There's no sign, no name. What kind of place is it?'

Without answering, Dad opened Kurtcebe's door and we all got out. An old woman holding an empty bucket was standing in front of the garden wall, beneath a dim lightbulb. On seeing us, she muttered something from her toothless mouth, after which we followed her into a stone building and up to the top floor, to a small room with two beds. The wooden floor was faded from having been scrubbed with coarse soap over many years, and on it lay a large kilim patterned with red and green birds. In the glow of the lamp, which sat on the table between the beds, the birds seemed to fly. Who would sleep with who, I wondered? I wanted to sleep with Dad. The dwarf wouldn't touch me if I was with him. Putting the lunchbox on the floor, I lay down on the bed next to the wall. The sheets were light and cool and smelled of pine resin.

'It's too hard! I can't sleep on such a hard bed!'

'But hard beds are better for you, Melike, my angel.' Dad sat down beside me, patting the bed.

I smiled. He was going to sleep in my bed. I'd snatched him! From the corner of my eye, I watched as Mum sat down on the edge of the other bed and gazed at the beads and bells hanging off the wooden bedhead. Cem went over, sat down beside her, and began inspecting the mud stains splattering his white socks.

'We've come a long way today and our weary bones will enjoy a good rest on these mattresses. Tomorrow, all our aches and pains will have passed. Isn't that right, Gulbahar? Tell the kids how a hard bed eases the body.'

Without saying anything, Mum stretched out on the bed. The bells tinkled and the beads quivered.

'Are you going to sleep before we eat, honey? Kismet Hanim is cooking beans for us. She told me when she brought up the towels.'

How had Dad understood what the toothless woman was saying? I hadn't been able to make out a single word coming from her puckered mouth, which looked like a bag. I glanced over at Cem. He shrugged. Mum didn't answer. She was already asleep. She always fell asleep as soon as her head hit the pillow. Maybe she had a migraine. She was very sensitive to light, noise, movement, crowds. They gave her migraines just like that. Putting his index finger to his lips, Dad motioned with his hand for us to follow him outdoors. Cem turned off the lamp.

It was dark outside, and chilly, but I didn't feel cold. The smell of the beans Kismet Hanim was cooking wafted out from the chimney. I lifted my head to watch the rising smoke. The sky above the snow-capped mountains was filled with stars. I was awestruck. Dad was excited too. Only Cem remained unmoved.

'Just look at this hullabaloo! The stars are on top of each

other. What a magnificent sight! Look, kids, that's the Milky Way right above us. Do you see it? Those stars crowding together in a shape like an arch, a great flood of them, like a river.'

Cem nodded and traced an arch above his head with his finger. I didn't see the Milky Way; I saw bulls butting heads, birds, butterflies blinking. The bright stars were swallowing the little ones, getting really fat and scattering light in the most fantastic show. In the distance, dogs were howling.

'Pick me up, Dad!'

Dad lifted me in his strong arms and I wrapped my arms around his neck, my legs around his waist. Maybe in a while we'd play 'monkey swing'. I'd hold on tight to his arms and he'd swing me high, make me fly to the stars.

'The Milky Way is our galaxy, kids. Our galaxy is made up of thousands of stars and the planets that orbit them, including our solar system. Just imagine how enormous our universe must be – the universe in which we live. The closest galaxy to us is Andromeda. Shall I teach you how to find it?'

Cem nodded his blond head. I nodded too.

'Look right above us. There's a cluster that forms the letter "W". Straight up from the third star you'll see another really twinkly one. If you look carefully, you'll notice it's different from the others. It blinks, shines, then goes out.'

I squinted, trying to see the star he was describing.

'That's Andromeda, and it contains within it at least as many stars as we can see right now, with the naked eye. Once we've settled into our village, maybe we'll buy a telescope so that on dark nights we can observe this great spectacle. What do you say, Cem?'

Dad gave me a squeeze and I rubbed my cheek against his black moustache. Cem didn't say a word. He was much more interested in the thick books he could finish in two days than he was in stars in the sky. He was in Year 6, about to finish primary school. My maternal grandmother, Madam Piraye, had got very angry with my mother when she heard we were moving to a village. Just yesterday they'd had an argument in the kitchen. 'Let the boy finish primary school before you go, daughter,' she'd said. 'You don't make a child move schools halfway through the year, especially not to a village school. Are you out of your minds? Your father has arranged for Cem to go to the English High School next year. They said they'd enrol him this summer. I don't know for certain that they'll enrol him with a diploma from a village school.'

Mum didn't answer. Cem was in his room, so he didn't hear our grandmother say, 'If you must go, leave the boy with us. You can come and get him in the summer.' But I heard. I was roller-skating on the hallway's wooden floor and my grandmother's huge blond bun bobbed in and out of view through the frosted glass of the kitchen door. My grandmother, Madam Piraye. In my mind that was her name. Dad's mother was Safinaz; Mum's mother was Madam Piraye.

I hugged my dad and whispered in his ear, 'The one with the ring around it is Saturn.'

'Bravo, my Melike! Saturn has a ring. What does Jupiter have?'

I waited for Cem to give the answer, but he was watching an aeroplane pass over us. He didn't even hear the question. His mind was probably full of secret agents, spies and intelligence services.

'Jupiter has a red spot.'

'Bravo, my little girl. Mars?'

I hesitated. Mars was our neighbour, not on the sun side but on the other side. Mercury, Venus, Mars. But what was special about it? I had to make up something or Dad might not love me.

'Mars has Martians!'

Dad laughed. Then he hugged me tight and kissed me. I was still in his arms. Cem laughed too and snuck under Dad's arm. As we stood there in a huddle, Cem and I were both positive that he would never, ever leave us.

Or were we?

Did we in fact both sense, with the sort of intuition that only children have, that we had embarked on a journey that could have only one outcome?

By the following afternoon, we had reached Antalya. We stopped for something to eat. Mum had driven Kurtcebe that morning, when the roads were straight, but once they got more twisty, she gave the wheel up to Dad and fell asleep in the back seat. The boat that would take us to our village would depart from Kas. I was sitting beside Dad, feeling carsick from the curves but happy that we were driving along the coast now. I opened the window wide and took a deep breath to help my nausea pass. The smell of cool sea and seaweed filled my nose. Cem was in the back seat, buried in a book. Dad turned on the radio. A joyful song in a foreign language filled Kurtcebe. Dad kept time with the song, beating out the rhythm on his knees with his gear-changing hand. He began to sing along in Turkish.

'How do you know this song, Dad?'

'My mother used to sing it, Melike, my angel. That's how.'

'Safinaz?'

'Why do you call your grandmother by her name – did she ask you to do that?'

I didn't reply.

'She has a really beautiful voice. Does she ever sing to you?'

'But the woman on the radio is saying different things.'

'It's the same song in Greek.'

'Why?'

'Because we're listening to a Greek radio station. Do you see that island out there? It's called Castellorizo, and it belongs to Greece. The radio station is broadcast from there.'

'Let's not listen to it, Dad!'

'Why not, sweetheart? See how beautifully she sings. Let's sing along. Some parts are in Turkish anyway.

'*Karabiberim, esmer sekerim...*'

'No, Dad, let's not sing.'

My eyes filled with tears. I reached out and turned off the radio. Kurtcebe's grumbling filled the silence. A dark cloud passed over Dad's face. Of course, he didn't know all the stuff our teacher had told us about the Greeks. How they were our enemy, how they attacked our country and threw babies up into the air so that they could catch them on their swords like shish kebab. I was very frightened of the Greeks, but if I told Dad that, I was sure he'd get upset, even if I wasn't sure why.

This sea was so big! It went all the way to the horizon then rolled up into the sky. I had to make things right again between Dad and me. The silence was scorching my heart.

'Dad, are we inside the earth or outside it?'

Without letting go of the steering wheel, Dad reached out to open the glove compartment by my legs. Thinking he was going to pat them, I was happy, but he just searched around for his packet of Birinci cigarettes. When he found them, he withdrew to his side. I drew my knees up under my chin. If I turned the radio back on, would our connection be repaired? The smoke stung my eyes, my nausea got worse. I reopened the window I'd just closed. The cool air smelled of pine trees now. When Mum shifted around in the seat behind me, her knees poked into my back. I was just going to ask how long it would be until we got to Kas when I heard that song again. But this time it wasn't coming from the radio.

Dad was singing the song.

He was singing it in Greek!

Ash from the cigarette he was holding in his left hand was falling onto the plastic floormat, but Dad, watching the road with narrowed eyes, didn't seem to care. A sweet smile had spread across his lips, the same smile I'd seen on Safinaz's face in the doorway that last night. He wasn't even aware that he was singing.

I felt the sense of security from the previous night, when under the stars he'd held me tight in his arms under the stars, shatter. It was then that I knew that, sooner or later, my dad would leave us.

7

Night

When I stretched out naked on the cool sheets of the tightly made-up bed, I was exhausted from having been hurled unexpectedly into the past. And confused. And it was all Petro's fault. He'd brought back memories of my grandma, and, by association, of my father too. With one glance of his honey-coloured eyes, he'd opened windows long closed, windows I'd thought would never open again, being too rusty, too swollen, too stuck from disuse.

Safinaz had a history that was full of secrets, but it was forbidden in our family to speak of her life before she had come to Istanbul. The fact that she was Pasha's mistress was mentioned only very rarely, when Mum and Dad were fighting.

That cold March night had been the first and only time I ever saw Pasha. He would never normally set foot in Safinaz's house. On certain Sunday afternoons, Safinaz used to leave my father and Aunt Zeyno with Irini while she and Pasha went off to a remote village somewhere up the Bosphorus. That was it. With the skill of an acrobat walking a tightrope, my grandma managed to keep her relationship with Pasha a secret from the neighbours. She successfully maintained her image as a respectable widowed schoolteacher with two children.

Most probably Safinaz was a Greek girl who had somehow eluded the compulsory population exchange between Greece and Turkey in 1923. This was not hard to surmise. She had a close relationship with her neighbourhood Greek Orthodox church, the Bloody Church, and she'd spoken Greek with the old caretaker, Pavli, at the church, who alerted her to the coal shed as a potential hiding place should she need one. Since Dad's birth certificate listed 'Bergama' as his birthplace, I had always assumed that was her village. She'd somehow managed to stay there when Bergama's local Greeks ran away or were forcibly exiled. Then she must have married a Muslim man and given birth to Dad. After her husband had died – her ID card stated that she was a widow – she must have met and fallen in love with Pasha while he was stationed there. Then when Pasha got sent back to Istanbul, she must have followed him.

This was the story I'd put together from the bits and pieces I'd heard. But no one had confirmed it – because in our family, secrets were buried deep like treasure, never to be spoken of. Still, enough clues had seeped into my consciousness – there had been words bandied about in a quarrel, the odd insinuation, an ID card slipped hastily from one drawer to another. Pasha had set Safinaz up in a house in Fener, in the Fatih district of Istanbul – since Istanbul Greeks were exempt from the compulsory population exchange, it remained a Greek neighbourhood until midway through the 1970s. There, he had taken care of her and protected her for the rest of her life.

Now, a stranger speaking my grandmother's language had

come into my life, and the sealed windows of the past were springing open one by one. I smiled, thinking of the way Petro pronounced my name – 'Me-LI-ke', with the stress incorrectly placed on the second syllable. It sounded like he was singing a song. I passed my hand over the tight, cool sheet. Why did I feel so close to him? Probably because of his childlike curiosity, his openness, the unjudgmental look in his eyes that made me want to open up to him. Maybe when I was next face to face with him, I'd be able to admit, without feeling worthless or lost, that my father had abandoned us when I was a child. If I saw outright curiosity spark in his eyes, rather than simply pity; if he didn't immediately tell me that this would 'explain a lot about my problems' – maybe then I would gather my courage and tell him, with utter sincerity, how my father had pursued a young woman and made a new life for himself. How he never once got in touch with us.

For whatever reason, I couldn't get Petro out of my mind. But that was always the way with a new man – the head trumped the heart, right? I sometimes wondered whether I'd actually fallen in love with any of the men I'd had affairs with or whether I just pretended that I had. Perhaps that was why I always found it so easy to leave affairs behind. For me, the seduction game loses its appeal as soon as the man falls in love with me (though I'd still have sex with him a couple of times just for the sake of it).

Lately, though, I'd not even had the patience for that. It wasn't for nothing that I'd decided to explore the mysterious world of fidelity. At a recent conference in Izmir, for example, I'd set my sights on an Iranian professor in his fifties. After three days of electrifying tension, I arranged for us to be seated next to each other at the gala dinner. But when he put his hand on my knee under the table, I was so taken aback that I immediately and instinctively pushed my chair back and shook off the fingers that were creeping up between my legs.

When a man beds a woman, he thinks he's won a victory. He doesn't realize that the woman has been directing the whole scenario, like an air-traffic controller, while he's actually had no idea where he's going to land. She orchestrates the whole thing, using all the tools at her command – the initial indifference, the carefully choreographed gestures, the slips of the tongue, the sudden silences – so that in the end she offers the man not herself but rather a space in which he can enjoy the pleasures of the chase. That's all.

I must have fallen asleep. For the first time in years, Safinaz appeared in my dreams. She was wearing an astrakhan fur coat with a wide belt around her waist. She was hatless and had gathered her hair into a bun – which was strange, because my grandma's hair was short. But the hair and fingernails of the dead continue to grow, I reminded myself. She looked anxious. I noticed a fatty growth on the left side of her top lip – perhaps that was making her appear anxious. She was sitting in the armchair by the window of my hotel room. She looked like she'd been there for a long time and had taken over the place, as if it were her room and I was her guest.

'A woman who seals her womb of her own free will is the most dangerous creature in the universe,' she said in a voice that was not her own.

'I'm not going to sleep with Petro.' I volunteered the information, as if in response to her comment. My heart was beating madly with the stress of having to explain myself.

Safinaz was laughing. This was a first. What began as little hiccups quickly gathered force and became a chortle, then developed into uproarious laughter so intense that she bent over with the effort of it. As she put her head on her knees,

I saw that there were spikes around her bun. Of course, that was perfectly normal, I said to myself. If it came to it, she could remove her bun and throw it, use it as a weapon. She was doubled over with her chest on her knees now, guffawing. The poppy-patterned curtains behind her chair were parted just enough to allow the silvery light of the moon to spotlight her spine. Her laughter didn't let up. Even the spiders on the ceiling stopped weaving their webs to listen.

'If the woman who turns her back on the soil doesn't dedicate herself to God, the dark forces of the netherworld will swallow her up.'

Shouting 'Witch! Witch!' I woke up. My throat was dry, my mouth like mud. I felt around for the glass on my bedside table but couldn't find it. I wasn't inside the mosquito netting of my bed on the island. Reaching out, I turned on the lamp. My watch, which I'd taken off before I went to sleep, showed 3 a.m. The watch had been Madam Piraye's and was not reliable. It stopped if you didn't wind it up. It could be 4.30 or even 5 a.m. Should I get up? It was still dark outside, no moonlight. Only a wavering yellow glow from the streetlight in front of the window seeped in through the gap between the worn curtains.

I dozed off and woke to knocking on my door. I was covered in sweat. My grandma's watch still showed 3 a.m. How long had I slept after the Safinaz dream? Five minutes? Three hours? The streetlight had gone out. Behind the coffee-coloured curtains the darkness had lifted a little.

Dazed at not knowing the time, I got up, wrapped the sheet around me and walked to the door. With my fingers on the handle, I hesitated momentarily. Could it be a stranger at the door, a pervert who'd heard there was a single woman staying in one of the hotel rooms? I drew the sheet more tightly around myself. From the other side of the door came a slight 'tick, tick', which made me forget everything. I turned the handle.

Petro was standing at the door. The first thought I had, despite my muddle-headedness, was that he was not here to make love to me. For one thing, he was dressed. In fact, he hadn't even got undressed. The trousers he'd had on the night before were wrinkled, his shirt collar was askew and his beard seemed to have grown longer. He obviously hadn't even tried to sleep. For the briefest moment, a whiff of unease clouded my mind.

Without unwrapping the sheet that covered my nakedness, I walked over to the man standing on the threshold and leant my head on his chest, as if it belonged there, right against his heart. He smelled of thyme and marijuana. I could hear his inhalations beneath my ear. He sighed as if raising a flag of surrender and rested his hands on my shoulders, bare under my hair. I felt the dough-like softness of his palms. I nestled close into him. His arms were so long they could have wrapped twice around my sheeted body. I was small, oh so small in his arms, and, surprisingly, instead of disliking the sensation of feeling so tiny next to a man, a part of me accepted it, even relished it – the part of me that felt like crying when we touched. His hands sank into the curls of my hair, which had stood on end during my dream about Safinaz. He traced one strand of hair all the way down to the base of my spine. I gripped the sheet, closed my eyes and let him carry me to the bed.

Our hearts beat together in sync, our breathing was as one. I didn't have to make much effort. I was female, after all. I could surrender into his arms.

With his soft hands, he spread my hair over the pillow,

unwrapped my arms and freed my naked body from the sheet. I didn't help him undress. A breeze wafted in through the open window and lifted the threadbare curtains. Guided by ancient wisdom, my body opened up to him. As he rested his weight on me, I felt light; I softened against his hardening. I held him close, to once more hear the sound of his heartbeat, pulled his chest to my face, then lay back on the bed.

A tiny woman like me could obviously not make love eye to eye with such a tall man – at least not in that position. With my ear on his chest, I watched the play of shadows on his collarbone in the dim morning light that was now filling the room. I wiped drops of sweat with my thumb. I hid my face in my arm.

As I lay on the bed, rocking softly in harmony with Petro's movements, the part of me that believed that lovemaking was an exchange of pleasures – the part of me that knew that the best sex required both partners to give and receive in equal measure – was melting. I was evaporating in bright blue sea salt. I couldn't remember ever having surrendered so completely the first time I went to bed with someone. I yielded to passivity. Involuntarily, my body swelled like a lake of fresh water, and my main sensation was one of surprise. Lifting my arm off my face, I began to laugh. He paid no attention. Without taking his half-closed eyes off my Medusa hair fanned out across the pillow, he continued what he was doing. Seeing that his attention was focused not on me but on himself, I was suddenly turned on. I squeezed him between my legs. The swollen river inside me was about to burst its banks.

Hurry! There's no stopping now! Go for it! Keep on climbing until you've run out of breath! It's you who will carry us both to the mountaintop.

When we came at the same time, I was still laughing.

8

The Prophecy

'Witch!'

That's what Mum said when she heard that Safinaz had died. 'Witch!' came out of her pretty lips like spit.

I was in the kitchen of our village house, preparing the tomatoes I'd picked from our garden for bottling. I'd put the tomatoes in boiling water to soak. Once the skins had softened in the hot water, they'd come off with one pinch of my fingernail – no need for a knife – leaving a single, thin piece, like a membrane, in my hand. I was going to fill the jars with skinned tomatoes, make them airtight, then line them up on the shelves in the pantry for us to use through the winter.

Auntie Naciye, the wife of the *mukhtar*, the village chief, had taught us how to preserve tomatoes when we finished primary school. Girls of that age in the village weren't treated like kids any more. Naciye's middle daughter, Fatosh, was in my class at school, and she knew not only how to bottle tomatoes but also how to roll dolma. Although, in fact, Fatosh never did complete Year 6. Our new teacher, Miss Sabahat, realizing that Fatosh didn't know how to read, had given her a fail. Miss Sabahat wasn't lenient like our old teacher, Mr Ibrahim, had been before he left the village. Even though Fatosh pleaded with her, 'Please, Teacher, if my father finds out I haven't graduated, he'll beat me till I bleed donkey water,' she was not given a diploma.

Mum pushed open the screen door and came in. Behind her, the evening sun seeped into the kitchen, making a triangle on the floor where the rays converged. Dust motes caught in the sunbeams looked like icing sugar being sprinkled on a slice of cake. Mum pulled a cigarette from the packet on the table, lit it and took a few angry puffs where she stood. Had she not seen me?

The door opened again. We both turned at the same time and stared. It was Dad. His face, like his collar, was crooked, the pupils of his eyes frozen. He collapsed at the wooden kitchen table, his face in his hands. Mum remained standing, the cigarette between her fingers.

'She threw herself off a cliff, Gulbahar! Her body got caught in a fishing net.'

Only I saw Mum spit out the word 'witch'; her lips were hidden by smoke but had become visible for a second between puffs. She said it not to Dad, but to the window overlooking the sea. 'Witch!'

Leaving the tomatoes, I washed my hands and dried them on the stained kitchen towel. The smell of cloves came to me from somewhere, the smell of the thin little cigarettes from India that my grandma used to smoke. I realized that the person my father was talking about was Safinaz. It was Safinaz who had jumped off a cliff. But why?

I reached for the loaf of bread on the counter. My hands were shaking so much, I couldn't cut it, so I tore off the end instead and stuffed it in my mouth. The bread swelled as I chewed.

Dad got up, went to the pantry, which was a couple of steps from the kitchen, and returned with a bottle of raki. His eyes were bright red. Taking a bucket of ice from the fridge, he set it down between them. Usually they drank raki by themselves, in secret – taking it from the cool pantry, filling a water glass and then swiftly gulping it down – but this time it looked like they were going to drink together.

'Why would a woman in her sixties commit suicide? Tell me that, Gulbahar. Huh? Why would she go and throw herself off a cliff?'

Mum stubbed out her cigarette and sat down across from Dad.

Dad's head was bowed and he kept rubbing his black curly hair. 'Oh, Mother, couldn't you have waited for death to come to you? Did you not consider us at all? How will we live with this weight on our shoulders?'

My mother said nothing. They both drank their raki in silence. The sun set and the golden dust above the table settled. For a time the only sound was the putt-putt of fishing boats. After a while Dad spoke.

'I have to go back there, Gulbahar. It took the police two weeks to find Zeyno. They had no idea that we existed, no idea who was who. The body was discovered way out beyond Rumeli Kavak. The funeral's going to be a problem, you know, not only because she committed suicide, but for other reasons too. Who will take the service? Which cemetery will we bury her in? My God, Mother! Why do this to us right now?'

I placed the tomato I'd been skinning into a bowl and sat down near them. I tried to put the bowl down quietly, but it hit the table too hard. They both turned and looked at me, as if they'd just noticed I was there, in the small house. Mum gestured with her narrow chin and Dad refilled the empty glasses with raki, gazing vacantly at the metal bucket, whose ice had already melted.

They were going to tell me what had happened, weren't they? They surely hadn't forgotten that I knew Safinaz. Okay, I hadn't seen my grandma in three years, and during that time the conversations we'd had on the *mukhtar*'s phone had been filled with boring, cool, truncated words. But Safinaz was my grandma. Mine. Mine more than Cem's. She had left her unique mark on my soul. Only I knew how the aroma of cloves from her cigarette, mixed with the scent of the rosewater she sprinkled on her neck, went to your head. If I wasn't allowed to know what happened to Safinaz, then who was?

My anger spread to my eyes. I swallowed a whole tomato from my bowl without chewing.

'What happened, Dad? Mum?'

Dad sighed. Mum covered her mouth with her hand as if she was about to sneeze, though she didn't. I felt like a fish in an aquarium, a creature who was seen but not heard.

'Go and find your brother, daughter. Your mother and I need to talk to each other.'

He knew very well that I didn't like being called 'daughter'. Miss Sabahat called me that at school. I'd told him so many times. Even though he teased me, saying, 'But you are my daughter. If I don't call you "daughter", who can I say it to?' he knew exactly what I meant. I pushed the wooden chair back noisily and stood up.

Go and find your brother!

Cem would be in some secluded spot with Mina. Where else would he be, the wannabe Romeo! My brother had turned fourteen that summer. He'd got tall, his voice had broken, and he was more self-conscious than ever. He didn't know where to put his arms or what to do with his hands, and he didn't talk to anyone except Mina, who'd come to live with us.

'The young gentleman is holed up somewhere with your orphan, no doubt.'

Dad raised his head and gave me a look that made me recoil as if I'd been slapped. I actually would have preferred a slap – then I wouldn't have had to carry the memory of the pain and disillusionment in his sad eyes for the rest of my life. He could have slapped my face and left, and that would have been that. But that's not how it went.

I opened the screen door and went out into the garden barefoot. The heat hadn't abated one bit. Bees were buzzing around the red geraniums Mum had planted in tins that first year, when she was interested in flowers and the soil, and there was an intoxicating smell of roses and dry grass. The sun had already vanished behind the castle, taking with it the reds and pinks of the sky. Under my feet the earth was bone dry. I picked up the hose at the edge of the vegetable garden. It was caked in dry soil. I wasn't going to water the garden. Let the tomatoes, peppers and courgettes shrivel up! Did anybody except me care anyway? Dad just dozed in the hammock all day, Mum sat around with the *mukhtar*'s wife in her house, smoking contraband cigarettes and waiting for the television hour to begin. She didn't care about anything, not even the geraniums. Cem had Mina. What about me?

I heard the click of Mum's cigarette lighter through the open door of the kitchen. Hose in hand, I walked closer. The clink of glasses. The smell of raki.

'... No, you stay here with the children, Gulbahar. Please don't make things worse. What would the four of us do in Istanbul in this heat?'

I turned my head and looked at the castle on the top of the hill, taking our village under its wing. Safinaz had thrown herself into the sea from a rocky cliff. Which cliff? Had the fish eaten her face? I tried to imagine Safinaz with half her face gone. What about her hair – the grey hair she wound around her fingers to make curls? My eyes filled with tears. Was Dad going to see her dead body? If I asked, would he cut off a curl and bring it to me? No, I wouldn't ask him for a thing. Let him suffer for treating me so coldly, so distantly, for calling me 'daughter'. My anger intensified when I remembered how offended he'd looked, the expression that had said 'Is this the way I brought you up, Melike?'

Dragging the hose behind me, I walked over to the middle of the garden, then flung the hose against the fig tree where Dad's hammock was suspended. A couple of drops of water dripped out. I flung it against the tree again. Inside me, somewhere near my stomach, something foamed and swelled. I liked it. I thrashed the hose again and again. The villains in the comic books Cem read came into my head – the really evil men who whipped slaves and everything. I was a bad person too. I'd been born that way for sure. I wasn't a fairy queen like my mother, or angel-faced like Cem. When I'd dunked our transistor radio in the sea, given Mina the flat battery and told her to lick it with the tip of her tongue, Mum had yelled, 'Orhan, I cannot handle this girl. The devil himself couldn't dream up such devious behaviour.'

Gulbahar and Orhan's bullshit friends, the ones who used to fill our house in Galata in the evenings, would laugh and say, 'Girl, did your mum and dad get you from the gypsies?' just to make me mad. Thinking of them, I whacked the fig tree again. Laugh! Laugh! I thrashed the memory of them. I hoped Pasha would catch all of them and stuff them in prison.

Suddenly a thin voice came out of the sky. I dropped the hose as if it were on fire.

'That's enough, Melike, girl! If you make it shake any more, I'm going to fall out.'

Squinting, I stared up into the branches, which were trembling with milky green fruit.

'What are you doing up there, Mina?'

No answer.

'Mina?'

When I peered more closely, I could see the ribbons of her skirt. She was sitting on one of the middle branches, by herself. Earlier that day she'd gone into the city, and she was stubbornly still wearing – even in the heat – white socks, and the blue plastic beach sandals Mum had bought her from the market. I climbed up barefoot. Her head was bowed, her black plaits falling on her chest. When I sat down beside her, she began to sob. This was all I needed.

'What's wrong, Mina?'

Something had definitely happened with her and Cem. But what? I'd never once seen the two of them have a row – may God preserve their friendship. Even on beautiful sunny days they'd sit side by side on the couch in the kitchen like vampire bats, reading books.

'Why are you crying?'

Silence. That morning she and Mum had gone to Antalya – once a month Mum would take Mina to Antalya to see her mother, who worked as a carer in someone's house, and Mum would go to the bank to pick up the rent from the apartment in Galata. They'd come back on the evening boat. When Mum got back, she always put the money in the drawer of the bedside table in their room. We'd pretend we didn't know about this because Dad had yelled, 'I won't touch the money from your father's love nest, Gulbahar!' (The house in Galata used to belong to our grandfather Nafiz. He gave it to Mum when she got married. I learnt all of this from Mum and Dad's quarrels after we'd moved to the village. Just as we never talked about Mum going to the bank in Antalya, we also pretended we didn't see Dad opening the drawer once a week.)

'Where's Cem, Mina?'

'I don't know. I haven't seen him since we got back.'

Mina's nose was blocked and her voice sounded different. I thought over what had happened that evening. What had made Mina so upset that she was hiding up a tree? She probably wasn't crying about Safinaz's death. Even *I* had only just heard about that. Plus, how would Mina even know Safinaz? She'd been living with us for less than three years.

My secret suspicion – that Mum loved Mina more than me – came to me again. I was the devil; Mina was pitiful. If I pushed her now, she would fall. And she wouldn't tell on me. But they'd know anyway. A lump formed in my throat. I hated all of them.

'Do you want to go to the castle?' I asked.

'You go.'

'Why?'

'Just 'cause.'

'What are you going to do? Aren't you going to get down?'

'Don't know.'

'Okay. I'm going then.'

'Melike, girl, don't go.'

She put her hand on my leg. In the twilight I saw that her fingernails were bitten right down, just like mine. When school finished, she and Mum had sat down at the table under the fig tree and painted their fingernails. You could still see the pink polish at the cuticles. While Mum painted Mina's nails, they chatted quietly, laughing together like a couple of old friends. Mum listened to Mina like she was a wise friend, not a twelve-year-old foster child, nodding her head from time to time. When she noticed me watching them from the garden gate, a towel over my shoulder, she called out, cigarette dangling from the corner of her mouth, 'Come, Melike, let me paint your nails too. You've finished primary school – you're a young lady now.' Mina was gazing at Mum, her hands stretched out in front of her, with so much love and respect. I was going swimming. Without bothering to reply, I ran off down the dusty hill to the sea.

'Melike, girl, I have something I want to ask you,' Mina said, lowering her voice.

'What?'

'When we got off the boat from Antalya, you told Mummy darling that the *mukhtar* came, didn't you?'

'Yes. My father got a phone call from Germany. The operator put it through. The *mukhtar* came all the way over to our house to tell us himself. He didn't send Ali.'

I had raised my voice. As we sat side by side up in the fig tree, Mina began to tremble. The red-hot ember of jealousy that had been scorching my heart suddenly dissipated and turned into a shiny red feeling, like a boiled sweet. I put my arm around her shoulders like I used to in breaktimes that first year we met each other. Laying her head on my shoulder, she began to cry. Tears dripped onto her skirt – she was still wearing the navy blue one, with white ribbons down the side, that she'd worn with such pride to the city. Mum had had Auntie Naciye sew the same skirt in red for me, but I never wore it because I didn't want to dress the same as Mina.

I replayed in my head how Mum and Mina had got off the evening boat a couple of hours ago, their arms full of packages and baskets. I'd gone down to the shore to meet them. Mina was laughing, as she always did when she'd just been to visit her mother. The sun was setting behind the castle, painting the village gold from the hilltop to the shoreline. Whenever she went to Antalya, Mum would bring us back books, watercolour sets, magazines, and, if the weather wasn't too hot, chocolate umbrellas. Cem and I would go down to the dock and wait impatiently for the boat. But that evening it wasn't excited anticipation that took me down to the shore to meet them but the need to tell Mum as soon as possible what had happened that afternoon. The *mukhtar* had come to our house! He never went to anybody's house – everyone always went to his. He had a television and a generator, and Auntie Naciye would invite all the women of the village there and they'd watch Greek television that nobody understood. You couldn't watch Turkish television because there wasn't a relay station near enough, but Castellorizo, the Greek island, was really close to us.

Mum would buy red Marlboros from the *mukhtar*'s house too. His sons were in the boat business. When I told Dad that I knew they took tourists out on boat trips to see the underwater tombs and hidden cities encrusted with sea urchins, he laughed. 'The *mukhtar*'s tourists come from Castellorizo, Melike,' he'd said. 'Those trips are money-makers all right, and they do transport Johnnies and Jims, it's true, but they're not the sort of tourists you're familiar with.' He'd laughed and laughed at that, but when the *mukhtar* had appeared at our bougainvillea-wreathed garden gate a few hours ago, Dad had leapt out of the hammock where he'd been dozing.

'What did he want?' asked Gulbahar wearily, unmoved by my excitement. She'd disembarked from the boat and was already making her way up the hill with the basket. Mina was walking behind us with the bags.

Hearing the coolness in her voice, the field of flowers inside me faded. I stared hopelessly at the dusty hill rising in front of us. The important thing was not what he had wanted, surely, but that he had come to our house himself. For someone unused to climbing our hill, especially in that summer heat, that was quite a challenge. Leaning against the wall beside the doorstep as he tried to catch his breath, the *mukhtar* had reached his hand out to me and said, 'My child, is your father home?'

'He came to say that there was a telephone call.'

'My goodness. Why didn't he just send the boy? Who was calling?'

Suddenly I saw the world through my mother's eyes – in her world, the *mukhtar* was just one of the villagers, she an educated, urban woman. So what if he had a television in his house? My excitement died. We headed up the hill back to the house, Mum scaling it at a speed you wouldn't have expected, given the weariness in her voice. Her blond head was bent low and her multicoloured silk dress – the one she only ever wore on the days she went to the city – was stuck to her skin with sweat. She was so thin, I could have counted her vertebrae through the low back of the dress.

Leaving Mina behind, I caught up with her, ran in front, and yelled breathlessly, 'It was from abroad! It came via the operator. Dad went to the village to see about it and Cem went with him.'

Gulbahar put the wicker basket down on the dirt road and looked directly into my eyes. The sun, setting behind the castle, lit up her blond eyebrows, her eyelashes. She waved her hand as if to push the light away. Mina caught up with us and the expression on her face changed instantaneously. A dark shadow passed across her eyes and her lips began to quiver, but I didn't care about Mina. I was busy trying to figure out whether Mum was angry with me or not. Her eyes were fixed on me. What was on her mind? All at once a light that I couldn't interpret flickered in her beautiful face – she was going to laugh. That scared me. It had been such a long time since Mum had really laughed that for her to start now, out of nowhere, could only be a sign that things were not going as they should.

I grabbed her basket off the ground then raced on home, through the dust. By the time first Mum and then Dad had come into the kitchen, where I was peeling the tomatoes, Mina had been nowhere to be seen.

'Melike, girl, do you know why they phoned your daddy?'

Two stars had become visible in the sky through the branches of the fig tree. In a little while the moon would show its face behind the uninhabited island. Venus had already set. Mina's head was still on my shoulder. I opened my mouth, but just like in my dwarf nightmares, no sound came out. It was as if by stating it out loud I would make Safinaz's death a tangible reality and deep down the part of me that knew this had tied my voice into a knot in my throat. I shrugged. Mina began to cry again. The smell I'd noticed three years earlier when Mr Ibrahim had first sat Mina beside me filled my nostrils once again. It was Mina's village smell.

'Why are you crying, Mina?'

'Don't act like you don't know, Melike, for God's sake.'

I was upset. 'The other day, when Mum gave you a whole pile of bits of fabric in secret, over by that outhouse, and you saw I was watching you and you looked at each other and smiled – is that what this is about?'

'Course not – this has nothing to do with that.'

I suddenly felt very lonely. It seemed that everybody had secrets. They shared them with their dear ones. Clearly, since nobody confided their secrets with me, I wasn't worthy of hearing them. I was always trying to guess what was being hidden from me.

'How much longer are you going to sit here, Mina?'

No answer.

'Are you hiding from somebody?'

She raised her head and for the first time looked into my face. She looked dreadful – her eyes were shining with tears and her plaits had fallen over her face. Mum brushed her hair every morning and braided it into two long, thick plaits that hung down her back. Since school had finished, I hadn't let Mum touch my hair and it was now all over the place, like a patch of weeds, shrouding my face. Just as the smoke from Gulbahar's cigarette hid her from the world, so my curly black hair hid me. Mina's hair was straight and silky; mine was like an electric shock, a curly chaos.

'Don't kick me out, Melike! Don't send me away! Please!' She was screaming now, like she did whenever she had a nightmare.

It was then that I understood why she was so afraid. It was because of the phone call from Germany. Germany was Mina's nightmare. Her older brothers, who lived there, wanted to marry her off. A candidate had come forward, an elderly relative, and so she had clearly thought it was her brothers who'd phoned. But of course, I knew who the caller was… the caller was my Aunt Zeyno, sharing the news of Safinaz's death.

Remembering that Safinaz was dead, a knot tightened in my stomach. Without saying anything, I got down from the tree. Sniffling, Mina followed.

When we went into the house, Dad lifted his head up out of his hands and stared at us with bloodshot eyes. Kerosene lamps were burning in the middle of the table and on the windowsill.

'Are you all right, Mina? Your face is so pale.'

'I'm fine, Mr Orhan. I just feel a bit dizzy. It'll pass if I drink some water.'

Before she'd finished her sentence, Cem had jumped up from the couch where he was reading a book by torchlight, filled a glass of water from the tap, and was at Mina's side with it. Mina was trying to tie the sash of her skirt, but suddenly she began to sway back and forth like the poplar trees over by the cemetery. The pupils of her eyes rolled into her eyelids. While she was trying to grab hold of Cem's arm, the glass fell to the ground and shattered noisily into many fragments. Cool water ran over our bare feet.

'Oh, my God! What's happening, children? Step away or you'll cut yourselves.'

Mum ran to the pantry for the broom. Dad stood up.

'Mina, my girl, what's happened? Did she faint? Cem, lay her down carefully.'

Cem did so. She had fallen into his arms and now he set her down on the couch with great tenderness, as if she were a glass statue. Dad came over with a lamp in his hand and examined her. She was barely breathing and her head had dropped to one side. Dad knelt down, held her wrist in his hand and took her pulse.

'Her blood pressure must have dropped. Do we have any *ayran*? Yogurt drink with salt will regulate it. Melike, go and check. Gulbahar, where are you? What's happened to this child? Is it heat stroke?'

Mum emptied the dustpan of glass shards into the red plastic rubbish pail in the corner. Instead of taking the broom back to the pantry, she left it on the floor beside the bucket.

'Don't walk around barefoot, Melike. Go and put your slippers on.'

Nobody moved. Mina opened her eyes a little. Cem lifted her dangling, toothpick legs onto the couch, then handed Dad a pillow to put under her head.

'Mr Orhan...' Mina mumbled. She had grabbed Dad's thick, dark wrist covered in black hairs. 'Dear Mr Orhan, don't go.'

Dad tried to smile, but in the light of the kerosene lamp we could all see that he was uneasy.

'Go where, Mina, dear? You have a fever – probably from staying out in the sun too long. Going to Antalya in this heat must have exhausted you,' he said, giving Mum a cross look.

'Mr Orhan, do not go. It's like hell over there.'

'Where?' I said, coming right up to the couch. 'Where is it like hell, Mina? Where should Dad not go?'

She gestured at the door. Dad was now looking extremely uncomfortable.

'Okay, kids, let's let Mina rest for a while. She's running a high fever and she's delirious. You all go to bed now.'

'Mr Orhan...' Mina's voice had dropped to a whisper. As she moved her head, one of her silky plaits dangled over the couch and onto the floor. She closed her eyes. 'Mr Orhan, if you go, you won't ever come back.'

Then she passed out.

9

The Dream of Love

When I woke in the morning, I was head over heels in love.

Propping myself up on one elbow, I gazed at Petro, who was bathed in the light seeping through the old, milky-brown tasselled curtains. He was sleeping like a baby. His lips were slightly parted and his wide, hairless chest rose and fell softly. What a calm sleeper. His eyelids didn't even twitch.

The bed looked like a warzone. I got up, put on the blue dress I'd draped over the armchair the night before, and tiptoed out. Downstairs, as I tied the ribbons of the espadrilles I had hurriedly slipped onto my feet, I caught my reflection in the lobby mirror. I hadn't washed my face and my hair was gathered on top of my head in a crazy mess, but I looked beautiful. Exhausted, but really very beautiful. My cheeks and lips were red and my eyes were large and dark. A fierce, melancholic beauty had settled on my face.

I went outside. A sweet morning breeze rustled my dress and moved on. Stopping under a washing line stretched between two houses and hung with clothes of different colours and sizes, I stared up at the sky. I couldn't contain myself. I wanted to run, to sing, to laugh – to laugh without stopping. In this state, I reminded myself of someone. Who? A character in a novel? Maybe Emma Bovary – Madame Bovary, who, after recklessly making love for hours, looked in the mirror and murmured, 'I have a lover. I have a lover.' Weren't the eyes she saw in the mirror also darker than usual? I loosened my hair with one hand, letting it fall down my back. It spiralled all the way to my waist. Putting my hands in the wide pockets of my dress, I twirled around, giggling.

J'ai un amant.

'I have a lover.'

No, not a lover. An *amant*. One who is loved. *Amant* comes from *amour*. Love. There is someone I have fallen in love with. I could still feel Petro's palms passing over my neck, my back, my belly; his lips buried in my neck; his voice moaning 'darling', 'sweetheart' over and over in his own language. Should I go back to the room? No, not yet. It was still too soon. Anyway, my body, my poor little body, couldn't take another session like that. It would break in two. What an appetite the man had! Now was the time to step back and give myself the chance to really feel what I was feeling. It was so strange – you felt love most acutely when you were by yourself, when you had the space to process your feelings.

I turned onto the street behind the hotel, where some children were playing noisily in front of three-storeyed houses that had leant into each other. When they saw me, they fell silent. A little girl of five or six with matted hair was drawing hopscotch circles on the pavement. Seeing me, she squeezed the chalk in her hand and poked the friend squatting beside her. The two girls stood with their mouths open, staring at the madwoman who'd appeared on their street. A shaven-haired boy near them began to cry. Witch! They must have thought I was a witch! Safinaz's witchy granddaughter. Ha, ha! Run away, children! From the dark interior of a house, a hand pulled the boy inside. I left them and continued round the corner.

My legs seemed to have doubled in length overnight. I felt as strong, as agile and as light as an Arabian horse. I strode up the hill at lightning speed and soon reached the crumbling city walls. At this rate I could walk all the way to Egrikapi and back. It was such a long time since I'd last come to this district that I had almost forgotten about that historic stone gate in the city walls, my beloved Egrikapi. Back in my university years, I used to take refuge there. That old Byzantine gate, which very few people knew about, knew me. It welcomed me into its sanctuary. It was a special place for me. Pigeons used to make their nests on top of the gate, and when you stood right under it, the dark green pine trees leaning over the tombs made you forget which era you were in. The prospect of leaning against the gate and seeing that timeless scene again made me speed up.

'Wait! Wait! Do you like poetry?'

I turned and looked. A man with a sack on his back who was loitering alongside the walls, in front of the Palace of the Porphyrogenitus, was coming towards me. He was obviously crazy, but I smiled. Love's glow had vanquished all fear, and I was trusting in that old-fashioned view that if you engaged with a person, talked to them, they wouldn't harm you. Besides, if a woman in love didn't like poetry, then what hope was there for poetry? He was happy that I didn't run off. Setting his sack on the ground, he stood to attention in front of me, staring straight into my face. Then he began to recite from memory.

'Wear the beauty of Istanbul and come, for my sake.
Let evenings at Kalamish be kohl for your eyes.'

I laughed. He laughed too. He was missing a tooth.
While he was continuing with his poem, a flock of sparrows
took off from the top of the dilapidated Byzantine palace.
I followed their flapping with my eyes. They were heading
to a wooded area behind the palace. There was a wall I had
never seen before extending parallel to the old Byzantine
city walls. In among a stand of sedate cypress trees a single
linden tree remained, its branches drooping. A strange,
magical light shone through its leaves. My heart raced. Life
was so beautiful, so enchanting. Without ever giving up, it
tirelessly persisted in showing us the way, lifting the edge of
the curtain on the next scene by means of miraculous signs.
I was part of a gigantic consciousness, a perfect particle in a
magnificent universe!

As soon as I got back to our room, I would share all of this
with Petro. He would be waiting for me in bed with the sheets
wrapped around him, naked, languishing, full of desire, ready
to take his lover, bringing news of the outside world, into his
arms. My head spun remembering how he had carried me from
the doorway to the bed. I missed him already. Wasn't that what
love was? Forever yearning, forever longing to be reunited?

I left my street poet with his bag at his feet and walked
towards the light that was calling to me insistently. I advanced
through piles of scrap metal, barrels filled with sand, rubbish.
Everywhere was dusty and dirty, but it wasn't long before I
found a gap in the wall. Pushing aside bushes, oblivious to
brambles that scratched my neck, I stuck my head through
the gap. It was a cemetery. A Greek Orthodox cemetery with
crosses standing guard over the dead. The hole in the wall

was exactly my size. Maybe it had opened for me. Gathering up the skirt of my blue dress, like Alice entering Wonderland, I passed through the hole.

As soon as my feet touched the dry leaves carpeting the ground on the other side, all sounds in the cemetery ceased. The sparrows on the branches, the chattering crickets, the ichneumon flies scurrying across the gravel all held their breath and looked at me. A lizard crawling up a gravestone, seeing me fall into its world, froze where it was. Brushing twigs and leaves from my skirt, I stood up. The light from the linden leaves that had drawn me in became a flood, cascading down onto my head, spotlighting me for the whole universe. Look! Here is a woman in love – madly in love! Bowing to the ground, I made my greetings to the dead who slept there, under the sombre crosses and marble stones. The world was blessing my presence with all living and non-living creatures.

As I began to walk around, leaves rustled beneath my feet. Moss had gathered on the north sides of the crosses. The faces of angels whose wings stretched over the dead had become blackened and the paths between the graves were clogged with thorny branches and the underground bumps of vast tree roots. Beside the graves lay forgotten empty vases, pots filled with dried-out earth, rusty frames containing now indistinguishable photographs. A familiar void ached inside me, but even that gave me pleasure. Death had its own elegance. Just as the longing to reunite made love sweet, so death gave meaning to life. I made a mental note to explain all this to Petro.

There was a small chapel in the centre of the graveyard. As I peered through the dirty window, I was suddenly conscious of being entirely alone in that vast cemetery. Raising my head, I watched the light falling on the gravestones through the century-old cypress trees. Sparrows were chirping and with their tiny beaks were pecking at the fruit on the branches of a fig tree that had grown up beside a fountain.

I glanced at the dates carved into the gravestones around the chapel. Most were from the first half of the twentieth century. As far as I could see, the most recent death was 1955. This was a rather large grave near the fountain. Forty-eight years ago. Leaning down, I read out the name on the tomb using the ancient Greek I'd learnt at university.

LU-KI-A-NOS 1904 ~ 1955

What a shame, he'd died so young, at only fifty-one, which would have made him a mere twelve years older than me. I felt as if my life was only just beginning. I glanced up at the sky. My childhood seemed no more than a stone's throw away. Did everyone feel that way – as if they were still only just starting out – right up until the day they died?

I sat down beside the grave, clearing the dried leaves and dirt from the marble lid inscribed with a cross in bas-relief. The vase at its foot had turned completely black and was silted up. It was obvious that no one had visited the deceased in a long time. I swung my feet purposelessly for a while. Two crows had perched on the arms of a cross in front of me. They watched me without fear. I winked at them, then leant towards the lid.

'May I sing you a song, Mr Lukianos? It may not be appropriate, but given the derelict state of your final resting place, I do not think you will judge me.'

The fig tree, rustling its branches, bent towards me. I raised my head. The crows turned their beady little eyes to see what I was looking at. The figs were small, hard and wrinkled. How sad. Like dried-up breasts that had never produced milk. My own breasts, which had never produced milk, raised their nipples rebelliously under the dress I had hurriedly slipped on without a bra. They were still aching from last night. Throwing my head back, I started murmuring the words of an old song that came to me from somewhere.

'Bend down, weeping willow, bend down.
It is not just love, what I have.
Bend down, rain and wind, bend down.
It is not just love, what I have.'

We never know when or how love will come into our life, do we, Mr Lukianos? We think the decision to love is ours. At least, that's what I used to think. If I wanted to fall in love, I could; if I didn't want to, I'd take precautions and it wouldn't happen. Ha, ha! Yes, you're laughing down there, beneath the earth, aren't you? I've known a lot of men. But did I ever really know them?

Okay, let me correct that. I have had sex with a considerable number of men. I know the breathless charms of seduction games, secret affairs, forbidden sex. And I love it. A woman must keep her spirit fresh with little adventures. As you know, one man is never enough. Clearly, I heard that once somewhere and hid it in a dark corner of my soul.

But what I loved was the game, not love itself. I didn't fall in love with the men I had sex with. I believed that in this way I could keep on being faithful to Sinan, to my husband. So what? Are you laughing again? Yes, it's nonsense. You're right. This morning, I woke up madly in love with a man I don't know at all. You have seen the world beyond, Mr Lukianos – can you give me a hint? Had I seen something special in Petro? Is it because I gave myself without a thought into those soft hands that I now cannot imagine a life without him, that I am saying all these things to him in my head? I beg your pardon, Mr Lukianos, it is to him and not to you that I am speaking. It's as if he is the only person in the world who can understand me.

I raised my arms to the sky, which I could see through the branches. I wanted to fly, to twirl and twirl, faster and faster, to rise above the branches, to reach the sky, the clouds...

I began to laugh.

All of a sudden, Barish, my first ever lover, came into my mind. Remembering him, my swinging feet and the thoughts in my head came to an abrupt stop. All sounds ceased. I lowered my head as if to hear the tune playing inside me. This was it – I had found it! I recognised the state I was now in from back then. From the time of Barish. It wasn't the carefree Emma Bovary that I'd reminded myself of earlier, when I was dancing in the empty street with my hands in my pockets, laughing like a madwoman. It was my younger self. Melike, under the spell of her first love. Melike, waiting in her small bedroom in the waterfront villa, lying on her back on the narrow bed that smelled of lavender, listening for the creak of a door opening. Repeating to herself every word that Barish had spoken, scouring those words for the tiniest expression of love. Fifteen-year-old Melike, recalling the imprint of Barish's lips on hers as she sat on the school bus the following morning, trying to work out a new theory of relativity that would balance the short time she spent with him against the time spent without him.

Ah, Barish! Barish and his crooked smile – when did that duo first appear in my life? Wasn't it sitting at a round table in that fish restaurant in Baltalimani one September evening?

'Get to know each other, you children. We're all going to

be living together under the same roof. Melike, Cem, Barish, from now on you will be siblings. Go for a walk along the shore together while we wait for the food to arrive.'

'Ha, ha.'

The thin black line above Barish's lip. His wonky, adolescent face, his lovable laugh. Dr Chetin had proposed to Mum two days earlier, and now he was whispering in her ear about the September moon rising like an orange ball behind the opposite hills. My nipples ached under my white blouse. I got cramps in my legs at night. These things happen as you grow up. The sarcastic laughter of my new big brother triggered a flutter of bird's wings in my heart. Was this also a side effect of growing up?

I lay face down on the marble, my ear resting on the lid. The sunshine shimmering through the fig and linden leaves had heated up the marble. My bare knees felt warm. My hips ached. Seeing me lying down, the crows took flight. After they left, everything seemed very deserted. I closed my eyes. Barish's voice echoed in my head.

'The dream of love is sweeter than love itself, Melike.'

How about that! How had a knee-high adolescent come up with such great pronouncements? I can laugh about it now, but at the time it made me terribly sad. I believed that he, and he alone, was my one true love. He wasn't a dream – he was flesh and blood. Being without him was death. On Monday mornings, when he went back to his boarding school, I would burn inside. Maybe he'd read that saying somewhere and was selling it to his fifteen-year-old lover.

Could we really have been called 'lovers'? What should we have been called instead? Siblings who were secretly making love?

Melike, Cem, Barish, from now on you will be siblings.

Blessed Dr Chetin! It was hard to believe that he – a reclusive dreamer, the gentleman resident of a waterfront villa – had fathered a boy like Barish, a good-for-nothing playboy. But in this story, it wasn't the maids that the young master of the villa fucked – it was his stepsister in her little street-side bedroom.

Have you finished this story, Melike?

Is that how you remember Barish?

No, not like that, of course.

Not at all.

At first there were two children. They dangled their feet in the dark waters of the Bosphorus off the end of a rotten wooden jetty. The moonless night smelled of salt and seaweed. Phosphorescence glowed on their intertwining bare feet. The girl kept throwing pebbles into the water, creating ring after ring after ring. Her pockets were full of pebbles. As for her throat, it was dry. She had never kissed a boy in her life, but when the boy put his hand down the front of her dress and held her left breast in her palm, it seemed like the most natural thing in the world. Her nipple became erect, reaching out to the finger that was touching it. She wasn't embarrassed at all – why was that? A familiar smell came to her. Was it because of that smell that when she undressed by candlelight in her room on the street side of the villa, when the boy lay on top of her on the narrow bed, she felt no shame?

At first they were just two children. The mother of one of them had died; the father of the other had gone away. Only smells remained.

Two children taking refuge in passion, relieving their despair in each other.

*

I had dozed off. When a fig dropped onto my back, my eyes sprang open with a start. I sat straight up on the grave. The hard little fig that had woken me up rolled off into a mess of sticks and twigs among the tree roots. I stood up drunkenly, sweeping the dry leaves from my dress. When I gathered my hair on top of my head, a familiar coolness spread from my sweaty neck down my back. I remembered Safinaz putting a white muslin cloth on my back to draw out the perspiration.

As I knelt down to retie the laces of my espadrilles, my eyes were drawn to the grave onto which the fallen fig had rolled.

1910 ~ 1974

Ah, Lukianos, my friend, do you see that? There's someone here who closed their eyes on life after you did. I paused abruptly. Why did these numbers feel familiar?

Probably because I'd played so much sudoku, sometimes my mind would get stuck on a sequence of numerals – the number plate of the car in front of me in a traffic jam, for example. I'd see a pattern in the numbers, feel like there was some mysterious connection. But just as when trying to recall a dream, the more I racked my brain about the dates on this gravestone which had given me pause, the more the clue eluded me. The brain cells that stored all of this knowledge tingled one by one, but somehow I couldn't find my way through the complex labyrinth.

I walked over to the gravestone, trying to figure out what the dates 1910 and 1974 meant to me. Two names were engraved on the stone. My eye went to the second name, which was in parentheses. I recognized Σ – sigma – right away. Then an alpha, *α*. S-A. *Φ* fi. S-A-F-I... The modern Greek alphabet was different from the ancient Greek – that I knew. I was probably getting something wrong. I traced the letters with my fingers, checking their authenticity. The marble had been carved with care, the letters painted in black, though most of the paint had peeled off. Next *v* – which translated as n. S-a-f-i-n-...

I turned around anxiously, took two quick steps towards the gap in the wall. But my brain had already registered the last two letters: in Greek, they were alpha and zeta; in Turkish they were a and z – a beginning and an end. *Σ-α-φ-ι-ν-α-ζ*. In despair, I stepped back onto the dry leaves and looked down at the unornamented, angel-less, abandoned, single-person grave.

No, I had not been wrong.

The name hidden inside the Greek letters was 'Safinaz Kutsi'.

My paternal grandmother's name.

Running back through the bushes and twigs, I hurled myself out through the hole in the wall. As I reached the hill, I remembered that there'd been another name carved on the gravestone as well. It was too late now. I was already beside the city walls.

Something was very wrong! The world had stopped making sense. Or maybe it was me. Was I going mad? Hadn't I lain down on graves and talked to the dead? It was as if a secret hand had put that gravestone there for me to see. A secret hand. Petro's hands on my breasts, my belly. Was that a sign, Mr Lukianos, that I was descending into Wonderland? Miraculous signs to show me the way? What was Safinaz's grave doing there? All those old memories – Dad's telegram and everything. Safinaz's ghost appearing in my dream.

Her ghost? A woman who seals her womb of her own free will is the most dangerous creature in the universe. The birds that led me to the cemetery. The crazy poet. *Wear the beauty of Istanbul and come, for my sake.* The tricycle in the churchyard, the still-burning candles. Was someone trying to send me a message? Angels? Divine beings? A gift from the magnificent universe to its perfect particle? Safinaz's grave. The gravestone. Alpha and zeta. A to z.

You are losing your mind, Melike!

When I got to the hotel, I flew up the stairs in a single breath and plunged into the room. The sweet smell of coffee filled my nostrils. The bed, denying the night before, was immaculately made up, pillows puffed and settled at the head. Petro was sitting in the armchair by the window holding a small cup in his hand. He had showered and shaved and was wearing a spotless, ironed, light green linen suit. He reacted to my rushing into the room all flushed as if it were the most normal thing in the world. Sitting in the armchair where in my dream last night Safinaz had been doubled over laughing, he said with perfect composure, 'We need to talk, Melike, *mou*.'

10

Gulbahar's Dimple

Mina's prophecy couldn't have stopped Dad.

And it didn't.

The day after we learnt of Safinaz's suicide, he set off for Istanbul.

He never came back to us.

Who knows, maybe he'd been longing to unearth the secrets of his mother's past for years. Or maybe he was tired of lying in the hammock reading books all day in the piece-of-paradise village he'd come to with so many dreams; tired of Gulbahar's increasingly bitter resentment. So he made the most of the opportunity and left. Given the circumstances, were the delirious exhortations of a feverish twelve-year-old village girl going to stop him? True, Mina seemed to know many things that we didn't. When Cem had inadvertently poisoned himself by eating potato seedlings and began vomiting with a bright green face, it was Mina who gathered herbs from the mountains, boiled them, and brought him back to health. But that didn't mean we had to take her nightmares seriously.

I hadn't given any thought to Mina's predictions until

years later, when she suddenly reappeared one evening at the door of Dr Chetin's villa on the Bosphorus. I'd not seen her since the day, six years prior, when we'd left her at a boarding school in Antalya. The fact that she'd then come to find us was not surprising. My mother had supported her throughout her time away, and Mina had written her long letters, sent holiday cards, and telephoned on occasion. The strange thing was the timing. The very evening she'd appeared, Dr Chetin had been bringing Mum home from the clinic in Switzerland where she'd been convalescing. Mina was standing at the door of the villa with a small earth-brown suitcase in her sweaty hand.

'I saw her in my dream, Melike. Madam Gulbahar had got tangled up in some seaweed at the bottom of the sea and couldn't break free. So I've come to take care of her. She's done so much for me. Please, Melike, let me look after her.'

It was then that I remembered Mina's prophecy. If Mina had foreseen the trouble that had come to Mum, could it also have been the case that the place Dad had gone to, the place from which he'd never returned, had really been hellish, like she'd said?

Oh, come on! When Mina arrived at Dr Chetin's villa, I was seventeen years old. I knew very well by then that my father had gone off somewhere and fallen in love with a young girl, erasing us from his life with a single stroke of his pen. Cem knew it too. So did Mum. We never discussed it, but we all knew. In fact, it was Mina who knew nothing. Dr Chetin must have searched for Mina, found her, and arranged for her to come and take care of Mum after her return from Switzerland. That was the explanation. She was just acting as if she had all these intuitive powers, as if she was a medium of some sort.

As I showed her into the house, that familiar smell from my childhood came to me. It was a smell like Mum's leather bag, like pickled meat, and it took me back to the day when our teacher, Mr Ibrahim, brought her to our house that first time.

It was not long after we'd settled in the village, three years before Safinaz's death and Dad leaving us. We had sold Kurtcebe to a car mechanic in Kas. Our new house was small, but on our first sunny morning there Mum had set the table for breakfast in the garden under the grapevine arbour. There were olives and cheese that we'd bought on the road. Dad had strung up a hammock between two fig trees. He and Mum would lie together and swing, laughing like children. Cem and I were attending school in the nearest town – there wasn't one in the village. In the mornings all of us children of the village would line up in single file behind Mr Ibrahim and follow him along a goat track smelling of sage and thyme to get there.

At the National Children's Day ceremony on April 23rd, Cem had carried the flag. People coming from nearby villages, seeing my brother's blond curls and the noble way he held the flag with both hands, whispered to each other that he must be a prince. Nobody except Mr Ibrahim noticed that I recited my poem in front of the bust of Ataturk without faltering at all. When the ceremony was over, he stroked my hair. Everybody was on edge that day. Along with the whispers that my brother was a prince, there were other rumours going around, something about the military taking over the government and imposing martial law. When I asked Mum what everyone was talking about, she said, 'Oh, it's too difficult to explain now.' Somebody had done a speech on television the previous night, but we didn't watch it – in our village there was no television at that point. The *mukhtar*'s television arrived later.

I had been happy when Mr Ibrahim – followed by Mina – showed up at the garden gate of our new house the next day. As usual, Dad was lying in the hammock and Cem was on the couch inside, reading. Mum and I were hosing the vegetable patch.

During those early days in the village, Mum was as excited as a little girl. The first time she ate fish fresh from the sea and strawberries with earth still clinging to them, roses bloomed in her cheeks and she hugged and kissed Dad. With the help of the *mukhtar*'s wife Naciye, she was raising tomatoes and peppers, and she'd sown parsley, dill and basil in pots bought from the local market. She was also planning to make a flowerbed right behind the fig trees. She would get down on her knees in the glittering sunlight, digging into the earth, pulling weeds, removing bugs and other insects, marking a border with rocks we'd picked up from the shore. Thanks to her work, by summer the garden wall was going to be adorned with bougainvillea, the alcove with jasmine. She also cooked a lot. In the stone kitchen of our little house, which also served as the sitting room and the office, she enthusiastically dredged fish with flour, cooked tomato pilaf and made salads. Sometimes the two of us together would consult the cookbooks her mother sent from Istanbul and bake orange or almond cakes. Mum would even let me lick the sugary remnants at the bottom of the bowl.

When I saw my teacher at the gate, I jumped up and stood to attention. Mum glanced up from where she was kneeling on the ground. She was wearing baggy trousers, the same as Mina's, only Mum's were purple, not red. Her head was

covered with a scarf of the same colour. As the sun set behind
the castle it was casting a red glow across the very part of
the garden where Mum was kneeling. The curly ends of her
blond hair had slipped from her scarf. Forgetting that she was
covered in soil up to her elbows, she'd tried to wipe the sweat
from her forehead with her arm, leaving a muddy streak
across her eyebrows. I giggled. When Mum laughed, her
dimples showed. Mr Ibrahim stood frozen to the spot at the
garden gate, his face whiter than the whitewash of the wall.
Mina, meanwhile, was waiting some way back on the dusty
path. I was the only one who'd seen her. Dad's book had
fallen onto his stomach and one of his hands was dangling
down from the hammock.

Mum stood up.

'Welcome, Mr Ibrahim. Please come in. I hope our children
haven't been up to any mischief.'

Unhurriedly, she washed her hands under the hose I was
holding and gave me a tiny wink that no one else could see.
Her hands were so soft then, the skin not yet ruined from
washing clothes with toxic soap. She walked to the gate,
drying her hands on the scarf that she'd just taken off. The
evening sun was setting her hair alight from every angle,
creating a halo of sparks around her face. For a while, Mr
Ibrahim failed to notice her extended hand.

'Please excuse our appearance. Melike and I were just
planting kale. They say it doesn't like the climate here, that
it's a Black Sea plant, but we're going to try. I love kale stew
and we'll make kale-leaf dolma too. Please, come in.'

She gestured to the alcove where we ate our meals. Then
she saw the hand dangling from the hammock.

'Orhan! Orhan, are you asleep?'

When no answer was forthcoming, she lowered her head

and gave Mr Ibrahim a look as if to say, 'Please forgive us.' Then she became agitated.

'Melike, quick, wake your father up. We have no idea when he drifted off. Oh, my God, has it been longer than twenty minutes?'

If he napped so long that his breathing deepened, Dad always felt disoriented and irritable when he woke up. Mr Ibrahim, who was unfamiliar with this family concern of ours, looked questioningly from me to the hammock. Just then, Mum noticed Mina hiding behind him.

'Ah, who is this little child, Mr Ibrahim? I didn't see her there. Why are you hiding, child? What is your name?'

'Mina,' she whispered, moving closer to the teacher. She too was unable to take her eyes off my mother. Since it was not a school day, Mina wasn't wearing her three-sizes-too-big uniform, nor the stiff collar like the ones the boys wore. But she was wearing the red baggy trousers that always protruded from underneath her uniform, and a pair of brown rubber beach shoes on her dark feet. She and Mr Ibrahim took a few steps into the garden. Dad had woken up and was smacking his lips.

'Mina is Melike's new seat-mate in class,' said Mr Ibrahim.

'Oh, how nice!'

Of course, Mum didn't know how hard it had been for me, sitting in that great big row all by myself. We'd been in the village for more than a month now, and Mina had turned up at school a week ago. Right away, Mr Ibrahim had seated her beside me. Until then, it had been just me on my own in the front row of the crowded classroom. The girls would stare at my fancy lace collar and the smocked uniform my maternal grandmother had had sewn for me by a seamstress in Osmanbey, and they would snigger. The boys would corner me at breaktime and wiggle worms they'd caught in the coal cellar in my face. And when we went back into the classroom, they'd squeeze three or even four people into a seat meant for two and leave me to sit in the front row all by myself.

'Please sit at the table under the arbour. It's cool here. I'll bring the tea. Orhan, dear, Mr Ibrahim is here. Melike's teacher.'

Dad was sitting up in the hammock now, sulking. He had definitely slept longer than twenty minutes. He was going to be cross with me for not having woken him up earlier, before his alpha brainwaves had become delta waves. It was my duty to keep an eye on him. When the fluttering under his eyelids stopped, I had to poke him. But I'd forgotten. I went over and held the hammock rope.

'Oh, hello,' he grumbled, throwing one leg out of the hammock. His feet were shoeless and he'd rolled his trousers up to his knees like a fisherman. Rubbing his eyes, he came and sat down at the table across from Mr Ibrahim. Compared with Mr Ibrahim, who looked smart in his blue suit, my father was unruly.

The previous Monday, when Mina had arrived for her first day at school and been seated next to me, she'd whispered to me that she'd counted six suits in the teacher's wardrobe. She was staying with him because the gendarmes had come and taken Mina's father to Antalya. Mina and her mother had also gone to Antalya, but Mr Ibrahim had since brought Mina back to the village. I got scared when I heard that story. What if the gendarmes came and took Dad? It wasn't that long since we'd left Istanbul. The memories of our final days were still fresh in my mind – Pasha whispering to Safinaz while I eavesdropped from beside the cupboard where the dwarf hid; the doorbell to our apartment ringing at midnight;

Dad lying against Mum's legs in the lilac morning light of our living room and saying, 'I feel nervous, Gulbahar. They are watching everyone. Let's get away from here.' I thought we were safe since our village was accessible only by sea, but Mina had explained that they came via the goat track – the same path we took to school every morning.

The screen door to the kitchen opened. Mum was carrying a tray loaded with tea things. Behind her came my brother carrying another tray stacked with plates. 'Here you are,' said my mother.

I looked to see what was on the tray Cem had put on the table. There was the cake that Mum and I had made that morning, figs, grapes, little bowls of orange and sour-cherry jam, and some hard biscuits.

'As you can see, Ibrahim Bey, we are never allowed to forget that Gulbahar grew up in a mansion in Istanbul. Her hospitality is always matchless, even out here in the middle of nowhere. Pay no attention to the fact that she came here with me. She is a real lady, so she is.'

Did Mr Ibrahim sense the sarcasm in Dad's voice, which back then was still pretty mild? Even if he did, he responded as politely as ever, smiling first at Dad and then at Mum. Dad was looking at the teacher's immaculate fingernails as his elegant hands sliced the cake on his plate with a knife. Then Dad yawned, not bothering to cover his mouth with his hand. In silence, we listened to the buzzing of the insects.

Mum thought our teacher was a sensitive soul. I had heard her saying to Dad, 'Ibrahim must have come here on account of a broken heart. Perhaps his story is a modern-day *Calikusu*, a sad affair of crossed wires and thwarted love, so let us hope that he too will eventually find happiness. He's a cultured man. He has classical music tapes at his house which he plays for the children on his battery-operated tape recorder. Just imagine, Orhan!'

Dad had yawned when she told him this too. But Mr Ibrahim really did invite us village kids to his house in the evenings to listen to music. Sometimes he would roast chestnuts on his woodstove or read books to us. Before the books which my grandmother posted to us from the house in Galata arrived, Cem read books he borrowed from Teacher Ibrahim, big books. After Cem finished them, Mum read them, then they would go on to Dad. They weren't given to me.

After he'd drunk his sugary tea, Mr Ibrahim said in his teacher's voice, 'Children, go and play in the garden. We adults need to have a chat now.'

'Melike, Cem,' Mum prompted, 'go and show Mina your books. Run on inside now.'

Hearing the 'b' of 'books', Cem was already up and heading for the little bookcase in our kitchen. Mina dashed after him. Dragging my feet, I followed them indoors. Cem was on his tiptoes, passing his index finger over the books on the shelves Dad had fixed to the wall between the couch and the woodstove.

'Here it is!' he said, drawing out a thick book with a brown cover. He turned his angelic face and smiled at Mina. Mina couldn't take her eyes off the bookcase. Her nervous fingers lingered over Mum's collection, most of which were in English. When she came to Halide Edip's *Heartache*, she stopped.

'That's a grown-ups' book. It's not for us,' I said.

'Let's look at this one together,' said Cem, walking over to the couch with a thick book under his arm. He had caught the scent of a fellow book lover. Mina followed him. They sat down on the couch side by side, their backs resting against the blue-painted windowsill, their legs stretched out. When Mina pulled her baggy trousers way down, her bare feet got lost in the material. As always, Cem was the little angel – he'd left his rubber shoes in front of the door and was now in his socks, which were snow white. If a person stayed indoors all day, of course their socks stayed clean too.

'This is my father's book, but as long as I don't take it outside, I'm allowed to read it.'

I knew Mina read very fast. I'd realised it the first day she'd sat down next to me and we shared my social studies book, which was covered in some rustly blue paper of Mum's. It was like she wanted to swallow the pages. Probably she was afraid the bell would ring and I would throw the book into my schoolbag and take it home before she could finish reading.

Now, watching Cem read *The Journey of a Musician*, with its tiny print, I understood that Mina was again trying to store the secret world of the pages in her mind in the shortest possible time. She moved her wet lips as she read and every so often made a sucking noise, like she was eating spaghetti.

'This is my favourite book. It's so funny!' said Cem. 'Can you read type this small?'

Without taking her finger from the paragraph she was reading, Mina nodded. Then my brother whispered to her, as if sharing a secret, 'I've read the whole book, from beginning to end, and now I'm reading it again.'

Mina raised her head and looked at my brother with a mixture of surprise and awe on her face. Then she turned the page. This time it was Cem who was surprised.

'Did you finish that page?'

'Yeah.'

The dusk light filtered in through the kitchen window

behind the two heads bent over the book, one blond, one black and speckled with dandruff. Annoyed, I went back outside. The adults were having a discussion under the arbour. I heard them say 'martial law' again. They were talking about people who'd been caught by the police and put in prison. Dad was saying, 'They're just children, for goodness' sake.' Mum and Mr Ibrahim were shaking their heads sadly. Who were 'just children' and what was going to happen to them? The talking stopped when they saw me.

'What are you up to, Melike?'

'Nothing.'

'Where are you going?'

I had no intention of going anywhere. I was just standing beside the door. I leant down and picked up my blue plastic bucket that was under the tap where the hose was connected.

'I'm going to make mud pies.'

'Fine. Go and play, daughter.'

'Don't dig in the vegetable garden and don't go near the outhouse. Play in the soil in front of the kitchen.'

'Okay, Mum.'

'She probably got bored around the other two,' Mr Ibrahim said quietly.

I pricked up my ears. Silence. I patted down the soil I'd shovelled into my bucket. They resumed their chat.

'They started Mina in school late this year. Maybe her birth date was registered late. It's impossible to know how old she is.'

'At least they registered her birth. They could have been negligent about going to the registrar's office when they saw she was a girl... You know what I mean,' said Dad.

Again, there was silence. I imagined Mum looking at Mr Ibrahim with an expression that said 'Please do excuse him.'

'To cut a long story short, Mr Orhan and Mrs Gulbahar—'

'There's no need for the "Mr" and "Mrs", Ibrahim. We're all equals in this village. Please just call us "Orhan" and "Gulbahar". No formalities.'

Silence again. Then the clicking of cigarette lighters. From where I was squatting, I could watch the alcove out of the corner of my eye. Mr Ibrahim was retying his burgundy scarf with his long, thin fingers. He wouldn't call them anything now. Dad had made him uncomfortable. A flame shot through my temples. Mum put another slice of cake on the teacher's plate. My stomach growled.

'They're demanding life imprisonment for the father. A blood feud. The brothers all fled to Germany, but the father's old and couldn't leave the country. They came here last summer, for some reason, and Mina started school in the autumn. According to her birth certificate she's eight years old. She'd never been to school before, but she taught herself to read, so I put her in Year 3. That's the morning session, as you know, with years 2, 3 and 4 all taught together. Mina's mind is as sharp as a whip. She's like a sponge, absorbing whatever she's shown. After the gendarmes took her father, she didn't come to school for a while. Then there was the March 12th coup and the schools were closed.

'Mina's mother took her to Antalya so they could be near the law courts. The brothers, meanwhile, wanted the girl to go over to Germany. There was someone there who wanted to marry her, someone from their own village, a relative on the father's side, I believe. When she heard that, the poor mother contacted our *mukhtar* and asked to speak to me. That was at the end of last week. I went in person to Antalya. It seems the mother has found work there as a carer for an invalid who doesn't want the child around. She gripped my hands and pleaded with me. "Only you can save my daughter, Mr Ibrahim." What could I do? I took Mina and brought her back to the village. She stayed with me that night, and the next day we moved her to the *mukhtar*'s house. On Monday she started back at school and I sat her next to Melike. But now the *mukhtar* is saying that he already has five mouths to feed and that we should be sending word to the brothers for them to come and get her.'

'The bastard!'

'Orhan!'

Mum refreshed the tea. They sat without speaking for a while.

Even though the *mukhtar* had lent us his fishing boat, Dad didn't like him. I remembered something Dad had said last Sunday morning when we'd gone out fishing early. We'd got our tackle together and set out before sunrise. It was cold. I was sitting at the front of the boat with my hands in Dad's, watching our fishing lines hanging off the side. Without taking his eyes from the sky that was turning red behind the island, Dad had said, 'Have you ever seen the whites of the *mukhtar*'s eyes, Melike?'

'No, Dad, I haven't.'

'You can't, because the *mukhtar*'s eyes don't have any whites, they are yellow.'

'Ah, like an egg.'

'Yes, exactly like an egg, my smart daughter. Like an egg, but an egg with no white, only yellow. And do you know why? Because his liver is ruined. Alcohol makes the liver work hard, much too hard, and the exhausted liver then loses its power to send white to the eyes. Do you understand?' He bent down to my ear, his black moustache tickling my neck. 'Because every night our *mukhtar* sits down with the passengers his sons bring over from Castellorizo – passengers named Johnnie Walker and Jim Beam. That's why. Taking tourists out to see the tombs of ancient kings? Ha! Who are they kidding! He's drinking all the time.'

'But you and Mum drink raki every night.'

'That's different. And what do you mean, we drink it every night? We clink glasses from time to time, when we're happy. And raki's white! Surprised you, didn't I, you monkey? Because raki's white, it never turns your eyes yellow – the eyes stay white! Teeth too. Show me your teeth.'

'Melike, what are you doing over there?'

Over by the kitchen door, where I was squatting with my bucket in my hand, I was showing my teeth to an imaginary Dad. Mum's shout startled me.

'Nothing. Making a mud cake. A birthday cake.'

I quickly inverted the bucket, emptied out the soil, sprinkled the last few drops of water in the hose onto the top and patted it with my blue plastic spade. When we'd come to the village, my bucket and spade were the only things Dad had allowed me to bring. And my inflatable rubber ring shaped like a swan. All my other toys had been left in Istanbul. I missed my dolls. When I thought about how lonely they must be without me, I felt like crying.

When Mr Ibrahim began to speak again, his voice sounded foggy.

'I would take Mina in myself. I would happily take care of her, raise her as my own child. I wouldn't hesitate, but it wouldn't do.'

'Why not?' asked Dad.

This seemed to embarrass my teacher. I blushed.

'Mr Orhan... oh, excuse me – Orhan... you wouldn't believe how many villages and towns I've been forced to leave. In one village, they said I was trying to convert the children to an infidel religion because the music of Bach sounded to them like church bells. In another school, when I suggested that we put on a play, they accused me of trying to turn their daughters into actresses and they called me – excuse me – a pimp. A dead rat was placed in front of my door in one village because I allowed the girls and boys to play dodgeball together in PE class. At another place, there was a similar situation to Mina's, where a very bright student was orphaned, and I, in all innocence, took her into my house, under my protection. The whole village congregated outside my door, which is how I ended up here. They almost threw the poor girl into the river to drown, but a man twice her age from a neighbouring village said he would take her, so they let her go. Within a week they were married.'

I froze where I was, kneeling there with my blue plastic spade. Mum and Dad's mouths were shut tight.

'You are good people. I've read your articles, Orhan. You write of humanity, brotherhood, a return to nature, simplicity, innocence and purity of heart. Save this child. Let her live with you, at least until the autumn. Then perhaps her mother will return to the village, in which case we can all support them here.'

Dad cleared his throat. I stood up and looked over at them. Beneath Dad's black moustache his fleshy lips were twisted into a proud smile. Mr Ibrahim had read his writing. I crept over to them and without saying anything crawled onto Dad's lap. He didn't object. The others just glanced at me. Automatically, Dad wound his fingers through my curly hair.

'Well, we'll have to discuss it, won't we, Gulbahar? It's not something we can decide on just like that. Right, Gulbahar?'

He was stroking my hair, but he wasn't really aware that

I was sitting on his lap. Mum buried her face in her slender white hands and inhaled, like she always did when she wanted to say something but was restraining herself. The ash on her cigarette, lying forgotten in the ashtray, got longer.

'I don't know, Orhan. If the child has nowhere else to go... It's not as if we're going to legally adopt her. Just a summer, maybe a winter. Things are so complicated now anyway. They're talking about martial law. Soon—'

'Mina is a hardworking girl,' Mr Ibrahim interjected. 'She was born in a village near Silifke, in the Taurus Mountains, quite some distance east of here. She learnt how to survive in very difficult conditions – she can bring the wood in, light the stove, help with the cooking and washing. She knows how to behave properly.'

'Stop right there, Mr Ibrahim!' Dad had raised his voice. He sat up very straight in his chair and I thought for a moment that he was going to push me off his lap. A lighter clicked. Forgetting the cigarette burning in the ashtray, Mum had lit a new one.

'If Mina were to come and live with us for even just one day, she would live here as our child. She would be treated exactly the same as Cem and Melike, not differently in any way. That's how it would be.'

Mr Ibrahim tilted his head and, at an angle that only Mum could see, gave a small smile. Exhaling a stream of smoke in Dad's direction, Mum answered the smile with the dimple at the corner of her beautiful lips.

Only I saw that exchange of glances, and how it momentarily bonded the two of them.

11

Intrigue

On the ferry back to Buyukada my insides were burning.

Knowing that tea on an empty stomach made me dizzy, I had a glass anyway, and, as if that weren't enough, I asked the skinny, long-haired young man sitting next to me if I could bum a cigarette. He clearly understood my situation. He looked at my messed-up face and said, 'Keep the packet, I have another one.' Sitting on the open deck at the back of the ferry, I drank tea and chain-smoked. Like my mother, I was hoping that if I hid behind the smoke, maybe I could just cry inside. The old Yalova ferry from Sirkeci always took ages, thank goodness, stopping at every island until it finally reached ours after two hours. I needed the time. Time to unravel the knots inside me and find a way forward. Time to clear my disordered head, to calm my soul. How could I face Sinan in the state I was in?

I looked at the shimmering blue city, roasting in the afternoon heat. The haze had erased the definition of the shoreline, removed all colour. Only the minarets, reaching up into the blue sky, had escaped the low pressure that was holding the city in its claws. To distract myself, I tried to find the mosques built on the seven hills: Yavuz Selim, Fatih, Suleymaniye... I couldn't do it! The dilapidated old ferry was going faster than I'd hoped and the pain in my heart couldn't bear the sight of the old city walls alongside which I had skipped just that morning.

My eyes filled. I chewed my lips.

Son of a bitch, Petro! He'd cheated me, deceived me. No, 'deceive' was too mild for what he'd done. The bastard was a liar from head to toe. And me? I was the epitome of a fool. Oh, sure, he was producing a documentary film about Byzantine churches. Yeah, he found my name on the internet. I should have sussed him out from the start. When you typed 'Byzantine churches' into Google, was it only my name that popped up, as if I was a world-famous professor in the field? Tricksy bastard. And to top it all, he had sex with me. Beast!

'Melike, I beg you, please be reasonable. The reason I knocked on your room door last night was to tell you all this. I couldn't sleep for worrying that if I told you the truth, you'd react exactly as you are doing now. I swear to you, that was my intention, but you—'

We were facing each other in the room. No, he was sitting where I had found him, in the armchair by the window, perfectly composed, and I was standing across from him, barely able to restrain myself from grabbing his neatly pressed linen suit by its starched collar and ripping it to shreds.

'Then you should have told me. You didn't look like you were at all eager to talk! What a hypocritical bastard – you used me.'

'Don't do this, Melike. *Eleos!* Have mercy! You came on to me at the door, so warm, so soft, so irresistible. What could I do? I couldn't control myself.'

He stood up to embrace me. I pushed him away with all my strength. He didn't even stagger. He turned and sat back down, picked up the empty cup, sniffed it, put it back on the table beside the armchair.

Remembering all this, a teardrop escaped from the corner of my eye and rolled down my cheek. I turned and looked at the city, fading into the distance so quickly. Did he really say, 'I couldn't control myself'? Did he really lose all self-control because of me? Despite myself, I smiled. A second teardrop rolled down my cheek, then a third. I finished the tea in the glass I was squeezing in my palm.

Goddamn you, Petro.

'Would you bring me another tea?'

'Right away.'

God, Melike! Are you trying to console yourself with the flattery of his 'I couldn't control myself' like some stupid schoolgirl? Are you trying to find crumbs of love in a story that has been a lie from start to finish? The bastard turned out to be an impostor. Wandering around Safinaz's old neighbourhood, jumping over the wall of the locked-up school, whispering the names of people long forgotten – what were you thinking?

What I'd thought were simply chance scenes in a sweet romance had in fact all been carefully planned. If the whole thing had been his idea, then, okay. But who was his accomplice? Huh? Who was the architect of this intrigue?

Orhan Kutsi.

My father!

The tea scorched my mouth and throat like a dragon's tongue, making my insides churn.

Think, Melike, think! Orhan Kutsi and Petro put their heads together and prepared this deception to trick you, soften you up, prepare you, if only a little, for what you would hear. It all made sense, of course. Petro had known so much about the Bloody Church, the Red School, that square that holds so much meaning for me.

'Your father sent me, Melike.'

'What?'

When I heard that, I almost fell off the edge of the bed. A foolish smile settled on my face. If Petro was going to invent things, he should try and be more credible. But he was serious. Upset. The moment he finished his coffee and set the cup on the table, I realized he was for real.

'There was some truth in what I told you. It's true that I am a documentary producer and I am doing a project on Byzantine churches. But…'

From the window behind him came the sound of children playing on the street and with it a surge of stiflingly hot air. My ears were burning. I stood up, but a part of me stayed there on the edge of the bed watching us trancelike as Melike walked towards Petro. Petro wiped a few beads of sweat from his forehead with the back of his hand. He had got smaller, his head had retracted into his body like a tortoise's; his neck had disappeared.

'What did you say?'

Putting my two hands on the arms of the chair, I thrust my face close to his. He was discomfited, trapped, and squirmed where he sat. His face was perspiring; little beads of sweat were popping up all over it – on his freshly shaved top lip, on the sides of his nose, around the roots of his hair.

'Melike, your father is very ill. He has leukaemia. He's in the last stage now, he's at home, waiting to die, and…'

'And?'

'He wants to see you one last time.'

When I leant over, the front of my dress gaped open. So as not to stare at my braless breasts, Petro turned his head towards the bed. On purpose, I leant over even further.

'Melike, you're frightening me. Don't look at me as if I'm your enemy.'

I drew back. My brain was taking in what he had said, each word spreading through my blood like deadly poison.

'The poor man is at death's door and he keeps repeating your name.'

Another cigarette. The woman sitting beside me on the crowded Sunday ferry waved away the smoke with her hand and gave me a cross look. On any other day, I would have done the same. I was against people smoking on the ferry. They said it would soon be prohibited. But today? Today was different! As I inhaled the smoke, puff after puff, my heart groaned like a train coming into the station.

You, Dad? After all these years? *But, no, let's not do this too fast. To smooth things over, let's send Petro first.* How thoughtful. Thank you so much! You dropping all those little details about our shared past into his head was intentional, so that I would think about you, right? You suggested he go into the church before I got there and light two candles. An inspired touch. Bravo! It worked. I've thought about you more in the past twenty-four hours than I have for years. But, my dear father, if you were hoping that in remembering you I would forgive you, there you are badly mistaken. The memories that came back to me were not sufficient to soften my heart. Perhaps you anticipated that, too. Perhaps honey-eyed young Petro knocking on my bedroom door at midnight was also part of the plan. So then what? When I woke up the next morning madly in love, was I supposed to wrap my naked arms around my lover's neck and say, 'Oh, my darling father, what a lovely gift you've sent me'? Was that your marvellous plan? The stories you used to tell us when we were little always began well, Dad, but you never could tie up the endings properly. Which means clearly you haven't changed at all.

As the ferry approached Kinali Island, the salty breeze dried the teardrops on my lashes. I smiled bitterly, thinking of my lovesick state earlier that morning. *J'ai un amant.* Ha! Even Emma Bovary was shrewder than you, Melike. Twirling around under washing lines strung between houses with colourful clothes hanging from them, your hands in the pockets of your blue dress. Just a few hours ago... How many more secret adventures I would have had with Petro! I would have run off into his arms and he would have been waiting for me in our hotel beside the city walls. Every so often, I would have hopped onto a plane and flown to Athens. While the sun was setting behind the Parthenon, we would have drunk a toast to Dionysius with the most delicious wine in the world. Strolling around the ruins, among street musicians, our arms around each other, we would have stayed sweethearts forever. Not sweethearts, lovers. Madly in love forever. Petro could have married if he wished, had many children. He would never have left me. On secluded, faraway islands in old-fashioned hotels overlooking wintry seas, we would have made love, keeping alive the secret love that only the two of us knew about. We would have remained fresh lovers (*les amants!*) whom time and habituation could not tarnish. Ah, Melike. Naive, foolish, stupid Melike. How was I the daughter of this father who had dreamt up such a complex plot, such intrigue?

'If you agree, I will take you to see him.'

'I do not agree.'

Like an angry panther locked in a cage, I was circling the room – the room in which our breath, our sweat, our skin had mingled – from the door to the window and back again.

'Melike, *mou*, you are angry. You are hurt. And you're right, I should have been less impatient. But... suddenly... I couldn't stop myself. Go home, think about it with a clear head. As you know, I'm here for two more days. If you want to come—'

He got up from the chair and walked to the window. His trousers were wrinkled from sweat, his hair tousled. Good! I stood in front of him, my hands on my hips. My lips and eyes were burning, as if I'd eaten a hot pepper.

'Where is my father?'

He avoided my eyes. I walked around the armchair and squeezed him into a corner. He tried to escape to the window, but he was too big to get past. He shrank. His chest, level with my head, was heaving.

Oblivious to the open window, I shouted, 'Tell me! Where are you going to take me? Ha, you won't even tell me that! You're a coward as well as a liar!'

The sounds of children playing on the street ceased. Several windows creaked open.

'Your father asked that I tell you where he is only if you agree to go and see him.'

'Well, thanks a lot. Come on, Petro! So you do everything he says, like a little lamb, do you? Why? Are you his son or something? If you are, believe me, I will not be surprised. You come here, screw your sister! There you have it – a Greek tragedy! It fits. Tell me, ye gods, did I make love with my brother last night?'

'Melike, please don't shout. It's nothing like that. Your father raised me, but you and I are not blood relatives. If you come with me, you can hear it all directly from him.'

No, I would not listen to any of it! I grabbed my bag from the floor, slammed the door and left, heading straight to the ferry.

While you were bringing up Petro, Dad, who did you think was bringing me up? My melancholic mother with the vacant eyes who kept moving us from one house to the next? Her husband, the villa gent, Dr Chetin? My maternal grandparents, who adored Cem but pretended I didn't exist?

Goddamn you, Dad!

We had arrived at Buyukada. I jumped off before the ferry had properly docked. Even as a child, I wouldn't have been able to run up the hill to our house as fast as I did now. I was surprised when suddenly I found myself at the kitchen door. Sinan was on his own inside. He was bent over the counter, whistling along to a tune on the radio while dipping anchovies into flour in a transparent bowl. When he turned to take a sip of the wine he'd placed on the breadboard, he saw me. The wine stuck in his throat.

'Melike, my dear. Princess! Early… you're home early. What's happened? Melike, my darling, what's happened? Let me look at you.'

At the sight of my husband's floury hands reaching out to me, the sobs which for so many hours I had held in tightly were suddenly set free. Tears began to course down my cheeks like a river that had breached its banks. Sinan became very anxious.

'Melike, for God's sake, what's happened? Are you all right? Did you have an accident? Have you had some bad news? Speak to me!'

Shielding my chest with my fists, I nestled close to him, like a baby. 'It's nothing – nothing to worry about,' I murmured between sobs. Holding his hands in the air so as not to dirty my dress, Sinan put his arms around me. I closed my eyes and rubbed my face against his grey beard. My feet were on the ground, my belly relaxed. Here was a man who was the same height as me, the same age as me. Here was a man who made my heart feel like it had come home. No other man had been able to do that. What business did I have being out on the streets or in the arms of strangers?

Suddenly I got panicky. Strangers' arms! I hadn't changed my dress or even showered. I was never this negligent. My hair smelled not just of cigarettes but of marijuana; beneath my fingernails was another man's skin. I hadn't even looked in a mirror properly; there might be purple bruises on my neck. I tried to draw back, but as I thought about the night before, I wept even more. I couldn't leave Sinan's arms.

'Oh my God! What happened, Melike? Come on, say something. You're driving me crazy, sweetheart.'

'It's nothing, Sinan. My nerves are frayed, that's all.'

I couldn't say any more. Saliva, snot, sobs. I was making a childish racket.

'Okay, okay, my one and only. Let's just calm down and go to our room. Then we'll talk.'

I nodded my head, which was resting on his beard. Without letting go of me, he washed his hands in the sink and together we left the kitchen. He grabbed the bottle of wine he'd left on the counter as we passed. I was burying my face in his shoulder like an ostrich. Footsteps approached down the corridor. Mina was coming to the kitchen. I didn't lift my head as she passed us. If I had, she would have seen everything in my face, the witch. Sinan shielded my face with his arm, as if protecting me from paparazzi. He and Mina spoke briefly about the anchovies and pilaf.

Sinan and I went into our bedroom. A hot, humid breeze danced in through the two open doors, causing the gauze curtains to billow like a wedding dress. The light of the setting sun painted the bed's white mosquito netting pink. Kneeling down on one knee, Sinan untied the laces of my espadrilles and lifted the edge of the netting. Still wearing my dress, I slid under it and took the wine glass Sinan held out to me. In his green shorts and white T-shirt he sat down cross-legged on the bed in front of me. I glanced briefly at his face, trying not to catch his eye. He had rested well in the past few days, got tanned in the sun. All of a sudden I recalled how his eyes had lit up the moment he saw me at the kitchen door, as if a lamp was burning behind his beautiful wide-browed face.

I used to think my husband also had little adventures in my absence. For example, while I was away on this so-called business trip, he could have taken the opportunity to call a friend, or one of those research assistants who were so in awe of him. He could have had a fling – not there in the mansion, under the nose of Mina and my mother, but, I don't know, maybe in one of those newly opened boutique hotels up in the pine forest. To me this would have been a distinct possibility. But no, taking advantage of my not being there in that way clearly hadn't entered my husband's mind. Instead, he prepared a feast of anchovies and pilaf for his elderly mother-in-law and her carer and met my unexpected early return, not with the anxiety of a deceiving husband, but with innocent joy.

Thinking about this, I was engulfed by a new wave of tears. I had ruined everything! I was a truly terrible person. Of course this wasn't the first time I'd cheated on him, but it was the first time I'd been so enthralled. And by whom? A son of a bitch! A liar, a deceiving fraudster. By God, Petro, the way you duped me. How you took advantage of my good intentions. You used me, you low-down bastard. Ah, my dear Sinan, my darling husband, how can I tell you the real reason my heart is raging? How can I tell you that I am crying like a schoolgirl because the fantasies I have, about a man I met just yesterday, have been smashed to pieces? You, who laugh at my flirtatiousness – even take your share of the credit – feel proud of your charming wife, can't believe that I might sleep with the men I flirt with in front of your eyes. Would you stay with me, even for a second, if you knew how much truth there was in the jokes you used to make about jealous husbands?

In my mind, though, I've always remained faithful to you. I have been without sin because I never fell in love with any of those men, never had real feelings for any of them. If I told you this now, you wouldn't believe me, but I was going to leave all that behind, had promised myself that I wouldn't make love with anyone but you. I had even cut down a lot. And then... Ah, Sinan, how can I tell you that I fell in love with a lie?

'Shhh, shhh... Calm down, sweetheart. Let me pour you some more wine. There, there. Cry as much as you want to. It will relax you. Your nerves are shattered. All of us are irritable in this heat – it's easy to get upset about trivialities.

When you tell me about it, we'll see what a tiny thing it is, and we'll laugh about it.'

He got up and refilled my glass from the bottle on the bedside table. Still crying, I tried to think quickly. How could I explain this nervous breakdown to him now? I had to have a rational reason for crying like a child who'd had her toy snatched. The emotional stability of women in our family was a questionable subject – I had no right to give my husband further cause for concern. But I couldn't say, 'The man who was going to make a documentary film on Byzantine churches turned out to be a liar and that's why I'm crying.' Still, I had to tell him some element of truth. And I could do that. My brain quickly started to rewrite the story of the past twenty-four hours, cutting out the romantic scenes. It did this so well, and so quickly, that even I almost believed my story.

Sinan came back under the netting and sat cross-legged in front of me. I stretched out like a cat and put my head in his lap. I couldn't look him in the face. The sun had set, fading the pink of the netting. Holding his wine glass in one hand, Sinan stroked my hair with the other. From time to time he held the glass to my lips. I would raise my head to take a sip of wine, then again lay my head on my husband's suntanned legs. Feeling his hand in my hair, I thought that my heart, already softened by so many tears, would melt. The wine was also beginning to have an effect. I was starting to distance myself from my broken heart. I closed my eyes.

'My father...' I said in a voice like a whisper. 'My father is dying.'

Sinan's fingers wandering through my hair came to a halt.

'What are you saying? Oh, Melike, oh, my darling, sweetheart. Come here. There, there. Oh, God! Let me hug you.' He picked me up and held me like a baby in his arms. I rested my head on his chest, the volume of my tears surprising even me. 'My darling princess, but of course you would be upset about that. And I was so tactless to say it was just a small thing. Your father, uh? Dying? I didn't even know he was ill. What's wrong with him?'

Maybe it was that easy. Maybe the question of how I had learnt this news wouldn't even come up. While I was in Istanbul, I stopped by the house in Galata and found a letter there, or something like that.

No, no. Stick to the truth as closely as you can, Melike. Don't expose yourself. Don't make it harder than it needs to be.

'Petro came here to tell me.'

I sighed. I could hear the beating of Sinan's heart beneath my ear. He bent down and brought his face close to mine. His grape-green eyes darkened in the shadows pervading the room.

'Who is Petro?'

Safinaz's grave came into my head. Had I really seen that grave, or was it a vision? All those miraculous signs that had seemed entirely feasible in the morning now, in the calm of my marriage bed, didn't seem believable at all.

'Melike, who is Petro?'

I slipped out of Sinan's arms and sat across from him, taking a sip of the wine he held out to me. My insides were still and silent. The storm had abated. Winding my hair around my neck, I raised my head.

'Petro, you know… that so-called documentary producer, the one who hired me as a consultant for a film he's making about Byzantine churches.' Sinan's eyes, which were always so sharp, became dull for a moment. 'I went to Istanbul for that job about Byzantine churches, remember? It was meant to last three days.'

'Of course. I knew that. But I didn't know... the producer's name...'

'Forget it. It's not relevant.'

'Why? What happened, Melike? What does all this have to do with your father? What do you mean when you say Petro came to tell you this?'

I held my back very straight. I felt very calm now; strong and good, very good indeed. I was sure my eyes were blazing with an insane light. Lines of worry appeared on Sinan's ever-darkening visage. I spoke with forced levity.

'Darling, it was my father who sent this impostor Petro.'

As I waited for him to take that in, I laughed drily. He was very confused. He sat there for a long time, rubbing his chin and his beard as he tried to work it out, to come up with a logical chain of events. I continued.

'My father is very ill, with leukaemia. He's had a relapse and it's terminal. He's set his heart on seeing me. Does he think he'll go to heaven if he apologizes? He knew that if he were to call me himself, I wouldn't come. So he sent Petro, who is his son – or something like that... I mean, probably. I don't know. I didn't listen to the details. When I realized I'd been tricked, I came straight home, to you.'

'What are you saying, Melike? Your father has another child and sent him to find you? You mean, you met your brother?'

Bad move. A very bad move, Melike! The point of telling Sinan that particular detail was to quash any suspicions he might be harbouring about me and Petro having had sex, but I hadn't taken into account that I might then need to give him more information. Everything was developing too fast. My brain was slowed by the wine and I couldn't fabricate things as expertly as I had before.

'No,' I stammered. 'I mean, I'm not sure. No, he's not his real son. My father isn't his birth father, but it seems he brought Petro up.'

Waves of anger flashed from my cheeks. The last rays of the sun had left the room. It was dark inside the netting. Sinan wouldn't be able to see my flushed face.

'Okay, so who is his real father?'

'How should I know, Sinan? Anyway, that's not the point. I hope I never set eyes on Petro or his adopted father again.'

I was gradually warming to my new role. Yes, it was true. I never wanted to see either of them again. The two of them had conspired to trick me. And Petro had taken advantage of the situation and inveigled himself into my bed. My eyes were blazing. I was suddenly starving hungry. Sinan and I been sitting across from each other under the netting for some time. Evening had turned into night. The sounds of knives and forks, of television sets, were coming from the next-door neighbours' balconies. I remembered that I hadn't had anything to eat since I'd woken up.

'What's happening with your anchovy pilaf, Sinan? Mina put it in the oven, didn't she? It must have been ready a while ago. Let's get up and eat. No, better still, why don't you make up two plates, put them on a tray and bring them in here. Let's eat in bed, darling. When you come, bring the radio, open another bottle of wine, and let's not leave our room till morning.'

From where he sat among the shadows, Sinan sighed. My going from such great upset to this gaiety did not signal good things about my stability. Without saying anything, he got up and switched on the bedside light.

That was when we saw her.

My mother was sitting in the velvet armchair in the corner of the room. I put my hand over my mouth to suppress a scream. She was wearing a pink robe, her long grey hair falling over her shoulders, her eyes focused on the dark window in front of her. How and when had she slipped into our room? How much of what we'd said had she heard?

Sinan rushed over and took her blue-veined hand.

'Mother, dear, are you all right?'

Mum turned her head imperceptibly towards him. Oh, she's alive. Gathering up my dress, I jumped out of the mosquito netting, almost falling flat on the floor. 'Mum, when did you come in here?'

It was an inappropriate question, of course, and she gave me no answer. I motioned with my head for Sinan to leave the room. Hesitantly, he looked at me, then at my mother.

'Shall I take you to your room, Mother, dear?'

I waved my hand. *Go on out. We'll handle it.*

When the door closed, I sat on the floor beside Mum's knees, raising my head to look into her face. How much of our conversation had she heard? Did she know that Dad was dying? Had she been there when I'd said that Petro might be his son? Oh, my stupid brain! Why couldn't I have held my tongue?

Gulbahar cleared her throat and sat up straight. With a customary movement of her head she threw back the hair that had fallen across her face and shook herself, transforming her shape; gone was the ghostlike presence. Maybe when we'd first caught sight of her, when Sinan had switched on the lamp, she'd been dozing, and was just now waking up. I hoped so. When she began to speak, her voice was clearer and more direct than it had been for years.

'Melike, go and clean yourself up. You smell like a whore. I don't know how your husband tolerates it. Then come to my room. You and I will eat together this evening, just the two of us. There are things we need to discuss.'

12

I Was Going to Run
Off with Him

While I was showering, Mum had set the small round table in the middle of her gloomy room for two. Standing at the door, I glanced in. On a white tablecloth she had arranged linen napkins, silver knives and forks that had belonged to her mother, and gilt-edged plates that she'd kept hidden in the sideboard in her room in case I put them in the dishwasher. A candle had been placed in a silver candlestick.

I found all this careful attention odd, but the effort pleased me. It had been years since I'd seen her lift a finger to do anything. While she was lighting the candle, she looked up and our eyes met. The match fizzled out as she held it. When her lips twisted into something resembling a smile, I didn't know how to respond. Although we spent the summer months under the same roof, the two of us were never alone together. She whiled away the long days watching television on the glassed-in veranda. I managed to keep busy even during my summer holidays. When I came home, Sinan and I would go down to the club or I'd shut myself up in my office on the top floor. I might go into her room once or twice a day, to wish her a hasty goodnight or to leave some medicine on her bedside table.

'Let's not leave the food to get cold, Melike. Come in and sit down.'

I walked over to the table and lifted the lids of the ceramic serving dishes. Sinan's anchovy pilaf sat in one, and there was shrimp casserole in the other. My mouth watered. I sat down on the uncomfortable high-backed wooden chair. The chairs were so old that when I was a child I used to fantasize that, before us, they had been used by the Knights of the Round Table.

'If you plait your hair while it's still wet, you'll get a headache.' With her head she indicated the long plait falling down my back. After my shower I had hastily braided it so it wouldn't get all tangled. I made no reply.

Mum sat in the chair opposite. She had taken off her robe and put on a navy blue short-sleeved dress with white buttons. With her hair gathered up on top of her head and secured with combs, she looked ten years younger. She had been a pretty woman. And she still was – behind the webs that spiders had spun across her face over the years, her cheekbones were still elegant. Even in the dim light of the lamp hanging above the table her eyes were lively, intelligent.

I hoovered up all the food on my plate without a word. Sinan's anchovy pilaf melted in the mouth. I hadn't eaten the shrimp casserole before, but *eline saglik*, health to the hand of whoever had made it. I reached for my wine glass so I could take a sip. It wasn't there. I searched around for the wine. I had forgotten that alcohol was absent – banished – from my mother's dinner table. It did not go well with her tranquillizers. She was now so dependent on her meds that without them it was impossible for her to be happy. If she didn't take them, she would fall into a dark hole, and we knew what happened then. We had all seen it.

'While you were bathing, I asked Sinan to leave us alone, just the two of us. He went to the club, and Mina has gone to her room.'

Wiping my mouth with the linen napkin, I nodded. As always, Mum was picking at her food like a bird, rotating the shrimp round and round in her mouth for minutes, then swallowing it with difficulty. She had never had a good relationship with food and was always surprised by my appetite, my love of eating. She was skinny and her collarbones stuck out sharply from beneath the collar of her navy blue dress. Despite her age, she still had that fine-boned elegance that I'd been so jealous of in my youth. Only her spine had shrunk a little, so we were now the same height.

'That's good. I was thinking last night that I'd like to have some time alone with you.'

For a while, neither of us knew what to say. For a mother and daughter as disconnected as we were, this was a novel situation. I glanced around the room; it had remained unchanged in half a century. The ageing, deep-cherry-coloured curtains made everything dark, the trifold mirrors on the dressing table were still set at my grandmother's preferred angle, and the surface was still littered with bottles of cologne, silver-backed brushes and a cut-glass ashtray filled with hairpins. The contents of the wonky drawers had also remained unchanged. I didn't need to get up and look; I knew from the smells that permanently laced the air of the room that they were still brimming with bits and pieces from my grandparents' time – with ribbons and bows, pages torn from old calendars, desiccated rubber bands and empty brown medicine bottles.

A flock of screeching seagulls passed over the mansion. I placed my napkin on my lap.

'Do you know what happened to your old teacher Mr Ibrahim, Melike?' Mum's eyes were focused on the flickering flame of the candle between us. 'He died.'

I was surprised. I'd not heard my mother mention Mr Ibrahim's name in thirty years. If she was just now bringing this up, after all this time, did that mean his death was recent?

'Do you recall the day we left the village, the day we left Mina at the boarding school in Antalya? Then you and Cem and I—'

'Yes, of course I remember it. We got on the night bus back to Istanbul.'

Mum nodded. That night on the rickety old bus came alive in my memory. It had stunk of cigarettes and dirty feet. The toilets in the rest stop areas were so filthy I had to hold my pee all the way to Istanbul. Still, I was happy to be returning there, and to Dad. The prospect of being with him again was enough to make me endure any hardship. Of course, I hadn't known at that point that he had already left Istanbul, on the trail of Safinaz's secret. I had forgotten Mina's prophecy – or, at least, I thought I had.

Mina was going to be leaving us – she had passed the entrance exam for the tuition-free state boarding school and would stay in Antalya. Mum, having got rid of the greedy brothers in Germany, would cover any extra expenses until Mina completed senior school.

We had left the house in the village with all our stuff and books still in it. 'What will happen to our vegetable garden?' I'd cried. The jars of tomatoes were still there in the pantry. 'Naciye will look after all of it, and we'll come back next summer.' We had stuffed our clothes into the brown leather suitcase. One suitcase between the three of us. And a beach bag of things for Mina. We left Dad's clothes in the wardrobe. Cem had been as white as a statue, and as silent as one too.

But what did all this have to do with Mr Ibrahim?

Mum spoke up again. 'Do you remember how we settled Mina into her dormitory before we got on the bus? They wouldn't let Cem go inside because it was a girls' school, so he had to wait for us in the garden. You, Mina and I were alone in that spacious dormitory.'

I remembered. Mum had taken the sheets with butterflies on them out of the beach bag she'd packed for Mina. The two of them stretched the sheet across the thin, spongy mattress and folded a yellow wool blanket at the foot of the bed. The smell of lavender momentarily filled the room. I had loved those butterfly sheets and was mad at Mum for giving them to Mina.

'Well, he died that day.'

'Who?'

Finally, she stopped gazing at the candle and turned to me. Her blue eyes were like beads, her long, thin chin was trembling.

'Ibrahim, of course! Ibrahim died that day. Even as we were saying goodbye to Mina at the school gate, he was already at the morgue.'

She paused, glancing at her cigarette. I got up, brought her the packet from the bedside table, and lit one for her and one for myself. The menthol made my nose tingle as the smoke drowned my lungs. Behind the smoke we stayed silent, facing each other for a while. Was it good for her nerves to rake up all these old memories? Maybe she should go to bed now, and we should continue our conversation in the morning.

'I was going to run off with Ibrahim.'

What?

'If your father had not acted first, it would have been me who'd gone away and left you.'

'You're joking, Mother, aren't you?'

'Why would I be joking? The whole village knew we were in love with each other. Surely you were aware of it. Don't you remember?'

Yes, of course I remembered. It was well known in the village that my teacher had fallen desperately in love with my mother. The girls who lined themselves up along the school walls would nudge each other when they saw me. The boys would yell 'Melike! Melike!' from the corner of the schoolyard, and when I turned to look, they'd run off into the back garden. There was always an insinuation of something dirty in the way they looked at me, in their tone of voice, in their laughter. And that dirty thing concerned my mother.

Still, I had never imagined that this love might have been reciprocated. Mum was like a queen; many people admired her, and she, in turn, bestowed her dimpled smiles on every one of those admirers. Mr Ibrahim was just another recipient of this gift, that was all.

Then I realised. It was around the time that Mr Ibrahim 'left the village' that Mum stopped doing anything in the kitchen, stopped attending to the flowerbeds and the vegetable garden. It was around the time she began neglecting us, instead spending all day in the *mukhtar*'s house, where she would smoke black-market Marlboros and wait for the television programmes to start.

The rumour at the time had been that Mr Ibrahim and

the *mukhtar* had had a falling out. Some thought this was to do with the election, the first one in many years. Mr Ibrahim was an ardent supporter of Bulent Ecevit – the leftist writer, scholar and leader of the social democratic CHP – the Republican People's Party. It was said that, should the CHP be successful, Mr Ibrahim would be given a role in the new government.

I had been in Year 6 that year – our last in the village. Miss Sabahat, who had just moved to town, took Mr Ibrahim's place when he disappeared. She would pull the boys' ears and knock their heads together, but she didn't touch the girls.

'When I took Mina to see her mother in Antalya every month, I would meet up with Ibrahim. We would spend the whole afternoon, behind faded curtains, making love in cheap hotels.'

'Mother!'

'What? Have you become a prude all of a sudden?'

I dropped my head, squashed cold grains of rice on my plate.

Gulbahar was revitalized; she'd regained her erstwhile beauty. Raising her voice, she said, 'I was going to run away with him, Melike. Do you hear me? He was everything to me. Every night, I would fall asleep thinking about which dresses, books and pieces of jewellery I would take with me in my beach bag when I went. I would set off for Antalya in a fishing boat beneath a dappled dawn sky. Orhan would take you all to Istanbul and raise you, with the help of my parents and Safinaz. But your wicked father got there first. Safinaz's death put butter on his bread, for sure. The opportunity he'd been waiting for dropped out of the sky and straight into his basket.'

'How?'

'He left to arrange the funeral, so why do you think he didn't come back? He was desperate to be free of me, of us. You're an adult woman now, so even though you don't have children, which makes a difference, you've no doubt realized that marriage condemns a person into forever being a narrow, constrained version of themselves. That was certainly true for your father. The dreams of his youth, his urge to do something significant in the world, were lost beneath the daily round of domestic drudgery. Even God, who, when you're a child, watches your every discovery with pride, forgets you once you reach adulthood. Your father and I got married so young. I fell pregnant with Cem, and before I'd even finished university I found myself in an apartment in Galata, defined now as a wife and mother. But the heart cannot sustain itself without passion, Melike. What do they say? "Living life fully can only happen by loving." For me, it was Ibrahim, though it could as well have been someone else. Ibrahim came into my life at the right time, when I was ready to give myself to whichever man was saying what I needed to hear. You understand what I'm telling you?'

'I'm going to have a glass of wine. Would you like one?'

'Open the sideboard. On the bottom shelf you'll see my decanter of cherry liqueur. Pour me a glass of that. Have one yourself too, if you like.'

Well, how about that! We'd been counting the empty pill boxes to be sure she was taking her medication properly, and all the while she'd been secretly knocking back cherry liqueur. I stood up wordlessly. To think that I'd scolded her like a child when she'd asked for a glass of raki to drink with the fish Sinan had cooked. I brought the hand-blown crystal decanter over to the table along with the glasses. The liqueur shone like rubies in the tiny glasses, lighting up our sombre table. We clinked glasses softly, the crystal tinkling like gentle laughter. The crease between Mum's eyebrows relaxed. I felt a similar softening in my own face, my own muscles.

'After Safinaz's funeral, your father called me from Istanbul. I went down to the *mukhtar*'s hut. The only phone in the village was there. "I want to get to the bottom of this, Gulbahar," he said. "Why would a sixty-four-year-old woman commit suicide?"

'He was confused, and in a way he was right to be. Take me, for example. I am now sixty-three years old, and, as everyone knows, certifiable. But even I don't think about suicide any more. When you have less than a quarter of your life left, you don't think about hastening death. "There are secrets here," Orhan insisted. "There's something odd about all this. I'm going to go to my mother's village."

'I was on the phone in that claustrophobic hut, covered in sweat. The *mukhtar* was staring into my face as if that might allow him to also hear the voice at the other end. I wanted him to leave me be, give me some privacy, but he didn't. So let him hear then! Without lowering my voice at all, I said, "I want a divorce, Orhan." Yes, just like that. "I want a divorce."

'Not a single sound came out of your father at the other end of the line. I repeated, "Orhan, I want a divorce." There was a scratching on the line then – interference. The lines often got crossed in those days, and the operator would have to reconnect you. I was just about to say, "Get yourself a lawyer before you leave," when the line suddenly went dead.'

I was in shock. I didn't even notice the mosquito buzzing in my ear until it began sucking blood from my neck. Mum, taking her empty glass and the crystal decanter, stepped lightly towards the balcony door, like a deer, and opened the curtains.

'Let's sit outside for a bit. None of the neighbours are around so we can rest easy.'

Dazed, I stood up and followed her like a sleepwalker. With the decanter in her hand, she settled herself on the wicker chaise longue on the balcony. I sat in the chaise longue next to her. Mosquitoes got started on my ankles straightaway. The moon had risen, casting a silvery light over the balcony. We didn't turn on the lights. Kicking my slippers off, I lay back on the chaise longue. I heard the sound of a cigarette lighter beside me.

As she let out her first exhalation, Mum spoke.

'After that, I left the *mukhtar*'s hut and walked down the goat track into town. At that time Ibrahim was hundreds of kilometres away in Mersin, teaching Yoruk nomads how to read and write. I went into the post office. Counting out all the money in my pocket, I sent the express telegram we'd agreed on: "The girl has passed her exam for the state boarding school. Monday 2pm." Two days later the village postman, Sabri, rang our doorbell with the reply telegram. I opened it right away. "Yes, with immediate effect." My heart did a somersault and I almost hugged and kissed Sabri. I immediately packed all our things into a single suitcase and prepared a bag for Mina. I was as light-hearted and joyful as a bird. I could forget all about the witch Safinaz and her suicide, and Orhan's pursuit of her secrets.'

I closed my eyes. In my mind I could see Mum in the *mukhtar*'s sauna-like hut, with the telephone in her hand, telling Dad, 'I want a divorce.' Our entire family history was upended. My stomach churned, and I tried taking deep breaths. The familiar sour smell of jasmine and fallen mulberries filled my nostrils.

Mum's voice shook.

'Ibrahim had got on the pre-dawn bus from Mersin; it would take half a day to reach Antalya. But the driver fell asleep at the wheel and crashed into an oncoming truck. Ibrahim was sitting in one of the front seats. He was thrown through the windscreen and propelled several metres in the air. When we got to the bus station in Antalya, the bus boy told us the whole story; the accident was recorded in his mind like a movie. He remembered Ibrahim distinctly too. Ibrahim hadn't wanted any of the cologne the boy was giving out to all the passengers at the start of the journey, but he offered the boy some mint candies from his pocket. After learning the boy's name, Ibrahim shook hands with him like an adult. When the boy said, "It was Mr Ibrahim, the teacher. His hands were very white," I wanted to tell him he was lying, force him to remember things differently. But he had a list of the dead in his hands. That night on the bus, while you and Cem slept in the seat behind me, I cried all the way from Antalya to Istanbul.'

I didn't know what to say. I wanted to reach out and hold her hand, but I didn't. I refilled our liqueur glasses. On the neighbour's dark rooftop, baby seagulls, not yet able to fly, were meowing like cats. I laid my head back down and stared up at the sky. The moon had risen higher. I wasn't sure whether it was full or not; there seemed to be a little piece missing. My stomach ached. I put my glass on the ground. So Mum had been planning to abandon us. *If your father had not acted first, it would have been me who'd gone away and left you.* Then I would have spent a lifetime missing Mum, not Dad. I was suddenly pumped full of rage, up to my ears. Incandescent now, I jumped up and strode to the other end of the balcony, but even the cool of the stone floor passing through my bare feet and into my bones could not suppress the fire rising within me. I pressed my forehead against the rusty railing entwined with jasmine. From the roof came an anxious flurry of wings.

She had envisioned it, spent countless nights envisioning it. She'd thought carefully about what she'd take with her in that bag of hers, but had given no thought at all to what would become of us. We mattered so little to both of them that one was off with a man and the other was off chasing a mystery. That feeling of insignificance, of smallness, which had taken root inside me that early morning, when I'd watched my father disappear in that boat, returned with all its force, sitting like a fist in my stomach. I made myself take a couple of steps back for fear that I might otherwise end up beating my head against the jasmine railing.

I'd felt insignificant ever since that day my father left. And now, rather than erasing that sense of irrelevance, my mother's story had reinforced it. I was an unimportant, inconsequential little thing, a superfluous creature that got under my parents' feet. And Petro had treated me in just the same way. He didn't appreciate me either. He was a bastard whose only aim had been to get me into his bed.

Why was I even still thinking about him? My eyes filled with nervous tears. I gripped the iron railing with both hands and squeezed with all my might. Closing my eyes, I followed the hot flow of anger down my cheeks. As the jasmine stroked my face, I felt sorry for myself, which made me hate myself even more. I pressed my forehead against the railing until it hurt. I must have looked like I was having a breakdown.

I turned, sat back down on the chaise longue, and downed another glass of liqueur. Its mix of syrupy sweetness and alcohol was making me nauseous. Mum had fallen asleep. She would have to be carried inside and put to bed. It was lucky that she was a birdlike thing – Sinan could pick her up with one arm. I reached out and took the glass from her fingers. Then, leaving her there with the mosquitoes, I went down into the garden with the decanter under my arm.

13

Under Egrikapi

Our garden, which in the daytime was alive with the buzzing of bees and other insects, was now buried in silence. Only the occasional scream of a seagull tore through the night. I sat down on one of the swings that hung from the iron poles, supporting the grapevines. Setting the decanter on the ground near the swing, I pushed off from the grassy ground like I used to when I was a child and began to swing. My legs looked as white as marble in the moonlight. Stones tickled the soles of my bare feet. A gentle breeze had picked up. I threw my head back and let the breeze kiss my breasts through the open neck of my dress. As the swing gathered speed, my feet left the ground. I could see stars in between the vines.

If your father had not acted first, it would have been me who'd gone away and left you.

So be it, Mother.

All through my youth, I'd been so ashamed of myself for being angry at my neurotic mother when I should have felt sorry for her. This was a source of shame that I hadn't been able to share with anyone. And now I could relinquish that shame! She wasn't innocent either! We'd always tried to protect her. And not just Cem and I – Dr Chetin, Mina, and even Barish were all exceptionally tolerant and forgiving of Gulbahar and her fragile nerves. Oh, dear, let's not talk about anything unpleasant, we don't want to upset her. And for what? Who were we protecting you from, Mum? We were children. Your children. It wasn't you who needed protecting, it was us.

The swing slowed and my feet met the ground. My cheeks were cold, my breathing had quickened. I picked up the decanter and took a swig. In my mind I saw with total clarity the events of that fateful afternoon. That cursed day in early summer, when Barish and I returned home together to find mother on the kitchen floor.

I was seventeen. The day had been an important one for me – did you know that, Mum? Of course you didn't know – how could you? You were wandering around Dr Chetin's damp waterside villa like a ghost, forever with a novel in your hand. I, meanwhile, had been falling madly in love with my stepbrother. That day, for the first time ever, Barish and I had spent time together during daylight hours. Not like siblings making love secretly at night, but like two sweethearts.

The first time – and, thanks to you, Mum, also the last time.

Did you know that your stepson came to my little room overlooking the street, whenever he felt like it, for two whole years? On those dark nights while all of you were sleeping – you, my brother, my stepfather, all of you – Barish would steal into my bed, my body, my soul, my heart. Then, in the mornings, he would stretch out in his chair at the breakfast table, and say with a crooked grin on his face, 'Bring me a glass of very strong tea, sister. Let me have a drink from your hand.' As if it wasn't he who, just a few hours earlier, had buried his face in my hair, whispered dirty nothings in my ear, and, excited by his own words, had made love to me again and again between the damp sheets, until I couldn't stand it any longer and screamed from deep inside my body, just as he'd taught me to. When I gave him his tea with shaking hands, he would tweak my cheek. Cem would look the other way, and you didn't even see.

Ah, if you only knew how in love with him I was, Mum. I wanted to be able to tell you. On the nights when he was home from boarding school, once everyone's lights were out, my heart would beat hard as I waited for my door to creak. What if he didn't come, or was bored with me, or had found a more experienced lover? I would eat myself up inside. On the nights when I was going to be with him, I would wash my hair in lavender water, pinch silk nightdresses from your drawer. You didn't notice. Barish didn't see them anyway. The villa was so cold, we never came out from under the satin quilt.

If there'd been the slightest flicker of interest in your eyes, I would have told you everything, Mum. But you sat in front of the kitchen window staring out at the magnolia tree, drinking your tea and never even looking into my eyes. If you had looked, would you have realized that my heart was on fire? Or did you know already and choose not to mention it? You were very intelligent, after all.

My stepbrother never once told me he loved me. When he'd finished his business, he would go back to his room, the one with the sea view. The two of us couldn't have fallen asleep together in my narrow bed, of course. I would console myself with that thought. He never once looked directly at me or kissed me during daylight hours, never walked down the street holding my hand. I couldn't mention him to anyone.

What we had together wasn't a simple, straightforward thing like other girls had. It was a relationship that had to be kept secret, concealed. Who would have understood? Our relations were shameful. We were siblings.

Melike, Cem, Barish, from now on you will be siblings.

Ah, Dr Chetin! Would it ever have occurred to you that your son might be having sex with your stepdaughter under your own roof? And for three whole years! I kept the secret of our love close to my chest. If I blabbed, I might have had to give him up. But if *you* had asked, Mum… if you had looked up just once and said, 'What's the matter with you?' I would have told you everything.

So, on that day – you know the day I mean – just as I was about to get on the school bus, the villa door opened and Barish came out. It was a Monday. He should have been going to school too, but he was wearing a pair of faded jeans and a light green shirt instead of his uniform. And he wasn't carrying a school bag. His black hair was tousled.

He was at my side in two strides. Effecting a most paternal attitude, he said to Oktay, the school bus driver, 'We'll be taking Melike to school today.' He had put his hand on my shoulder. I acted like that was no big thing. With his head, he indicated the chauffeur, Hamdi, who was washing Dr Chetin's white Mercedes. Hamdi waved to Barish.

A girl who was dozing with her forehead resting against the window of the school minibus opened her eyes and gave Barish the onceover. I wanted her to see Barish's hand on my shoulder. We had gone into short socks a while ago, so my legs were bare under my school uniform. The fresh spring air lifted my skirt and I was filled with happiness, like when you have your first ice cream of the season.

Oktay grumbled something under his breath and hit the

accelerator. The dilapidated old school bus drove off, leaving a cloud of black smoke in its wake. Barish's hand stayed on my shoulder. As we walked side by side to the ferry landing, we kept glancing back at the villa. Dr Chetin would be coming out soon, getting into the car Hamdi had just washed and heading for the American Hospital. Cem wasn't around any more. He'd gone to Australia for university.

We bought bagels at the Kirecburnu landing and boarded the ferry. I was so excited, I didn't even ask where we were going. One possibility was that Barish would drop me off at school. Our schools weren't that far from each other. He took a ferry to go to school every Monday morning and came back on Friday afternoon, so he could quite easily walk up from Karakoy to Taksim and leave me at my school in Harbiye. While I was stirring and stirring two lumps of sugar into my tea, I prayed. Please, God, please don't let him do that. Let him not take me to school. I am begging you, God, allow us to spend just one day together, like proper lovers. It doesn't matter if the principal calls my mother, or if Dr Chetin interrogates me this evening. I can lie. I'm just asking for one little day. Please, God, let me skip school with Barish today.

Probably because the ferry was at the start of its route, it was quite empty. We sat on the open deck at the back. The rain that had begun the night before, just when Barish was leaving my bed, had turned the waters of the Bosphorus a gloomy green. The air smelled of seaweed iodine and salt. How beautiful life was, for all its imperfections!

Gathering my courage, I asked, 'Where are we going?'

My voice sounded normal. I was glad. I hadn't spent much time with Barish in daylight. On the rare occasions when we'd had breakfast together or shared a holiday meal, I always had trouble speaking to him. I felt like a talentless actress. I was always worried that my audience – my mother, Dr Chetin, Cem, the servants, and most of all Barish – would think I was playing my role very poorly.

Barish didn't answer. He had spread his long legs wide and was chewing big hunks of bagel, reading the sports news on the back page of the newspaper that the man sitting across from us was hidden behind. I wrapped the navy blue cardigan that covered my grey school uniform around me and clamped my bare knees together. Attractive girls didn't care if the men they were with fell silent. They just laughed and shrugged it off. The man opposite us folded his newspaper carefully and looked us over. I turned my head towards the sea so he couldn't see my eyes filling with tears and watched the people boarding the ferry from a dock on the Asian side of Istanbul.

Our ferry continued making its way from one side of the Bosphorus to the other, picking up its full complement of passengers: men who, from their speech, were obviously tradesmen in the Grand Bazaar; students anxiously finishing their homework on the boat; elderly ladies all dressed up; little children dragged along by exhausted-looking working women. It was now packed to bursting point. A tea-seller passed by, rapping on his tray. Even though I was cold, I didn't ask for another tea.

Just then, Barish put his arm around my shoulders and pushed a piece of bagel between my lips. It was as if the sun had suddenly emerged from behind the clouds. A surge of joy coursed through my veins and I almost fainted from happiness. The sesame seeds on the bagel stuck in my throat, and my heart thumped. Barish drew me in close, his breath licking my neck.

'Let's you and me wander around doing nothing today. What do you say?'

I turned to him in joy. I wanted to put my arms around him and kiss him. God had answered my prayers. I nestled close. He squeezed my shoulder. Was I really the same girl as the one who'd felt so sorry for herself a few minutes ago? My eyes met those of the man sitting across from us. Raising my chin, I turned my face to the sea. The murky colour of his small eyes stayed with me. I couldn't stop myself from smiling. I was the happiest person on earth.

When we got off the ferry at Eminonu, Barish held my hand, as if that was something he did every day. I was used to his hand passing over my belly, my breasts, my neck, at night-time, but in my palm his hand felt strange. Bigger, bonier. Hand in hand, we went in and out of street markets in ancient, forgotten courtyards I never knew existed. We didn't speak at all. Barish stopped once, to look at two canaries in a cage, and again, to inspect a brass samovar in an antiques shop. Side by side, we browsed through books on the counter of a second-hand bookshop. Without him seeing, I opened and smelled the old English novels.

When we left, Barish didn't hold my hand again. Maybe it wasn't proper to hold hands in such a conservative neighbourhood? The serious-faced girls to our right and left weren't touching the boys walking beside them, and there was no kissing or hugging at the tables under the large plane trees of the crowded coffeehouses.

We'd just come through a confusing maze of streets, past a row of shops selling metal lunchboxes, teapots, robes for the pilgrimage to Mecca, and prayer beads, when Barish turned to me and said happily, 'See where we are!'

I looked around, trying to catch my breath. We were at the courtyard entrance to a mosque. It was spacious, airy, silent, a place designed to inspire inner peace. I was embarrassed that

I didn't known which mosque it was. I was very ignorant of Istanbul's history. In the years when a child would usually be taken on field trips to museums and mosques, I'd been living out in the village, and then I'd spent Year 7 at the middle school on Buyukada Island. When I finished Year 7, Dr Chetin paid for me to go to Notre Dame de Sion, the private French high school for girls in Istanbul, where there was no opportunity to make up my gaps in Ottoman history. I took a step into the courtyard, hoping the name of the mosque would be written somewhere. Willow branches hung over the wall; cats slept in the shade of the giant plane trees. Was it proper for me to be walking around this courtyard in my school uniform, with bare knees? I stayed away from the row of fountains beside the door into the mosque, where a couple of men were performing their ablutions.

Barish caught up with me in two steps.

'Come on, I want to show you something.'

We made our way round to the back. Before us stretched a hazy view of Istanbul, but Barish paid no attention to that, instead pulling me around the tombs and into the cemetery. As we rushed past the tombs, I glanced at the names inscribed on them. Sultan Suleyman the Magnificent lay in one, Hurrem Haseki Sultan in another. I relaxed. We were at the Suleymaniye Mosque, of course! I stood a little taller. Barish pushed open the black iron gate of the wall surrounding the gravestones adorned with turbans and fezzes. I followed him. We came to a standstill in front of a white, ornamental gravestone.

'You see this? It's a woman's grave.'

'How do you know?'

'From the carvings of flowers and spring blossom. It's what's called a "lady stone".'

I looked. There was a decorative band right across the stone, like a necklace.

'This is a very special grave.'

'Why's that?'

'Because it was carved by an Italian sculptor. Guess who wrote the inscription?'

Barish's black eyes shone like beads as they wandered over my face. Of course I didn't know the answer to his question. In desperation, I took a look at the Arabic letters on the gravestone, but I couldn't understand anything. My cheeks flamed.

'Halide Edip!'

'What?'

'Halide Edip wrote the inscription. I wonder what it says. If I ever manage to learn Ottoman Turkish, I'm going to come and read it.'

I looked again at the gravestone, this time with a different eye. The famous feminist Halide Edip was one of my mother's favourite authors. It wasn't only that they had gone to the same school. When Mum was a child, Halide Edip would visit the mansion on Buyukada; she used to stroke my mother's blond hair. Ever since then, Mum had adored her. She studied English literature at university because Halide Edip had founded the department.

While I was wondering whether to tell Barish about this, he brought his lips close to my neck. I almost fainted.

'If a woman dies when she's still a young bride, they carve a broken rosebud on the footstone. Let's see if there are any of those here.'

He went off to look. Where had he learnt all that? Did they teach it at school? Did he read encyclopaedias?

'Melike, come, I've found one.'

Hearing my name in his mouth, I was ecstatic. He'd never spoken my name before. At night, when his head was buried in my hair and he was moaning, he had never once spoken it, instead growling 'You're so beautiful' and 'You're going to kill me.' At breakfasts in the morning, I would be 'sister'. When he first started addressing me like that, I thought he was treating me like a nursing sister in a Catholic hospital or something and I wondered what special nurse-like quality he saw in me. It took me a while to realize that he was referring to me as his sibling sister.

I ran over to him and we stood staring at a headstone that was notably whiter than the grey stones around it.

'Look, do you see? At the foot of the grave.'

I couldn't see anything. I leant down. Again, there were carvings of roses, other flowers and blossom. All of a sudden, Barish grabbed me by my waist, turned me towards him, and pressed his lips against mine, trying to push his tongue insistently into my mouth. I moved uneasily but didn't dare try and wriggle free of his arms. I just mumbled, 'What are you doing, Barish? We're at a mosque!'

His face wore that crooked grin again. I lowered my head. With one hand he lifted my chin and turned my face towards his. He was very tall. My neck hurt from trying to look into his eyes.

'We do other things that shouldn't be done, sister.'

His black eyes shone with hunger and desire. He was drawn to anything forbidden. He again put his arms around my waist, pressed his groin against mine. My head spun.

'Are you hungry, sweetheart?'

Sweetheart! First 'Melike' and now 'sweetheart'! The world had suddenly become such a tender and friendly place. God had not only granted my prayer but had given me a bonus.

'Are you ready to eat the world's most delicious beans and rice?'

It wasn't at all the right weather for beans, and they might make me gassy, but I was not about to curb the enthusiasm of Barish – my sweetheart. I doubted I'd be able to eat a thing, but since he'd asked, he must be hungry.

As soon as I took my first forkful of the beans that had been placed in front of me, I realized how hungry I really was. Barish doused his plate with paprika. They were truly the best beans I had ever tasted. I closed my eyes as the spices, the smell, the tomato sauce suffused my palate in perfect harmony. When I opened my eyes again, Barish was looking at me, not with that crooked grin on his face but with a new smile. It was a little childish, a little uneasy, but still somehow like a flower that had opened just for me. I held it close to my heart. I thought of saying, 'I love you', like the people in *Dallas* did all the time. He would have to answer, 'I love you too.' I smiled. Who could ever say that sentence out loud except for the characters on that American TV show that the whole country was now addicted to?

Barish suddenly stood up. Something in the distance had caught his attention. He squinted to get a better look. I turned around as well. A small, bespectacled young man with a book bag on his back was walking towards our table. When he saw Barish, he smiled and hurried over.

'What are you doing here, my friend?' Barish shouted joyfully. 'Come and sit with us, don't be shy. Let me introduce you. Melike, this is Sinan. Sinan, Melike.'

He winked at me. The friend saw it too. Something bubbled inside me, like a fizzy drink. He hadn't said 'my sister' and nor had he resorted to nonsense like 'the daughter of my father's new wife'. There was a Melike in Barish's life that everyone should know about. And that was me! This boy would definitely think I was his sweetheart.

Sinan extended his hand and directed his green eyes straight at me. 'Pleased to meet you, Melike.'

His hand was thin, white, cool.

Barish was beside himself with happiness. I laughed to see him so glad. He insisted that Sinan sit with us.

'Melike, this is my old dormitory friend. He snored beside me every night from the age of eleven. And how he snores! I tell you, do not be duped by his gentlemanly appearance; in his sleep he turns into a tough guy. Sinan, old chap, what year are you in now?'

With his beautiful hands, Sinan picked up the heavy water pitcher from the table and filled his glass. When he replied, he looked not at Barish but at me.

'I'm in the third year, economics department,' he said.

There was something clear and honest about his face. The more you looked at him, the more you wanted to look. I dropped my gaze to the table. Barish mopped up the sauce on his plate with a huge hunk of bread and threw it into his mouth.

'Naturally, Sinan didn't have to keep repeating classes like I did. He finished school quickly and went on to university.' He turned to Sinan. 'When are you going to take over the chain of hotels in Bursa, Sinan? Melike, Sinan's family are huge property tycoons in Bursa – they own the Ishik Hotel chain. They're the famous Ishik family. Have you heard of them? When Sinan finishes university—'

'Hold on a second, Barish,' Sinan interjected calmly. 'I don't know whether I'll go back to Bursa or not. I might work towards getting my doctorate.'

'You'll get it, my friend. You can do anything. Melike,

Sinan is a maths genius. When he was just twelve, he could multiply three-digit numbers in his head. He doesn't have a brain, he has a calculator in his head.'

Sinan laughed modestly. Barish stood up, glanced around for a waiter, and took some money out of his back pocket to pay the bill.

So as to break the silence at the table, I said, 'Do you have any ski resorts in the mountains, up at Uludag? My school is organizing a ski trip to Uludag next winter. We're staying at Kirazliyayla, at the State Waterworks camp.'

Sinan's green eyes shone behind his glasses. 'Yes, we have a hotel at Kirazliyayla. There's a hot spring there. If you go, be sure to let me know. My aunt can open up one of our private family baths for you. We're very near the Waterworks camp.'

He wrote his number on a napkin, put it in front of me and stood up.

'I should get going. My class is about to start.'

He hugged Barish and shook hands with me. Barish smiled as he watched his friend disappear in the direction of Istanbul University. It made me happy to see him happy. I folded the napkin with Sinan's number on it and tucked it into my uniform pocket.

It had got really hot. I took off my cardigan and tied it round my waist, praying that the blue shirt I was wearing under my grey uniform didn't have sweat stains under the arms. As we crossed the narrow streets around Suleymaniye Mosque, Barish put his arm around me and drew me close. Arm in arm, we wandered around the madrasa courtyards, past the churches converted into mosques and the fountains still flowing with cool water. I felt intoxicated with it all. Even the poorest neighbourhoods seemed beautiful to me: the old wooden houses with decoratively carved windows that showed they'd been built with great care, the hills, the hazy views of Istanbul glimpsed between stairways, the screech of seagulls. Everything made me laugh.

On one street we saw some ragged children rolling a rusty barrel. Three of them were sitting inside the barrel while two burly kids pushed it. The street rang with their laughter. With a sadness in his voice which I found strange, Barish muttered, 'What good would it do if we went over and told them off, warned them about tetanus? As soon as we were out of sight, they'd just carry on as before.'

I couldn't think of a reply.

He continued, as if talking to himself. 'Will the revolution change any of this? Sometimes I have my doubts. I'm not as optimistic as my friends.'

I prayed that my palm wasn't getting sweaty inside his hand. It was as if I'd been asked to talk about a subject I knew nothing of. Those friends of my father's who used to wander round our house when I was little came to mind. They were revolutionists too. Supposedly. I never liked them. They acted like I didn't exist. When Mum used to empty the overflowing ashtrays the following morning, she'd refer to them as 'useless dreamers'. I was suddenly angry. No, I wasn't going to let Barish get upset by all that stupid revolutionary talk and have that ruin our day. No way.

At the end of the street, right in front of us, was a narrow, ancient, Byzantine gate. I went over and read the name of it – Egrikapi. Grabbing Barish by the hand, I pulled him inside the gate, out of the sun, and leant my back against the inner wall of the stone passageway. It was damp from the centuries of moisture it had absorbed. Shadows passed across Barish's face. Two doves that had made their nests in the ceiling of the gate above our heads grumbled. I reached up, grabbed the collar of Barish's light green shirt, pulled him to me, and, standing on tiptoes, wound my arms around his neck. He pressed his lanky body against mine and our bones pressed against each other in a dance that felt familiar, despite my school uniform. His hands clutched my face. We kissed for a long, long time, until everything else was forgotten.

At that very moment, you, Mum – in imitation of Sylvia Plath, that favourite author of yours – decided to end your life. And to top it all, you failed.

As soon as we stepped through the door, we knew that something wasn't right. The smell of gas burnt our nostrils, and there was an ominous silence in the house. It wasn't just quiet because the cook, Atesh, who took Mondays off, was absent. It was something else. It was, I now know, the silence that comes before an explosion.

Hand in hand, wary, we followed the smell and came to the kitchen. The door was closed. You had stuffed a towel under it. When we went in, gas scorched our faces like fire, burning our eyes and noses. Barish rushed to the window while I stood frozen to the spot. I kept thinking that it was quiet because the kitchen window was closed, as if understanding the reason for the silence was the most important thing just then. The towel you'd stuffed under the door got tangled around my feet.

Barish ran into the kitchen. A howling sound filled my ears. He turned off the gas valve behind the oven. He was yelling something to me, but I didn't hear him. The gas was destroying my nasal passages, tears were flowing from my eyes. Maybe that's why it was a while before I got sight of you, Mum. The skirt of your quilted yellow robe had opened; your blue-veined legs were splayed out on the stone floor of the kitchen as if they were made of porcelain. All around were trays, pots, pans... Barish knelt down beside you. I couldn't seem to understand what he was saying. My hand was stuck to the door handle. The two of you in front of the oven were like Sleeping Beauty and her prince.

The lovely white blossoms of the magnolia tree had unfurled in front of the window, and, Mum, your face was so beautiful, too beautiful for death, as you lay there on the floor with your long hair fanned out, shining.

Everything beautiful was breaking and falling away.

I hated you.

Because, that day, after Barish and I had breathlessly hailed the first taxi we saw at Egrikapi and returned to the villa, instead of making love to our hearts' content, we had to take you to hospital. Because you turned Dr Chetin into an old man overnight. Dr Chetin, who raced to the emergency room without even pausing to wipe his mouth, and hugged me with sauce on his cheek. Because, in the hospital corridor that smelled of medicine, I had to apologize on behalf of his neurotic stepmother, over and over, to Barish, whose eyes had become bowls of blood.

Do you know, Mum, after that day Barish never came to my room again? You scared him off. He never again wanted to be close to me.

That kiss under Egrikapi was our last.

You were responsible for all the men that had disappeared from my life.

But we weren't allowed to get angry with a psychologically damaged mother. We had to tiptoe around her. Doors couldn't be slammed. We had to talk quietly. Over time, where I'd previously been angry, I now began to feel ashamed. I was guilty of an inadmissible crime. But you... It turns out that

I'd been right to be angry. As a mother, you had mentally deserted us a long time ago.

So, Mum, lift this burden of shame from my shoulders and set me free!

14

Love Is a Door

The last ferry of the night was blowing its whistle when the garden gate opened, causing our bell to tinkle. Sinan was back from the club. I was still sitting on the swing in the moonlit garden, my bare toes in the earth, the glass decanter in my lap, but I didn't call out to him as he walked up the path of multicoloured pebbles and into the house. His keys jangled in his pocket. The moon was lighting up the garden like a lantern. If he'd turned his head, he would have seen me, but he didn't. Good. He'd find my mother on the balcony and carry her to her bed. I would go back into the house after they'd all gone to sleep. I didn't want to talk to anyone.

When the door to the house closed, I drained the last of the cherry liqueur. The sweet-sour liquid scalded my throat as it made its way to my stomach. I lifted my head and gazed up at the stars. How many there were. And how silent. I felt dizzy on the gently swaying swing. It was such a long time since I'd thought about that day with Barish at Egrikapi. I had never before felt such righteous anger towards my mother. A strange lightness had come over me, maybe from the alcohol. I thought of Petro. His long arms around my body, his face taut with desire as he thrust deep inside me. My cheeks felt hot. I gripped the decanter tightly. Then the cemetery came to my mind. Safinaz's gravestone.

The beginning and the end.

I felt a wry longing.

Something rustled in the bushes. Ugur. When Safinaz died, we brought her pet tortoise to Buyukada, to my grandparents' garden. He'd been with us now for twenty-nine years, living out his days among the grass and flowers, the fallen apricots and mulberries. He used to follow Safinaz around her back garden, through the dry weeds, and put his head on her feet; now it was Mum he followed, appearing whenever he heard Mum's voice, dragging his huge shell behind her. It was from Ugur that I learnt how loyal tortoises are. I turned in the swing to look at Ugur, and froze. It wasn't Ugur in front of the mulberry tree but a ghost with a quivering white halo. As the moonlight shone through the leaves, it appeared and disappeared, its slender hand reaching out towards me.

My scream cut through the starry silence like a knife.

'Calm yourself, Melike. It's me.'

I put my hand on my heart, which was beating wildly. I was holding my breath. It was only later that I realized I'd jumped down from the swing. I was still clasping the empty decanter.

'Mum! You scared me half to death. You shouldn't creep up on a person like a thief.'

My mother's familiar face appeared from among the shadows. Her hair, gathered into a chunky bun on top of her head, really did look like a halo in the moonlight. She came over to me.

'When Sinan couldn't find you in the house, he was

worried. I guessed you'd be out here, so I came to look for you. Are you all right?'

Without waiting for an answer, she sprang forward like a deer and sat on the empty swing. She was wearing high-heeled mules. Putting the decanter on the old cistern, I walked over to her. My breathing was still irregular. There was a rustling in the grass and Ugur appeared. He began making his way over to the swing. Mum's voice immediately turned liltingly sweet. I felt crushed inside. My mother had never loved me.

'Darling Ugur, my love. Come, come. Let me see you.'

I leant against the grapevine's iron post. She hadn't loved me and she would never love me. Ugur had stuck his head out of his shell and was sniffing the high-heeled mules dangling from the swing. The upstairs balcony door squeaked and we heard Sinan's voice.

'Melike, are you out there? Is everything all right? Did someone scream?'

'I'm fine, Sinan. Don't worry. I got startled and yelled out when Mother came down. Go to bed. I'll be up shortly.'

The balcony door closed. Mum bent down and took Ugur onto her lap. In a sudden reflex, he retracted his head and legs into his shell. Seeing him on Mum's lap, I realized how much bigger he was now than he had been in my childhood. He must have been just a young thing when he was wandering around Safinaz's garden. He would outlive all of us. I looked around at our neglected garden extending into the distance.

Death.

Dad.

Petro.

In the moonlight, Mum and I looked at each other. The whites of her eyes and the buttons of her dress shone.

'Is there any cherry liqueur left?'

'No. I finished it.'

Without lifting her feet off the ground, she began to gently swing.

'I want to say something to you, Melike. Love is a door. Do you hear me? You don't know where the door will lead you, but you step through it anyway.'

'What? Why are you talking about this now?'

In truth, I knew very well why she was talking about it.

'There is more to love than the affection you feel for someone. That someone is a vehicle, a way for you to find the door. The secret is hidden somewhere in the story that you'll find beyond that door.'

'What?'

Putting Ugur on the ground, she pulled a packet of cigarettes from her breast pocket. When I was little, Mum never talked to me like this. After Dad left, her language changed, influenced by those old novels she immersed herself in. Her mind also retreated. She became a person of the past, a person suited to her old-fashioned name.

'What do you mean, Mum?'

Smoke swirled between us. Ugur disappeared into the whispering grass.

With her eyes closed, Mum murmured, 'A woman grows into her own story. She finds her story and discovers how to spread her wings and fly. Most people spend their whole life behind the door, making do with passing pleasures. But some go through it and find their story.'

I grabbed the thin rope and stopped the swing. On the street two cats were getting ready to fight. Fierce growls were rising in their throats. Soon one would scream, then the noises would cease.

'Stop speaking in riddles, for God's sake. Stories, doors, wings... what are you trying to say? You heard everything that Sinan and I talked about, didn't you? Are you trying to tell me to go there? Talk to me straight.'

Silence. As she smoked, she gazed into the distance. Mum looked good when she smoked, and she knew it. She used to choose long cigarettes because they enhanced the shape of her slender white fingers. When her hand went to her lips, everyone would hold their breath, wishing they could be the smoke that was being sucked down into her lungs. My hands, like everything else about me, were like Dad's. My fingers – Sinan's beloved little doves, childish hands that got lost in Petro's huge palm – were short and dark.

'I heard not only what you said to Sinan, but also what you didn't say, Melike.'

'What do you mean?'

'Tell me, is Sinan anything more to you than a shoulder on which you can shed your tears about other men?'

Staggering backwards in fury, I let go of the rope. My mother retained her composure. She raised an eyebrow. How well she knew exactly where the moonlight would strike.

'That's how your relationship began. And that's how it will always be, daughter.'

I froze. She was referring to Barish. *That's how your relationship began. And that's how it will always be.* But how could she know? She hadn't even been with us throughout those sad autumn evenings after the bloody military coup of September 1980, when they took Barish away and we received no news of him for weeks. Dr Chetin had taken Mum to Switzerland and checked her into a sanatorium for psychiatric patients in the foothills of the Alps. In that peaceful care home, they set about repairing my mother's soul, patching over the great voids that were full of pain. How could she know that I, meanwhile, was waiting for Barish in Dr Chetin's empty villa, alongside Barish's old schoolfriend Sinan? The two of us would sit there listening to the swoosh of dry leaves in the howling wind, thinking about Barish, too scared to share our fears for him, images of police torture vivid in our imaginations.

Then one night, as we waited, our lips met, and then our arms and legs. We found comfort in the warmth of each other's bodies and stayed there, seeking comfort and distraction as we feared the worse. But once we started, we couldn't stop. We did not disentangle ourselves for weeks.

Who told you about all that, Mum? Mina had not yet reappeared. Cem was already in Australia. Dr Chetin? Impossible. Before he could get over the shock of his wife's suicide attempt, his son was arrested. Leaving my mother in Switzerland, he rushed back to Istanbul. When he realized that none of his friends in the old Istanbul aristocracy could save Barish from the terrible basements of the military police, he took residency in front of the window at the villa and counted the shipping tankers coming and going, his eyes blank.

And upstairs, while I was crying tears for Barish in his arms, Sinan was stroking my hair. He loved me even though he knew that when the lights were out, in my head I was fantasizing about lying in someone else's arms.

He loved me so much. Enough to say, 'All I want is to spend the rest of my life with you, Melike.'

Mum spoke up again. 'You know, don't you, that your paternal grandmother went through her own door and turned into Safinaz.'

'What?'

I leant forward to see Mum's face, but the moon had disappeared behind a cloud.

'Your grandmother followed Pasha to Istanbul. She knew that he was married and had a family. But still she tucked Orhan under her arm and left her village and her husband. She took a boat and a train and travelled all the way to Istanbul.'

'How could that be? Didn't Dad's father die? Safinaz's ID card listed the marital status as "widow" – I remember it.'

Mum elegantly threw her head back and gave a dry laugh. Then she slid over to one side of the swing.

'Come and sit beside me, Melike. Don't just stand there like that. My neck hurts from looking up at you.'

When we were children, Cem and I used to sit together on the swing, one of us facing the mulberry tree, the other facing the street. I could easily sit the same way beside my skinny mother. The thin rope grew taut and creaked, the wooden swing beneath us sank a little. We began to sway very slowly. My mind was on Safinaz.

'What is the truth then?'

'They asked the camel why its neck was so crooked, and he said, "What is there that is straight about me?" Your grandmother's identity is like that.'

'I don't understand.'

Our faces were very close. Too close for comfort. I smelled the familiar scent of lavender on her skin. She raised one thin eyebrow again.

'Pasha was clever. Back then, Safinaz's name was Anastasia. When she followed Pasha all the way to Istanbul, he didn't only buy her that house with all the clocks, he gave his mistress a new identity. The new surname law had just been passed. The country was in such chaos, nobody cared what anybody else was doing; everybody was registering at the public registration office with whatever name they liked. "Anastasia" was changed to "Safinaz". The father of young Anastasia, whom she'd left in the village, had been nicknamed "Kutsos", which apparently means "lame" or "crippled". In his honour she chose "Kutsi" for her surname. And there you have it – Safinaz Kutsi!'

My mouth dropped open. I brought the swing to a halt. Under my bare toes, the ground was soft and moist. Mum lit another cigarette and the smell of smoke mingled with the scent of lavender.

'How do you know all this? Did Dad tell you?'

I squirmed uneasily. This was the first time I had asked my mother something concerning my father.

'No, of course not. He didn't even know himself, though I'm sure he's found out by now. Much later, your aunt Zeyno put the pieces together. Pasha is Zeyno's father.' Seeing the shock on my face, she smirked. 'Don't tell me you didn't know that either. How else would Safinaz have had enough money to send her daughter to the German High School? Your father resented that so much. Your aunt Zeyno began to visit Pasha at the end of his life. When she made it clear that she wasn't after his inheritance, Pasha's other children left her in peace. At any rate, Pasha was all alone then, stuffed into an apartment. In his final days he poured out his heart to his illegitimate daughter.'

My nose filled with the scent of the jasmine entwining the railings of the balcony. As my eyes wandered over the mansion's dark windows, I said quietly, 'And Dad? Is he Pasha's child too?'

Silence.

'Mum?'

Quickly I tried to think. No, Pasha couldn't be Dad's father. Aunt Zeyno, okay. But Dad? No! If that was the case, surely he would have been sent to the German school too?

'I don't know if Pasha is Orhan's biological father or not, but he is definitely the father of his name.'

'What do you mean?'

She leant back and exhaled a stream of smoke. The moon peeped out from behind a cloud and lit up her slender neck, her bony ribcage. Her feet in their high-heeled mules began to rock the swing slowly.

'God, Melike, would a Greek woman ever have a son named Orhan? When Pasha transformed Anastasia into Safinaz, he gave the baby the name Orhan.'

'What are you saying, Mum? What is Dad's real name?'

She looked up and met my gaze. The sharp bones of her hip were poking into my leg.

'I don't know. I asked Zeyno. She didn't know either. Either she'd forgotten to ask or Pasha himself didn't know. To find out, you'd need to go to the village where your father was born.'

'Where is that? Bergama?'

'What? Bergama?'

She threw her cigarette to the ground and stepped on it. The swing stopped.

'Isn't that the village where Dad was born? Bergama. His birth certificate... Oh, is that a lie too?'

Mum began to laugh.

'Oh, Melike, you were such a smart little girl, honey. When did you become so naive? If you hadn't been so angry, if you had been even the slightest bit interested in your family, I would have told you Anastasia's story a long time ago. I would have told you that the place your father disappeared to was not Bergama. But you didn't want to hear anything about him. You cut him out completely. You said, "I've erased that man from my life." So I just left it at that. And you and I didn't exactly sit down for cosy chats together, did we, for God's sake.'

I felt dizzy. I stood up, leaving her on the now unbalanced swing, and went over to the mulberry tree. Lies! You're lying, Mum! I never asked you where he was because I wasn't allowed to. You'd forbidden that question. You and your mother, Madam Piraye, never allowed us to ask anything. The whole subject was out of bounds. The eyebrows raised to the sky, the puckered lips, the meaningful silences. At eleven years old, I learnt that it was imperative not to speak about taboo subjects. So don't you dare try and make it my fault that this secret has been kept hidden from me for years.

'Where is it then?' I stuttered, leaning against the mulberry tree. 'Where is Dad now?'

Mum raised her feet and the swing flew into the darkness. Her mules dropped off into the grass. She shouted over to me.

'I don't know the name of the village, Melike. It used to be in the north. But then when the army invaded, the whole village fled and settled somewhere else. Your – what was his name? Petro? – certainly knows more than I do.'

'Shhh! Not so loud, Mum!'

I walked towards her, my curiosity piqued, and stopped where I could see her face. She was swinging high. The grapevine's rusty old iron poles creaked.

'What place are you talking about?'

My mother looked down at me from on high, the swing climbing up and up amid the dusty, worm-eaten vine leaves. The moon had again changed its position. Its light struck Gulbahar's dimples as she laughed.

'Safinaz's village, of course, Melike, dear. I'm talking about the place to which your father went, and from where he never returned. I'm talking about Cyprus.'

15

Viranbag

I opened my eyes inside the mosquito netting. The house was silent. I was surprised. Even the television was switched off. I got up, slipped on the white cotton dress I'd left on the armchair and called down the stairs: Mum? Sinan? Mina? No answer. Where had they all gone? Sinan had probably gone down to the beach after his tennis game. But on a hot day like this, it was unheard of for my mother to leave the house. I checked the clock on the wall. It was noon already! Well, naturally, if you stayed swinging in the garden until daybreak...

I made my way down the hall to the bathroom, barefoot, pushing open each room door as I went, one after the other. The walls of the wooden mansion were oven hot, so hot that my poor lungs hurt when I inhaled. The table in my mother's room that we'd eaten from the previous night had been cleared, the pillows had been fluffed, and the old cherry-coloured curtains had been tied back with their velvet ribbons. The air in the room, trapped there because of the closed windows, smelled of the inside of drawers. The next room, the library, held a Far Eastern smell – a mix of Sinan's books, old papers, incense, marijuana and herbal tea. I shut that door quickly. Across the hall, Mina's room was neat. A single bed against the wall, a tower of books on the bedside table, with a glass of water alongside it, covered with a saucer. A tasselled, well-cared-for Milas rug lay beside the bed. I felt sick. Imagining the cool of the marble floor beneath my bare feet, I ran to the bathroom.

My face was puffy with sleep, and pale, the eyelashes glued together. Even my hands and feet were swollen. I bent over and stuck my head under the tap, giving my neck a good wetting. It wasn't enough. Shaking off the cotton dress, I stepped into the shower. Even the cold water ran warm. Still, when I came out into the hall with my hair dripping, I felt refreshed.

I dried myself, dressed quickly and went down to the kitchen. I could hear Mina and my mother talking in the back garden. So there they were. Mina was hanging out the washing and, strangely, Mum was laughing at something Mina had said. Did they always laugh together like that at this time of day? As I emptied coffee beans into the grinder, old childhood emotions resurfaced. Mum loved Mina more than she loved me. She always took the side of the underdog, against me. In fact, she had never loved me... Just stop it, Melike!

I ground the beans and made myself a frothy cup of coffee, no sugar. Cup in hand, I walked into the living room and took the opportunity to sit down in the flowery armchair in the glassed-in veranda. My mother had taken over the veranda so completely that I hadn't even set foot in there for years. Over time, it had become like a shop window that you peer into from a distance.

Like all the other windows in the house, the ones in there

were closed. On hot days Sinan was very particular about leaving the windows open all night and closing them in the morning. Since the mansion's electrics could not cope with air conditioning, this ensured that the cool night air was captured and the hot and humid daytime air couldn't seep in. I looked at the small television standing on the table across from me. It was turned off. A flat and wide Melike with puffy face and eyes was reflected back at me from the grey screen. In the living room itself, Sinan had set up a hi-tech multimedia system with a giant screen, and leather sofas and armchairs so comfortable you could get lost in them. But my mother would not be prized away from that miserable tiny television and her glassed-in veranda.

I stretched out on the chair, picked up one of the magazines stacked neatly on the coffee table – Mina's doing, of course – and absentmindedly flipped through it. I couldn't concentrate on anything, had no idea what I was even looking at. I needed to make a decision about my father.

Cyprus. So he was in Cyprus. He had gone to Cyprus and he had stayed there. Safinaz's real name was Anastasia. She wasn't a local Greek girl who'd dodged the forced migration. She was Anastasia from Cyprus. Okay. So what was Petro's connection with my father? With Safinaz? The heat and too much sleep had numbed my mind and I was finding it hard to think clearly.

Your father raised me.

Idiot!

I drew my knees up to my chest, laid my head on them and closed my eyes. My wet hair formed a shampoo-scented tent around me. Dad's expressions, his gestures, the way he ran his fingers through his hair, the way he tugged at his black eyebrows, his weird intonations, all the things I thought

I'd forgotten long ago had come alive in my head and were parading through it now. I felt like I was becoming smaller and smaller. I hugged my knees tight.

That morning, when Dad got into the boat and left the village, I lost the battle that I'd been fighting the whole of my short life. After that day I was an insignificant detail, a war veteran, dragging my wounded heart behind me for all eternity. Was I really going to travel all that way just to experience that loss all over again?

Pushing my hair away from my face, I stood up. Oh, never mind, Melike, you can think about that tomorrow. Where was my handbag? I'd been so full of anger when I'd got back last night, where had I put it? I went into the kitchen and saw I'd left it on the shelf beside Sinan's pickles. My phone battery was about to die, but nobody had called. I felt sort of crushed. Come on, Melike. You slam the door in the boy's face and then expect him to call you?

While I was in the kitchen charging the phone, I played with its buttons. It was new and I hadn't got used to it yet. It was very fancy – silver-plated, a limited edition. It made a 'schack' sound when you opened or shut the cover. Sinan gave it to me for our fifteenth wedding anniversary. He was always afraid I would drop and break it.

I looked at the last numbers I'd called. Petro's wasn't there. It wouldn't be, of course. We had never talked on the phone. We'd made our arrangements by email, and after that we'd been with each other the whole time. Until I slammed the door and left. All of a sudden, I was anxious about not having his number in my phone. I ran up to my office on the top floor. As soon as I opened the door, a wood-smelling heat lashed my face like a whip. Throwing myself at my desk, I opened my computer. It took ages for the machine to wake up and connect to the internet. Come on, come on! Even though I'd showered, sweat was now dripping off me. I quickly scanned my emails. Scrolled up, scrolled down. Nothing. And again. No, nothing. He hadn't emailed.

My insides deflated like a balloon. My shoulders slumped. I tried to re-ignite my anger. It didn't take. There was just a familiar disappointment smouldering inside me, like smoke from a fire that had been extinguished long ago. I found his number in an old email and made a note of it. For what purpose?

I closed the computer and went downstairs. In this heat, the only thing to do was go swimming. The sea would restore my equilibrium. Yes, the sea, at the back of the island in a bay nobody ever went to. Right now. I stuffed my swimsuit, a towel and my sudoku cards into a basket, grabbed my phone from the kitchen and rushed out of the house.

At the boathouse, Osman Usta was elated to see me.

'Where have you been, Melike, for goodness' sake? I fixed your boat up – it's as good as new. She's all painted and ready to go. The summer's coming to an end now, and she's still waiting there in the water with her head bowed, like a bride. What a shame, what a sin! Other summers you used to take her out so often. Where is Mr Sinan? Hey, boy, go and get Madam Melike's boat ready; fill the tank... That little fishing boat – yeah, *Misket*, that one.

The old boatman and I walked together to the end of the dock. He was right. This summer we had neglected the poor thing. Years back, when I'd first bought the boat, with money left to me by Dr Chetin (may he rest in peace; he was a generous man), I'd take her out every day, showing Sinan the captains' tricks I'd learnt in the village and improved upon in my adolescence. We'd go all the way out to Yassiada and back.

Osman Usta untied the rope. Ignoring his outstretched hand, I jumped into the boat, slipped to the stern, arranged the new green-and-white-striped canvas cushions on the seat and yanked the starter cord. It fired up with just one pull. I grabbed hold of the tiller. The blue wood was warm.

Osman Usta frowned. 'Be careful, daughter. Lots of know-nothings have started a new trend: they take boats from the landing and go round to the back of the island. Then the ones who can swim, and also the ones who can't, jump into the water wearing long underpants on their butts – excuse me. You should see how they thrash around and bellow. They'll get in your way and you won't know what to do. People like that can turn a person into a murderer just like that.'

'Okay, Uncle Osman, I'll be careful. I know which bays they anchor in and I know where I'm going. To Viranbag. Don't worry.'

I turned the tiller. Osman Usta's dark, wrinkled face, leathery from a lifetime in the sun, broke into a smile. He placed his hand over his heart.

'Be back before dark.'

Turning the nose of the boat towards Nizam, I waved to Osman Usta's diminishing figure on the dock. I'm forty years old now, Uncle Osman, not the fourteen-year-old girl who used to steal her grandfather's boat and go out fishing while you were taking your afternoon nap under the awning.

I steered towards Dilburnu, following the coast. Two packed boats set off from the landing and passed me in the open sea. They'd turned up their music as loud as it could go and a group of young people in the back were beating time on a drum. One of them pointed at me and they all crowded round the railing to look at the woman sitting in the back of the little fishing boat, steering. I waved to them. They turned at the cape and were lost from view, leaving me with *Misket*'s putt-putt. Under the cloudless, pale blue sky, the sea spread out like a sheet. Well-kept mansions shaded by ancient pine trees, terraced gardens that ran down to the sea, arbours, decorative pools – the island was a green oasis untouched by time.

A fibreglass speedboat which Sinan's friend from the club, Shefik, had recently bought was tied to the dock of the old Ververoglu mansion. Shefik commuted to the city, to Kabatas, in this boat every morning. He said that now that he had this boat, he could live on Buyukada all year round, through the winter as well as the summer. What a stingy guy he is! Try staying one winter in the island and see how you will freeze in the damp cold. Even the most expensive central heating system couldn't stave off the merciless chill that funnelled down the chimneys of those old wooden mansions.

I knew all about that. That first winter, when Mum and Cem and I came back to Buyukada from the village, I was forever burning my hands while I huddled beside the woodstove doing my homework. Mum had brought us straight from the bus station to the island, to her parents' summer home. After Dad's telegram, she had made the hasty decision: she and I would be spending the winter on the island, and Cem would go to high school in Istanbul. He would live with my grandparents in their apartment in Harbiye. I would go to middle school on the island. Even my grandmother, Madam Piraye, lost her cool when she heard that, and entreated Mum to reconsider, but she paid no attention. 'Melike is used to a village school. There's no need to evict the tenants from the apartment in Galata.' And the subject was closed. Then, in front of her mother and father, she lit a cigarette and blew smoke in their faces.

When the schools went back in September, my grandparents took Cem and returned to Istanbul. Nobody was left on the island except a few tradespeople and horse-carriage owners. Fortunately, Fati, the faithful old nanny, remained with us. She cooked for us. Every morning it was she who put a cheese sandwich in my bag in case I got hungry at school. In the evenings she would prick chestnuts with a sharp knife, soak them, and then roast them on top of the stove. The smell of the chestnuts, the way the shells opened like a flower when they were ready, reminded me of the evenings at Mr Ibrahim's house, when we would listen to classical music and read books. My childhood had come to a premature end and was now just a series of sad memories. Nothing passed my mother's lips except the tea brewing on the stove and the tobacco in her cigarettes. While I was sniffling and studying in the only room in the mansion with a woodstove, trying to ward off the chill from the insidious wind, she was buried in the novels of her youth.

What a lonely, lifeless time. I paced the concrete schoolyard on my own, impatient for breaktimes to be over. I took an interest in my lessons purely because they made my days slightly less tedious. I was so bored and unhappy that finally I became top of my class. This didn't achieve anything except that the other girls now completely avoided me. Plus I was the girl with the weird mother. When she came to pick me up from school, her long, blond, uncombed hair reaching down to her waist, my classmates would stare at her with a mixture of fear and awe. She was a fairy child in faded blue jeans and handmade sweaters, someone from a different universe.

I had no idea what other girls and their mothers who came to get them at midday talked about or did. Actually, other mothers didn't come and pick their daughters up from school. But the two of us would set off into the forest, along Lovers' Road. Mum would point out to me where the heroines in books I knew nothing about had wandered under the pine trees. I memorized the paths made-up people I didn't know had walked down, the bushes behind which they had secretly kissed. It was not reality but her fictive world that excited my mother then. While I was at school, she spent all her time with those characters from her novels. When we were together, she wanted to talk to me only about them. Not about Dad, or Safinaz or our old village.

Now, in light of what I'd learnt the previous night, I felt I understood my mother a little more. She had punished herself. If she hadn't sent that telegram, if she hadn't summoned Mr Ibrahim to Antalya, he would still be alive. Having caused her lover's death, she did not deserve to live either. For that reason she buried herself on Buyukada, where life came to a halt in the winter. She did not care at all about the difficulties her bewildered children were facing as they tried to adjust to their new schools. Why should she? She had given up her children anyway. *If your father had not acted first, it would have been me who'd gone away and left you.* The first sign of psychosis was a lack of empathy towards others, wasn't it? Which meant that the disconnection began way back. But who could have understood that in the winter of 1975, when Nanny Fati, the gardener and I were running around putting buckets under the leaking roof?

After Cem stopped making his weekend visits, supposedly because of this wind, or that wind, or homework, Mum and I hunkered down on the lonely island and established an odd sort of life woven of silences and forbidden questions, like two strangers who'd lost their memory. If Dr Chetin had not appeared in Mum's life the following summer, we might have continued like that for years. He rescued the two of us from the lonely island when he moved us to his villa on the shores of the Bosphorus.

When I turned into the back of the island, a light breeze sprang up. Viranbag Bay was completely empty. I dropped anchor in the shelter of some pine trees that were bending in the breeze. The whole world fell silent when the engine stopped. The sun roasted my skin with all its might. I quickly put on my swimsuit and descended the ladder. I slipped my legs into the water, then let myself go, sinking into the sea from my toes to my head. The chill of the water worked into my bones; my hair floated right and left like seaweed. I let out all my breath and dived to the bottom in a ray of sunlight. In that underwater world, with its roof of blue glass, life was so silent, so slow. The light was fractured, scattering rainbow colours into the hushed water. Even the school of little silver fish darted in slow motion between the rocks. If I could hold my breath, how long could I stay down there in the depths? If only I could live down there, just me, with no past, no future, having forgotten everything, not even remembering that I had anything to forget. In that fairy-tale world of sparkling light, if I could only jump onto a seahorse's back and find a secret palace hidden behind the velvet seaweed.

The soughing of the glittering water became my father's voice. I couldn't understand what he was saying. I dived deeper. Instead of getting quieter, the soughing intensified, squeezing my head from both sides like a vice. Behind the seaweed on the seafloor I found not a palace but our house in the village. The beam of light I was diving into shone onto the sweaty neck of my childhood self, asleep on a narrow bed. Dad was kneeling beside me, bending over my face. One of his hands was on my cheek, his lips were whispering something. The whispers filled my brain, but my head couldn't contain them; it was throbbing, about to burst.

All at once my body took control and shot me up to the surface like a firecracker. Air rushed in through my nose and mouth, replenishing my lungs. I lay on my back, my arms and legs spreadeagled. My breathing was erratic, my ribcage swelling, swelling, and deflating. What had I seen down there on the seabed? Was the lack of oxygen down there making me hallucinate? First Safinaz's grave, now my father at the bottom of the sea.

Mum's riddle about doors and love doesn't make your sin any slighter, Dad. You betrayed us all.

I flipped over onto my stomach and began to swim. My breathing had calmed. Yielding to the embrace of the water, I swam with long, slow strokes. I began to feel lighter. I slid through the water like a sailing boat. My mind kept returning to Petro and our lovemaking, to the passion that had suffused my entire being at the moment of full surrender. Nectar, not blood, had flowed through my veins. Even now, as the sea wrapped my legs, my arms, my body in its cool membrane, warmth vibrated inside me. I took faster strokes, quickly reached the boat and climbed the ladder. With water dripping from my fingertips, my hair, my nose, I lay down on the towel I'd left spread out at the front of the boat. Shaking my salty, wet hair over my face, I blocked out the light. The sun passed its fiery hand across my shoulders, my back, the backs of my legs, sucking out the water, leaving the salt. What if the hand were not the sun's but Petro's? I would lie like this, he would lower his whole weight onto my back, one hand spreading my legs... I opened my eyes.

My phone was ringing.

In a flash, I threw the imaginary Petro off my back and jumped up. Stepping over the seats in the middle of the boat, where the oars were, I ducked under the awning at the stern and fumbled for my phone in the basket I'd left beside the tiller. It had stopped ringing. I tried to read the shining screen. It said there had been seven unanswered calls. Seven! And the low-battery indicator was flashing. I pressed some keys and Sinan's name appeared, again and again. Sinan, Sinan, Sinan... Seven times Sinan. God help you, Sinan! What's up with you? He'd also sent four messages. I should just hurl that expensive phone into the sea! The phone rang again. Sinan, of course. He was breathing heavily.

'Where in the hell are you, Melike, for God's sake? We've all been worried sick. How many times have I asked you to leave a note or send a message before you just take off like that.'

'Don't be angry, Sinan. You're right. I apologize. My phone battery is about to run out. Don't worry.'

'Where are you?'

For a moment I hesitated, as if it wasn't an imaginary Petro that was waiting for me on the towel but the flesh and blood version.

'Where are you, Melike? You're back in Istanbul, aren't you? What are you up to? You're starting to really test my patience now.'

'No, Sinan, I'm not in Istanbul. I'll tell you, but you can't get angry, okay?'

Sinan growled something at the other end of the line.

I made my voice softer. 'I took the boat. I'm at Viranbag Bay.'

Silence. Taking the phone from my ear, I glanced at the screen to see if the battery had died and we'd been cut off. Sinan was still there. I squinted up at the sky. The Monastery of St George was glowing pink at the top of the hill.

'Why don't you come over, Sinan? It's so beautiful here. We can swim. It's cooler now.'

'Where? All the way to Viranbag?'

'Yes! Get on your new bike and come. You'll fly here on that.'

'I don't know, Melike. I'm tired. And in this heat…'

'Oh, come on! Don't be lazy! We can eat at the taverna on St George's Hill. What do you say, sweetheart? We can watch the moonrise.'

'If I come on my bike, how will we get back?'

Typical Sinan, needing a plan for everything. At least his anger had passed.

'We'll find a way, honey. Worst case scenario, we'll leave the boat here for the night and walk home with the bike. We can come back and get it tomorrow. Let's not worry about the details. Just come!'

He sighed.

I spoke hastily. 'Listen to me, Sinan. Put a dress in the bike bag for me, and some underwear, no need for a bra. And some shoes – my leather sandals. Come to the Viranbag tea garden, on the Grand Tour Road. You know it, right? There's a track that leads down to the beach, a dirt road. I'll swim to the shore and wait for you there. We can swim for a bit, then walk up St George's Hill. The sunset is so wonderful from there, it never disappoints.'

'The way you just left your dress on the bathroom floor

and took off again, Melike… You could at least have taken it back to your room, even if you didn't hang it up—'

'I can't hear you, Sinan. The battery must be dying. I'll be at the Viranbag tea garden in forty-five minutes. Did you get that? Don't be late. I'll be in my swimsuit, barefoot, bareheaded. Okay, sweetheart?'

I shut the phone and went back to the front of the boat. The wind had picked up and was beginning to whip up the sea. I breathed in the smell of hot earth, of pine trees and pinecones that had been cooking in the sun all day. The smell of summer. The smell of the sun. Then I lay back down on the towel, where the imaginary Petro was waiting for me. As the boat rocked like a cradle, hidden behind my hair, I completed our half-finished lovemaking.

16

Calculations of Probability

It turned out to be one of those rare summer nights when the moon rose just a few minutes after the sun had set. When I'd tried to convince Sinan to come over, telling him that we could watch the moonrise, I hadn't known that – I just got lucky.

We were sitting side by side in the taverna at the top of the hill, looking out over Heybeli Island. A bottle of local red wine, sealed with wax, had already been brought to our table. The sun was melting like a scoop of orange ice cream on the horizon, leaving behind a purplish-pink sea. The wine in our tumblers flashed like jewels. My hand was in Sinan's, my head resting on his shoulder. My skin, roasted in sun and salt the whole day, was smouldering. Maybe because it was local, the wine was sliding down my throat like water.

When I looked around for a waiter to ask for bread, I saw the tip of the moon peeping out from behind Sedef Island. No one else had noticed it. First, a corner of Sedef Island reddened, then the moon emerged from the sea, like a precious gemstone being held up for approval on a tray.

Tipping my head back, I watched it rise out of the corner of my eye. It too glowed red, but it didn't make a great spectacle of its glorious light like the sun did. It was calm and coy. I took a deep breath, as if to draw the light inside me.

The moon and the sun. Selene and Helios. Two siblings. One a faithful goddess, the other a promiscuous god. Though the goddess might be faithful, she was also mysterious. Not only did she smile at the world from behind a screen of frosted glass, she also never revealed her dark face. Her redness was actually a lie, and, like all lies, it became less tenable over time. Even now, as the sky darkened, her cheeks were turning pale. Selene's face was encircled by a blue veil. As for Helios, god of the sun, he was wide open, he wore no mask, sheltering in his brave heart his heat, his light, his colour. It was obvious what he was and who he was. Nothing was hidden.

Selene and Helios.

One female, one male.

Two siblings, each only visible when the other was absent.

'Oh, look at the moon! When did it rise? Damn! How could we have missed it?'

The crowds filling the tables of the taverna built on the island's highest hill turned their heads as one, from the western horizon to the eastern. They laughed and clinked glasses, then dropped their voices and fell silent. Sinan put his arm around my waist. Leaving our table, we walked over to the other side of the hill. Without saying a word, we watched the moon climb slowly over Sedef Island. A magical silence reigned. We were even loath to bring our glasses to our lips. Sinan had brought me the multicoloured silk dress that my grandmother's seamstress had made for her, years ago. He stroked my back through it as we stood there. I laid my head on his shoulder and he drew me close, planting a kiss on my temple. He smelled of coconut. I felt totally safe, secure in his love.

'Come on, Sinan, our sausages have arrived. Let's go back to our table.'

This time we sat across from each other. In the glow of the colourful lightbulbs threaded through the vines, my husband looked very handsome. He was wearing a short-sleeved navy blue shirt that I hadn't seen before, ironed to perfection, of course – Mina's handiwork. Even the cycle ride hadn't wrinkled it. His hair was tousled and his green eyes shone with a different intensity. Was that the wine or the moonlight?

The chubby son of the restaurant owners brought out our side orders of chips, green salad, and beans cooked in olive oil. My mouth began to water even before he'd lifted the dishes off the tray. I threw a chip and a piece of sausage into my mouth right away, not caring if my tongue got burnt. Sinan poured the last of the wine into our glasses. Everyone else had returned to their tables too, and the taverna began to buzz like a beehive amid the clatter of knives and forks. I stuck my fork into another sausage. Sinan was spooning the food onto his plate in an orderly way. When the sausages, chips and salad were arranged so that they didn't touch each other, he picked up his fork in one hand and rested his cheek on the other.

'I have to go to Bursa sometime next week, to one of the hotels. My brother called this morning and was complaining again.'

Worry lines appeared on his beautiful, wide forehead. For a while now, Sinan's brothers and cousins had been putting pressure on him to get more involved in the ever-expanding

Ishik hotel chain. As the youngest brother, Sinan was in a difficult position; he felt guilty and didn't know what to say to them.

'Remind them that you are now a professor, darling. They think you're just having a good time, and that annoys them. Would they really be any happier if you joined the family business full time and made your life as boring as theirs?'

Sinan's face puckered. I stopped talking. He didn't like me sharing my thoughts about his family so openly. As I saw it, his elder brothers and cousins wanted to control their sons and grandsons, tell them how they should live their lives. Sinan had separated from the herd and they couldn't bear that; they wanted him to be just like them, so they used all sorts of dirty tricks to try and quash his free-spiritedness. But Sinan didn't want to hear any of that. To do so would introduce disharmony into his life, like causing a piano to go out of tune. I softened my voice and shifted to a flirtatious frequency.

'Joking aside, you've completed a whole year at university, Professor Sinan. Let's have another bottle of wine to celebrate.'

I pointed out our empty bottle to a boy running from table to table.

Glancing at his glass of wine, still half full, Sinan said quietly, 'Do you really think my family takes my university work seriously, when even I don't?'

'Why do you say that?'

'Three hours a week at a private university, filling the board with statistics and graphs while a bunch of kids stare dozily back at me? Can you really call that teaching?'

'I don't understand why anyone would sleep through your classes! What's not to love about using statistics and graphs to solve universal problems? And mathematical induction!

Not to mention probability theory, your specialist subject. I'd have loved it if we had classes like that when I was a student.'

His face relaxed; he smiled.

'Not everyone approaches life like they're solving a sudoku puzzle like you do, darling.'

I reached under the table, found his hand and placed it on my bare knee with a giggle.

'Professor, may we discuss the probability of relations between us in your office?'

'Ah, Melike, you devil! How many professors' marriages did you break up at university?'

'You're the devil. I never broke up anyone's marriage.'

We laughed together. Our second bottle of wine arrived. We asked for another round of sausages.

'When my brother Kaya called this morning, he said they're thinking of opening a spa hotel in Cekirge, central Bursa. It'll be a boutique hotel, and he wondered if I'd consider running it. I'd only have to go there once or twice a week, and there's that new ferry service from Istanbul to Mudanya now. Anyway, I'll go and see what's involved. And I can visit Mother as well. She's very upset that Aylin isn't receiving any marriage proposals. They're still making her go to all kinds of religious people, fortune tellers and all, even though she's over thirty years old now.'

I took a sip of my wine, then dipped some bread into the sausage fat. 'Kaya should let Aylin run the boutique hotel,' I said with my mouth still full, knowing that Sinan would disapprove of such poor table manners. 'Then everyone would get what they wanted.'

He reached over the plates and took my hand. 'You should come too. It's been so long since we went to Bursa together.'

The moon was suspended above us like a lantern, with a

very pale, ice blue halo around it. Selene had mounted her two-horse chariot and was galloping from one hilltop to another, leaving a silver trail across the dark waters. A big group at a long table in the back were singing an old Turkish folksong together:

'Every night on Heybeli
We'd go out and enjoy the moonlight...'

I wondered why we islander locals couldn't let go of the past. We were a community of mansions, pine forests, horse-carriages, and songs like this one that kept alive the dreams of a different time. Wasn't that why we loved this taverna, because it was a relic of days gone by?

'What do you say?'

'About what?'

'Shall we go to Bursa together? In this heat, I can't tempt you with a thermal bath or kebabs, but maybe we can go to Kirazliyayla. We could stay in one of the honeymoon bungalows and go walking every morning in the fresh air. Or cycling. It's cool there now. Pure—'

'I can't come, Sinan.'

He leant back, rubbed his hands together, stroked his beard in the mosaic glow of the colourful bulbs. I was sure he was rolling a joint in his mind. But Sinan was careful. He wouldn't roll a joint and light up in a public place like Petro did.

'My father... I need to see my father.'

He sat up straight. The mosaic on his face changed colours.

'Are you serious?'

'He's dying. I told you that yesterday.'

'You told me, but it didn't seem like you were in a rush to go and see him.'

'He's in Cyprus.'

'Cyprus?

I took a big gulp of wine. Sinan looked at my glass but didn't say anything.

'And he's been there ever since? How many years is that?'

'Twenty-nine.'

'Wow! All that time passes without so much as a peep and then he suddenly reappears and sends word to you via this documentary producer son. Interesting man.'

'You said it!'

'So now you're going to Cyprus right away?'

'Looks like it.'

'Do you want me to come with you?'

I shook my head so vehemently that a piece of sausage got stuck in my throat. Grabbing my glass, I drained my wine in one go. After a coughing fit, I spoke in a hoarse, shaky voice that didn't sound like mine.

'No. I need to deal with this by myself. I'd rather go alone.'

'But there'll be someone with you, won't there? This documentary fellow – what was his name? Pavlo?'

My cheeks burned red to match the wine I'd been guzzling.

'Will he be with you? But... Melike?'

You're finished now, Melike. You're damned, my girl. Your husband isn't dumb. He knows what's happened here, of course. He teaches classes on probability at a university.

'Ye... yes.'

'Is your father in the south or the north?'

'What?'

'Is your father in Northern Cyprus, or in the south?'

'North, I guess. How could a Turkish citizen be in the south?'

'If your father's in the north, how does this Greek chap

– what was his name? Petro? – know him? Didn't he say your father raised him – like a son? Isn't that what you said last night? Melike, sweetheart, take it easy – you're drinking very fast.'

'Aren't there any Greeks living in the north?'

'I don't think so. After the Turkish army's takeover of Northern Cyprus, all the Greeks fled to the south. People brought over from Turkey moved into their abandoned houses.'

I shrugged. 'I don't know where they met each other.'

'Oh my God, Melike…'

My head was spinning. I held onto the sides of my chair.

Sinan's eyes had widened. He brought his face close to mine and lowered his voice, like a detective who'd just discovered an important clue. 'Do you remember what month it was when your father left? You were living in the village, right? And he set out, supposedly, to arrange his mother's funeral. What month was that?'

'It was summer, but I don't remember the month. Around now, I think. Maybe the middle of summer…'

'What year was it when you finished primary school? 1974, wasn't it?'

'Yes. So?'

'If your father went to Cyprus then… Do you realize what that means?'

I thought about it. No, I didn't think. I narrowed my eyes and tried to locate my boat, *Misket*, on the waters washed silver in the moonlight. The neural pathways in my head were all tangled up. Feeling nauseous, I reached for my wine.

'Melike?'

'Yeah?'

'That summer, your father…'

'… was there during the invasion,' I mumbled absentmindedly.

'Slow down, Melike! Okay, please, let that be your last glass. You know, don't you, that referring to the Cyprus landing as an "invasion" is offensive. Don't say that word out loud in a public place. It might even be illegal.'

At any other time, I would have had a fierce argument with paranoid Sinan about that, but right then my mind was on something else. What would have happened if my father had been there when the Turkish army landed on Cyprus? If his mother's village was a Greek village and Dad was there at that time…

Mr Orhan, do not go. It's like hell over there.

I pushed my chair back abruptly. It wobbled on the uneven ground. The tables around us had emptied. The group at the back who'd been singing were now talking quietly while they ate watermelon and cherries.

'Do you have a cigarette on you?'

'What kind of cigarette?'

'A normal one, sweetie. You carry tobacco with you sometimes.'

'Have you started smoking?'

'I just feel like one.'

'I don't have any with me, but when we get home, I'll roll you a proper one. Listen, Melike, if your father was there that summer, there's a good chance—'

'Shh, Sinan, enough! I don't want to talk about that any more. I also don't want to go home tonight.' I spoke slowly, trying not to slur my words. The wine had majorly gone to my head.

'Okay, then what should we do?'

'Let's sleep on the boat!' I gestured loosely in the direction of Viranbag Bay, as if I could see in the moonlight the spot where my *Misket* was moored.

'You're drunk.'

'Yeah, so what? Come on, don't disappoint me. Let's go down to the shore, swim to the boat, make love all salty, and sleep buck-naked.'

'Crazy girl! What about our clothes? Will we swim in them? My phone? My wallet?'

'Oof, Sinan, I don't know! We'll work it out. We could hide them under a bush or something. Come on, please. Don't be such a killjoy.'

Even though I was so drunk, I still had enough sense not to tell ultra-cautious Sinan that I'd left my expensive phone, with its dead battery, and my handbag on the boat.

He stood up, putting his wallet in the back pocket of his shorts.

'I swear to God, you're crazy, Melike. But in a very cute, irresistible way. Okay, let's walk. We'll see if you still insist on your mad plan once we get down to the shore.'

As we walked down the path which, in days gone by, ascetics had climbed barefoot, my feet kept tripping over each other. If Sinan hadn't grabbed me around the waist, I would have fallen flat on my face. Maybe I was drunker than I thought. It wasn't until I saw the Tower Mansion at the top of our street that I realized I was sitting in the back seat of a horse-carriage with my head on Sinan's shoulder. The bicycle had been loaded onto the carriage. When we got home, I observed, as if it were a scene in a film, my husband unzipping my silk dress and slipping it off me, carrying me into the mosquito netting, spreading my hair out on the pillow, and taking me in his arms in the moonlight. Later, as he drew a white cotton blanket up over my bare shoulders, he leant towards my ear. Did I really hear him whisper, 'Go, my princess. Pursue your dreams,' or was I dreaming? Next morning, when I woke up alone in the bed, I wasn't sure.

PART TWO

17

Safinaz's Clocks

A week later, I was in Athens, sitting in a café overlooking the ancient Agora and waiting for my aunt Zeyno to arrive from Germany. At the summit of the steep hill to the left, the marble pillars and pediments of the beautifully proportioned Parthenon glowed pink and red in the evening light, a perfect testament to the golden ratio. The temple's goddess, Athena, watched over the city and its people, reminding those who knew to look that the world was indeed a place of much beauty.

The statue of Athena was stolen from the temple centuries ago, but her spirit still hovered over the city, imbuing it with her wisdom and bestowing her blessings on the arts and the pleasures. I glanced around at the attractive young women and good-humoured men sitting at the tables in the café. They were all talking excitedly, gesticulating with their hands and arms, laughing easily and heartily, as if they had never in their lives known shame. Jokes passed from table to table. It wasn't only the laughter and uninhibited chatter of the women that impressed me. They were also self-confident; they carried themselves with pride, sure of their place in the world.

I smiled. Dante was right: beauty inspires the soul to action. I was happier than I had been for a long time. I was almost thankful for the bureaucracy that had made it necessary for me to come to Athens.

As Sinan had surmised, Dad was living in a village in the Republic of Cyprus, the southern part of the island, the Greek part. As a Turkish citizen, I needed to apply for a visa from the Cypriot Embassy in Athens. Petro had contacted the embassy as soon as he got home and sent me a list of the documents required. He recommended that I bring with me Safinaz's birth certificate with the name 'Anastasia' on it, along with any other paperwork I could find bearing that name.

Since that morning in the hotel – the morning I'd woken up so madly in love – we hadn't spoken to each other. It had only been ten days, but it seemed like months. In our correspondence, Petro assumed a very distant tone. His two-paragraph emails contained only information on tickets, documents and the visa. As he persisted with this coolness, my heart vacillated between longing and anger. A classic 'HELL' scenario. Hunt-Enticement-Lust-Loss. It seemed that, having lost his self-control that night, he was now trying to put as much distance as possible between us and act as if it had never happened.

To hell with you, Petro.

I'd sent him a coolly brief message as soon as I'd arrived in Athens, and had then spent the rest of the day wandering around the ancient city by myself. We were due to meet the following morning at the Cypriot Embassy. I considered what to wear. I'd brought with me a strappy, dark blue top and white linen trousers, a combination that made me feel beautiful and strong. I knew I looked good in that outfit; it was simple, elegant and flattering. I wondered how he would feel when he saw me. Had he thought about me in the last ten days, missed me? *Come on, Melike!* So what if he thought about you, missed you. Why would you care? The bastard is a conman, have you forgotten that? Not to mention cold and detached. You need to forget him, for God's sake.

'Here's your frappé. If you don't like it, I'll bring you an *ellinikos*.' The waitress indicated with her head the cups of Turkish coffee on her tray. She had put a tall, thin glass of what looked like melted ice cream in front of me. Seeing my blank expression, she said, '…You asked me to choose for you, to bring you whatever I recommended. Frappé is our most popular coffee.'

I raised the glass to my lips. The top half was all froth, the bottom half was full of sweet coffee. The froth melted in my mouth, dispersing caffeine across my palate. I nodded, smiling my approval. She had a cheeky face. Tossing back her long, black hair, her tray balanced on one hand, she set off to serve the *ellinikos* to the old men in the back who were simultaneously reading newspapers and chatting between tables.

A train clattered by beneath us. I checked my watch. It was almost 8.30. Aunt Zeyno was going to miss out on enjoying the legendary Attica twilight. Her plane would have just landed and it would take her at least an hour to get into the city. In spite of her advanced age, she had insisted that she'd be taking the metro from the airport into the centre.

'It's from living in Germany all these years – I can't bear to waste money on a taxi. Wait for me somewhere around Monastiraki. Anyone will be able to tell where that is; it means "Little Monastery". I'll meet you there.'

Her voice was just as I remembered it – a little husky, low, subtly commanding. When was the last time I'd seen her?

She'd come to my wedding, brought a very classy watch for Sinan from Germany – an IWC. The new groom loved it. For days he walked around without taking his eyes off his left arm, saying, 'What great taste your aunt has.' That was the first time it occurred to me that, in marrying me, Sinan had gone up in the world. Was that why he'd proposed? Were there other powerful reasons for his desire to spend the rest of his life with me, behind his love and affection for me? Before he'd been with me, Sinan was simply the son of a wealthy Bursa family. After me, as it were, he was the son-in-law of a well-established old Istanbul family. Just like… just like Dad, the son of a widowed art teacher, who had moved up the social ladder when he married Mum. By joining my family, Sinan had been catapulted into the city's top social circle. Had he actually made that calculation, or was this just me and my devious mind again? I didn't know.

My genius of an aunt, on the ball about everything, had pinned a diamond brooch of Safinaz's that I had never seen before onto my wedding dress. And after that? Had we not seen each other since? Fifteen years had passed. Fifteen huge years! When I was a child, so much would happen in the space of just one year that fifteen years would have been a lifetime, but so little had changed in my life since I'd got married. Winters were the apartment in Galata, film festivals in Beyoglu, movies, cafés, bars; summers were the island and the club. Maybe Mum was right. Marriage really did constrain a person into being a narrow version of themselves. Was that why, in my head, each of the New Year's celebrations of the past fifteen years seemed to merge one into the other? In the old days I used to store events in my memory by the month, by the week. But since my marriage, I hadn't been able to distinguish one year from the next.

As a child, you were so full of magic.

Oof, Mum! Always talking in riddles.

I remembered Mum and my aunt clearing out Safinaz's house. For some reason, I could picture very vividly how my aunt was that day. My mother and I had taken the ferry from Buyukada to the city. It was a windy day in late summer – the summer Safinaz died, and Dad left and never came back. Because of the Cyprus operation, it was also the summer in which there were blackouts at night. The Sirkeci ferry rocked back and forth in the wind. I was petrified that I would vomit and ruin the new red dress that my grandmother had bought me. By that time we were living with my grandparents on the island, and it was during this time that my aunt had telephoned the island and said, 'Come and take whatever you want. The rest of it I'll sell along with the house.'

We found Aunt Zeyno on the first floor. She was sitting in the beige wingback chair by the window, leaning back, her eyes closed, Mavri on her lap. She had cut her hair, which I remembered as having been like a wild forest. Now it was short, like a little boy's. She was wearing a long dress of purple batik, and silver earrings with blue stones. Seeing her sitting there, I remembered Pasha's car and his shiny black boots that the snow hadn't stuck to. The last time I'd visited the house, I was eight years old. Pasha had been sitting in that wingback chair. In her fluster, Safinaz had put the salt cellar instead of the sugar pot on the tea tray. It had been snowing outside, the woodstove was burning away. Now Safinaz was dead, and my father had abandoned us. My short-haired aunt was sitting in that chair.

The house was deserted and gloomy.

Sensing Mum and me approach, Mavri jumped to the floor; my aunt opened her eyes. A couple of lines, like little incisions, had formed on either side of her mouth. She had lost weight. She and Mum embraced without speaking. Zeyno laid her head on Mum's shoulder, and Mum closed her eyes. It was their first meeting since the New Year's Eve when my aunt and my father had had their big quarrel.

They stayed like that for a long time, clasping each other tightly, like lovers reunited. Orhan was gone now, taking the anger with him, and they were once again inseparable friends, the erstwhile celebrated literature students of Istanbul University.

Leaving them to their reunion, I went over to the window. The fig tree in the garden was all dried up, its leaves curled inwards like claws. The trough that Safinaz used to plant flowers in was now just a pitiful piece of old marble, discarded in a corner of the garden. I pressed my nose against the wall, sniffing for the scent of rose oil and cloves, but all I got was dust. Just as the breath had left my grandma's body, so the air of the house had been sucked out. I felt as if I was suffocating. I opened the window. Ugur was moving very slowly through the dry grass. He seemed perplexed. Did tortoises get sad? Did he even notice that my grandma was gone? Of course he did! How could he not? In my mind, I saw Ugur sticking his neck out of his shell to take peach peelings from Safinaz's hand. While he was hungrily chewing the velvet-furred peel, his wrinkled face would stretch into a smile. My eyes filled with tears. I raced to the stairs to go down into the garden to be with him, and at that moment I realized what was really missing from the house.

It wasn't the light, or the smells or even the fresh air. It was the sound that was missing.

The clocks!

The clocks were silent.

Jumping down the stairs two at a time, I reached the entrance hall. With trembling hands I opened the glass door of the giant grandfather clock, whose chime used to shake the whole building. I touched its heart. The clapper didn't make a sound. I took two steps back in fear. The giant clock was buried in a deathly silence. With my ears ringing, I ran up to the first floor. My mother and my aunt had pulled apart, but they were still standing there, talking in whispers. When they saw me, they stopped. Sliding my hand over the dusty bannisters, I went on up to the top floor, where the dwarf cupboard was located. I had grown up now – I was eleven years old – and wasn't afraid of the dwarf, but when I saw the cuckoo clock's disgruntled face in the hall, my heart constricted with the same terror that the dwarf used to inspire. The door to the living room was open. I rushed through it.

The shutters were closed, the sofa and armchairs covered with white cloth. Striped shadows fell on the rug with its bird designs. I passed by the table in the centre of the room without looking at the crystal bowl containing mint and milk-chocolate sweets. At any other time I wouldn't have left the living room without stuffing at least two into my mouth. But that day I had to reach the clock with the sun, the moon and the stars that was waiting on the mirrored console table. It was my favourite smiley-faced clock. The image of Safinaz winding it with the key which hung on the end of a chain came to my mind. On Sunday mornings the two of us would do the clock-winding tour. No matter how much I begged, my grandma would never give me the little keys. It was her fingers alone that could make the delicate adjustment.

Leaning on the marble console, I brought my face up close to the clock's glass door. I saw that it too had stopped. On the little blue clock face, the half-moon showed that it had halted at the first quarter, who knew when. A cold sweat broke out down my back and my neck burnt as if it had been touched by ice. I was shaking. I picked up the huge clock. It was very heavy. Losing my balance, with the clock in my arms, I fell to the floor in front of the console table. I scraped my knee, but the glass didn't break. With my arms still hugging the clock and my head resting against its cold, yellow metal, I lay there on the bird-patterned rug in Safinaz's shadowy living room, the room that was only ever opened up when visitors came, and for the first time since my father left I cried, until eventually I fell into an exhausted sleep.

18

Yamas!

As soon as Aunt Zeyno's curly head appeared at the corner of Monastiraki Square, my face broke into a smile. What was it that connected us to our blood relatives, I wondered? Was it simply the similar facial features, the particular gait, that made me feel close to this woman who was walking towards me, dragging a red suitcase behind her, a closeness that neither time nor distance had diminished? Or was there a deeper connection, a shared destiny, even a shared sadness? Perhaps something had passed from Safinaz to my father and my aunt, and from them to me. A vague longing, like a wisp of smoke still rising from a long-extinguished fire.

I stood up. My aunt took my face into her palms like a lover and gazed into my eyes for a long, long time. Her hands smelled of cigarettes and jasmine. My eyes filled. In front of me stood a mixture of Safinaz, Dad and the reflection I saw every day in the mirror. We hugged each other. She was so small. Inside the faded blue jeans, her hips were as narrow as a boy's. She seemed to have no breasts under her teal silk shirt. This was the fate of a childless woman, I thought. As the uterus shut down, the body relinquished its womanliness and shrivelled up like a raisin.

'Melike, my darling girl, who would have thought! How long has it been? Ten years? Fifteen?'

My nose filled with the smoky aroma of sweet cognac, which I remembered from my childhood. When my parents' rude friends used to wander around our house, teasing me about my having been brought in by the gypsies, my aunt would take me on her lap, press me to her bosom and whisper huskily in my ear that I was more beautiful than the lot of them, even my mother.

We sat across from each other at a small, round table. My aunt quickly lit a cigarette and offered me the silver case, which I declined. When I was a child, people use to say how alike we were, and they were not wrong. Zeyno and I were more like mother and daughter than Gulbahar and I. We had the same wild hair, small-boned physique, black eyes, thick eyebrows that met in the middle, and childlike hands and feet. But what struck me now was how my aunt resembled Safinaz, not me. Zeyno had turned into a blue-jeaned copy of my grandma. Her olive-black eyes were deep-set, just like Safinaz's, with faint bags beneath them. Her grey hair even had finger waves like Safinaz's used to. A few curls had fallen across her temples, like question marks above her cheekbones. If she hadn't pushed back her chair and crossed her legs, I would have sworn I was in a time warp.

'Who would have thought I'd be seeing you in a café on the streets of Athens! God works in mysterious ways. How are you? How's your mother, your handsome husband, everyone in Istanbul? You've got so pretty. It's not for nothing that they say that a boy takes after his mother's brother and a girl after her father's sister... If I didn't know your age, I'd say you were a young girl. So, what's going on with you?'

I looked down so she couldn't see me blushing. I always turned into a shy adolescent in the face of my aunt's cheery frankness.

'Uh oh... What are you mixed up in now? You know I'd never tell anyone. When a woman is this radiant, there has to be a reason.'

I bit my lip to keep from laughing.

'Nothing's going on, Aunt Zeyno.'

'Liar. It's that Greek man, isn't it? I knew from the moment I read your email. The boy who's helping you get a visa. What was his name?'

'Petro. But...'

'But what?'

'There's nothing between us.'

'Tell that to my hat. Anyway, introduce me to him and then I'll get both sides. He's coming to the embassy tomorrow, isn't he?'

'Yes.'

Thinking about seeing Petro the next day made my foolish heart start to beat like one of Safinaz's clocks. A silly grin took over my face, impossible for my clever aunt to miss. I was dying to fill her in about that night, and couldn't help but tell her everything. As she asked and I answered, the details of our lovemaking would come alive again in my imagination and the insecurities that Petro's coolness had aroused in me would be swept away. For one night at least I would once again believe that I had been desired and loved, and then... Yes, and then what, Melike? Would I then turn into a better person? More admirable, stronger, more lovable?

I changed the subject.

'Were you able to find the documents?'

She leant back, waving the cigarette in her hand.

'Oh-hoo… more than you asked for. I've brought her baptism certificate, her high-school diploma and a whole bunch of other papers that I don't know the meaning of. And an envelope full of photographs that I found in a drawer before I sold the house and moved to Cologne. I knew they'd come in handy one day.'

'Did you bring everything?' I asked excitedly. 'Including the photos?'

'Of course. They're all here.' She patted the red carry-on bag she'd set down beside her feet. 'I haven't even looked at them properly yet. I don't know how we're going to prove that these papers belonged to Safinaz Kutsi, citizen of the Turkish Republic, but your Petro must know something. Tell me, how did you two meet?'

She stubbed out her cigarette and brought her face close to mine.

I waved my hand. 'Aunt Zeyno, thank you so very much.'

'What are you thanking me for, girl?'

'For coming here all the way from Germany. You could have sent all this by post.'

She leant back, crossed her legs. She was one of those women who know how far they can push things.

'Are you crazy, Melike? I was looking for an excuse to get out of Cologne for a couple of days, to get away from your uncle Christoph. Would I have missed the chance to come to Athens? Don't even ask! He's old now, and entirely dependent on me. I told him, "Melike can't get a visa for Cyprus without me. I have to go." So here I am! Don't ever let it slip out within earshot of your uncle that we could have done this by post.'

She laughed. Uncle Christoph was my aunt's husband of

forty years. They met when she was at the German High School in Istanbul. Zeyno was nineteen, Christoph was thirty. She was a final-year student and he was a maths teacher at her school, with a wife and two sons waiting for him in Germany. Throughout that last year of high school, Zeyno and Christoph made love secretly in his apartment in Tunel. Then my aunt went on to university. Their love did not die, but it took Christoph four years to convince his wife to divorce him. Meanwhile, Zeyno continued studying German literature at university, and visiting his Tunel apartment without her mother's knowledge. She even lent Orhan the key to Christoph's apartment so that he and my mother could make love in comfort. The pregnancy that obliged my parents to get married began there, in Christoph's one-room apartment.

'Tell me, *yavri mou* – my child – do you serve ouzo here?'

My aunt was speaking to the cheeky-faced waitress in German-accented English interspersed with Greek words inherited from her mother.

'*Malista*. Of course, madam.'

'Bring us a single shot of ouzo each. What would you suggest to go with it?'

'Whatever you feel like. We have fresh sardines, squid, octopus, shrimp—'

I hadn't expected that a street café would have a bar menu. Then I noticed that the young people at the surrounding tables had moved on to small glass carafes of wine or ouzo.

'Okay. Make up a plate for each us with a little bit of everything. Except octopus – they are artistic creatures.' She turned to me. 'Ever since I read online about how they decorate their dens, I've not felt like eating them. I've stopped eating meat too, did you know? I haven't put meat in my mouth for almost ten years. I only eat seafood – and now I've wiped octopus off my menu.'

The waitress gave us an impish smile, as if she'd understood what my aunt had just said. I looked at the stream of people flowing down the street. Now that it was evening, the cafés and restaurants lining the walls of the ancient Agora had filled up. African immigrants lingered in front of the tables with bags of merchandise in their hands, trying to tempt tourists into buying anything from lemon squeezers to contraptions that could sew on a button for you. They left armfuls of colourful handmade bracelets on tables as they passed, then came back to see if anyone was interested. Some of the bags were full of pirated DVDs. Those were for locals, not tourists. Nobody was rude to the vendors, not even the restaurant staff. People who weren't interested in buying anything would just shake their head with a smile. Was this good-naturedness a side effect of the luminous halo spreading over the city from the Acropolis, I wondered?

Feeling my aunt's eyes on me, I returned my attention to the table.

'So now, tell me how all this came about. What's made you suddenly decide to go and see Orhan? Is it just that as you've got older you've got more interested in finding your father? I also started visiting Pasha, my father, in his final years – did you know that?'

'I did know that. My mother told me. It was Pasha, wasn't it, who told you about Anastasia's escape from Cyprus, her changing her name and religion, becoming Safinaz?'

'Yes, it was Pasha. But he was quite senile by then. On my final visit, as he lay there on his sickbed, his eyes glassy, he grasped my hand and cried as he said, "Take the burden of what I did to your poor mother from my shoulders, I beg you, my child." I suppose he held himself responsible for my mother's suicide.'

Our little plates of sardines, squid and shrimp arrived.

I put a tiny red shrimp into my mouth. I'd never had one before. It was crunchy, like a nut, and so fresh it melted in my mouth. These were special shrimps from the island of Symi, our waitress told us as she set down on our table the four plates she'd carried over to us on a tray balanced in one hand. My aunt filled our glasses with ouzo from the carafe.

'Come on, raise your glass! Welcome to Athens, Melike!'

'What shall we drink to, Aunt Zeyno?'

'To our being together again, of course. To all reunions. *Yamas!* Do you know what that means? It means "To our good health" and also "To us". The way you write it might be different, but to us it is all *yamas*. Yes, we are drinking to us. *Yamas*, Melike, dear!'

When my aunt and I clinked glasses, the young people at the next table also raised their glasses. We all shouted '*Yamas!*' together.

I took a big gulp of ouzo. Raki without the aniseed. It slipped down easily. A sweet, familiar melody came to my ears. An old man was walking through the square pushing a fancy, shiny black barrel piano. It was painted with a picture of an old-fashioned girl in a hat. I stole a glance at my aunt. A nostalgic, yearning expression had descended over her face like a veil. If I missed my grandma, having shared only a brief period of my life with her, how much more intensely must Zeyno feel her loss?

'Were you very surprised when you heard Safinaz's story from Pasha?'

My aunt stared at her ouzo glass and thought for a little while before answering.

'Well, actually... every detail I heard from Pasha just confirmed what I already knew. Mother would take us to church, not on Sundays of course – that would have been too risky – but in the evening during the week. She spoke Greek fluently. If anyone asked, she would say she was a refugee from Crete and that she'd been settled first in Bergama, in western Turkey, and then, after her husband's death, she'd moved to Istanbul. This was her story, which I believed, of course. So, yes, the Cyprus part was a surprise to me. I knew she was homesick for a large island, but I thought that island was Crete. That she left a husband and followed Pasha to Istanbul, that he arranged new names and identity cards for her and Orhan – those details I did not know. But that she was a Greek girl who had found a way to become a Turk... What can I say? I sensed it.'

'Did you know her name was Anastasia?'

The sound of the barrel piano had faded into the distance. An upbeat Greek song was now coming through the café's loudspeakers. Holding a sardine by its tail, I dropped it into my mouth, bones and all. Sea, salt and seaweed mingled in my throat. My aunt did the same. We closed our eyes and chewed. Sinan came into my head. My aunt was like him; she didn't speak with her mouth full.

'We had a neighbour – Irini. You wouldn't remember her. She was one of the thousands of Istanbul Greeks who were forcibly deported to Greece in 1964. They had to pack up their entire world into one suitcase, which was all that they were allowed to take. Whenever there was tension in Cyprus, it was the Istanbul Greeks who suffered. It was all about retaliation. "You evicted our Turkish Cypriots from their homes, so we'll expel your Greeks from Istanbul." Oh my God, our fates are forever in the hands of idiot politicians...

Anyway, Irini was Mother's closest friend. She was a teacher at the same school. In the evenings, Safinaz would run over to Irini's. Irini rarely came to our house. She lived on her own. When you're a child, you never give such things any thought, of course. Who was she? Where were her relatives? All she had was a cat. When she was deported, she left the cat with Mother.'

'I remember – Mavri.'

My aunt laughed. 'Well done, you! I'd forgotten the cat's name. Yes, Mavri. She disappeared before I sold the house, otherwise I would have taken her to Buyukada, to your mother's garden, along with Ugur the tortoise. When I was very little, maybe in Year 2 or 3, Mother would take me with her when she popped over to Irini's in the evening. That's what she used to say: "Children, I'm popping over to Irini's." Irini's house had occasional tables with lacy cloths on them, and console tables, and photographs in silver frames, and mirrors, mirrors, mirrors. There were other cats too – Mavri's mother or grandmother or whatever. Oh, those olden days, Melike! You've brought them back to me now. Anyway, from hearing those two whispering together, and sighing, and reading their coffee grounds and telling each other's fortune, I worked out that they were probably speaking Greek. Irini called Mother "Anastasia *mou* – my dear sister". But I didn't let on that I knew. Children somehow have an instinct for when to mention something and when to stay quiet about it.'

Didn't I know it! Didn't I work out all by myself that I wasn't to ask where Dad had gone, and why he'd gone, and whether he was ever coming back? I turned away and looked at the sky. The first stars were becoming visible in the east. Just then the lights of the Parthenon came on. The peerless temple appeared on the hill once again, the Goddess Athena emerging in all the elegance of her evening garb to greet the city.

'Anyway, that's enough about the past for now. Tell me about Orhan. What happened? How did it happen?'

I sighed uncomfortably. I'd managed to avoid the subject up to now. I skewered a piece of squid with my fork and held it there. The laughter from the surrounding tables and the piped music was giving me a headache.

'Like I wrote to you, he's sick. Leukaemia. He wants to see me one last time.'

'I understand that much. Was it him who found you? Did he phone you?'

I put down my fork and looked her in the eye. She shook her head questioningly.

'Dad sent this Petro to Istanbul to find me.'

Her eyes widened. 'Seriously? How come?'

Then her expression changed. I realized she knew something that I didn't.

'Aunt Zeyno, do you know who Petro is, and what his connection to my father is?'

She pulled on her chin, scratched her throat with her short fingernails. Her skin was now like Safinaz's had been, like the thin layer on top of rice pudding.

I took a deep breath. 'Petro said, "Your father raised me."' Despite my efforts, my voice still shook. I reached for my glass and took another sip.

My aunt had stopped eating and was playing with her silver lighter. She lit a cigarette.

'And then?'

'Then...' I was suddenly overcome with exhaustion. I couldn't continue. I'd been travelling since dawn, by ferry from Buyukada to Sirkeci, from there to Istanbul airport, then

Athens, the hotel, the Acropolis in all that heat. Determined to greet my aunt when she arrived, I'd worn myself out. Now I felt nothing; I was emptied out.

'Just forget about it, Aunt Zeyno.'

She reached across the table and squeezed my fingers with her tiny hand. 'Let's finish our ouzo and go for a stroll.'

It was easier to walk side by side than to sit opposite each other. Taking my aunt's suitcase, I held her arm as we wandered the narrow streets of the Plaka district, past rows of pastel-coloured stone houses whose ground-floor shopfronts were hung with strands of blue beads, sponges, vacuum-packed olives, blue and white Greek flags. I felt my energy returning.

'See what a beautiful place we've come to, Melike.'

We'd arrived at a little square enclosed by two-storey stone houses. In the middle of the square stood an ancient column surrounded by bitter-orange trees. In among the trees were tavernas, restaurants and teagardens. We rested on a bench across from an elderly couple who were holding hands as they sat in the soft yellow light illuminating the column. I inhaled the sweet smell of citrus. For a while we listened to the haunting tune that was coming from the restaurant behind us. I felt a yearning for something – for someone; it came from deep inside me, but I didn't even know who it was I was missing.

'Aunt Zeyno, you buried Safinaz in a Christian cemetery, didn't you?'

She was startled. 'How do you know that?'

'It's a long story. But I'm right, aren't I? You buried her in the Greek cemetery by Egrikapi. On her gravestone—'

'We wrote both "Safinaz" and "Anastasia". That's true. It was Pasha's idea.'

'Pasha's?'

'Of course. Just after Mother died – threw herself off a cliff – Orhan and I were pacing at her house in Fener, trying to work out what sort of funeral we could have, how to handle it, where we could find a *hodja* who would agree to say prayers for a woman who'd committed suicide, and then the door opened—'

'And…?'

'My father, Pasha, came in. He'd already made the funeral arrangements.

'What are you saying?'

She laughed. I met the eyes of the old woman on the opposite bench. What happiness it must be at her age to still be sitting holding hands with her husband on a park bench. Would it be? I thought of Sinan and myself, growing old together. On the island we walked around hand in hand. But somehow I never pictured us as old people; we were forever young, a strong, handsome, childless couple with no problems. Modern. Too modern. A husband and wife with time for themselves.

'It wasn't the first time we'd met Pasha, of course. We knew him. When we were children, very occasionally he'd take us for a drive in his car along the Bosphorus with our mother – once a year. One time we went to Emirgan, on the Bosphorus, and he bought me a purple and yellow balloon. I remember Orhan shooting at the row of balloons which were lined up facing the sea. We were shy around him, but we so looked forward to that one day in the year because we got to ride in a car. Later, I realized that this one day a year was always Easter Sunday. Pasha did it so that my mother wouldn't feel sad. For that one day, Pasha would set his own fears aside and risk being seen on the streets with his mistress and her children. He was a strange man. He always felt guilty for cutting Mother off from her religion and her traditions. I think that's why he arranged for that gravestone. That day, Mother's doorbell rang... No, the bell didn't ring; he had a key. He opened the door, came in, and told us that he'd arranged a place for her, that she would be buried the next day. That baptism certificate you wanted and the photographs in this suitcase made their appearance at that point.'

I was beginning to understand. Safinaz's grave was like a knot at the heart of a puzzle comprising multiple threads that had yet to be unravelled. Even as my grandma's secrets were being buried, my father had decided to do some digging.

Aunt Zeyno lit another cigarette and continued. 'I made tea and the three of us sat together on the first floor. Pasha told us the Cyprus story, about Anastasia becoming Safinaz and so on. Orhan got very excited. He quizzed Pasha about everything – the name of her old village, how to get there, and on and on. Pasha seemed reluctant to tell him much, I thought – perhaps he knew that things in Cyprus were about to take a terrible turn – but he didn't try to stop Orhan. The next day the three of us went to the Greek Orthodox cemetery near Egrikapi. There was a small chapel there. Pasha had arranged for a priest. Prayers were said and we buried her.'

In my mind I saw Safinaz's small grave, unadorned, with no angel statue watching over her, alone in a distant, long-forgotten cemetery. Sparrows were chirping in the branches above our heads. The elderly couple stood up. Arm in arm, they left the square and turned into one of the narrow side streets.

I pictured Orhan, Zeyno and Pasha drinking tea in Safinaz's house. Pasha would have been sitting in the beige wingback chair. Across from him was the young Zeyno. With her olive-black eyes and curly black hair, she must have looked just like Safinaz. And Dad, having finally discovered a clue that might help him disentangle his mother's mysterious past, would have been fidgeting with excitement, the prospect of this new adventure helping him to forget the pain of losing his mother. Bored now with his village adventure, he was racing towards the first exit to present itself.

'Aunt Zeyno, will you come to Cyprus with me?'

My hand went to my mouth anxiously. Where had that come from? What had happened to the woman who'd told Sinan, 'I need to deal with this by myself'?

'I cannot come, my beauty.'

'Why not?'

My voice was trembling again. When I thought of my father lying in a hospital bed hooked up to tubes and drips, my courage failed me. My heart tightened with an old pain. Everyone abandoned me in the end. The wound of the fatherless. The wound of the rootless. Where had all this come from? Hadn't the whining child inside me died a long time ago? I was strong; the beautiful Melike. I was a woman whom other women envied, whom men desired. Petro! The cause of all this was that damn Petro. He'd undermined my self-confidence. He'd brought the insecurities I'd buried to the surface, one by one, and then left me in the lurch.

'Everything else aside, my heart won't let me leave Christoph for more than a couple of days at a stretch. Pay no attention to what I said earlier. Your uncle might be dependent on me, but I'm also far too nervous that something might happen to him while I'm not there. He's almost eighty now, after all. He's in good health, thank goodness, but still...' She knocked three times on the wooden bench we were sitting on. 'And, Melike, Orhan summoned you to his side, not me.'

I started to object, but she stopped me with her hand.

'Orhan and I closed our account years ago. Once we'd sold the houses, got rid of everything, our relationship was over. That was his wish and I respected it. Now it's time for you and him to be reunited and effect your own closure. My being there would upset the balance. And anyway, you'll have your guide with you.' She winked.

I persisted. 'Are you still annoyed because of that row?'

'Which row?'

'That big row you had on New Year's Eve, at our house in Galata. The night we were welcoming in 1971.'

My aunt threw back her head and laughed.

'I swear, Melike! How do you remember that row? Even the year! You were just a squirt of a child then. After that row... Oh-hoo... A lot of water has flowed under the bridge since then. It's long forgotten, *yavri mou*!'

In the mellow light reflected off the ancient column, Zeyno looked so much like Safinaz had on that last night, when I'd seen her through the crack in my bedroom door. She reached out and took my hand.

'Melike, don't forget that you'll have Orhan with you over there. This is between the two of you. You'll work through the hurt between you together. You are not as alone as you think you are.'

When I heard that, my eyes filled with tears. My aunt stroked my cheek and nodded, as if to reinforce the truth of her words. I was not alone. That's what she was saying. Inside me, however, the wound of my fatherlessness told me otherwise. Everyone abandons you in the end, it was saying. Petro had already left. Sinan would leave one day. How much longer could he ignore my insatiable search for attention, disregard the hours I spent apart from him?

We stood up. Dragging the suitcase behind us, we left the square and turned into the narrow streets, now overflowing with people holding drinks in their hands, young people shouting to each other, older ones singing along to the live music from their tables. Tourists, toasted by the sun, were staring in surprise and confusion at the food set in front of them. Hearing us speaking in Turkish, the restaurant barkers invited us to their tables with calls of 'Merhaba!' and 'Buyurun burada!' My aunt responded with a few Greek-style sirtaki dance moves that she knew. She was in good spirits. She wanted to sit and eat and drink some more. If I hadn't pulled her away, she'd have stayed up until dawn, going from taverna to taverna, belly dancing with some spruced-up old headwaiter. She sang along to every song we heard as we walked down the street, half in Turkish, half in Greek. When we got to our hotel room, she fell asleep as soon as her head hit the pillow.

As for me, I lay on my back, gazing up at the lazily rotating ceiling fan in the glow of the streetlight, and thought about the day when she'd been cut off from us.

19

The Row

I was seven that New Year's Eve, when the row had erupted. My maternal grandmother, Madam Piraye, my grandfather Nafiz, Aunt Zeyno and Uncle Christoph had come to our apartment in Galata. Safinaz was not present. She did not enjoy the company of her son's mother- and father-in-law – maybe that was the reason. But thinking about it now, I don't remember her ever coming to our home in Galata. She had never been with us at previous New Year's Eve celebrations, or at other family gatherings. Safinaz always stayed in her own neighbourhood, around Red Square, with her clocks. It was even hard to imagine her leaving her children with Irini on Sundays and going to meet Pasha in some distant neighbourhood.

That day, schools were on a half-day. I was in Year 3. After I got home from school, Mum and I had gone out. We met her mother at the fish market in Beyoglu and bought a turkey. Madam Piraye had a special turkey-man from whom she had ordered one days before. 'Why are turkeys sold at a fish market?' I asked Mum, and she laughed. I didn't persist. I was so happy that they'd taken me – and not Cem

– shopping. I was walking between them. The weather was very cold. There was a thin dusting of frost on the carrots, cabbages and lemons outside the greengrocers' shops, but seeing the colourful lightbulbs strung across the doors of the shops made me feel warm inside. I was going to wear my purple velvet party dress with a lace collar and patent-leather shoes in the evening. The streets smelled of burning coal and roasting chestnuts.

My grandmother was wearing a stylish hat. When we went into one shop, to buy Madlen chocolates, the man inside stood up and kissed her hand, saying, 'It is lovely to see you, Madam Piraye.' I giggled. I was wearing a black overcoat with shiny metal buttons. It was a bit long for me, so I'd be able wear it the following year as well. (At this point, none of us knew that we'd be spending the next three years in a village with no electricity.) Before returning home, we went into a fancy shop, sat on high stools and ate pumpkin dessert with walnuts on top. Mum looked beautiful. She had straightened her long hair and let it fall down her back. She looked like a blonde version of Jenny in the film *Love Story*. Just like Jenny, she was wearing a beige wool overcoat with a red checked scarf around her neck. Looking at her, my happiness multiplied. When she helped me down from the stool, she gave me a hug and a kiss. I was so happy, I decided that New Year's Eve was my favourite day of the year.

When we got home, Mum and my grandmother shut themselves up in the kitchen and began preparing the turkey, making the dried apricot and almond pilaf, and Uncle Christoph's beloved German potato salad. They were still in the kitchen when the television came on. The celebrations opened with the singing of the national anthem and a military salute, and our grandfather told Cem and me to stand to attention. Cem was to put his hand to his temple; I was to stand very straight with my arms glued to my body.

Dad, Aunt Zeyno and Uncle Christoph were sitting in armchairs across from the television, drinking cognac and eating nuts. When they saw us standing in front of the dining room table like soldiers on duty, they started to laugh. My grandfather glared at them. I was confused about what I should do. My face was itching, but I wasn't supposed to move. Beside me, Cem was standing perfectly still, saluting the flag like a real soldier. Looking at the light grey skies on the screen with the dark grey flag flying, I wished that the national anthem would hurry up and finish. I was sweating inside my purple velvet dress with its lace collar. I definitely looked very comical, whereas when I was getting dressed I had felt like a princess. Mum had tied ribbons in my hair, tiny little ribbons in red, pink and blue. When I saw the faces my aunt was making in order not to laugh, I wanted to pull them all out and throw them away. I tried to focus on the noises coming from the kitchen instead, on the clanking of the plates and bowls and the murmurs of my mother and grandmother. My stomach growled.

The national anthem finally came to an end and my grandfather said, 'At ease!' Dad and Aunt Zeyno looked at each other and laughed.

The kitchen door opened and my grandmother's huge blond bun appeared. Shooting a quick glance at the table, she said, 'You could at least set the table. We're not going to do all the work.'

Dad must not have heard her. He was filling my aunt's glass with cognac.

Grandfather Nafiz cleared his throat. He seemed to have a

perpetual tickle in his throat. 'Cem, Melike, come on, let's lay the table together. Your mother and grandmother are worn out. Open the sideboard and get out the knives and forks.'

Since our apartment used to belong to my grandfather, he knew where the tablecloths and cutlery were. While we were setting the table with the silverware, he shot another resentful glare at Dad, who was showing no interest whatsoever in the table or the food.

'Knives on the right, forks on the left, and serving spoons in the middle, where your grandmother can easily reach them. Cem, put candles in the candlesticks, son. Little one, let's see you put the cloth napkins in the silver napkin rings.'

Dad and Aunt Zeyno were talking about the janitors' protest march. Our janitor, Veli, had joined the march, and Dad said he was proud of him. He didn't tell my aunt that Cem had got sick because the heating wasn't on.

'Grandfather, I'm not going to go to sleep until the new year comes. I'm going to watch the belly dancers.'

Suddenly everything went quiet in the living room. Even the television. Dad moved around uneasily. What had I said? Mum and Dad had been making jokes about the dancers for days, saying the whole country had been hypnotized by the vision of a belly button. Back then I didn't know belly dancing was forbidden on TV, with the one exception being on New Year's Eve. It was considered too orientalist for modern Turkey, too erotic for children to watch. I shot Cem a desperate look. He was standing still with a match in his hand.

Grandfather cleared his throat again. 'Come on, children, let's put some cotton wool on the branches of this aeonium plant. It will look nice – like snow. Cem, run to the bathroom and bring us some cotton wool. Go on, son.'

Upset, I went over to the dining room window. The TV was showing adverts, and although I adored them, I didn't even sneak a look out of the corner of my eye. I had embarrassed Dad for sure. I had made him ashamed in front of my grandfather. Trying to forget about the belly dancers, I counted up how many hours there were before midnight. Four and a half hours to go. Counting was easy, but four and a half hours was a long time. I added up the numbers of the new year: 1971. It made eighteen. I was very upset.

The Italian family who lived across the courtyard had put a big fir tree in front of their balcony door and decorated it with shiny red glass balls, little bells and brightly coloured lights that blinked on and off. Even though I wanted one so badly, I couldn't go on about a fir tree. Decorating a tree for New Year's Eve was a bourgeois tradition, and Dad didn't like bourgeois traditions. Cem had whispered in my ear that if I made a scene, we might not get any presents. If I lay down on the floor and cried, Aunt Zeyno might not even give us the presents she'd brought from Germany. So I'd had to forget about a New Year's Eve tree. Maybe we wouldn't get our presents anyway because I had mentioned the belly dancers. Were dancers a bourgeois tradition too? I felt guilty.

The row erupted suddenly.

The adverts had finished. Dad got up angrily from the brown leather sofa where he'd been sitting all evening and walked over to the balcony, grumbling, 'Did your German husband put these thoughts into your head, Zeyno?' When the balcony door opened, the curtains were blown inwards by the wind. I ran towards Dad, but seeing that the floor of the balcony was covered with a thin coating of snow, I couldn't decide whether to go out in my new patent-leather shoes or not. Dad was cracking pistachio nuts in his hands and chucking them into his mouth. He was leaning over the iron railing and staring down into the courtyard; clouds of white steam were coming out of his mouth. When he turned and shouted into the living room, I hid behind the curtains.

'Don't waste your breath, Zeyno. We're not going to sell Irini's house. Mother doesn't want to anyway.'

'Cem,' my grandfather called from the dining room, 'run and turn up the sound on the television, son. Ali Kocatepe will be on soon and I don't want to miss him.'

Cem raced over to the wooden-framed television. The news was just starting. 'Good, good,' Grandfather said. 'Let's listen to the news.' But he didn't leave the dining table.

Aunt Zeyno shouted from the leather armchair, where she was sitting with a fat glass of cognac in her hand, 'It's easy for you to say. You're living the high life, after all. If it hadn't been for me—'

Dad stuck his head inside the door. Snow had settled on his black moustache and in his hair.

'Don't push it, Zeyno!'

While trying to escape from the curtain, I'd got all tangled up and was in a panic that I was about to pull the whole thing down on my head. When I finally found an opening and was able to breathlessly poke my head through, I saw that the wind from the balcony had blown out the candles on the dining table. My grandfather had disappeared. Cem had struck a match to light the candles again.

Dad came in and closed the balcony door. He didn't see my patent-leather shoes sticking out from beneath the curtain.

Aunt Zeyno was separating the raisins from the nuts and throwing handfuls into her mouth. She eased herself back in the armchair. 'Brother, just look at all this that you have,' she said, gesturing at the leather sofa and chairs, at the television set and the dining room with its stable doors. You have one hand in butter and the other in honey, am I not right? You want to donate Irini's property to the state and at the same time you go on protest marches and talk about leftist organizations, the Communist Party and the labour unions. That's hypocrisy, isn't it? *Was ist*, Christoph? What's up? Don't worry, I am quite calm. Give me a cigarette.'

From over beside the record player, Dad called out, 'Turn off that television, Cem. At least on New Year's Eve let me not hear those idiots pontificating. Christoph, another glass?'

With the television silenced, the living room felt very empty. My aunt said something in German to her husband. Running his hand over his sparse hair, he shook his head. I couldn't understand whether he was saying yes or no. Dad didn't understand either. He came back to the sofa with two drinks in his hands, gave one to his brother-in-law and settled the other in his palm. A record began to turn. Aunt Zeyno lit her cigarette. I tried again to free myself from the curtain. The soft, light-brown fabric smelled of dust. My purple velvet dress was going to be covered in it. Mum would be furious. I'd been banking on Cem to rescue me, but he had vanished into the hall after turning off the television.

Dad sat back and began to sing the song coming out of the record player.

'Maybe one day in this life
You'll look for comfort in past days.'

'Is the subject closed now, Orhan?' Aunt Zeyno said, raising her voice in order to be heard. 'Is that it? I'm not Gulbahar. You can't just feint punches at me – two to the right, two to the left – and move on. When Irini left the deeds with Mother, did she not say, "If I don't come back, the house is yours"? Huh? That's what she said. If necessary, we can hire a lawyer. Mum has power of attorney for Irini, she can sell the house on her behalf. The government is gradually confiscating the properties of all the Greeks who were kicked out of Turkey in 1964. Either way, we'll soon have gypsies, or peasants, or immigrants occupying it. They'll take over our beautiful building until the government confiscates it. We have to settle this business this year. Okay?'

'No, Zeyno. What are you saying? That's her home. There are still flowers in the tubs and wine in the cellar, just as she left it. What would we do if she came back and found that the house she had entrusted to Mother had been sold – and by us! How could we look her in the face? Do your ears hear what is coming out of your mouth? Has your heart dried up, living among the Germans or what? What is happening to you?'

'It's been seven years, Orhan. Seven! It's obvious that the woman cannot return. None of those people left Turkey because they wanted to. They were deported. Is the government just going to let the people they expelled keep their properties, for God's sake? You really are naive. You have children. Think about them.'

'Zeyno, *Liebling*, my love, do not quarrel on such a beautiful night, *bitte*.'

'Leave me alone, for God's sake, Christoph!' My aunt made a motion with her hand as if swatting her husband away.

I squeezed back into the curtain.

Dad slowly lifted his head and said the words that would forever sever the ties between himself and Aunt Zeyno.

'If you're so interested in Irini's house, why don't you go to your dear father, Pasha? I'm sure he will fabricate the deeds for you. Then you can sell the house and be rid of it. Rid of us, too.'

Everyone was silent. The curtain suddenly unwound itself. I stood nakedly before them. They looked at me, but they didn't see me. The smell of turkey roasted with oranges, and the crackly music of Cem Karaca coming from the record player, filled the living room. Without saying a word, Aunt Zeyno stood up. Her usually smiling face was dark with anger. Her lips were trembling. Seeing her like that, I wanted to hide in the curtains again, but before I could move, she had grabbed her handbag, and a bewildered Uncle Christoph, and gone out to the hall.

Just then the kitchen door opened and my mother and grandmother emerged, carrying the delicious-smelling turkey on a tray. Mum's cheeks were bright pink, her hair like a golden waterfall. Smoke was rising from the turkey.

'Okay, everybody, to the table! Children – Cem, Melike! Oh, where is Zeyno?'

In answer to that question, the front door slammed. I ran and hugged Dad's legs. The floor was littered with clumps of cotton wool. They must have been blown off the aeonium flower when the balcony door opened. As Dad stroked my hair, my ribbons came untied. Strips of red, pink and blue fell among the cotton wool. He didn't even notice. I bit my lip. I knew I shouldn't cry on New Year's Eve – if I did, I'd be sad the whole year. As we sat around the table without a word being spoken, I wasn't even able to eat the white turkey breast. I gave up on the belly dancers too and went to bed early. We never again celebrated New Year's Eve in our house in Galata.

20

High Fever

The mouse-faced clerk in the visa booth was yelling at the top of her voice from behind the word-muffling glass. The veins in her neck were bulging and her cheeks were flushed in anger. The Indian husband and wife who were waiting with their three children for their visas in the embassy's windowless processing room straightened up in their seats. I hung back beside the wall. My aunt was with me, shaking her head, eyes fixed on the floor.

In front of the booth, Petro wiped beads of sweat from his forehead with the back of his hand. When he glanced up, our eyes locked and I smiled for the first time since we'd met that morning. He just looked so desperate. I'd been keeping my distance until then. Even though my insides had bubbled with happiness when we'd met at the embassy door, I hadn't let him kiss my cheek. While we were walking down the long, high-ceilinged corridor, I'd made a point of speaking Turkish with my aunt, excluding him. But now, as I watched him struggling to try and jump through this heated, bureaucratic hoop on my account, I couldn't stop myself. His eyes rested on my face. I turned my head away.

The clerk pushed my documents away in disgust. Petro bent down to the gap at the bottom of the glass and tried again to explain something to her in a low voice. Ah, how young he was, such a novice when it came to dealing with bureaucracy. My aunt took off her glasses and wiped the lenses with a handkerchief. I leant my head against the wall. My temples were throbbing. The Indian mother in her purple sari, who looked young enough to be my child, motioned with her hand for me to sit down on the chair next to her. I really did need to sit down. Cold sweat was prickling my back under my blue blouse. I felt seasick. Sounds mingled with walls, walls with faces. The visa application neurosis that I thought I had overcome years ago had returned at full power, as if I were not a world traveller whose passport contained stamps and visas of all colours but again the child of a poor country peering through a crack at that rich garden called Europe. I needed these people. As the woman at the visa desk banged the knuckle of her index finger on my passport and Safinaz's baptism certificate and high-school diploma – Bam! Bam! Bam! – and shouted, I felt I was diminishing, losing my strength. I was exhausted anyway. I hadn't been able to sleep all night because of the heat, the worry, the family stories that wouldn't let go of me. I'd wanted to wake up feeling strong and looking beautiful, but when I finally got up at 6 a.m., my eyes were small, with bruises underneath. I had drunk three cups of free, poisonous, strong hotel coffee, one after the other, and now my hands and legs were shaking.

My aunt pushed Petro aside and made a space for herself in front of the glass. She put on her spectacles.

'My dear lady, what is the problem? We have brought you all the documents we need to obtain a visa. Is there something else preventing my niece from entering Cyprus?'

'Yes, madam, there is,' yelled the mouse-faced clerk shrilly in English. 'It is quite obvious why your niece wants to go. She will use these family documents as proof of ownership and inheritance, and as soon as Cyprus becomes a member of the European Union, she will apply for citizenship. We cannot permit this.'

Hearing this, I laughed out loud, despite my exhaustion. What a stupid idea it had been to include Safinaz's baptism certificate in the documents presented for my visa application. This proved Petro's childish lack of experience. I had taken him seriously and done what he said, but now here we were, arguing with this paranoid clerk who thought I was planning some sort of land grab. I should have applied as a university professor who needed to attend a conference. We didn't think of that. Now it was too late. We would just have to forget it. I walked to the entrance with trembling legs. All I wanted was to out of there. Who was I to go to Cyprus anyway? This plan had been ill-conceived from the start. I wanted to go home, to Sinan, to my mother, to the life I knew. I didn't want anything to do with doors, with stories – I just wanted the old Melike back.

Just then a door opened behind the clerk. A red-nosed, black-moustached face appeared in the crack. He and the angry clerk talked among themselves. The clerk frowned and handed him my passport and the other documents, explaining something to him with exaggerated gesticulations of her head, hands and arms. Her head was so small, sticking up above her shirt's padded shoulders – which made them seem extra broad – that it was impossible not to think that God had got it wrong, and put a head one size too small on her body.

I looked at Petro. His eyes slid to my neck, bare beneath my blue blouse, and stayed there. Although I was tired, my heart jumped. He still wanted me. He'd missed me while we were apart. He had thought of me, had dreamt of making love to me. The cool tone he'd assumed in our correspondence had been a mask. Propped against the wall, I smiled faintly at my foolish victory. It was embarrassing that, even at my age, I could still not tell whether a man was in lust or in love with me.

'*Epomenos, parakalo.* Next, please. Next!'

The Indian family stood up as one and warily approached the counter together. In the same movement, Petro blocked the Indian father and leant towards the glass, shouting, 'What about our visa?'

My chest swelled a little with pride.

Without looking at him, the clerk said, in formal English, as if delivering a recorded message, 'For further updates, return here tomorrow afternoon.'

As we left the embassy building, my legs gave way, and I had to grip Petro's arm to stop me from dropping to the ground like a lump of metal. How bright the sun was, how white the buildings and the steps. The whine of motorcycles drilled into my brain. I shielded my eyes with my hand. My head was spinning. Squeezing his muscular arm under my fingers, I murmured, 'Petro, I don't feel very well.'

He turned towards me and smiled. This was the first time since the night we made love that I had called him by name. But what he saw on my face made him suddenly anxious. He put his palm on my forehead, felt my temples. My aunt had paused on the top step to light a cigarette. When Petro hailed the first taxi that passed, she grumbled, but the driver motioned that she could continue smoking inside. We got in. The back seat was upholstered in leather, soft. I rested my head on Petro's shoulder.

Being ill can be strangely liberating, allowing you to act like a child again, like a different person. Nobody can expect a flawless performance from a student with a sick note. Since I was now sick, I could relinquish my anger for a while and surrender myself into caring hands. I didn't have to be myself today. With relief, I closed my eyes. Petro's huge shoulder was like a pillow.

My aunt turned to us from the front seat. When she saw Petro's arm around my shoulders, a little smile appeared on her lips, betraying the naughtiness of her youthful self.

'Melike, darling, are you okay? What's happened? Is it heatstroke?'

I murmured something that even I didn't understand. When I closed my eyes, I felt terribly nauseous. Petro held my hand. He leant towards the front seat and lowered his voice.

'Could it be something she ate?'

'She hasn't eaten anything. She skipped breakfast, just drank one coffee after another.'

'It's... nothing... my blood pressure... just need... a lie-down.'

'Let's go to my house. You can lie down comfortably there. Okay?'

I nodded. I was in no condition to refuse. Since I'd stopped having to be myself, I'd given up on forming sentences with clear beginnings and endings. I shut my eyes, but that made me feel so nauseous that I immediately opened them again.

'I feel very sick.'

'Are you going to throw up? Should the driver stop? Petro—'

'No, no, I won't throw up. I just feel nauseous, that's all.'

'Oh, Melike, dear, you were like this as a child. Stressful situations always went straight to your stomach. She takes after her mother. Gulbahar's migraines were famous. Do you have a headache too? Of course, after what that shrew of a clerk said...'

My aunt turned around and began telling Petro all about the oversensitive stomach I'd had since childhood. She told him about us driving in Kurtcebe to Belgrad Forest just outside Istanbul, and to further villages for a picnic, and how they'd had to repeatedly stop the car because I'd vomited. How neither the medicine Mum made me swallow before we set out nor the shame-inflicting suppositories up my bottom ever did any good. And so on. I tried closing my eyes again. The light was really bothering me. When the taxi finally came to a halt in front of Petro's building, I felt faint, but, not wanting to worry them further, said nothing. I almost never got a fever, so even a rise of just half a degree was enough to make me miserable. But now that I was in the old-fashioned, cage-like elevator in Petro's building, ascending the floors at a snail's pace, my eyes were burning and my temperature had shot up.

As soon as we were inside the apartment, I ran to the bathroom and tried to vomit. Nothing came out. I peed, splashed water on my face. Petro's bathroom didn't have a mirror, but through its tiny window the Parthenon was visible, like a statuette carved into a niche in the wall. The walls were littered with movie posters and I'd like to have stood there and enjoyed them, but I couldn't stay on my feet any longer. I made straight for Petro's large bed and threw myself on top of the un-ironed purple sheets.

Petro and Aunt Zeyno hovered around my bedside, fussing over me. Would I like something? What would I like? Water? Tea? Toast? *Go away!* All I wanted was to lie there. They left me alone, but they couldn't go very far. The apartment was tiny. There wasn't even a door, just a half wall between the bedroom and the rest of the flat, which comprised a kitchen, a living room and an entrance hall. From where I was lying I could see my aunt sitting on a high stool in front of a high table in the centre of the room. Right behind her, Petro was filling his coffee machine in the open-plan kitchen. He was apologizing for his apartment being messy, telling my aunt that he'd had to go to Cyprus a lot lately.

The apartment was surrounded by a spacious balcony. Petro obviously had no use for curtains, because light was streaming in from all four sides. I put a pillow over my eyes. A familiar smell of thyme and marijuana filled my nose. Desire was still lingering somewhere in my body, beneath my aching bones. I'd read somewhere that having a high fever could have that effect. On the one hand, you couldn't lift a finger; on the other hand, you wanted to make love.

As if coming to me from a dream world, my aunt's voice filled my ears.

'Look, Petro, guess who this is! Me, of course! In the garden of our house in Fener, trying to climb the fig tree barefoot. I still have a dummy in my mouth, see it? Oh, look, this is Orhan, reading a poem on Republic Day – and look at Mother, standing as straight as a soldier right behind him.'

Safinaz's old photographs had presumably been spread out on the table. I wanted to join them. With mugs of coffee in their hands, they were now whispering to each other, laughing every so often. I propped myself up on my elbow, but the wall turned black, so I lay back down again. The sounds grew faint. A curtain came down over my eyes.

Now I was in a little boat. Around me everything had turned purple – the sea, the sky, the small islands scattered across the water. Beneath that light the whole world was holding its breath, waiting for a miracle. On the shore, seagulls had ceased shrieking, swallows had stopped flapping their wings, tan-coloured dogs had left off play-fighting on the beach and were lifting their noses to the red dome of the sky. It was just before dawn, and Dad and I were off fishing. I swayed as I threaded bait onto the hook of my fishing line. The nose of the boat was cutting through the milky-blue sea. Now I was holding the end of my fishing rod. If a fish got hooked, the line would immediately pull tight. A bucket was ready in the hull. Smoke was vibrating around Dad's shoulders like a vision. From where I was sitting, when I raised my hand towards the purple realm, the same vibration encircled my hand, my fingers. I reached towards Dad's broad back and we merged, the two of us becoming one. I was the continuation of him; he was the previous version of me. The boundaries between us disappeared in the whirlpool of time. I was content, as if I had finally found the home I'd been seeking for so long.

Tuk, tuk, tuk. A fish was thrashing against the side of the boat. I yanked the line. It was very heavy, but for some reason we couldn't see the fish even though its tail was smacking our boat. Tuk, tuk, tuk. I tried to open my eyes. The branches of the olive tree on Petro's balcony were tapping the window behind me. My eyelids were on fire; my eyelashes were stuck together. I buried my face in the pillow. Oh, Dad! We always returned to shore with empty buckets. Not once did we reel in a fish. Not once did we have a fish thrash its tail against our boat. But there was an abundance of fish out there. The village fishermen would come down to the dock at the same time as we did, eyes downcast, buckets in hand, their wives following behind. Putt, putt, they would go out to sea and return later with buckets full of flapping fish.

But you weren't bothered by our empty buckets, Dad.

'We're still novices, my Melike,' you used to say. 'We're going to learn this business, aren't we, my lionhearted girl? Ismail Usta, give me two kilos of those. Are they red gurnard or are they seabass? Make it three kilos. What are these? Bream, aren't they? Put one or two of those in our bucket. No, don't bother to clean them; my daughter and I can handle that.'

You'd wink at me; I'd wink at you. This was a secret.

Our secret.

Safinaz was standing at the portal of a dark door, wagging her finger. Her hair was long, falling over her shoulders and down her back, to her waist. The hair and fingernails of the dead continue to grow. Witch! The word 'witch!' spewing out from my mother's beautiful lips like spit. Gulbahar had become a little girl, crying on the lap of her nanny, Fati. Nanny Fati's thick fingers, white on the inside, black on the outside, were caught in her golden hair. Dad's telegram held between Cem's trembling, thin, white fingers. Safinaz's finger, bigger now, was wagging at speed. If you dig around in the past so much, you'll be drawn into a black hole, Melike. Me-LI-ke. That dark door was the mouth of the black hole. Safinaz's name was carved into it in Greek letters: Σαφίναζ. See where we are, Melike? The burial ground at Suleymaniye Mosque. Halide Edip wrote the inscription on Safinaz's tombstone. They tore down Halide Edip's bust in the Sultanahmet district, which made Mum really mad. If you go into that grave, the black hole will swallow you. Stay where you are. Beneath the lid lie many secrets. Every woman must be nourished by an inner reservoir of secrets. I'm so thirsty. Petro! Sinan! One man is never enough. I must get stronger. Your inner reservoir is your treasure trove. Memory. Memory is your treasure. Hide it. Seal it up. Don't dare open it, don't dig it up. But it's too late now. Grandma, it's too late!

The spirals of the black hole were swallowing Safinaz. Grandma! Whirling around and around, Safinaz was being drawn into the darkness of the grave. Her hair was like seaweed. She was still wagging her finger. All of this happening because Barish and I had kissed in the courtyard of the mosque. No, she didn't say 'burial ground', she said 'treasure trove'. No, she said 'inner reservoir'; she said 'memory'. Inner. Voice. Children who hear their inner voice are sensitive. Everything was so confusing. It was so hot! There was a fire in my voice box. My throat was in flames. Grandma, don't go! I have things to ask you. Dad's name – what is my father's name? Dad! Mum! Grandma! STOP! STOP!

I woke up gasping for breath. My aunt was sitting on the edge of the bed, stroking my cheek.

'Did you have a nightmare, my beauty? You shouted out so scarily.'

Petro was kneeling on the kilim on the floor with a glass in his hand.

'Have some water. Shall we take your temperature again? Why don't you get undressed and get under the sheets? You'll be more comfortable.'

I was in no state to answer. My fever had shot up to thirty-nine degrees. I didn't say a word while they undressed me like a baby. Aunt Zeyno plaited my hair, allowing my neck to breathe. The purple satin sheets I wrapped around my body felt cool. When I raised my head to take a sip of water, my stomach cramped horribly. I just managed to push Petro out of the way and lean over the bucket in time. My aunt raced in from the kitchen and held my plait while I vomited. Later, I lay on my back again as Aunt Zeyno wiped my mouth with a damp cloth. I pulled the sheet up to my chin.

'I'm okay now. I've got rid of whatever was bothering

me. I'll be fine in a little while.' My voice was already much stronger. My nausea had passed. 'I could eat a piece of dry bread, if there is any.'

While my stomach was digesting the bread, I let myself fall back on the bed, succumbing to a sweet tiredness. Sleep embraced me like an octopus, pulling me into a vortex of purple satin sheets. I turned my face to the wall, drew my knees up to my stomach, and began to dip in and out of sleep, like a little rowing boat on a choppy sea. The low voices of Petro and my aunt in the kitchen came and went in my ears.

'What a beautiful woman my mother was, wasn't she?'

'Really beautiful. She looks just like you.'

'You charmer!'

'It's the truth. She looks so much like you. And like Melike, of course. Look at this picture – she's a carbon copy of Melike in that one.'

'Ha, ha. Yes. Look at the turban wrapped around her head, Charleston style. I've never looked at these pictures. They just stayed in a drawer for years. Give me that one in your hand. What is that?'

No reply.

'Petro, give me the one in your hand. Don't mix it up with the others. It's clearly an old photo, taken in a studio. Let me see it. Give me the one with the baby.'

My aunt had raised her voice. I opened my eyes. The light hitting the balcony had reddened. The olive branches above my head were rattling.

'What are you doing? What are you hiding, son? Give it to me. Don't! You're going to tear it. Ha! Okay, let me see now. This baby on Mother's lap is Orhan. Those are his eyes, nose and chin. Who's the man behind them? Mother's husband, of course. Orhan's father. Look at his eyebrows. God be praised! Ah! Ah! But...?'

Her voice was quite loud. I tried to get up.

'But this... in the arms of the man in the back... Petro? Petro, look at this.'

'Shh, shh, Zeyno, not so loud, *se parakalo.*'

I wanted to look too. What was in that photograph? I tried with all my might to stand up, but I felt dizzy and fell back onto the bed. My perplexed aunt was now shouting.

'One moment... But how could this be? Petro? This... this baby? You can explain this to us, I presume.'

What baby? What explanation?

Everything turned black.

21

Lightning

As we turned onto the narrow gravel road, the open-topped jeep we'd rented at Larnaca Airport rattled and shook. I grabbed the handbrake. The heat hitting my face through the open windows had left me dazed. Petro was holding the steering wheel with one hand and with the other was wiping his face with a green handkerchief he'd taken from his back pocket.

'There's someone I'd like you to meet before we get to our village. It's a little out of the way, but it'll be worth it. Shall we stop by?'

I nodded without saying anything. A strange shyness had settled over us. We spoke only when necessary. My aunt had acted as a buffer between us, but once we'd seen her off at Athens Airport, the silence had deepened. Which was why this surprise visit suited me. I was, anyway, more than happy to string the trip out for a bit longer. If he'd suggested that we should spend the night somewhere along the way, I would have said yes. The longer I could delay seeing my father again, the better.

Leaning my head back on the seat, I tried to take some deep

breaths. I wasn't completely recovered yet. I still felt weak and had a headache. I'd been terrified that I'd feel nauseous on the plane. Waiting in the passport line, I'd been trembling, which was not usual for me. As hard as it had been to get a visa – after all the fuss, they had eventually stamped a valid visa for the Republic of Cyprus on my passport – entering had been easy. The young official who'd stamped my passport had even smiled and welcomed me by saying '*Merhaba*' in Turkish.

The jeep jolted its way over a low rise. A sweet smell was coming from the lemon and carob trees on either side of the road. For the first time my stomach growled. I hadn't eaten anything in two days; it was as if my throat was stopped up. It wasn't only the high fever – anxiety and indecision had also worn me down. Was I actually going through with all this? The thought of seeing my father made my head hurt. I didn't want to see him. I had drifted into this crazy adventure with my eyes closed, following desire and love. Whenever my inner teenager got a tiny bit of attention, it was immediately led astray. Mum's words about doors and love had confused me still further. In truth, I was afraid that a memory I had buried deep inside me – no, not a memory, a pain – would surface again. All I really wanted was to go home and forget all about the past two weeks, and about Petro. Never in my life had I missed Sinan so much.

We came to a house with a white iron gate entwined with roses and parked the jeep beside an old scooter. When the noise of the engine ceased, the chirruping of the crickets intensified. In the distance a rooster crowed out of time. Wiping the sweat and dust from my face with the back of my hand, I walked over to the rose-entwined gate. The newly watered earth gave off a strong fragrance. My throat and skin were parched from the heat. I glanced around for a fountain of cool water I might wash my face in. The branches of the lemon and grapefruit trees, planted in orderly rows, were bowed to the ground, laden with fruit. In one corner there were thick-leaved banana trees, in another olive trees.

Swinging the car keys, Petro came up beside me and opened the latch with a familiar touch. Placing his hand on the small of my back, he gently pushed me inside. When Sinan did that, I always got really angry – such a macho thing to do – but on this occasion I said nothing. To the left of the house, in a small vegetable garden behind the olive trees, tomatoes shone bright red in the light of the setting sun. My stomach rumbled again. With a garden like this, you'd never go hungry, I imagined. I leant down to smell the lavender and rosemary growing in pots beside the steps.

'*Vay gaydouri! Kalos irthate.*' Hello my donkey! Welcome.

The door of the house opened. On the threshold appeared a small, dark young man in a blue vest. Withdrawing his hand from my waist, Petro was at his side in two strides of his long legs. His sulky face of the past several days broke into a wide smile and the two young men embraced in front of the door, wrestling each other in a well-honed routine. Finally Petro put his friend in a headlock, dragged him over and set him down beside me. He was in good spirits now, his face lit with that childlike spark he'd had on the day we met in front of the Bloody Church. He pushed his friend, who looked tiny under Petro's arm, in front of me.

'Melike, *ela*, I want to introduce you to my oldest friend in this life. My cousin Alex. My second bellybutton. When we were babies, we were rocked in the same cradle. Then we studied at the English school together. We shared an apartment in London, isn't that right, mate? *Maymoudaki*

Alex. That's his nickname – "Monkey" – because he climbs trees barefoot.'

The young man reached out and shook my hand. '*Harika poly*, Melike. Great to meet you. Welcome to Cyprus.'

He spoke with a clear English accent, like Petro, and he had the whitest teeth. His eyes shone. His dark face was really adorable. It was obvious that he'd been expecting us, as there was not the slightest sign of surprise on his face. I felt a light wave of anger swelling inside me. Again Petro had planned everything beforehand and then turned off the main road suddenly as if it had just occurred to him. The snake.

We followed Alex into the house. Insulated by thick stone walls, the building was dim and cool. The smell of mothballs and soap that seeped into the passageway from the rooms with tightly closed wooden shutters filled me with a bittersweet nostalgia. It felt as if certain things were slipping through my fingers and though I didn't know what they were, I still felt their painful loss. It was a strange nostalgia triggered by a smell like that of the inside of drawers and wardrobes and long-unopened sewing machines.

Alex had switched to Greek and was explaining things to Petro excitedly. I caught up with them and went out into a courtyard at the back of the house. It was spotlessly clean and had an old pomegranate tree at its centre. There was an old water tank on one side, but it was empty; probably used to collect rainwater. The last rays of sunlight were falling across the far wall, the rest of the courtyard was in shadow. The sight of the purple morning glory climbing the wall and blooming in the sunshine reminded me of the guesthouse where Dad, Cem and I had spent the night en route to the village, when running away from Istanbul. That was an old stone house just like this one. Who knew where it was, whose it was. We had sat on the roof and recited the names of the stars in the sky. The air there had been so pure it had made us dizzy. I'd climbed into Dad's arms, convinced that he would always be there for me. Had that child really been me? Did that night happen in this life? I suddenly felt like a dog that had been sent into space, a dog with no home, no country and no idea which door led where.

Alex came over to me, smiling apologetically.

'Please excuse me, Melike. It's nearly election day here, and my mind is full of it. Seeing Petro, I got carried away, forgetting you were here.'

'Don't worry, Alex. Your language is so beautiful, it's like music to my ears.'

When he smiled, his beautiful white teeth showed. He tossed back a shock of black hair that had fallen over his forehead.

'I was really hoping that you'd stay here tonight, but Petro won't hear of it. Maybe you can persuade him. My mother and father are on holiday in England. The whole house is empty. Our guest suite is clean and ready. My granny will be so happy that you're here.'

Ah, it seemed that both Alex and his granny knew we were coming. I threw a suspicious glance at Petro, who was examining the pomegranate tree as if it were some very interesting specimen. Without turning his head, and with his hands shoved deep into the pockets of his shorts, he mumbled, 'Impossible, Alex *mou*. You know our situation... My mother is expecting us for dinner.'

Hearing this, I was startled. His mother? That hadn't been part of the plan. My chest tightened, my nausea returned and my eyes filled with tears, not of sorrow but of anger. It was hard enough preparing myself for seeing my very ill and lonely father in the hospital, without considering her too.

Suddenly a flash of lightning struck my brain, illuminating the scene. Ah, Melike! Stupid Melike! How had I not thought of this before? Petro's mother and Dad. Dad and Petro's mother. Of course. Oh, how dumb and naive I was. How had this brain, that had solved countless sudoku puzzles in record time, failed to see that simple connection?

Your father raised me.

Petro and my dad!

Jealousy began spreading through my veins like venom. I turned to Petro in fury. He was sitting at an oilcloth-covered table in the corner, wetting his green handkerchief with water from a pitcher and wiping his brow. I knew that Dad had abandoned us for another woman, of course, but the woman herself had never been mentioned. Dad was never mentioned either, but the woman never even featured. I'd forbidden myself from countenancing the idea of her. If I eliminated her from my imagination, if I rejected the idea of her, she would vanish into thin air. The best way to punish a person was to treat them as if they didn't exist, right?

The venom had already reached my ears. Tears which I thought had long ago passed attacked my eyes. I didn't even know who I should be jealous of, or why, but I was certain that I had to get out of there, right away. This was too much. I would not see my father. Let tonight pass; tomorrow morning I would take the first flight home. So much for love and doors, I would go back to the narrow version of my old self.

I went over to Alex and held his suntanned arm.

'Actually, Alex, staying here tonight is not a bad idea at all. I'm not feeling very well. The long trip has tired me and it'll be dark soon. If it's not too much trouble for your granny and yourself, I'd like to accept your kind invitation.'

I glanced at Petro from the corner of my eye. He'd bent over and was searching for something in the bag at his feet. A red-combed rooster was grumbling its way into the chicken coop in the corner of the garden – there were no chickens to be seen.

Alex clapped his hands like a child.

'*Orea!* Wonderful! Melike, please sit down at the table. You've come such a long way, you must be hungry. I'll bring some food and give Granny the news. She has trouble walking and is a little senile. Ever since we went back to our old village last April, when the borders opened, she's been confused about where she lives, but when she's talking about the past, the details she remembers are extraordinary. When she was reunited with her old neighbours in the coffeehouse, the Turkish that she hadn't spoken in years came back. You're in luck, Melike! While losing today, yesterday is gained, I guess.'

I smiled brokenly. He had spoken with sensitivity, but I was in no state for thinking about Alex's granny or her visit to her old village. After he disappeared out of the courtyard, I went over and stood across from Petro. He looked up from where he was leaning over.

'Sit down, why don't you?'

He was very calm. His honey-coloured eyes were clear, as if he was entirely at peace with himself. Of course, he was in his own country again now. I shifted my weight from one foot to the other. A flock of birds – I didn't know what kind – were chirping from inside the pomegranate tree.

'You know why I'm not sitting down, Petro. You arranged to come here, yet you pretended it was a last-minute decision. I am sick and tired of you tricking me.'

My voice sounded shaky, nervous, like something was caught in my throat. The things I wasn't saying were strangling me. My dad and your mother. Your mother and my dad. How could you not have told me this before now, Petro? How could you hide such an important detail from me? But, no, don't say it! Once I said it out loud, it would come alive, be real. Let it remain a secret. Them. My father, your mother.

'That's your opinion, *canim*.'

He had said '*canim*', 'my dear' in Turkish. My foolish heart jumped. I pressed my lips together.

'If that's my opinion, what is the truth?'

Petro looked into my face for a while. Then, putting his bag back on the ground, he sat up and sighed.

'Alex's granny is also my granny. My great-grandmother, to be precise. Her name is Niki; she's called "Nana Niki". When you got your visa, I called Alex and told him we'd stop by here to see Nana Niki. You were still sick and I didn't want to burden you with details. I thought you might want to get a little more information about Safinaz before seeing your father. When she was younger, when they lived in Northern Cyprus, in their old village, Nana Niki was Anastasia's closest friend.'

My legs began to tremble. I pulled out the chair next to him and sat down. There was a glass of water on the table, and without questioning whose it was, I drank it all. My heart was beating fast. Safinaz's closest friend – her childhood friend? Still alive... here?

Petro slowly pushed the photograph he'd taken out of his bag towards me.

'Look at this. It was in the envelope your aunt brought over from Germany. Look carefully and you'll see what I mean. Nana Niki is the person best placed to tell you this story. I didn't trick you, Melike. Maybe... maybe I just wanted to surprise you.'

Avoiding his chin, which was approaching the bare shoulder by my vest top strap, I took the photo in my hands. It was a sepia studio photograph printed on cardboard. In front of a backdrop of deer and trees, Safinaz – or Anastasia – was sitting on a high stool wearing a dark-coloured dress that came down to her ankles. Although her hair was gathered on top of her head, as was the fashion of that period, escaped strands had fallen right and left over her forehead and neck in familiar curls. The likeness between us was striking. It was as if Safinaz, not my mother, had given birth to me. Not even given birth; I looked like her clone. We even pursed our lips in exactly the same way.

The baby on her lap was about four or five months old. My father. I would know those round black eyes, and that curly black hair, anywhere. The man standing behind the stool had to be the grandfather I never knew. He looked like Dad. A sterner-faced version maybe. His hair, his moustache, his little ears were all the same. He was holding a baby in his arms. My aunt? No, that was impossible. Or could it be? I brought the photograph close to my face to see better in the dim light of the shadowy courtyard. Were my eyes deceiving me? Petro was holding his breath, watching me. Even though I couldn't see his face, I felt his unease. Tension, like heat, passes from body to body in waves.

I looked very carefully at the photograph again. My ears were ringing. Yes, I'd seen it correctly. Now I understood why my aunt had screamed in surprise while I was lying feverish in Petro's bed.

The baby at the back of the photo was also my father.

22

Inherited Memory

I turned to Petro in shock, holding the old photograph in my hand. But before I could open my mouth, the door beside the chicken coop creaked, and out came Alex with a tray full of food and wine. Behind him, leaning on a cane, was a tiny little white-haired woman. Petro immediately jumped to his feet. In three steps he was at her side and embracing the old lady in his vast arms. Nana Niki hugged Petro tight. As she only came up to his waist, Petro had to crouch down, almost on his knees. His granny took his cheeks in her hands, read his face with her moist eyes, and blew into the air.

Alex put the tray he was carrying on the table. I stood up, my mouth dry from excitement, unsure what to do with my arms and legs. I examined the picture I was grasping tightly in my fingers once again. No, I was not mistaken. The man at the back was holding in his arms a baby that looked exactly like the baby at the front. Hoping for an explanation, I raised my head, and came eyeball to eyeball with the old woman.

'Oh, my Lord! Anastasia *mou*!'

A strange scream came out of Nana Niki's throat. In fear, she clamped her liver-spotted hand over her toothless mouth.

Dropping Petro's arm, she hurriedly made the sign of the cross. Alex rushed to her other side and tried to seat her on a chair.

'*Ase me.* Leave me be.'

With unexpected strength, Nana Niki threw off her grandson's grip and took a step towards me without her cane. Taking my chin in her hand, she examined my face in the dim light of the courtyard. Her head was cocked to the side, like an owl's. The smell of bay leaves and lavender came to my nose. I felt like a desperate concubine being assessed by a master at a slave market. My eyes sought Petro. He had sneaked behind me to his place at the table.

Alex touched his granny's arm gently. '*Yiayia mou, ela.* Come, Granny.'

We sat down side by side. The old woman was staring into my face as if bewitched. Her little black eyes were like currants. Our knees touched under the table. Petro had taken a thick slice of bread from the tray in the middle and was spreading it with tomatoes and halloumi, unable to suppress his appetite any longer. Alex filled my glass with wine.

Nana Niki, resting her elbows on the oilcloth, leant over and spoke to me in broken Turkish.

'You're Anastasia's grandchild?'

I nodded.

Her voice was like a whisper. 'What might your name be?'

'Melike.'

She closed her eyes, trying to remember something. 'Melike, *melaike*... Melike, meaning *angeliki* in Turkish? The angel?'

Petro, his mouth full, mumbled '*Ne, ne.* Yes.' He was chewing on a huge hunk of bread, not caring about the tomato juice that was dripping through his fingers onto the tablecloth. I handed the old photograph in my lap to Nana

Niki. Without saying a word, she put on the glasses that hung on a chain around her neck, brought the thick piece of tatty-edged card close to her face, and smacked her lips toothlessly. If she'd been my grandma's friend, she had to be over ninety. Could she see anything in such poor light? Would she remember what she was looking at? The back wall with its tracery of morning glory was now in shadow. Dusk had fallen.

Gathering my courage, I spoke. A vein in my neck was throbbing.

'Nana Niki, this baby on the lap of my *yiayia*, Safinaz – the one you know as Anastasia – and the other baby at the back...'

Petro said something with his mouth full. I couldn't tell whether he was speaking Greek or English. The three of us bent over the picture. Petro's breath was warm on my neck.

Nana Niki pressed her crooked index finger on the baby sitting on Safinaz's lap.

'*Ma vre*, little girl, you don't know your uncle? *Na*, just look here. They're like two drops of water. You could never tell them apart. Anastasia had a two-time baby. *Didimos...* How do you say it?'

'Twins?'

'Ha! Exactly. They were twins, these childs.'

'But how...?'

In one gulp I downed the wine Alex had placed in front of me. Without waiting for an indication from me, he refilled my glass. My cheeks and ears were on fire.

'You cannot know this,' the old woman explained. 'Anastasia, she tried very hard for a baby to fall into her womb. She waited, she went to the priest. Without Gianni knowing, she even went secretly to the Muslim side, to *hodja*. Even the magician, he prayed, he puffed air. Nothing worked. Finally, gypsy elixir did it. She gathered weeds from the mountains, made *maztouni,* herbal paste with roots. She made an elixir like poison. Anastasia drank it. She put yellow powder from the gypsy in Gianni's food. She'd said, on the first *panselinos* – when the moon is full – you should lie with your husband, and not one but two eggs will fall. And it happened.'

She stopped talking, took a sip of wine, and then, with one hand leaning on the table, the other on her cane, she closed her eyes. She was out of breath. As for me, I was dazed. Twins! Safinaz had had twins. But… how come no one had ever mentioned this to me – neither my mother nor my aunt? I felt a sudden panic rise. I turned to Petro and Alex. 'Where is my father's twin brother now?'

Silence descended on the courtyard. Nana Niki had dozed off. Alex had lowered his head and was staring at his glass. Petro finished his wine, put his glass down on the table with a bam, and wiped his mouth with his green handkerchief. I saw such dark anger in his eyes that I was almost tearful.

'What happened to him? Tell me. Why aren't you saying anything?'

They looked at each other across the table. Petro took a cigarette paper and a pinch of weed from his pocket. He began to roll a joint in the now very dim light of the courtyard. I'd never seen him so serious. I was confused. Had I asked the wrong thing? Licking the paper, he pressed it into place, put the joint in his mouth, lit it and inhaled deeply. As he slowly exhaled the smoke through his nostrils, he threw his head back and stared up at the darkening sky. Right above us a huge star had appeared.

Alex cut up a tomato on the oilcloth and pushed it towards me.

'You have to taste this, Melike. You won't find another tomato like this in Greece or Turkey. They're from our garden – no insecticides, no chemicals, purely organic. Don't be shy; eat it with your fingers. You can wash your hands in the fountain later.'

Just to buy some time to collect my thoughts, I did as he said, laid a slice of tomato on a chunk of bread and put the whole lot into my mouth. It truly tasted like strawberries. To add some saltiness to the tomato, I took one of the oily black olives from the middle of the table. I closed my eyes and chewed.

'And then that Pasha-man came to our village.'

Nana Niki's voice, which up to then had been like a whisper, had suddenly loudened. I quickly spat out the olive pit in my mouth. I had to devote all my attention to understanding the Cypriot Turkish coming out of Nana Niki's toothless mouth.

'Anastasia *mou*, she was recovering from childbirth at that time. Darkness come over her. *Melankolia.* No milk flowed from her nipples. Every day she ran away, leaving the babies to me. I nursed them. How do you say it? Wet nurse? *Ya.* I was those babies' wet nurse. My milk always flowed. I tell you, when children suck milk from the same mother, they're like brothers. *Telos pandon.* Anyway. Anastasia, every morning she went, sat by riverside, looked at the water and – what did she see? We don't know. Pasha-man was the guest of a *Muslumanos* gentleman on the other side. Our village at that time was a mixed village. We lived together. Then they separated us all apart...'

Her eyes were fixed on the tablecloth; she sighed. I looked over at Petro and Alex, who were silently drinking their wine.

'Never you mind. Pay no attention to these things, my girl. *Ma*, you know, people who forget the past cannot know where they go in the future. We say that all the time in Cyprus. "Never forget," we say. You will learn Anastasia's life, tell your children. Your *yiayia* and I were *na*, like this.' She pressed two fingers together to show how close she and Safinaz had been.

As always when the subject of children came up, I squirmed uncomfortably in my chair. Uneasiness spread through me. I reached under the table for Petro's joint. For a second our fingers locked. I met Alex's eyes and he smiled sweetly. Half-turning my back to Nana Niki, I inhaled.

'This Pasha-man came to our village many times. Three months, five months. He was doing some work, but his job didn't stay in my memory. Some grape-thing, fig-thing, I don't know what. Every morning he made a circle in the forest, boots on feet, hat on head. He was very nice, clean dressing. He walked fast. When he saw us over by the church, he greeted us like this: "*Kalimera*, ladies. Good morning, ladies." He was a noble man. Rich, very rich. Like this…' She rubbed her crooked, bony fingers together. 'You understand?'

I laughed. After just one puff, I was stoned. In my imagination, I was picturing what she was telling me.

'*E, etsi*, so, early one morning, Anastasia and Pasha-man met in the forest by chance. The poor girl left her babies with me again, ran away.'

I raised my head and looked up at the sky full of stars. Pasha's boots came into my mind's eye. I saw him sitting in the armchair in the room on the first floor of Safinaz's clock-filled house, one leg crossed over the other, wearing his shiny black boots that snow didn't stick to. I again heard the chirping of some bird or other. Nana Niki's voice seemed to come from far away. In the light filtering through the branches, I saw Pasha's boots sinking into the earth, crushing the dry, rustling leaves underfoot. The young Anastasia was sitting like a forest nymph on a rock, staring at the flow of the river, unaware of the cautiously approaching Pasha, who was drawn by the elegant angle of her bent neck. She had taken off her leather sandals and her stockings and was dangling her feet in the water. Little silver fish were nibbling at her skin. Anastasia was not smiling. A vague longing, for what or whom she did not know, was searing her heart. Hearing the crackle of the leaves beneath Pasha's boots, she made a veil of her curls and hid behind them. Pasha approached in silence and stood behind her. Undecided as to what he should do, he chewed on the tobacco he'd lodged behind his bottom lip. He was in civilian clothes; his military status, his 'pasha-ness', having come to an end long ago, only the name remained. He was a businessman now. Did Anastasia see him? We would never know. Her long hair shrouded her whole face, but, even so, he greeted the young woman with a tip of his hat before continuing on his way. Pine cones crackled under his departing boots. Anastasia's bare calves seemed to flutter in the water like two white fish. Tomorrow, he said to himself. Tomorrow.

'Our village is very small, my girl. They told Gianni. "That *Turkos* Pasha will marry your wife," they said. You know one more thing – your grandad Gianni, he's a good man. But in the coffeehouse, in the town square, they said, "Those babies are not yours, they're Pasha's." Idiots, they washed his brain, turned his eyes black. With force they put a knife in Gianni's hand. His house was across street from the coffeehouse, next to the church. They shouted like tough guys. We were inside the house. One baby was on my lap, one was on Anastasia's.

The babies were not even baptized yet. Anastasia asked, "What's all this noise outside, Niki *mou*?" Then she said – ah, *mana mou* – oh dear, she went and opened the door.'

The old woman put her hand on her heart and swallowed. Her eyes filled. In the candlelight they looked like oily olives. In spite of the heat that smelled of dead flowers, I shivered. My head was spinning. I finished my glass of wine and took another puff of Petro's joint. Although Alex and Petro hadn't understood Nana Niki's Turkish, they sat there in sad silence. I put my elbows on the tablecloth, stray breadcrumbs pricking my skin, and buried my face in my hands.

'These men all come out of the coffeehouse together and leaned on our door. I knew all their faces, but I'd never seen them like this. My eye only saw the knife in Gianni's hand. *Mana mou*, my dear mama! My heart was in my mouth, *na*, like this. He's going to cut the girl's throat. That happened in our village in the old times. Then the babies started to cry. Once one of the little ones started, the other didn't stop.'

I shook my head. Behind my closed eyes a world was coming to life through the old woman's words. A long-forgotten dream was being revived in my brain. Maybe that thing they called genetic memory really did exist. It was as if I was there that noontime, with Nana Niki, Safinaz and the babies, the smell of the dry earth in our nostrils. I was terrified of the gang of men leaning against the door. I remained frozen. I would be hunted down. I would die.

'Anastasia stayed like that, stuck there, my sweet girl. I was pulling her inside, begging her, "*Ohi*. No." She didn't come. Gianni raised the knife up, like this. The sun fell, our eyes all dazzled. I screamed. Anastasia, she didn't move. You'd think her hand was stuck to door handle. *Na*. That moment, *katastrofi* came. Then there was a loud boom sound. *Panagia!* Mary, Mother of God! Our men were frozen. We looked. There in front of the coffeehouse was Pasha-man. With a pistol in his hand. He got out of his car. Our men divided, like a knife had cut them all in half. Like Moses did to the Red Sea. *Thee mou.* My God. Pasha-man passed through the men, reached out, took Anastasia's wrist. Nobody made one little sound. Gianni's knife stayed in the air. Then Pasha-man – with his pistol in one hand, Anastasia's wrist in the other – walked back to the coffeehouse, where his car was waiting. He opened the door. Anastasia *mou* was in front, with one baby on her hip. She got into the car with no question. I wanted her to turn and look. *Ohi.* No. She didn't lift her head. Our men became like statues. Did Pasha do black magic on them? The car left the village. They stayed like that. Then *mikrouli*, the baby boy in my arms, let out such a scream. You'd think his flesh was being torn out. Then everybody came to sense. Oh... But who did all this help? Not anybody.'

She stopped talking. In the flickering light of the candle, her face had got smaller. I leant back in the old chair; the wood creaked. The stars in the sky were twinkling in harmony with the insects buzzing beyond the courtyard.

So Safinaz escaped with one of her children and left the other in the village. The story she used to tell about finding Ugur came into my head. Seeing the baby tortoise walking along the railway track, she bent down and picked him up, put him in a matchbox and hid him in her bosom. Now I knew that she travelled, Ugur in a matchbox, first by boat from Cyprus to Turkey, then taking the train to Istanbul with Dad in her arms and Pasha by her side, the other baby left behind as the train rumbled further and further away. Safinaz's twins grew up ignorant of each other's existence.

Dad was half a person, Safinaz half a mother. Like all divided people, they were incomplete and unhappy, their whole lives spent longing to become whole again.

'Gianni said if she came back, he would cut her throat. She would not come back. I knew that a long time before I mailed Anastasia's papers to her in Constantinople. I wrote her new name so nobody would know who the letter in the envelope went to. Gianni knew later. Later he went, got lost, nobody knew where. The Second World War exploded. They say he joined the English army. I put the baby who'd been left behind with my own babies. He was a reminder of Anastasia. We called him Damianos, but we didn't know which one he was. Maybe he was Kosmas. I couldn't tell them apart. We told him, "Your mother died when you were born, your father died in the war, fighting at the front." After he grew up, *yavri mou*, my child, he heard the truth, of course. Our village is *mikro*, very small. Ah, ah… Damianos was a very quiet boy, no trouble. Many years passed. My heart still burned at thought of him. Why, oh why, they murder my boy…'

I opened my mouth to take a deep breath. My chest was tight; not a drop of air could enter my lungs. As if I were holding fast to a lifesaver, I pressed my knee against Petro's under the table. Our sweaty legs stuck to each other. When I felt his soft palm on my knee, I grew calmer. Nana Niki had closed her eyes.

I turned to Alex and Petro and whispered, 'What happened to Damianos?'

'He was shot.'

Petro withdrew his hand from my leg.

'What? Who shot him? Turks?'

'Forget it, Melike.' His voice was harsh again.

'Not the Turks. Our side.'

Petro muttered angrily to himself.

Alex paid no attention. In a low voice he continued explaining. 'Your uncle was the leader of a group that was fighting for an independent Cyprus. They wanted a Cyprus that would be governed by Turkish and Greek Cypriots together. They had many enemies. Damianos and his friends got into a street fight with a far-right organization supported by the junta in Greece. That's when Damianos was shot.'

I was confused. 'Junta? What year are you talking about?'

'July 1974,' murmured Petro.

'What?'

'The date Damianos was shot. 1 July, 1974.'

Why did that date feel familiar? I wracked my brains, but all this information had clouded my usually sharp mind. 'Okay, but how old were you then? How do you remember all this?'

'It's been passed down from generation to generation. Heroes are not forgotten.'

The candle flared suddenly. And just like that, it came back to me.

She threw herself off a cliff, Gulbahar! Her body got caught in a fishing net.

Safinaz must have known that the son she'd left in Cyprus had died. Someone would have given her the news. She had not severed her ties with her native land; she hadn't ever abandoned the child she had left here. She couldn't have. I remembered the letters in Greek she'd written, supposedly to her neighbour Irini. Those sheets of thin paper she used to fill, dipping her pen into the inkwell, did not go to Irini in Athens.

They came here, to Cyprus. I turned towards Nana Niki. Our eyes met.

'My dear Anastasia, she could not stand the pain,' she whispered. 'When she got the bad news, she let herself go into the sea from the cliff. Like King Aegeus, fishermen gathered her from their net. Your papa told us about it when he come here.'

The tears rolling down her wrinkled cheeks shone like diamonds. I reached out and took her hand. The liver-spotted skin covering her gnarled bones was so soft. She put her other hand over mine.

I saw Safinaz's face, that last expression as she'd stood in the doorway of my room painted orange by the fire in the woodstove. My eyes filled too. The wound in her conscience for having separated the child from her milk, her life, his brother, had never healed; over the years, it had only grown deeper. Damianos's pitiful death had been the final blow to Safinaz's wounded soul.

My hand was still enclosed within Nana Niki's curled fingers. Petro leaned over to wipe my cheeks with his green handkerchief, which smelt of dust and sweat. Alex pinched the wick of the candle between his two fingers, extinguishing the flame. In the flickering light of the bulb burning above the courtyard door that opened into the kitchen, he stood up and took the tray he had loaded with plates, glasses, olive pits and tomato skins. A half-moon had risen in the sky, the insects had ceased their buzzing. A deep silence enveloped the courtyard.

Petro leant towards my ear.

'Let's get to bed now, Melike *mou*. Nana Niki is tired out and you are just getting over your sickness. *Ela edo*. Come with me.'

Sniffling, I nodded and got to my feet. Nana Niki, leaning on Alex's arm, was walking very slowly towards the house. When the kitchen door closed behind them, the weak light also went out. I held the hand Petro reached out to me in the darkness. Without speaking, we went through the door.

23

The Last Roll

The guest suite was a little cabin separate from the house. After washing my hands and face in the small bathroom, I stretched out on the white sheets of the bed in the glow of the late-rising half-moon. We hadn't turned on the light. I was very tired. I wasn't just physically exhausted – now an earthquake had rocked the depths of my soul, and the emotions shattered by that shock had not yet risen to the surface of my consciousness. Was it sadness I was feeling, or grief, or something else that I couldn't find a name for? All I wanted now was for Petro to lie down beside me in the dark, take me in his arms and do whatever he desired. I would surrender to him, allow wild passion to subsume every other emotion. But he, like a ghostly giant, was just standing in the middle of the room, chewing gum, taking not so much as a single step towards the bed.

In the blue darkness, I reached out my hand.

'Could I have another toke of your joint? Is there any left?'

Taking the stub from his shirt pocket, he lit it, took a puff, put it between my fingers, then walked to the window, away from the bed. Holding the bitter smoke inside me, I buried myself in the bed. The sheets were cool. I rubbed the pillow on my face. It smelled of lavender and bay-leaf oil. The sound of Nana Niki's voice receded into one of the back chambers of my brain.

'Why don't you come over here?'

Not a word came from Petro, who was standing with his back to me. I was high. Maybe I'd spoken in Turkish. I tried again.

'Petro?'

Putting the joint in the ashtray on the table beside the bed, I closed my eyes and patted the empty space beside me. Come on, Petro. Don't be coy, for God's sake. Come and lie down. Don't be afraid. I won't bite. (Well, I might bite, but I won't hurt you, I promise!)

Footsteps approached. My side of the bed sank down. Good. Without opening my eyes, I reached out, found his hand, and, pulling up my T-shirt, placed it on my bare stomach. A current of electricity raced from his palm to my skin. Our bodies had already tuned in to the same frequency. That's it! Now, slide your hand down, darling; a little lower. I'm ready to be sparked into life like a toy beneath your fingertips. You'll see. With my free hand I took my hair from under my head, spread it out across the pillow and settled myself in the bed. Petro, however, suddenly drew back the hand that I'd been expecting to slide over my body, the hand that I wanted, that I desired. I opened my eyes, raised my head.

In the blue darkness, his bowed silhouette murmured, 'I can't do it, Melike. No. Afterwards it's too hard for me.'

I moaned, burying myself in the pillow again. The walls of the room were wavering. My whole body was on fire. For God's sake! Was this really the time, Petro? In this faraway country, behind a curtain of marijuana, I had forgotten everything: my father, my uncle, Safinaz, Pasha, and all the longings that burnt inside me. I was as light as a feather, so light that I was even able to forgive Petro. All I wanted was for him to give himself up to me, let nothing but desire and pleasure remain.

I tried to catch his hand again. He drew it back. Offended, I blew out my lips. He couldn't see me in the darkness. He wasn't looking anyway.

'If you don't want me…'

'Don't be ridiculous.'

'If you don't like me… If I'm not young enough for you…'

He raised his head and our eyes met in the shadows. I reached out to stroke his cheek.

'Please, Melike, *se parakalo*. I've never in my life desired a woman the way I desire you. Right now there is nothing I want more than to get lost in you.'

Hearing this, I sat up, purring like a cat, wrapped my arms around his neck and pressed my lips against his. Even after all the wine and cheese, his mouth smelled of fresh mint. Of its own accord, his tongue delved into my mouth. Taking advantage of this, I slid my body towards the hardness in his lap, but then, with his strong arms, he unwound my arms from around his neck and stood up. If I'd reached out, with one swift, skilful movement of my fingers, I could have left him unable to think straight. But I was magnanimous. I didn't touch him. I chose to use words, like a civilized human being.

'Petro, I really want to make love. Please. It won't be like before. I won't get angry with you about anything, I promise. Tomorrow we'll continue our journey as if tonight never happened. Come on. *Se parakalo*.'

He approached the bed again, grabbed my arm, and with

a harsh movement lifted me onto my feet. I was breathless with excitement. Yes! Like this! When I recovered my balance, I tried to stand on tiptoes and circle my arms around his neck. He didn't let me. He dragged me by the arm to the door. We went out into the courtyard. I didn't even have my shoes on. My excitement increased. We passed the entrance hall, the front garden, the rose-entwined gate. We were out on the road. All the houses and gardens in the vicinity were buried in darkness. We stopped in front of the jeep I'd rented at the airport. Were we going to make love in the back seat like high-school lovers? Was Petro worried that we'd make so much noise we'd wake up Nana Niki and Alex? No, we left the jeep behind us and continued onto a gravel track, turned blueish in the moonlight. Stones bruised my bare feet. Stumbling, falling over, getting up again, I struggled to keep up with him. I was out of breath. He paid no attention to my travails, did not shorten his strides at all, but continued hauling me along by the arm. This was a little too much, wasn't it? Couldn't he lower me to the ground between the trackside olive trees? The earth was moist and soft and smelled of lemons. I looked up at the sky. If I extended my hand, I could catch the stars scattered through space. Yes, yes! Under the stars…

The track beneath my feet suddenly turned soft. My bare soles sank into moist sand. The sound of waves came to my ears; the air smelled of seaweed, iodine and salt. Before I could ask him where we were, what was happening, Petro turned and lifted me into the air. I was confused. Finally I was in his arms, but there was something wrong. Suddenly he began to run, sinking and rising in the sand. I wound my arms around his neck, out of fear more than desire. The shushing of the waves came closer. A coolness hit my bare feet. I understood then what was going to happen. I struggled to get free, kicked the air.

'No, no! Let me go, Petro! No! Let me go, you bastard!'

He was as strong as a horse. My struggles were like mosquito bites to him. Laughing at my efforts, he speeded up. With his shoes on, he took three steps into the dark sea and threw me into the embrace of the waves with all his strength. My screams tore through the night before I sank to the bottom. My ears, my nostrils, my throat filled with salt water. Like a holed ship, I sank down into the sand. The bottom of the sea was darker than night, quieter than night. My hair stuck to my face like seaweed. Paddling my arms frantically, I rocketed back to the surface. With difficulty, I opened my salt-scorched eyes and began to laugh. Petro, up to the legs of his shorts in water, arms crossed in front of him, was grinning, showing all of his perfect white teeth in the moonlight.

'Has your fever abated now, baby *mou*?'

Spraying water from my mouth and nose, I yelled in Turkish, 'Damn you, Petro!'

Chuckling, he returned to the shore, stripped off and jumped into the water stark naked. I was almost back at the shore too. Ripping off my wet T-shirt, shorts and underwear, I balled them up and threw them onto the beach, then dived back into the sea. When my skin met the water with no obstruction, no barrier, a hundred per cent connection, even though my throat was raw from the salt, I was filled with an incomparable happiness. To think that tiny scrap of cloth we called a swimsuit diminished the pleasure of swimming so much! Slowly, with long strokes, I unfurled and caught up with Petro. We came face to face on an avenue of silver painted by the moon. Below the surface, in the darkness, our arms and legs paddled up and down like the limbs of an octopus, independent of our minds. I had planned to be angry with him, but suddenly I began to laugh.

'Is this so bad now?'

Instead of answering, I splashed water in his face. The cool sea had indeed doused my fire; in its place had come a sense of relief and a sweet happiness. Even if Petro had taken me in his arms right then, I wouldn't have felt like making love any more.

I turned and began to swim back to shore. We had no towels and my clothes were sopping wet. No matter. Even at that hour of the night, it was still warm. Petro came over beside me and we lay down on the smoothness where water and sand merged. A shyness had come over me. Even in the darkness I wanted to hide the front of my body. I turned onto my stomach. Petro, with the ease of a man who had wandered naked along beaches many times, stretched out on his back. With our heads on dry land, and the rest of us, from our shoulders downwards, in the waves lapping the shore, we began to rock backwards and forward. When a wave came, it covered us like a thin blanket; when it withdrew, it left us exposed in our nakedness.

'Do you see that constellation right above us?'

The stars were much lower now. A constellation I didn't recognize was perched above the hill to our left, only just visible. It resembled an animal with a long neck, like a dinosaur with a triangular tail.

'Which one do you mean? Andromeda?'

'How do you know which one is Andromeda?'

'You're not the only one who spent their childhood lying on dark beaches looking up at the stars. Wherever I am, I can always find that one.'

'How do you find it?'

Raising my hand, I pointed to the constellation right above us that formed the letter 'W'.

'Count from the third star in Cassiopeia. Right above it is Andromeda, our neighbouring galaxy. Why are you laughing? Don't you believe me?'

'No, I believe you. Why wouldn't I? I'm impressed. I didn't think Turks knew anything about the sea and the sky.'

'*Zevzekis!*'. Idiot.

He grinned at me calling him an idiot, but my mind once again went to that night at the stone guesthouse on our way to the village. That night, Dad had shown us Andromeda for the first time, explained to us how we could find it. In the following years in the village, when we went out fishing on dark mornings, he would teach me how to take a bearing by looking at it. Now, for the first time in decades, he and I were lying under the same sky again. He was so close. If I jumped into the jeep parked in front of Nana Niki's rose-entwined gate, I could be with my father in an hour, at most an hour and a half. I could be counting Cassiopeia's third star with him. At this, for the first time, something like joy stirred inside me. But then I remembered. He was dying. He was about to abandon me again. I would be alone once more. I sat up and wrapped my arms around myself, my joy soured.

'You can wear my shirt and shorts. Don't catch cold.'

Petro had stood up. He held out his shirt while I put my arms in the sleeves, feeling like a puppet. I slipped on his shorts without unbuttoning them. While I gathered up my hair and secured it on top of my head, he put on his only remaining dry item of clothing, his boxer shorts.

'Shall we sit here a bit longer? Are you cold?'

'Let's sit for a while. I'm not cold and it's such a beautiful beach. If we had a blanket, we could stay all night.'

'Shall I go and get one?'

'Don't worry about it. It's still warm and there's no wind. Let's just sit here.'

Side by side we sat on the warm, moist sand.

A long time ago, when I'd just married Sinan, he and I discovered a cove carved into a hidden valley while we were exploring the Mediterranean coast by motorcycle. We set up camp there, tying our tent down with ropes tethered to the poles stuck into the sandy beach. We were the only people camping on the entire beach. We stored our tomatoes and cucumbers in a plastic bag which we suspended in the ice-cold water of the stream that rushed down the valley to meet the sea. We lined up our dried beans, tins of tuna, bottles of wine and packets of pasta in the shelter of a good-sized boulder. The sea, so soon after winter, was very cold, but Sinan swam every morning, shouting and yelling. I would wait in my warm sleeping bag for him to get out of the water, make two cups of sugary Nescafé on our little camp stove and bring one to me. Then the villagers who lived at the top of the valley warned us about an imminent April storm, so we climbed the steep cliff to their houses.

Remembering this made my heart ache with a feeling not of guilt, but of loss. Would Sinan and I ever go back and camp in that valley again? Had we been since? We had talked about returning there, but we never had. Almost fifteen years had passed now. If we did go back, would I still think, as I had then, that the Nescafé in that tin mug, thrust into the hand I groggily stuck out of the sleeping bag, was the most delicious thing in the world?

It felt as if my youth had suddenly passed. Until that

moment, I'd assumed that that young woman, all groggy with sleep, was still waiting for me on that beach. I'd spent the past fifteen years believing that at a convenient time I could re-enter her body in a single bound, resume that life, refreshed, and continue from there. But a person's lifetime was so short. I was already at the halfway point – and even that was an optimistic estimate. The overwhelming inevitability of death now hit me with all its might, and for the first time I began to fear my own demise. What made a life meaningful was that it had a beginning and an end; an a and a z. Safinaz's grave.

The meaning of life was revealed in death: if there was no end to life it would carry no value, no meaning.

I looked at Petro – his strong chin, the perfect teeth visible though his parted lips. He was still young. Such thoughts wouldn't enter his head. If they did, he wouldn't feel the fear I felt yet. He was drawing circles in the sand with a stick.

'Melike, you've probably guessed by now. My mother…'

He spoke quietly, slowly, as if afraid of hurting me. Even so, a heavy weight settled in my stomach. This was jealousy, the kind children felt. The sort of jealousy you'd be ashamed of, that you'd never admit to. A silent jealousy.

'She's married to my father. Yes, I worked it out. Why didn't you say something earlier?'

'I was ashamed.'

'Ashamed? Why?'

'That you would think your father left you and your family for for my mother.'

'Isn't that what happened?'

He didn't answer, just kept on drawing circles inside circles in the sand.

'Is that not the truth, then, Petro? Look at me.'

He raised his head. His face in the shadows was sorrowful.

'Yes, it's true that your father stayed here because of my mother, but you need to hear that part of the story from him.'

'Why's that? Why don't you tell me?'

'I won't be able to convince you.'

'Of what?'

'That it wasn't your fault.'

'What wasn't?'

'I cannot convince you that your father leaving you was not your fault. You need to hear the real reason from him.'

Hearing this, my anger passed and I began to laugh. Petro really was such a child!

'My God, Petro, you think that I... that I...?' I gathered my thoughts, trying to organize them in English. 'You think that I, at this age, still believe in such sophistry as "My father abandoned us because of me; if he'd loved me, he would have stayed"?'

He didn't give a straight answer. 'With your adult mind you know it wasn't like that, of course, but—'

A wave of anger swelled inside me again. I interrupted him. 'I knew with my child's mind what was what as well!'

We stopped talking. I squirmed a little on the sand and drew my legs up to my stomach. My tongue had transformed into a poisonous scorpion, looking for an opportunity to deal Petro a cruel sting.

'Melike, I've noticed something. Concerning you.'

'What is that?'

'You took me to a restaurant the evening we met. Where I had sour-cherry compote.'

'The restaurant where you ate a mountain of food as well as the sour-cherry compote.'

In my head I saw Petro, under the awed gaze of the restaurant owner, ordering dish after dish: compote and mushrooms sautéed in olive oil and thyme, lamb stew with peas, dolma and mashed potato.

'That evening, while we were eating, I told you that I wanted to talk to you about something serious; do you remember?'

'Vaguely.'

'I was going to tell you that your father had sent me to you. I tried to get your attention several times, but you kept changing the subject, as if you knew where the conversation would go if we got serious. I don't think you did that consciously, but for sure you had some sort of intuition about it.'

'I don't remember.'

Actually, he was right. I remembered it perfectly well. Something had made me really uneasy that night, but I hadn't dwelt on it. I'd assumed it was my long-forgotten past coming back to haunt me – the corners of the church; the dark, narrow streets; the steps shaded by fig trees – not unlike my experience earlier tonight, when that dream had surfaced in my consciousness and caused my heart to beat anxiously. Plus there was the weed we'd smoked in the yard of the Red School, which had given rise to some very strange sensations.

'And because you felt uncomfortable, you switched the focus to a different plane, to an area where you felt comfortable and in control.'

He went quiet and searched amid the shadows for an answer in my face.

What? Was I supposed to say something now? So what if maybe I did sometimes switch the focus elsewhere. Normally, if I wanted to distract myself, I solved a geometry problem. Or did sudoku. But how would Petro have known that? When I said nothing, he continued.

'You seduced me.'

What! Was it me who'd knocked on the door in the early hours? Was it me who'd booked a room in the hotel, insisting that it would be too difficult to shuttle back and forth from Buyukada? I opened my mouth to object, but he silenced me with a motion of his hand. I picked up a handful of sand and squeezed it in my fist. There was a lump in my throat. He spoke softly.

'You have become an expert at that. You do it without realizing it.'

'What?'

'Hiding behind your sexual charm. I don't know how to explain it, but it seems to me that by having sex with a man, you're actually putting a distance between yourself and them. Just when a deeper connection is being forged, you switch to the sex circuit. So instead of getting closer, you detach yourself. And in the morning, you up and leave. Which means you're never the one that gets abandoned; you make sure that the thing you fear most never happens. In fact, while still holding onto your husband, you're able to take revenge on all men—'

Enough! Who did this Petro think he was? I would shut his mouth. 'You took your pleasure once and now you're trying to get rid of me.'

Petro stopped. The stick in his hand snapped in two, then into quarters. He poked each piece into the sand, one at a time, and sighed. 'Just now in the room you said a similar thing. If you only knew how much that hurt.'

I didn't answer. I fidgeted uneasily. Sand dribbled through my fingers. Petro's voice was very low.

'Melike, I have loved you since the first time I saw you. When I say "first time", I'm not talking about our meeting in front of the Bloody Church. Long before then. Years ago…'

I raised my head in surprise. The whites of his eyes were shining in the darkness.

'The first time I saw you was in a photo I found in your father's drawer.'

'What?' I gathered my legs under me and turned towards him. 'What photo? When was this?'

'I was just a child. In the photo, you were a child too. I remember every detail of that picture. It was black and white. You were sitting in a fishing boat tied to a dock. In the back of the boat were fishing nets, buckets and bowls. You were wearing a light-coloured dress with straps that left your shoulders bare. Your hair was as curly as ever, and long, falling over your shoulders. You were laughing. Your lips were parted, showing your teeth.'

I didn't remember any photograph like that, but that whole last summer Dad had walked around with a Kodak camera, taking a lot of pictures. Because there was nowhere in the village that could develop the films, he used to line up the rolls that were ready to process in their boxes on a shelf in the pantry. When Mum hurriedly packed up and took us to Antalya, we left all of Dad's rolls of film in the village house. All except that one last roll, which seemingly had gone to Cyprus with Dad, and been developed and printed.

'I had never come across a girl like the one in the photograph, not at school or in the village. Here in Cyprus, people married each other, so the children all looked the same. You looked like us, but at the same time there was something about your expression, the way you held yourself, that was not familiar at all. I was bowled over, enchanted. I kept going back to that drawer, which was out of bounds to me, taking your picture out from among the piles of paper and notebooks, and looking at it.'

I lay down, flat, on the beach. The stars were twinkling. Life was made up of such weird intersections. For those elements that had brought this moment into existence to have come together was even more complicated than the most complex puzzle I knew. If just one element had been different, this moment of ours would have been lost to the darkness of the universe. I wondered if there were other Melikes somewhere out there in that mysterious space that we called time. Other Melikes who were going through different moments, as we were right then. I thought of Petro, holding my childhood picture in his hand. That glance between us which existed somewhere outside the straight line of time.

I sat up. My anger, like the waves beating on the shore, had retreated; love and compassion now filled its place. I was so close to Petro that our shoulders, our arms, our sandy knees were touching. In the light of the half-moon, the lines of his long, bony nose and his hard chin had softened. He had turned into the boy looking at my photograph. Cupping his face in my sandy hands, I kissed his lips for a long, long time. I wanted to apologize for being so furious. He didn't respond, but nor did he retreat. When I drew back, his tone of voice was gentler.

'The reason I was obsessed with you wasn't just that you were so beautiful; it was also because I'd found you in a forbidden place. Children weren't supposed to rifle through the adults' belongings, especially not in a family like ours, which had so many secrets. There were many things I didn't know, but from when I was very small I'd realized that talking about the past created an unpleasant atmosphere. I wasn't the only one who'd discovered that. All my peers understood that talking about the time when they were born caused tension in the family. Many fathers had died during the war, had left and never returned, their bodies never found. My situation was not unique.'

I held his hand.

'Did you know who the girl in the photo was?'

'I didn't. How was I to know? I couldn't ask questions about the photo of a girl I'd found in a drawer I shouldn't have opened. That made you even more mysterious, of course. It was only years later that your dad told me.'

'He told you? How? Why? When?'

Petro sighed.

'I'm afraid that's also something you need to hear from him, Melike *mou*. I just want to tell you this: my boyhood was taken up with dreaming of you. For me you were in a faraway land, a dream world. A girl who came out of a drawer full of secrets. Eventually, I could stand it no longer, and I stole that photograph.'

He stopped. Taking my hand, he brought it to his lips, then turned and found my eyes in the darkness.

'But the reality of you, Melike... Even a lifetime of dreaming couldn't have prepared me for the real thing.'

A light breeze blew over us from the olive groves. My hair was still damp. I shivered. Clouds had appeared from nowhere, obscuring the stars and the moon. I hugged my knees under my chin and buried my face in them. In the darkness, he couldn't see the smile spreading across my lips, but I wanted to hide it from him anyway.

Petro pressed his beautiful lips to my ear and murmured, 'I am madly in love with you, Melike.'

21

Distraction Games

My phone was ringing. I reached for my handbag on the back seat and got my mobile out. It was Sinan. From the corner of my eye, I looked at Petro in the driver's seat. He was steering with one hand, like a taxi driver. With his left palm he was continually changing gears (unnecessarily, in my opinion). His hair was tousled, his face tanned by the sun. Once the roar of a passing motorcycle had quietened, I held the phone to my sweaty ear.

'Hello? Melike, my love, can you hear me?'

I could hear him. The reception in that godforsaken corner of the world was unexpectedly good. I was using a prepaid card that I'd bought at Larnaca Airport as there was no coverage for Turkish mobile phone providers in Cyprus. Sinan's voice was as clear as if he'd been calling from the next room. I could hear not only Sinan but background music, the clatter of forks and plates, laughter. He was obviously in a restaurant. All of a sudden this seemed weird to me. I turned and looked at the distant mountains visible through the open windows of the jeep. We'd been driving along this dusty, badly paved road for almost an hour. There was not a town or village in sight, just a few old billboards riddled with bullet holes, occasional long-abandoned single-pump petrol stations, and a never-ending ochre-coloured road. I felt like I was on Mars. Sinan, on the other hand, was on earth.

'Melike? Hello?'

Leaning down, I picked up the water bottle at my feet and stuck it between my legs, which had welded together in the heat. The glass bottle was already warm.

'I can hear you, Sinan. How are you? Are you in Bursa?'

'I'm fine, darling. No, I'm still in Istanbul. I'm going to Bursa tomorrow. I took the car to be serviced. Where are you? Have you seen your father?'

'Not yet.'

I paused. No, it felt more like a shift in time than in place. Sinan and I were not living in the same timeframe. Like a train switching tracks, my life had entered a different dimension. The life of the old Melike seemed like a movie I'd enjoyed a long time ago – drinking raki under the mulberry tree with Sinan, wrapping ourselves in light covers and dozing on hot, still afternoons, making love with familiar pleasure, gossiping as we walked home hand in hand from an art exhibition opening. It was as if that Melike was continuing her life in another square of time and I had slipped out and passed into a different dimension. It even seemed surprising that Sinan could reach me by phone as I travelled by jeep along a road in this new dimension. I let the bottle go and it rolled down to my feet.

'Melike, my love, are you there?'

'I'm here, Sinan. There's a delay on the line. We stopped for a break somewhere near Limassol at a cousin of Petro's last night. It was late so we stayed over. We're on our way to see my father now.'

I bit my tongue. Three sentences with 'we', one after the other. I changed the subject.

'Sinan, you won't believe who I met – a childhood friend of Safinaz's! A woman called Nana Niki, over ninety years old. Last night she—'

'Seriously? Darling, you can tell me all about it in detail when you get back. I won't keep you on the line now; I just wanted to hear your voice. I didn't have a chance yesterday. Call me after you've seen your father, please. Or leave a message and I'll call you.'

I sighed. Sinan was not the sort of man who'd notice that I'd said three 'we's, one after the other.

'Of course. Are you okay? How's Mother?'

'Everybody's fine, darling. Don't worry.' He laughed. 'I'm in Istanbul chasing a business opportunity. I can't explain on the phone now, it'll eat up your minutes and cost too much, but we'll talk this evening from a landline, okay?'

'Okay.'

I closed the lid a little abruptly and my silver phone fell to the floor and hit the glass bottle at my feet. That would have scratched it for sure, wouldn't it? Well, so what if it had. I leant my head back on the car seat. Sinan wallowed around in so much money, then counted the change. Damn it!

Petro glanced sideways at the phone lying next to my sandals.

'Your husband?'

I nodded.

'Is he worried about you?'

'Yeah.'

'Is he on Buyukada?'

'No. He went to Istanbul.'

What had Sinan meant by a business opportunity? Was

he going to open a boutique hotel or something? Maybe his sister was getting married. We were people from different dimensions now, Sinan and I. Different times. Maybe the squares we occupied in time would never fit on top of one other again. All at once Dad came to my mind. He must have felt the same way when he came to Cyprus. A new Orhan who had left the old Orhan behind like a shell. He was Kosmas. Mum, the house in the village, Cem and me, everything, all of us, would have been like frames from a movie he'd watched a long time ago. Just as I somehow couldn't even imagine living a future with Sinan now, he must not have been able to comprehend returning to us.

'Why don't you ever mention your husband to me?'

'What?'

'You act as if you don't have a husband.'

Ridiculous! I hadn't even taken off my wedding ring when we'd made love.

'What should I tell you?'

'I don't know. Tell me something. Like how did you two meet?'

I didn't answer. In the distance a village of dilapidated houses came into view. Was that where Dad lived? How much further did we have to go? More than an hour had passed since we'd left Nana Niki's house. We'd lost the chance to travel in the cool of the day by not waking up early. The sun was very harsh. I'd forgotten to bring my sunglasses and the white glare was blinding me. Hot wind blowing in through the open windows scorched my skin. Petro was no longer having to make rough gear changes when he overtook a bus or a truck; there was only the two of us on the road now, in the middle of this desert.

'Tell me about him. We still have some way to go.'

'He was a friend of my first lover,' I replied wearily. As soon as I'd said it, I regretted it. I should have played the stepbrother card, then my relationship with Sinan would have sounded clean, easy to understand. The girl went and married her stepbrother's closest friend, a boy who visited the house a lot; a proper and romantic love story.

'Wow! So it began as an illicit liaison, huh?'

If Petro only knew the half of it! Illicit liaisons were my speciality. That Petro was also my stepbrother made me feel like laughing. What a joke! I'd slept with both my stepfather's son and my stepmother's son. I wondered if this particular neurosis had been documented in psychology literature. Wasn't Zeus's jealous wife, Hera, also his older sister? Did I have a Hera complex?

'How old were you?'

'Seventeen.'

He was surprised.

'You've been with your husband that long?'

'No, that wasn't when we got married. I was seventeen when I first met him. We got married much later. In 1988.'

When a motorcycle suddenly appeared right in front of us, on a bend, I let out a loud scream and covered my eyes with my hands. I hadn't got used to the traffic driving on the opposite side of the road in Cyprus. We continued through an abandoned village. Roofs and walls had collapsed, grass had grown tall inside the houses. Pomegranate trees had reached their branches through the empty windows like thieves. Outside the ruined houses stood steps that led nowhere. Not a living creature, not even a bird, was to be seen anywhere. Even the air didn't stir.

'When you got married, what did your first lover do? Was he angry?'

Holding the steering wheel with one hand, Petro took a packet of chewing gum from his pocket and offered a piece to me. The sight of that ghost village obviously hadn't affected him. Maybe he was so used to that sort of thing that he didn't even register it. I put the gum in my mouth.

'He didn't do anything. We'd been split up for years. We didn't even see each other any longer. In 1980 there was a fascist coup in Turkey. All the leftist students and supporters were arrested and tortured, including Barish, my first lover. When they let him go, he fled to France and never came back to Turkey. Maybe he was happy for both of us when he heard we'd got married. Who knows.'

I was waiting for him to swallow my lies. Involuntarily, my hand went to my left cheek, where Barish had hit me all those years ago. A hot wave spread up to my ears. What was it that turned my cheek red? Was it pain or shame? Shame or pain? I had contemplated that as I'd sat on my messy bed in my little room in the waterside villa, rubbing my cheek.

They had let Barish out of police custody at dawn. Exactly forty days had passed since they'd seized him and taken him away. He walked with difficulty, like boys did after they'd just been circumcised. His face and eyes were unrecognizable. As soon as he got to the villa, he rushed to my room, not because he'd missed me so much, but to get money for the taxi that had brought him to Kirecburnu.

Sinan, asleep at my side, opened his eyes at the sound of the slap. He immediately sprang out of the bed and stood in front of Barish in his rumpled shirt and trousers.

'Look, my friend, you've misunderstood. I didn't want Melike to be on her own... As you know, her mother's in a clinic and your father isn't very well, and what with martial law, we were hanging out together... The curfew... We fell asleep.'

He was tugging at his shirt so that Barish could see – look, we didn't even get undressed, mate. While I was comforting your girlfriend – your girlfriend, who is your stepsister, by the way – I was wearing my trousers. If you don't believe me, just look and see.

Barish was looking only at my narrow little bed, which he had got into so many times, but in which he had never once stayed until morning. From where I was sitting, sleepy-eyed amid the quilt, blanket and sheets, I felt sorry for Sinan. He was wasting his words. Barish knew. Our arms and legs had given us away. They'd been twined around each other as with any couple who were used to sleeping together. As soon as Barish had come into the room, he'd focused not on Sinan's trousers or my dress, which by chance we'd not taken off the night before, but on the familiar togetherness of our bodies. Even if Sinan had waved a magic wand, he could never have convinced Barish that we weren't lovers. He shouldn't have even tried. He and I made love so beautifully, but right then I wanted him to leave. Immediately. Barish and I needed to work things out. It was a family matter.

'So what did you do during that time?' Petro shifted down a gear, jolting me forwards. If a pregnant woman was to ride in this jeep, she'd have a miscarriage, it shook so much. I held onto the dashboard bar.

'During what time?'

'Your first lover fled to France in 1980. You got married in 1988. You probably didn't sit around for eight years waiting for your first lover to come back.'

'No, I didn't wait for him. I slept with whoever happened to come my way.'

He was startled. Without letting go of the steering wheel, he turned and looked me up and down. I swivelled towards the window and stared at the old tyres lined up along the roadside. The sun was high in the sky now. My face was hot all the way up to my ears. I had been unfair to that young girl whom I had cruelly portrayed as a slut in my story, disregarding all that she had lost. The truth was that she had sex in order to forget. That might even have been the only reason she had sex. She thought she would find love in each embrace, but then, afraid of the rejection and disillusion that might follow, she moved on straight away. Petro was right. Seducing men was my way of numbing the pain, my coping mechanism. I'd been doing that since way back then. Over the years, I'd become an expert. I didn't even notice I was doing it any more.

Slipping my feet out of my leather sandals, I drew my knees up to my chin and hugged them. My voice was muffled between my legs.

'Barish fled the country. Sinan went to America for graduate studies. I finished high school and started university. Those were awful, dark times, Petro. Just forget about it.'

Petro nodded but didn't say anything. We were now on a winding mountain road. Instead of rough, brown wasteland, there were pine trees. I breathed the cool air into my lungs. An emptiness left over from long ago smouldered inside me. I pictured my mother when she had come back from the clinic in Switzerland. The medication she was taking had turned her into a ghost, a skeleton, not even a shadow of the old Gulbahar. And there was Mina, with an earth-coloured leather suitcase in her hand, at the door of the villa.

I saw her in my dream, Melike. Madam Gulbahar had got tangled up in some seaweed at the bottom of the sea and couldn't free herself. So I've come to take care of her. She's done so much for me. Please, Melike, let me look after her.

Mina's reappearance was for me a heaven-sent blessing. It released me from having to take care of my sick mother. Mina had always wanted to be with my mother, and now they could be together to her heart's content. Meanwhile I, with my pockets full of the generous allowance Dr Chetin gave me, could check out the newest Istanbul bars with my wealthy university friends and drink and dance until the small hours. I didn't care whose house I ended up in; it was enough that I didn't need to go back to the villa, to my mother, to Dr Chetin, to the room where the walls still rang with the sound of Barish's slap.

When I came home in the early morning, reeking of alcohol and cigarettes, I would bump into Dr Chetin in the kitchen. The poor man never asked where I'd been, returning home in such a state, but I'd make up something anyway, like that my exams had started and I'd been up all night in the library studying with friends. My stepfather, coffee cup in hand, *Cumhuriyet* newspaper open in front of him, would glance up from the table in the coffee-scented kitchen. Seeing my cheeks smeared with black mascara and my mini-dress stained with whisky, he would only sigh. My mother's suicide attempt and his son, who had first been detained by the police and then had to flee the country, had numbed him. Besides, right from the start, Dr Chetin had never paid much attention to me. Maybe because I was just an ordinary student, maybe because I looked like my father and not my mother, our stepfather had embraced Cem, not me. Dr Chetin had enrolled Cem in the high school he himself had gone to, had helped him fill out the application forms for foreign universities. His devotion to Cem increased greatly when it became clear that Barish had not even completed high school. I remember how disappointed he was when my brother chose to go to Australia. He had hoped Cem would choose a university in England or on the east coast of America, somewhere within relatively easy reach. Cem had been accepted by all the universities he'd applied to, but he chose the one furthest away from us. I understood that; Dr Chetin did not. His spirits were very low.

I was overcome with a deep weariness. Maybe it was the wine I'd drunk the night before, the hangover from the weed, or a delayed reaction to the startling revelations I'd heard from Nana Niki and Petro. As we twisted our way up the mountain road, I scanned the distant clouds and tried to determine how far we were from the sea. What kind of village was it that my father lived in? On and on, and still we kept going, when supposedly in Cyprus nothing was more than two hours away. A broad-winged bird was diving languidly among some rocks. A hawk, maybe, or an eagle. A sign of life, at least.

'Then what happened? When your husband-to-be returned from America, did you get married?'

'No, of course not. We didn't even write to each other. I thought I'd never see him again. After Barish fled to France, there was no longer any reason for us to stay in touch: the thread that tied us together was gone. In those days, if someone went to America, they never came back, and even if he did come back, he wouldn't look me up.'

'But...?'

I couldn't decide whether to tell him the rest of the story or not. Something was holding me back. Petro turned and gave me a quizzical look. I sighed and reclined further back in the seat.

'One night we bumped into each other at a nightclub, a place called Studio 54. I was so surprised. It was the only place in Istanbul where young, rich kids like us went. Almost everybody knew each other. Sinan had just recently returned from America and was there with his friends. I was happy to see him because I'd been having a very bad night.'

'Why?'

Let him hear it, Melike! What are you hiding from this boy? You may as well – he can see inside your head anyway.

'There was a man I was very much in love with. At least I thought I was in love with him. He was nine years older than me and insanely jealous. He would get furious with me: "You looked at that boy; you made eyes at this boy; is he one of your ex-lovers; did he fuck you too?" Humiliating comments like that. But for some reason I didn't leave him. He was engaged and was going to be getting married soon. The girl lived with her family. He would take her out in the evenings for dinner, then leave her at her house and summon me to his bed for the remainder of the night. I would go running to him.'

I stole a glance at Petro. A healthy young man. How could he understand such a destructive relationship, my addict's craving for such searing, humiliating pain? I couldn't tell him. He wouldn't get it.

'How were you able to both sleep with any man that came your way and be the slave of such a jealous man?'

With both hands on the steering wheel, his close-set eyes squinted; he seemed to be giving all his attention to the curves in the road as it snaked its way through the pine trees. Was this a reproach, or was he trying to catch me in a lie? I couldn't tell from his face.

'After I met him, I didn't so much as look at anyone else. He would have gouged my eyes out.'

'Wow, the bastard had so much power over you. What was his name?'

'Tarik. Tarik Tunca.'

I hadn't said his name in so long that I felt like laughing. I repeated it several times, like I was stuttering: Tarik Tunca, Tariktunca, tariktuncatariktunca. Had he even existed, was he a real creature of flesh and blood, or had he been a figment of my imagination? In my youth I'd thought about him so much, had wasted so many words trying to prove my innocence to him, that the real Tarik Tunca was lost to me. Was he really the man who once upon a time had made love to me on sheets smelling of raki, had slept beside me in bed while I cried, as rain streamed down the window pane in torrents in the dim city light?

'This Tarik… What was his name again? Tarik Tunca? His fiancée – did you know her?'

'We were never introduced, but I saw her a few times. That night, Tarik had even come to Studio 54 with her.'

Petro laughed and shook his head, reminding me once again how young he was. He hadn't been around this type of man yet. For him it was unbelievably absurd that Tarik Tunca would bring his fiancée to a bar knowing that I would be there also. In time, some of Petro's friends, and maybe also Petro himself, would turn into a Tarik Tunca, but for now the whole concept was new to him and therefore intriguing.

'He used to do that sometimes.'

Petro puckered his lips as if to say, 'What a nerve!' We hit a pothole and the jeep shook. From somewhere over the mountains a truck grumbled.

'And?'

'While he was sitting in a corner clinking glasses with his fiancée, he always had one eye on me, of course. That night he was scowling. If ever my gaze wandered in the direction of another man, I knew I would pay for it the next day. I was talking with some of my girlfriends, pretending to laugh, swaying to the rhythm of the music, but inside I was crying tears of blood. My eyes kept getting stuck on the fiancée, a made-up, dressed-up, dried-up girl not worth my fingernail. Horse-faced, but a virgin. I had my sexual freedom, but she had him. I was drinking tequila shots, one after the other. Lemon, salt, shot! I was perched on a bar stool like a bird with my elbows on the damp, dirty counter. The bar staff knew me, of course. Did they feel sorry for me, or were they messing with me? I wasn't sure, but the moment I finished one shot, the next one was slid in front of me. Wheee! I drank that one down. With Dr Chetin's money in my pocket I was easy, you know. My friends were cheering me on. My eyes were fiery. I turned and looked over at the corner where he was sitting with his fiancée. He was shaking his head as if to say, 'I'll show you tomorrow.' I was the only one who saw that, of course, that one-millimetre movement of his big head. Even that made me happy.'

'Sort of like, "He's angry with me, therefore I exist", which was better than him acting as if he hadn't even noticed you?'

Well, look at that! It seemed Petro did understand destructive relationships – at least a little.

'So I'd just downed yet another shot and was wiping the salt and lemon from the corners of my mouth when someone grabbed my arm. I turned and looked. I still had this foolish hope that it would be him. He wouldn't have left his fiancée at the table, but maybe he'd put her in a taxi and sent her home and was now ready to turn his attention to me. Obviously a girl from a decent family couldn't stay out too late. He'd understood how much he'd hurt me, how miserable he'd made me... But it was a vain hope. Of course it wasn't him.'

'It was Sinan.'

When I heard Sinan's name in Petro's mouth for the first time, something like guilt quivered inside me. I yanked the seatbelt, which had been cutting into my shoulder.

'Yes, it was Sinan.'

'He was so handsome,' I was going to say, yet decided against it. But Sinan really had looked immensely handsome that night. Young, and spick and span. He'd removed his glasses and was wearing a white, short-sleeved shirt, sparklingly clean and ironed with razor-sharp creases. Blue jeans, obviously bought in America, and a brand of trainers I didn't know. His eyes shone in that dark club full of drunk people, a pearl among the shameless. His smile was like a fresh breeze inside me. Forgetting for a moment the big head watching me from the corner, I hugged him.

'You were happy to see him. At the least he was an old friend whom you hadn't seen for years.'

He was not an old friend. He was the first man who had loved me as a woman. It was his lips, his slender white hands, that had with kindness taught my body the pleasures of togetherness, a body that, until him, had known nothing other than the rough touch of Barish's hurried midnight visits.

'Sinan had completed his master's in business administration, but he didn't want to go into his family's hotel business and was trying to settle in Istanbul. We chatted for a while. But when I ran to the bathroom, leaving him at the bar, he realized what a miserable state I was in. "Come on, let's get some air," he said. "No, no, we can't leave together," I insisted, in tears. "You go first; I'll follow." My eye was still on Tarik, sitting in the corner with his fiancée. By now he had forgotten his fiancée and was staring straight at me. He'd seen how happily I hugged Sinan, of course. I even thought at one point that he might get up right there and start shaking me on the dance floor. When I picture him doing that, I felt like laughing. He would be gripping me by my shoulders under the silver disco ball and shaking me. So embarrassing! Would his horse-faced fiancée faint or would she pull my hair? The more I laughed at this vision, the angrier Tarik Tunca got. The angrier he got, the more I laughed, like a wild animal just discovering its strength. He moved as if he wanted to get up from his chair but couldn't. I laughed more than ever. Anyway I was drunk as a coot.'

'A proper tequila high!'

'Exactly.'

Yes, Petro, tequila – and more… I kept my mouth shut. A sudden tenderness towards Petro swept through me. He was a child who'd fallen in love with my photograph. *But the reality of you, Melike… Even a lifetime of dreaming couldn't have prepared me for the real thing.* I needed to protect him. From myself. From my defects, my destructive side.

Catching sight of my mobile, which was lying at my feet, I spoke rapidly.

'While I was laughing like I was having a nervous breakdown, Sinan suddenly noticed Tarik. Did their eyes meet in the darkness? I don't know what happened, but in an instant he understood everything. He grabbed my hand, then…'

Again I stopped. My mouth was dry. Leaning down, I picked up the water bottle, took a few gulps, then handed it to Petro. The bends in the road had come to an end and we were now descending a steep hill with sharp grey rocks to either side. My insides were like jelly from the jolts of the jeep. I gripped the door handle. I'd never told anyone that story before. It was all so long ago that the events of that night hadn't come into my head in years. My memory must have stored a lot of details, and presumably the ones I froze back in the day were now thawing out, as fresh as they were on the night. Sinan entwined his long, beautiful fingers with mine, held them tight, and looked straight into my eyes. He held my hand so tightly, looked into my eyes so intensely that I stopped laughing and suddenly saw what he was seeing. I was very beautiful, very young, and unique in the world. I was too precious to be shedding tears over a man who could not see that, tears for a love that man could never give me. Sinan's eyes had become a clear mirror. I had found a home.

'Then what? Go on. You've stopped at the most exciting bit.'

Petro's lips were smiling, but between his close-set eyes a furrow had appeared. Maybe from the sun – it was shining through the leaves and hitting the front windscreen with ferocity. I sat back and closed my eyes.

'It was a beautiful spring night. We walked down to the Bosphorus hand in hand, then on from Bebek to Arnavutkoy. It wasn't far, but in my drunken state it seemed as if we'd been walking all night. I was also really hungry. We found a kiosk that was open and Sinan bought me a huge hotdog and a bottle of *ayran*. Do you know what *ayran* is?'

'Come on, Melike. I'm a Cypriot, not an American. The salty yogurt drink, right?'

I laughed, but didn't fail to catch the harsh edge to his voice.

'Okay, okay. Understood. Don't get angry. Anyway, with the hotdog and *ayran* in my hands, we sat down on a bench overlooking the sea. I immediately got busy with my food. It was the most delicious sausage ever, with a wonderful red, slightly hot sauce. I drank down the *ayran*. Sinan didn't let go of my hand. By the time I took the last bite, we had decided to get married.'

I turned towards Petro to gauge his reaction. He'd stopped the car. He looked tired. The sun had withdrawn, but the furrow between his eyebrows was still there. Because of me! I'd told him more than he could take. I shouldn't have told a very young man, who had just last night declared his love for me, about that romantic night I'd spent with my husband-to-be, about the gratitude I felt to Sinan for pulling me out of the darkness. My own kind of faithfulness. Whenever I lost strength, I caught my breath with Sinan lying beside me. Having heard this story, Petro would have understood that, would definitely be feeling hurt.

'Petro, I...'

He turned off the ignition and put his hand on my knee. Crickets immediately filled the void now that the engine had gone silent. I turned and looked around us. We were on a narrow, shady street, in front of a two-storeyed stone house. After all that desert and dust, all those stones and curves, how and when had we happened upon this immaculately clean, cobblestoned street? What kind of place was this? Were we in a hidden valley between the mountains? My heart began to beat really fast. Petro was looking at me.

Suddenly I realized what he'd been doing. He'd been distracting me. He'd made me forget about where I was going by keeping my head busy with the past. He didn't give a damn about what had happened to me on a dark bench in Arnavutkoy. While I was carefully choosing my words to protect him from myself, he was once again blindsiding me.

Goddamn you, Petro!

Without saying a word, he let go of my knee and got out of the jeep. Left alone in the passenger seat, I felt a wave of panic rising to my throat. I hung onto the seatbelt. Petro turned around, came over and opened my door. Putting the green handkerchief he'd wiped his forehead with in his back pocket, he extended his hand.

'We're here, Melike. Are you ready?'

I shrank down in my seat, still trembling inside. I opened my mouth, but no sound came out. I shook my head. No, I was not at all ready.

25

Mice in a Maze

The door opened before we rang the bell. A tall, smiling woman appeared at the top of the steps leading down to the street. I recognized Petro's mother at once. She had the same close-set, honey-coloured eyes as her son, the same arched nose. The nose, which gave Petro the air of a hawk, created an owlish effect on his mother. The two of them embraced. She was heavy-boned, strong. Although I often made the mistake of assuming that if a person was tall they had to be older than me, I realized at one glance that this woman was not many years my senior. She was young, too young to be my father's wife. Resentment surged through me.

'Melike, this is my mother, Eleni.'

Without waiting for Petro to finish his introduction, she hugged me, clasping me tight, with sincerity, as if we knew each other and hadn't seen each other for a long time. Her short, black hair smelled of lavender. She knew me. She might even have known quite a lot about me. But what did I know about her? Who was she? The woman who stole my father. The devil who seduced him. In the eyes of my grandmother Madam Piraye, just a simple village woman.

Gulbahar, daughter, didn't we warn you from the start? That woman is no more than he deserves, a simple village woman. Your father's lawyer will sort out your divorce in a single session of the court. You can do so much better than him.

Well, now that woman had a name and a body. Eleni. Eleni, an island woman, within whose powerful arms I felt very small, very helpless.

'Welcome, Melike! You have made us so happy.'

Like Petro, she spoke good English and pronounced my name with a soft 'k'. Her voice was deep. Maybe she wasn't as young as she looked; maybe it was the clean air and nutritious food that were keeping her strong.

'Please come into the kitchen. I just made some cherry syrup and it'll be cool by now. I'll go and check on your father. He's been so excited all morning, knowing you were coming, that he wore himself out and fell asleep a little while ago.'

Hearing this, my throat began to burn. With my thoughts on the cherry syrup, I followed Petro into the stone-walled kitchen. It was old but immaculately clean and well organized. It was also cool. There was a smell of dill and mint in the air. In the back part of the kitchen, where the oven was, copper pots and pans just like the ones in Safinaz's house were suspended from ceiling hooks. Glass jars holding almonds, sesame seeds, dried sage and other nuts and seasonings were lined up along the shelves. Petro opened the fridge in the corner and checked out its contents. He threw some grapes into his mouth, then lifted the lid of the pot on the stove and mumbled something happily. From the smell I understood that Eleni had made chicken-liver pilaf in anticipation of our arrival. My stomach growled, but I didn't feel like eating anything. I had lost my appetite again.

I sat quietly on the edge of a wooden chair. The jolting of the jeep, the skin-roasting heat and all that talking had worn me out. I needed to pull myself together before I saw my father, but my eyes kept closing. I rested my cheek on the table and looked out at the courtyard. Red and white geraniums were growing in the window. White sheets that had been hung out to dry on taut lines strung between orange trees were swaying in the gentle breeze. My eyelids were getting really heavy as I gazed up at the dried peppers hanging from the ceiling. A tremendous force was pulling me into sleep. I was sinking gradually to the bottom of a muddy lake. A five-minute nap would be enough. It had always been like that with me. As a child, I would often doze off when I was faced with a difficult situation. Once, I even fell asleep while I was walking. I was holding Safinaz's hand as we came home from the market, and just as we were climbing the steps up to Red Square, my fingers slipped out of hers and I collapsed in a heap on the ground. She didn't know what to do. She prodded me, shook me, pinched me, but she couldn't rouse me. In the end she just sat down on the step beside me and waited until I woke up. For some reason Dad used to find that story hilarious and would relate it to his friends at every opportunity. He particularly enjoyed the part where his famously strict teacher mother perched herself on a step beside the school walls and waited for her granddaughter to wake up from her sleep coma. That used to make him cry with laughter. Ah, Dad! From behind my closed eyelids, the copper pots trembled on their ceiling hooks. Then sleep drew me in and swallowed me up.

I woke up to the scraping of a chair. Petro was sitting across from me. Between us was a misted glass pitcher full of cherry syrup. I wiped saliva from the corners of my mouth with the back of my hand and sat up straight.

'Was I asleep?'

'You were even snoring.'

'Don't make things up!'

He put a glass of the cherry syrup in front of me. My brief nap had disoriented me. I held my glass up to the light. The cherries hadn't sunk to the bottom yet; they were dancing gently in the sparkling liquid, like rubies. The cool of the liquid passed to my hand. My mouth had turned to mud. I drank down the syrup in one gulp, burst the pitted cherries between my tongue and the roof of my mouth and swallowed them without chewing. Delicious! It had just the right amounts of sugar, coolness and strength. A freshness spread from my throat and throughout the rest of my body; I felt reborn. Petro refilled my glass from the pitcher. A door in the corridor opened and then closed again.

'I think we came just in time, Melike,' Petro murmured. 'My mother has a feeling that the end is approaching, judging by his condition. When he left the hospital, they said he had two months left, at most two and a half. He's on non-stop morphine for the pain now, and… he's just waiting.'

His eyes filled with tears, accentuating their honey colour. He propped his elbows on the table, dropped his head into his hands and ran his fingers through his thick hair. I examined my own response. What was I feeling? Not much of anything. It was only Petro's sadness that was causing me to ache inside. It was as if he was grieving for the untimely death of a distant uncle I barely knew. I felt like reaching out to take his hand, to comfort him. I was ashamed of myself. It was as if Petro was Dad's only child. He was the only one who would genuinely cry when he died. Cem and I both took after Gulbahar; we were cold, unfeeling, selfish souls, concerned only with our own troubles, insensitive to others' pain.

There was a light rattle. I turned towards the door. Eleni. She smiled, her face exhausted.

'You can go in, Melike. Your father has woken up and is waiting for you.'

I looked over at Petro in fear. He had better not leave me on my own! He stood up and nodded. The half-opened door of the room opposite was casting a shadow across the floor of the corridor. Petro pushed it and it yielded with a slight squeak. My nose filled with the smell of hot wood and medication. I used Petro's body as a shield. In spite of the closed shutters and the fan rotating above the bed, the room was hotter than the corridor or the kitchen.

Petro left me at the door and went over to the bed. A man was lying in the middle of the bed under a blue cotton blanket, a man wearing a lightweight white shirt, with two thick pillows supporting his head, a dark-skinned man with no hair save a few white strands at his temples and a white beard. A small, shrivelled man. Petro leant over and whispered some words in his ear. As I looked at him, it suddenly seemed obvious to me that everything that had happened in the last few weeks was a joke. No, not a joke but a huge mistake. The Melike Petro had been looking for was someone else. I had come all this way through a misunderstanding. Because this man... this man was not my father. This man was another, totally different person.

I gripped the doorknob so as not to fall. My eye caught my reflection in the mirror above the dressing table right across from me. Was that frail child in the white cotton dress me? How thin I'd become! My breasts were shrunken, even my shoulders were narrower. My hair, unfettered, like a wild river, surrounded a tiny face with huge black eyes. A weird, unfamiliar, spicy smell was coming off my skin. Something was changing irreversibly.

Petro came over and put his hands on my shoulders. Unwilling to offend his soft palms, I took four or five steps, enough to get me to the side of the bed. The patient slowly turned his head and looked at us. The skin on his face was saggy and his cheeks were hollow. I avoided his eyes. There was a drip stand between the dressing table and the bed. A thin plastic tube led from the drip to the bed and disappeared into a bandage on his right arm. Morphine. Was it the morphine that made his eyes look lifeless, as if a film had been drawn over them?

Petro pushed on my shoulders and sat me down on a wooden chair beside the bed. I collapsed like a puppet whose strings had been cut, my head falling forward. I stared at the bedclothes. White sheets, a blue cotton blanket embroidered around the edges with yellow and pink flowers. A hand came into view. It was square and stubby. A hand with fingers. White hairs covered the fingers. Even the fingernails were short. It was a familiar hand. Fearfully, my eyes followed the hand. Was this arm, with its loose skin and veins full of puncture marks, the same black-haired, thick-wristed arm that I'd once held on to like a monkey? Was this dry twig now resting on the blue blanket the same strong arm that used once to pick up my child's body in one hand and whirl me in the air as I screamed and yelled, in what we called the 'monkey swing'?

I lifted my head. Petro? Where was he? I glanced around the room, in shadow because of the closed shutters. He wasn't there! He'd left me there and gone away. I turned around in fear, coming eye to eye with the man in the bed. A tiny smile appeared on the left side of his lips. Then a whisper.

'You look so much like my mother, Melike, my angel.'

A hiccup stuck in my throat. I gripped the chair with both hands.

He raised his voice. 'I didn't think you would come.'

His voice filled the body on the bed like water running over earth. The empty shell in front of me shook itself and revived. Dad's eyes, his mouth, his expressions appeared on the face of the sick man. The voice hadn't changed. Dad's voice! That was the first thing I'd forgotten. For a long time I could remember what he looked like, but no matter how hard I tried, I hadn't been able to recall the way he talked, his turns of phrase, the tone of his voice. It might have got a little weaker, but it still had the same soft, nasal timbre. Very deep down, audible only to a familiar ear, was an offended note. Lowering my head, I rested my cheek on the hand lying on the blanket. His skin had got darker, rougher. I turned my head towards the door and closed my eyes.

'How is Cem? I wanted to call him too, but... Your mother?'

Without moving my head, I shrugged. What could I say? As soon as Cem finished high school, he fled to the furthest place on earth and never came back. He became a citizen of that distant country and apparently had even changed his name. If you'd called him, he wouldn't have come. As for Mum, she tried to kill herself. She couldn't cope. My first lover had to carry her to the hospital, after which he never came near me again. He was my stepbrother, by the way, the son of the man Mum married after you. I went ahead and wed his closest friend, and before the ink had dried on my marriage certificate, I began cheating on my husband. That's the full account. Do you want to settle up now? Or later?

I sighed.

'Everybody's fine, Dad. Just muddling along in their own way.'

Dad! I'd said it! Dad. I swallowed. After all these years, my tongue had said it just like that, without any hesitation. I screwed my eyes shut even more tightly. He drew his hand from under my cheek and touched my hair. My breath was caught in my ribcage, like a bird. A wave of heat spread across my face. He ran his fingers through the curls of my hair.

'Melike, my angel…' His voice had again become a whisper. 'Thank you for coming, my daughter.' I sat up straight and looked into his face. He was smiling. Then he winked. 'You don't like it when I call you "my daughter", but what can I do? You are my only daughter.'

As I laughed, my eyes filled with tears. How did he remember that? I wanted to get up and wrap my arms around his neck, but I was afraid to with all the tubes in his veins. What if, when he wanted to hug me back, they came out? I reclined in the chair, kicked off my sandals and drew my knees up to my chin. My hair fell over my face. I wanted to cry my heart out. Or laugh hysterically. But I could do neither. I could only sit soberly on an uncomfortable wooden chair. I was a cowardly, dried-up daughter with her arms around her knees, hiding behind her hair. I couldn't lay my head on his thin, rasping chest. I could only touch love with the tip of my finger.

'Melike, I am dying.'

'Shh, Dad, don't talk like that.'

'But it's the truth, my beauty. There are things I need to tell you. I'm not looking for forgiveness, but what I have to say can only come from me. No one else can tell you what happened. Not Eleni, not Petro. I want you to hear it from me.'

Taking a handkerchief from under his pillow, he covered his mouth and coughed for a long time. I handed him the glass beside his head and he took a sip of water.

'Don't tire yourself now, Dad. We'll have time to talk. I've only just arrived.'

'There is no more time, my Melike. None at all. I want to tell you everything, from the beginning. Maybe starting with my mother's life, or before that – our ties to this land. But—'

'I know, Dad. I know about Safinaz's story, why you came here in pursuit of that, the murder of your twin brother... They told me all that.'

He shook his head.

'There are other things. Horrible things. I came here at the most awful time, Melike. This beautiful island suddenly turned into hell. Do you remember little Mina's prophecy? When I witnessed the most horrendous cruelties, her words echoed in my ears: "It's like hell over there, Mr Orhan," she said. "If you go, you won't ever come back." She was right.'

He closed his eyes, buried himself a little deeper into the bed. The only sound in the room was the hum of the ceiling fan and from time to time my father's rasping breath. When he again began to speak, his voice was very quiet.

'At first everything was calm. I was in Mother's village. Not here, a village in the north. It was a beautiful, green, well-tended place. There was a coffeehouse under a plane tree, a church, a stream splashing gently nearby. I was a guest in Nana Niki's house. You met her yesterday. She raised Damianos, my twin brother. Then... then everything got out of hand. Very suddenly. Disasters, my Melike, can happen in a split second. First there was a coup here, which they said was the work of the Greek junta, the regime of the colonels. A woman ran out into the village square, very distressed, shouting, "Makarios has been murdered!" I didn't completely understand what was happening, partly because of the language barrier and partly because I wasn't really involved, Cyprus not being my country, but I did know that Archbishop Makarios was the president of Cyprus, the father of the nation. When a military coup happens in your own country, it feels as if everything in your life has changed, but when the same thing happens in someone else's country, you say, "Well, that's how the world goes."'

He'd mumbled those last words. I leant down to hear better, my face very close to his. He smelled of lemon cologne. The skin on his neck was like a frog's. Orderly shafts of light fell onto the bed through the shutters. We were quiet for a while. I thought he might have fallen asleep. His eyes were closed and his chest was rising and falling peacefully. I was surprised when he began speaking.

'Nana Niki and the other old people in the village had told me Mother's story. I had heard from Pasha that her name was Anastasia, but I was only now learning of the existence of my twin brother, Damianos. I was in shock, naturally. My entire past was being rewritten. My name wasn't even Orhan – it was Kosmas! Imagine, Melike, if at your age someone was to tell you, "Your name isn't Melike, it's Angeliki." How would that make you feel?'

I was about to reply that, technically, my situation wasn't all that different from his, but he carried on speaking.

'I realized that my mother had spent her whole life weighed down with this enormous burden of guilt. It seems your poor grandmother suffered from depression throughout her life. Nowadays, she might have been helped with medication, or therapy or something, but back then depression was viewed as melancholia and simply part of a person's nature. We didn't know that it could be a fatal mental illness.'

He looked into my face with hopeless sorrow. I didn't know what to say. I too had a mother who'd been dismissed as 'melancholic' and who had tried to kill herself. If I told Dad that, would that bring us closer together? No, he would be upset to hear of mum's nervous breakdown and I didn't want to make him sad now. That old protective instinct of my childhood – that I alone was responsible for Dad's mood – had been reactivated.

'A few days later we heard that the Turkish army had landed in Cyprus. Everybody was already extremely tense because of the Greek junta's coup, and this news terrified the village. President Makarios had been trying to keep Cyprus united and independent, with Greek Cypriots and Turkish Cypriots continuing to live alongside each other. But now our village, which was predominantly Greek, feared a huge massacre. The young men disappeared overnight. A rumour spread that prisoners of war were being shot at roadsides. Mothers hid their young daughters in attics and basements. One little word about something and immediately it would be translated into news of a slaughter. It was impossible to know what was the truth and what was a lie. Collective hysteria is such a weird thing. The whole village had lost its head. I went around saying, "Do not be afraid; nothing will happen," but no one listened to me.

'Nicosia had turned into a war zone, with roads closed and telephone lines cut. It was a divided city even back then, as it is now – a capital city split in two with barbed wires; south to the Greeks, north to the Turks. Nana Niki crouched in a corner praying. There were only old people, women and children left in the village. I kept telling them not to be afraid, that there was no need to panic. "The Turkish army will kick the Greek junta out and then leave,' I told them. "And, anyway, the English are here. Who would touch you, and why would they? Also, I'm here, so there's nothing to fear." Being the only man in a village of women has that effect on a person, my Melike. Makes you feel brave. Until…'

I bent over him, concerned. He sighed. His eyes were closing and the voice coming out of his quivering lips was barely audible.

'… until you hear screams shattering the night. Then you realize that courage and all of that are empty. When you feel the cold metal of the knife at your throat, your chivalrous fantasies evaporate. Your only struggle then is to save your own life. You're not fighting, you're not doing battle – that's the stuff of novels. You just freeze, petrified, and endure the cruelty that is inflicted upon you.'

He rubbed his temples. His face was tight with pain. I drew back. From elsewhere inside the house a door closed; then the noise of the jeep's engine filled the room. Petro must have gone off somewhere. In spite of the heat, I shivered.

'I want to tell you about that night, my Melike. That night they came to the village, and I… I need to tell you everything, but this head of mine… My head hurts so much, it's as if a red-hot poker is boring into my brain. Could you open the valve on that drip, give me some relief?'

I got up and did as he'd asked. The liquid began to flow through the clear tube, drop by drop. Dad took a deep breath. Perhaps I should have asked Eleni if there was a limit on the amount of morphine he was allowed before I opened the valve, but I liked the idea of being Dad's partner in crime. Returning to my place, I shifted the chair closer to the bed and covered his hands with mine. His eyelids closed; his breath deepened. What? No! You can't go to sleep now, Dad. Not now. Suddenly, I panicked. What if he never woke up?

What if he left me halfway through the story and died? What if he abandoned me once again?

I got up and closed the morphine valve. The drops in the tube stopped moving. My father did not wake up. In desperation, I stood beside him, observing his relaxed face. His breathing became deeper still. He wasn't going to wake up. Looking at his body, as empty as a hazelnut shell, a lump came to my throat. We thought time was a straight line, but it couldn't be. It was a mystery. A puzzle of moments in squares whose edges touched, side by side, one on top of the other, opening into each other. For I was certain that somewhere in time another Melike was still casting her fishing line into the milky-blue sea with Orhan, waiting for the sun's pink head to rise behind the uninhabited island. Threads more delicate than a spider's web were drawn taut between the different dimensions, a gauze curtain separated one square from another. Every so often, the curtain lifted a little, confusing us. My nose was filled with the aroma of dried seaweed tangled in the net. Seaweed, iodine, salt. The smell of the sea at the top of a mountain. If I followed the scent and found the way, I could get back there.

The room resounded with familiar snoring. I smiled. In a while it would intensify and the noise coming out of Dad's thick, blue-tinged lips would echo off the walls. There was a growth in his right nostril, which was why he snored so loudly. In the village house all those years ago, as I had lay in my bed in the room next to Mum and Dad's room, I used to imagine that the snore that had woken me up had risen to the ceiling and burst like a thunderclap.

I suddenly felt a great emptiness inside, a habitual longing. All roads led to this. It was in all the squares. I could fill my life with all sorts of things, but the loneliness would always be lurking somewhere. I might get distracted for a while, but as soon as I felt the tiniest bit fragile, physically or mentally, loneliness would go on the attack, like bacteria, and conquer my spirit. I had spent my entire life missing my father. That yearning had plagued me like a ghost, was in my blood, had made me an addict. Even now, although I was holding his hand and hearing his voice, I still longed for him.

A truth I had always known now appeared unavoidably clear: this longing, this burning emptiness inside me had settled in my heart long before Dad left us. Although I had come into the world as a loved baby, I had been an ill-tempered child. Anger had followed me like a shadow ever since. Sadness also. The void inside me would never be filled. It wasn't even mine. My inner reservoir held not only the memories of my own short lifespan but also those of my ancestors. Life was a never-ending yoke, passed from generation to generation. Disconnected ends never came together. Disillusion settled in my stomach like a fist. I collapsed onto a low, satin-covered stool in front of the dressing table mirror and took my head into my hands.

Wherever you positioned 'Melike' and 'Orhan' in time, in history – on a horizontal, running from right to left; vertically, with the one above the other; or within their own squares – they always ended up at the same place. A place of loneliness, emptiness and longing. Was this the way life was meant to be? We continued to scurry here and there, like mice in a maze, working hard to try and find an answer that had been determined long ago, looking for a pattern, for meaning. When we've filled all the squares, used every number from one to nine, we're so pleased to have solved it that we forget it's just a game. But you can't avoid the reality of time; it was right there in front of me: wrinkled skin, cells unable to renew themselves, bankrupt organs. The malignant tissue passed from one generation to the next.

I raised my head with the heaviness of my thoughts and came eye to eye with my reflection in the mirror. Now that the roundness of youth had been erased from my face, I really did look like Safinaz. Gathering my hair on top of my head with one hand, I peered more closely at my reflection. The mirror was old; the silvering was peeling at the edges. The glass had misted with my breath. I opened my left eye wide and examined it carefully. Red veins ran down from the centre of the white. In the light seeping through the shutters, I could see specks of hazel in my brown iris and a ring of milky blue around it. Iris: Electra's rainbow daughter; the messenger goddess who brought good news to mortals from the gods. These were my father's eyes. Now I understood why, in the years after he left us, I used to frequently get up close to mirrors and examine them. I was desperate to be with him, and though I didn't know it, I sensed somehow that it was this which connected me, not only to my father, but to Safinaz and the uncle I had never known.

The iris, heredity's representative. With a pupil at its centre. The black hole of Safinaz's door, which I had seen in my dream when I'd had that high fever. Your inner reservoir is your memory, the treasure trove spiralling from one baby to the next, then uniting in another. The door opening from Safinaz to the twins, from Dad to me – and after me? I sighed. I wondered if the reason I'd never wanted to have a child was because I didn't want to pass on this burden I was carrying from my ancestors. Was there no good news for Iris to bring us now?

In the mirror, the door to the room opened. I turned around in a frenzy, like a crazy person caught doing something. My hair, freed from the hand holding it to the top of my head, tumbled over my shoulders in a cascade of curls. My eyes met Eleni's. With her hand she motioned for me to sit down. She had come to check on Dad's drip. Seeing that Dad was sleeping, she silently walked away. I got up and slipped out behind her, barefoot on the cool stone floor. The corridor was bright with the afternoon sun coming in through the courtyard window. I rubbed my eyes. Through the open door, I glanced into the kitchen. A tray of grape leaves for dolma was lying on the table.

From beside the oven, Eleni called to me.

'Come in, Melike. Shall we make tea? Your father has some black-market Turkish tea. Fresh.'

I was surprised to realize she was speaking Turkish. The familiar smell of dill and mint wrapped around my brain. With a childish curiosity that suppressed every other emotion, I went into the kitchen.

26

Yalanci Dolma

While I'd been with my father the sun had moved. Heat was now blasting through the screen door of the kitchen and filling the room. Except for a fat black and white cat curled up asleep in the shade of a plant in the courtyard, there was no sign of any living creature. The silence and the heat were suffocating.

'You're speaking Turkish!'

When she smiled, Eleni's face shone with a childlike light, just like Petro's.

'I speak a little, *ne*. In the past our village was mixed. When I was a child, both Turkish and Greek were spoken, always. After the events of 1963 and '64, the Turks in the village left, one by one, but I did not forget my Turkish. Your father and I speak to each other in a mix of Turkish and Greek, and whenever I get the chance I still read Turkish books. But sometimes speaking it is difficult.'

'I think your Turkish is very good.'

Like Turkish Cypriots, she switched certain vowels around, but her making the effort to speak in Turkish was making me feel closer to her. I pulled over a chair and sat down at the table.

'My father is sleeping.'

She nodded. Standing on tiptoe, she took down a jar of tea from the shelf above the stove and filled the kettle from the tap. As she turned around, her hand suddenly shook, causing the metal teapot to slip and fall onto the marble floor with a clatter, exploding in the silence of the afternoon like a bomb. The cat asleep in the courtyard sprang up and raced away from the house. I knelt down beside Eleni to help, handing her the lid, which had rolled under the stove. My bare feet almost slipped on the wet floor. As we stood up, we came eye to eye and I could see that she was as tense as I was, maybe even more so. We both smiled. The white strands in her black hair glinted like silver.

'I'll make the tea, Melike. Do you see the bottle of cognac on that high shelf? You get it down. It's our Cyprus drink. I bought it in Limassol, but I've not had the chance to have any yet. They say it's eighty-year-old cognac. Let's see what it tastes like.'

A while later we were sitting at the kitchen table across from each other, drinking our strong Turkish tea and sipping Cypriot brandy on the side. After just one sip, both of us relaxed. The brandy was delicious. At first I thought we shouldn't be drinking brandy in that heat, but as the caramel-coloured liquid flowed down my throat, I realized that, just like tea, it too took the heat away. The beads of sweat on my brow had dried.

'Eleni, I need to tell you something. Just now, while I was with Dad, he was in a lot of pain. He asked me to open the morphine valve. Then when he fell asleep, I closed it.'

I stopped, trying to gauge how much of my Turkish she'd understood.

She nodded. 'You did well. At this stage we're just trying to keep him comfortable.'

'Is there nothing more that can be done for him?'

Biting her lip, she shook her head. 'He was in and out of hospital until a month ago. The doctor told us that there's no chance he'll get better.'

'So they've stopped all treatment?'

'We've agreed that he'll be at home now until the end of his life. Normally our doctors here don't say that sort of thing to their patients. They never actually say, "There's nothing more we can do for you, you're going to die." I got angry with the doctor. *Ma.* "Why do you hide the truth from the poor man?" "So that he won't be depressed," the doctor said. Is he a child that we have to lie to him, *vre*? Can that be right, Melike *mou*?'

As she spoke, three deep furrows appeared on her forehead, then disappeared when she stopped talking. I tried one more time to guess her age.

She waved her hand in the air. '*Telos pandon*. Forget it. We told him. We said to him, "Darling, you are dying." It's good that we told him. Why? Because he immediately wanted to see you. Dear Petro was here. He said, "I will go. I will find Melike and bring her to you." If we'd hidden the truth from your papa, if he'd thought he was going to recover, you would not have got together.'

Without saying anything, I lowered my head. In the heat, the water that had been spilt on the floor had already evaporated. Eleni reached across the table and raised my chin with her heavy-boned hand. We looked into each other's eyes.

Though she had slight shadows beneath hers, they were still shining.

'Melike, you are a very good girl. You love your papa very much.'

My heart felt crushed. That was false. She was wrong. I was not a good person. I was not at all a 'very good girl'. I did not love Dad very much. I did not, I could not, love anyone, particularly men. I was handicapped when it came to love. I was going to fill her son's heart with pain, then run away. A branch loaded with carob pods was tapping on the windowpane. Looking at it, my tongue remembered the puckeringly sweet taste, the slippery pulp around the seeds.

Eleni let go of my chin, sat back and took another sip of her brandy.

'I tell you, you remind me of your papa when he first came to our old village. His lips were just like yours – plump, like he was perpetually sulking.'

My eyes opened wide with curiosity. 'When Dad came to Cyprus, you were in the village?'

She stood up abruptly, picked up my half-finished glass of tea from in front of me, and went over to the stove. Had I asked something I shouldn't have? She fiddled around at the stove without speaking for a while, refreshed our tea, refilled the kettle. When she finally sat down across from me, a sadness had fallen over her face. She sighed.

'Yes, I was there.'

She was holding the narrow-waisted tea glass between her palms, seemingly unconcerned that it was very hot, and staring at the door behind me, no longer maintaining eye contact as she had earlier. She continued as if mumbling to herself.

'Last year, in April, when the border between the north and

south parts of Cyprus opened, Petro went to my old village. Other people are living in our houses now, and none of our animals are left. We used to have cows. We milked them, sold the milk. Actually, I only lived in the village during the summertime, when I went to stay with my granny, because my parents lived in Limassol. Nana Niki – you met her yesterday – she is my grandmother on my father's side.'

For a while Eleni moved the tea glass over her lips, lost in her dreams. I tried to remember what Mum had told me about Safinaz's village. When it passed into the hands of the Turkish army, did all the villagers flee to the south? What had she said? Or did something like the population exchange that had happened in Turkey and Greece take place in Cyprus too? A sensitive subject for sure. I decided not to say anything that would make my indifference or my ignorance obvious. I took a sip of my tea, which in that heat hadn't cooled at all, and then a sip of brandy. When your insides heated up, you felt the outside heat less.

'Orhan arrived in our village – you can picture the scene. There was a big *platanos* tree in our village square. How do you say that – a plane tree? Exactly. Beneath that tree was our coffeehouse and across from it was the church. We girls were sitting in front of the church. The bus stopped right there in the square. The men were in the coffeehouse and your *babas* got off it like a tourist, with a bag on his back. Everyone turned to look and what did they see?'

'What?'

With a tiny smile at the corner of her lips, she again looked into my eyes. Her cheeky, boyish expression made her look so much like Petro.

'*Fantasma!*'

'What?'

'A ghost!'

'What ghost?'

'Damianos's ghost, of course. He'd come back!'

'Damianos's ghost?'

Surprise had caused me to raise my voice, which made us both laugh. The brandy had begun to do its business. Eleni refilled our empty glasses. We clinked them and giggled as our eyes met.

'*Akrivos*. Exactly. We were all thinking that Damianos had returned. *Panagia mou!* Holy Mary, Mother of God! Back from the dead, like Jesus Christ. It hadn't been forty days yet. One of the girls ran and fetched my darling granny, and when she saw Orhan, poor thing – bang! She fainted. Ah!'

She had said 'bang!' with such a funny accent that I couldn't help laughing. This time Eleni only smiled.

'May he rest in peace, my darling Damianos. He was such a good person. Like my big brother, you know?'

I couldn't have known. But then I thought about it. Since Nana Niki had brought up Damianos, and since Eleni used to spend her summer holidays with her grandmother in the village...

'Damianos was older than me. I was a child, and he was a *palikari*. You know "*palikari*"? It means "young man". But he used to play my games with me and at night before I went to sleep he read to me. Then, when I became a young woman and he became a grown man, we would walk beside the river together. Our village was so beautiful, Melike. So green. There was a forest, and water splashing in the stream. Even when I was very little, Damianos always took me seriously. We talked for many, many hours. I adored him, Melike. Very much. *Parapoly.*'

I sighed. The light which had been pouring through the

windows of the kitchen dimmed, as if someone had turned down the lamp. A cloud must have passed in front of the sun. A sudden gust of wind lifted the blue and white checked curtains in the windows overlooking the courtyard. Maybe it was going to rain. Summer rain. This time it was I who got up to refresh our tea. I could imagine how Damianos's death had shattered Eleni. Then when Dad appeared so soon after...

'How old were you when Damianos was shot?'

I returned to the table with our tea glasses and sat across from her.

'I had just finished high school. I was eighteen and had come back to the village for the holidays. My father was working at a facility in Larnaca that year and my mother was in Limassol. At the end of the summer, I would go to England for university. The first tragedy happened in July. Damianos was shot. They brought the bodies to the village, piled up in the back of a truck. Nana Niki and I held each other and cried and cried. That was why when I saw Orhan getting off the bus, I thought it was a miracle. Almighty God had sent us Anastasia's other son. Because he was Kosmas, we all hugged him, loved him, embraced him, petted him. He didn't understand. He laughed. We thought: this is a miracle. But the tragedies were not finished, in fact they were only just beginning.'

She stopped talking. With her empty brandy glass in her hand, her eyes again focused on the door behind me. She stayed like that. In the courtyard, birds began to twitter nervously. The blue and white kitchen curtains again lifted in the breeze; the screen door slammed. A familiar wave of fury swelled inside me. I was thinking of the fresh, young Eleni just out of high school the summer Dad turned up at Safinaz's village. While Eleni was weeping night and day beside the body of her childhood sweetheart, Damianos, a miracle occurred. A man the exact duplicate of her one true love got off the bus. It wasn't Damianos, however. It was a miserable Orhan, who'd just had to identify his mother's body, discovered tangled up in a fishing net. A confused young man following the trail of his mother's suicide. And then, in front of him, there appeared strong, statuesque, shiny-faced Eleni. An eighteen-year-old island girl with pearly teeth. Eleni, a mere seven years older than me, Orhan's daughter, whom he'd left on the opposite shore... Seven. A mere seven years.

Were you seduced so easily, Dad?

The screen door slammed again. Eleni suddenly jumped up from where she'd been sitting dreaming and slapped her forehead.

'Oh, *Panagia*! Holy Mother! I got lost in my talking. I was going to make *dolmadakia*. You know them? *Yalanci dolma* – stuffed grape leaves, the small ones. My Petro loves them so much. I make masses and masses, and still he can't get enough of them.'

Now she'd turned into a Greek mother, devoted to her son. Squinting, I looked her over. I slept with your son, Eleni. Not only did I sleep with him, but he... Suddenly I felt proud. *I am madly in love with you, Melike. Me-LI-ke.* Good for you, Petro! I smirked. An eye for an eye, a tooth for a tooth. You seduced my father; I seduced your son. I went over and lifted the lid of the pot on the stove, smelled the chicken-liver pilaf.

'Did you put cinnamon in this?'

'Yes, I did. I put allspice in it too, *ma*, then I forgot about it.'

'Don't worry, we'll roll the dolma together.'

She looked into my face doubtfully. Somewhere in the distance, thunder rumbled. The kitchen had become very dark. She grabbed a purple plastic clothes basket from beside the door and ran outside to get the washing off the line. I took the grape leaves from the tray on the counter and placed them on a chopping board in the middle of the table. I scooped the pilaf into a bowl, washed out the pot, dried it and spread a thick layer of grape leaves across the bottom. Eleni came back in and stood in front of me with the clothes basket resting on her hip. She was smiling. She was a good-hearted woman. She didn't see the world through a lens of rancour like I did. You and I, Eleni, are from different worlds. You would get on well with Sinan. When people like me come across people like you, all we know how to do is compete with you. So, let's see which of us rolls the best dolma!

I settled at the table, put a leaf on the chopping board in front of me, filled it with pilaf, quickly rolled it up, wet the edges, and closed it. Eleni raised an eyebrow. My dolma was better than I'd thought it would be. I placed the thinly rolled grape-leaf dolma on top of the leaves in the bottom of the pot. She came over and looked inside the pot.

'*Po po po kukla mou!* Well, well, well, babe. We call dolma that are rolled that thin "*Poli*-style" because it is only in Constantinople that they are rolled like that. You are very skilled!'

There was a crash of thunder, this time right over the courtyard. The black and white cat leapt through the window. Eleni lit the lamp. I began to roll another dolma with pride. At the same time I was thinking about women who used their cooking skills to lure in men and keep them hooked until they died. By the time Eleni came back into the kitchen after having checked on Dad, I'd filled the entire base of the pot with my masterpieces. She sat down opposite me. Black clouds were lowering over the courtyard and, in spite of the light over the table, the kitchen was dim. We continued rolling dolma in silence.

It began to rain. As raindrops the size of grapes beat against the windowpanes and fell into the courtyard, from the corner of my eye I watched my stepmother's nimble fingers. She was working swiftly but couldn't roll them as thinly as I did. I sent grateful thanks to my husband, who'd taught me the fine art of dolma rolling.

After it had got really dark outside, Petro returned home to find Eleni and me in the damp kitchen that smelled of brandy and steeped tea, rolling grape-leaf dolma in competition. A wide smile, which he was unable to hide, spread across his face. He was soaked through. His hair was plastered down, making his head, which anyway seemed small above such broad shoulders, look like a hazelnut. He had just opened his mouth to say something when we heard Dad's voice from the room across the corridor. He had woken up and was calling for me.

Then the electricity went off.

27

The Scream

By the time I got to my father's room, the summer rain had turned into a storm. Lightning flashed in the distance, thunder rumbled and fat drops of rain were drumming against the windows. When I closed the door, the flame of the candle I was carrying stuck to a plate flickered. Dad was sitting up in bed, his back supported by pillows. A gas lamp was burning at his head. It seemed that in that remote corner of the world the electricity often got cut off, so gas lamps were kept handy. I glanced at the drip stand but couldn't tell whether there were drops passing through the tube or not.

'Come and sit beside me, my Melike.'

With his right hand he patted the empty side of his bed. Setting the candle down in front of the mirror, I went over, sat cross-legged on the blanket on the unused side of his bed and turned my face towards his. I was happy that for the first time since I'd arrived I felt almost chilly. I wrapped my arms around myself. The smell of wet earth filled the room from the screened window, which was slightly ajar.

'Were you able to sleep, Dad?'

'I swear, I don't know whether "sleep" is the right word;

it's more like losing yourself. Morphine takes you to very different worlds. One day, if we have time, I'll tell you about those worlds, between sleep and wakefulness, or, should I say, between life and death. Purgatory, an intermediary realm between heaven and hell, but... Oh, forget it. What have you and Eleni being doing?'

'We made dolma. *Yalanci dolma* – the vegetarian ones.'

He smiled. In the light of the gas lamp his eyes shone like they used to in the old days, then dimmed.

'Good for you, my daughter.' He pressed his handkerchief to his mouth. Between fits of coughing, he asked, 'Do you like Eleni?'

I didn't answer. Instead, I let my hair fall over my face and began plaiting it. He coughed a while longer, then folded the handkerchief and placed it on the bedside table.

'Melike, I want to tell you how I met Eleni.'

'Don't tire yourself. She's already told me anyway.'

'Really? How much did she tell you?' His voice was anxious – surprised, even.

Leaving my plait half-finished, I raised my head. 'She told me how everybody thought you were your twin brother Damianos when you first arrived. How she used to spend her summer holidays with Nana Niki while she was growing up and what good times she and Damianos had together. How she loved him very much. And so on.'

'Only that much, uh? She didn't tell you anything else?'

'Nope. Just that.'

He breathed a sigh of relief. He hadn't noticed that my voice had been shaking. I've worked out the rest for myself, Dad. How you bedded a woman who was just seven years older than your daughter. And how because of that you never came back to us. You made the land your mother had abandoned your own country. I bit my lip. He nodded without speaking.

'You need to hear the rest. It's not how you think it was.'

I took a pillow for myself and reclined against it, stretching out my legs. We were sitting side by side now. It was easier that way. We were both facing the door, which moved in and out of view from among the shadows. The house was filled with the aroma of grape leaves boiling in lemon-flavoured water. I had left Petro in the kitchen, winding around his mother like a hungry, wet kitten, waiting impatiently for the dolma to cook. For a while we sat there without speaking, listening to the murmur of mother and son coming from the kitchen.

A flash of lightning lit up the room. The mirrored dressing table, the wooden chair beside the bed, the door, the gas lamp and the water jug all flashed momentarily, as if they'd been X-rayed. Dad was muttering to himself, trying to remember where we'd got to in the story. He'd mentioned a knife, and screams shattering the night, and how fate dealt out different amounts of cruelty to different people, but I didn't want to remind him of that. He began to speak.

'The night that I want to tell you about... Nana Niki had taken me into her house as a guest. Eleni was also there. The Turkish army had landed in Cyprus. The war had begun. The village was ominously quiet, and dark because of the nightly blackout. Eleni's mother was sending her message after message to come back to Limassol, and Eleni was replying, "I won't run away and leave Granny. If I leave her, she'll die." Later, she was proved right. The old women who'd been left behind in the villages all died in their homes. When the incomers turned up, they had to throw their bodies into the wells.'

He stopped and reached for his handkerchief. The bed shook as he coughed. This fit was more violent than the previous one. I sat up straight. Not knowing what to do, I touched his hunched-over back. How thin he was. With the tips of my fingers I could feel every one of his ribs. He waved his hand to signify it was nothing. The coughing didn't stop. I tried to reassure myself that if there was anything to worry about, Eleni would have heard it from the kitchen and would run in and help. But what if she didn't hear him? Outside, the storm had become more violent. Rainwater was streaming down onto the courtyard paving stones from a gutter right outside the window. I got up and closed the window. My shadow on the wall was gigantic in the candlelight.

'Dad, please, don't wear yourself out.'

Wiping his mouth with his handkerchief, he sat up straight and drank some water from the glass beside the bed. I went back to my place beside him. He raised his hand with difficulty and put it on my leg. Through the thin cloth of my white dress I could feel its heat. He drew a scratchy breath.

'We don't know whether there'll be a tomorrow or not. Be a little patient, my Melike.'

I gave him a sideways glance. In the shadows he looked very diminished. His illness had hollowed him out, leaving only the dry husk of a tiny old man. But he wasn't the age yet to be old. If he'd been healthy, we might have climbed hills and mountains together. All of a sudden, the pain of the time we'd lost fell heavily upon me. Why hadn't I set my pride aside and searched for him earlier? Why had it never occurred to me that I might more fruitfully find the attention I'd repeatedly sought in the beds of countless men in a newly established friendship with my father? Don't die, Dad! Please, don't die now. Let the rain stop. Let's go out to the courtyard together and look up at the stars. Let me rub my face against yours. Let your beard tickle my cheek. I held his hand. It was bone dry. When he began to speak, his voice was shaking. I leant near to hear him, my head grazing his shoulder bone. I closed my eyes and waited in vain for him to stroke my cheek, but he had already returned to that ill-omened night and was insistently calling me to join him.

'I woke up suddenly. There was shouting and screaming in the streets. The sounds of fighting. I got up and went to the window. Everywhere was dark. Even the moon had conformed to the blackout rule and was hiding. In the distance a forest was burning, crimson flames devouring the foothills. When my eyes had adjusted to the dark, I was able to make out three men roughing up an old man in the doorway of a house across from the coffeehouse. It was a hot night, very hot. I was naked. I threw on a shirt, pulled on a pair of trousers and rushed outside. Eleni and I came face to face on the stairs. She was gripping a tiny candle in her trembling hands and her eyes were wide with fear. I put my hand on her shoulder. She gestured that she was going up to the roof, but first she ran to Nana Niki's room.

'By the time I got down to the street, one of the men had pinned the old man against the door and was pressing a hunting rifle into his chest. The others, with gas lanterns in their hands, were bringing out anything of value they could find in his house. What would they find in a poor villager's one-window house? Forks and spoons, a sack of dried beans, one or two candlesticks. They were drunk and speaking Turkish to each other.

'When I saw other men going in and out of other houses, I realized it was not just three or four people, but many. Several of them were wearing military trousers, but in the darkness I couldn't recognise the uniform. They might have been members of a paramilitary gang. I could tell immediately from their speech that some of them came from Turkey, but I didn't know how many of them there were. Much later, when they asked for witness testimonies so that they could try and capture the perpetrators, Commander Mete asked me these details, but I was unable to answer properly. Commander Mete worked very hard to find the suspects, but did they ever catch anyone? I don't think so. The only thing I could recall was that they had bats in their hands and were knocking down doors and breaking windows. Some were clambering over rooftops, some were shouting into dry wells. I approached the men across from the coffeehouse who were threatening the old man. One of them aimed his rifle at me. I put my hands in the air.'

I raised my head from Dad's shoulder and looked over at the candle, whose flame was strengthening as the candle got smaller. Its reddish-yellow light was reflected in the mirror, filling the room with strange shadows. Dad's face had also turned red. Anxiously, I squeezed his hand, which was quivering on my knee. His rasping breath settled.

'I spoke Turkish with them. When I told them I came from Istanbul, gave them my name, their attitude softened. One of them even came over and patted me on the back. "Holy shit!" he said. "You came all the way from Istanbul to lend a hand to us fighters for Islam. Come with us. This village has bugger all. There's only this old fart's milking machine. Let's get that and leave. The villages over in Omorfo will have more for us. The infidels left everything and ran away. We'll go and take the loot." I looked at the old man. He was quaking from head to toe, at the end of a double-barrelled rifle. I knew him. He was one of the men who'd been sitting in the coffeehouse when I got off the bus. Mr Hristo. He'd told me about my mother, about Damianos, about Pasha coming to the village. "Let the poor man go," I said. At first they laughed. "Aren't you ashamed of yourself, torturing an old man like that?" I continued. They stared blankly into my face, as if I was talking a different language. Then one of them, probably the ringleader, grabbed the collar of my shirt and pushed me against the wall of the house alongside Mr Hristo. "Hey you!" he bellowed. "Are you one of us or aren't you? Are you an infidel? Or a spy?" His breath stank of cheap whisky. His face was filthy. He had a beard, but he was young, much younger than I was. He took a knife out of his pocket and clumsily pressed it against my throat. It was so sharp, it pierced my skin slightly. Imagine it – I could feel warm blood running down my neck.'

I was holding my breath, my eyes fixed on the candle flame. When I was little, Dad used to tell me scary stories, then praise my courage. He used to say that other children would have wet their pants listening to those fairy tales full of demons. I used to hold my breath back then too, but a part of me always knew that it was a story and that the horror wasn't real. I was in my dad's arms and after a bit of a fright I could return to the safety of his lap. Now, however... Now, that safe lap was itself in a terrifying situation. I didn't know where to turn. Everything I knew was being pulled out from under me. Dad continued.

'Just then I heard a scream. The shattering scream of a woman... sharp, splitting the silence of the night in two. The eyes of the man holding the knife to my throat glittered in the darkness. His hand loosened a little and he turned and spat in old Christo's face. "You didn't tell us there were women here, you old fool." With his head he gave a signal to the man with the hunting rifle in the old man's chest. The rifle exploded. Mr Hristo, his eyes open, a surprised expression on his face, collapsed at the bottom of the wall. My tongue was frozen. Without removing the knife from my neck, the ringleader began to push me in the direction the scream had come from. Screams were coming from all over the place; young girls were crying, begging. But the scream I'd heard hadn't come from one of them. I knew it was Eleni. How was I so sure? I don't know. When your life takes a sudden swerve, you don't question your intuition. It's like fate winks at you momentarily. You see your life ahead for a second and all disappears into the void. I knew where we were going. The ringleader was right behind me, with his knife at my throat, and he was shoving me towards Nana Niki's courtyard.'

I closed my eyes. I didn't want to hear the rest. I didn't need to hear the rest. Please, Dad, that's enough. I felt sick to my stomach. Oh, God, let all this be made up. Let him be inventing a dramatic past to deceive me so that I'll forgive him. I would put up with being cheated and deceived by any man after this. Just let the scene he's describing belong not to the past but to his imagination. My father raised his hand with difficulty and stroked my cheek. The skin of his palm was rough and burning hot, and his touch wasn't comforting like I'd hoped. When he began to speak again, his voice was muffled, as if it was coming from the bottom of a deep well. He proceeded to tell the story very slowly. He was rubbing his ribs, as if every sentence that came from his mouth was piercing his chest.

'They had brought Eleni down to the courtyard and laid her on the table in the middle of it. Only a couple of days earlier, Nana Niki, Eleni and I had eaten supper at that table. The three of us had drunk homemade wine, raising our glasses to the memory of Mother and Damianos. Eleni had got Nana Niki to sing for us. And now... now...

'In the dim light of the gas lantern I saw everything. One of them was holding Eleni's arms, another was covering her eyes, a third was pulling down her pants. When the ringleader saw them, he got furious. Forgetting me, he yelled at his men. "Hey! Didn't I tell you that I would be the first!"

'I didn't know what to do. Somehow in the darkness I found an oar and attacked the ringleader with it, but his men caught hold of it. The bastard with his hand over Eleni's eyes turned to look at me and let go of her for a second. Eleni tried to escape. When she stood up, she saw me. "Orhan, is that you? Please help me!" she shouted. The ringleader heard this and smirked at me in a way that made my blood curdle. "This is your sweetheart, eh? You come all the way from Istanbul to get into an infidel girl's knickers and when we want to get in there too, you try and hit me over the head with an oar, eh?"

'His men held me tight by my arms. "Bring him close. Shine a light here," he ordered. Then... then he unbuckled his trousers. One of them covered Eleni's eyes, but they saw no need to suppress her screams. One by one, they all raped Eleni. Not just once either... As for me... I...'

His voice drowned in the bottom of the well. His hand, which had dropped down beside my leg, was trembling. I moved in close to him, put my arm around his shoulders and hugged him tight. It felt as if his bones would crumble in my arms. His whole body was shaking now. He was a child, small, shrivelled up, terrified. I pressed his hairless head to my shoulder, covered his mouth with my hand so that he would stop talking. Our gigantic shadow danced on the wall, a Melike and an Orhan in a fast embrace on the bed. A small piece in the puzzle we called time. Confession. Despair. Cruelty. Fate. Which was it? Thunder crashed directly above us.

'Shh, Dad. It's okay. Don't tell me any more now. I understand.'

He shook his head. In a tearful voice, he murmured, 'My… They wouldn't let me turn my head away. They made me watch from beginning to end.'

He began to cough again. On the one hand he was coughing as if he would suffocate; on the other hand he was struggling to form broken sentences. I had never felt so helpless. I loosened my arms. Reaching for the glass, I tried to get him to drink some water. His hand hit the glass, spilling water on the bed.

'Dad, please…'

'Eleni's clothes were torn. She was hurt. They had clumps of her hair in their hands. Even in that weak light I could see the imprints of their fingers on her neck. The knife. I turned my head. Screams filled my ears. They had rounded up the girls they'd found in empty houses, even in the church. From every corner of the village came shrieking, weeping, imploring. It was as if the men were rabid. One of them was yelling, "This is nothing compared to what your people have done!" Others were raping women in front of their children. I heard it all. It was as if the village was one huge, screaming mouth.'

He closed his eyes with his hands. His cheekbones were like razorblades; tears ran down his hollow cheeks. I had never seen my father cry. I didn't know what to do. I crawled across the bed and awkwardly tried to put my arms around his neck as I whispered, 'Dad, you're torturing yourself. This is enough. You don't need to say more.'

But he wasn't hearing me. With his hands over his eyes, he was crying hoarsely.

'There were soldiers among the men. One of them

was addressed as "sergeant". They were filled with an incomprehensible hatred. Screams… from everywhere screams were rising. It didn't stop. Why? Why didn't it stop? I thought she would have fainted with such unspeakable things being done to her, but…'

A sob caught in my throat. I tried begging. 'No more, please. Stop talking!'

'… her clothes were in tatters. There were cigarette burns on her breasts. Her face had gone purple.'

I closed my ears, began shaking my head back and forth. 'Dad, please. It's enough. Okay. I don't want to hear the rest.'

It was thundering outside, the windows were banging, and rainwater was draining noisily from the gutter onto the courtyard. But Dad's frail voice still found a way into my ears. Dad's voice. The only thing left to me of him. I was prepared to give even that up if only he would shut up.

'Between her legs was bloody… She was screaming, "Kill me!" They… they laughed shamelessly, then carved a star and crescent on her stomach with a knife. They couldn't get enough. They still wouldn't let me look away. The whole night, from the beginning, over and over again…'

'I said that's enough, Dad! I do not want to hear more. SHUT UP! SHUT UP! ENOUGH!'

The door to the room opened noisily. Gigantic shadows wavered on the wall. Petro came in. He looked anxious. Right behind him, Eleni appeared. I jumped from the bed barefoot and threw myself into Petro's arms. Dad was having another coughing fit. Eleni ran to his side, turned the morphine valve and knelt down next to the bed.

Petro took me from the room and carried me up the stairs to my room without unwinding the arms that I had circled around his neck.

28

United

In the darkness of the room I rested my cheek against Petro's broad chest. His heart was beating wildly. I closed my eyes. As he hugged me to him even more tightly, the sobs that had started to build when I was with my father and had then got stuck now leapt out of my throat and became a torrent. I gripped Petro's shoulders with all my might in order not to drown in my tears. Lightning flashed twice somewhere close by, one flash and then another, illuminating the old-fashioned bedstead in the middle of the room. Thunder roared. Then everything was buried in blackness.

I don't know when Petro wove his huge hands through my hair, when he pressed my back against the wall, when his lips slid down from my sweat-drenched neck to my breasts. He was still supporting me in his arms, and I was crying. It was dark. He pinned me between the wall and his body, held me there. He was naked above the waist, and he too was covered in sweat. I was holding onto him as if he was a lifebelt, clasping him with my arms, my legs, with all my strength – my whole being. The skirt of my dress had slipped up to my thighs. He wiped away my tears, whispered something into my ear in his own language. I softened. He glided slowly and softly into the opening door. I held my breath and waited. With a slight contraction my womb drew him into its depths; with one motion, he was joined to me. We weren't making love; we were doing something else, something that I didn't recognize, something greater than ourselves. We were together, but we were also alone in the darkness. My body seemed to have widened so much that it could take in not only a penis but a person, no, not just a person, all of humanity. We were melting in the heat of a fire more powerful than desire or passion, melting, separating into pieces, coming together again, then melting again. That familiar wave swelled inside me. I buried my head in his chest, wet with sweat.

'Shh, shh,' he said. Heavy raindrops were beating on the rooftop. 'Keep going like this. Let it come by itself.'

Another flash of lightning lit up Petro's face. A face that showed a mixture of pain and desire. For the first time in my life I was allowing a man to unite with me in the depths of my being. I no longer knew where I ended and he began. Our bodies were connected, with a single rhythm, a single heartbeat. This was intercourse with no beginning and no end, beyond all time. The two edges of the chasm inside me that I thought could never meet were coming together. He wasn't Petro any more. I wasn't Melike. We weren't even a woman and a man having sex. We were simply two bodies mediating for the unification of all disconnectedness in the world.

We were two flowing arteries about to merge.

I leant my head back, unwrapped my arms from around his neck, let the wall behind me take my weight. My legs were around his waist, my back against the wall. Beneath my skin the wave continued to swell. I took deep breaths, trying to slow my excitement. Petro covered my mouth with his hand. In the darkness, the whites of his eyes gleamed. I took the fleshy part of his palm between my teeth. Still my moaning wouldn't stop. I wanted him to hurry up. I was dying to explode, to break into pieces. My womb would cure humankind. Recovery would sprout in the deepest part of me and with a single burst would extend into the past, the future, the entire universe.

I don't know how many minutes we were able to continue in that position, my legs around Petro's waist, Petro supporting me with one arm, but our lovemaking seemed to last for hours. When it ended, we collapsed over by the fireplace, breathless, half-naked, both of us sopping wet. My ears were ringing and my head was completely empty. I was like the earth after rain – moist, soft, replete. A mature acceptance had settled within me, taking the place of my traumatised response to the horrors of the night that Dad had transported me to. Cruelty was real. It existed. It was in every one of us. The seeds of hate as well as the seeds of love were sown into the essence of what it was to be human. This truth might burn me inside, but it was irrefutable. It existed. That was all. To deny the existence of evil was to struggle in vain. The only thing I could do after this was to choose love over hate and anger. That would be my tiny contribution to the world.

Later, after we'd moved to the bed and I was lying with my head on Petro's bare chest, listening to the sound of the rain on the roof, I considered that I wasn't as alone in the world as I'd thought. Petro lifted his arm and hugged me. His breathing slowed and he fell into a post-coital sleep. The lightning was receding. Good things were going to happen. Even in the face of such brutality, something good could be salvaged. The night Dad, Cem and I had gazed up at the stars came to my mind. My brother's face appeared before me, getting mixed up with Sinan's. Dad's voice rang in my ears. He was young and strong. Thunder rumbled for the last time. Then I went to sleep.

In my sleep, I felt safe in a way that I never had before.

29

I Am the *Tragodia*

'But the real tragedy happened when Orhan and my mother got to Limassol.'

Petro was sitting cross-legged in the middle of the messy bed. We had woken at sunrise to the crowing of a rooster. The rain had stopped and the clouds above the mountain peaks were turning from purple to pink. Half dreaming, half asleep, we had made love one more time. Afterwards, I had wanted to lie there a while longer, enjoying the afterglow as we listened to the clinking of nearby cow bells, but Petro had got up and opened the window, determined to tell me the end of Dad's story, the part that involved him.

Holding onto the cotton blanket, I propped myself up on one elbow.

'For the love of God, Petro, what further tragedy could there be?'

Staring into my face with his honey-coloured eyes, he waited. He paused, sighed, and then continued with the story.

When he finished talking, an hour had passed. I hadn't shared an opinion or asked a single question, but had listened to the whole story in silence. Having been alerted to what had gone on, Turkish commander Mete had come to the village and rescued Dad, Eleni, Nana Niki and the other villagers who'd survived. He'd had them taken to a hospital in Nicosia. Petro described the hospital in the war-torn capital city at length, as if he'd been there himself – children coming in with arms and legs torn off, young men with their intestines ripped open, rape victims who'd lost their minds. Dad and Nana Niki spent days and nights on blankets spread out on the corridor floors, alongside the relatives of other victims. By the time they eventually set out for Limassol, Eleni had come out of shock, but she was still unable to walk. It would be two years before she could once more. 'She still drags her left foot, you might have noticed,' Petro said. I had not noticed.

'You were saying something about the real tragedy? Did something happen to them on the way to Limassol?'

'No. That is a story in itself. For your father to go to the south of Cyprus at that time was, in a word, insane.'

'Why?'

'The war, Melike. The war! Do you know how many fathers and sons there are whose remains have still not been found? Just think about that... Some Greek men were loaded onto ships, supposedly being sent to southern Turkey, to prison camps in Adana. Not a word was heard of them after that. On the other side, three Turkish villages, already emptied of men, were overrun and the women there raped for two days. Everybody was slaughtered – schoolchildren, babies still in their cradles – so that there would be no witnesses. That's the sort of times we're talking about, *yavri mou*.'

He sounded not angry but resentful, as if I had participated in the persecution myself by not knowing about such things.

'Okay. So how did Dad manage it?'

Of course, that wasn't the real question on my mind; instead I was thinking: since the situation was that dangerous, why did Dad take it upon himself to go with Eleni and Nana Niki to Limassol? When he had his own family, why did he risk his life for these women he'd only recently met? Of course, I couldn't ask that. If I did, it would show how twisted my soul was. It was obvious that Petro and his family saw my father as a hero, a knight in shining armour.

'It was Nana Niki who eventually came up with a solution. Your dad was sent back to the village from Nicosia. Commander Mete wanted him to testify as an eyewitness, to help catch the rapists, so your dad went back to Nana Niki's village with him. Everything had been looted, but Orhan found the deeds to the house and the baptism certificates among the books that Nana Niki had described to him. And also the student ID card belonging to his twin brother, Damianos.'

A dog barked outside. Noise from the chickens flapping about in the courtyard filled the room. My head felt like it weighed a tonne. I lowered it onto the pillow. Petro filled a glass of water from the pitcher in his lap. Without offering me any, he drank it down in one gulp, then wiped his mouth with the back of his hand.

'Did Dad use his twin brother's ID to cross into the south?'

He nodded. His swollen eyes and morning grogginess made his face seem more childlike than ever, perched on top of such a huge body. I reached out and touched the sparse hair on his chest. Sinan came to my mind. If he had called last night, he wouldn't have been able to reach me. I felt upset and covered my bare breasts with the blanket.

'And then what happened?'

He sighed.

'You don't have to tell me, Petro.'

'I do.'

His voice sounded very stern. I didn't know what to say.

'Okay. I'm listening.'

He swallowed and started talking very fast, as if he wanted to get it over with.

'Your father brought Mum and Nana Niki safe and sound to the house in Limassol, then handed them over to my grandmother. My mother's father, Akilleas, was an officer at the time, in the war. Actually, a ceasefire had been declared, but no one was allowed to leave the island at that point. Your father had to wait a few days, maybe a week or more, before ships and planes began operating again. Then Akilleas, my grandfather, returned home. He was Nana Niki's oldest son. He grew up with Damianos, but when he saw your father he didn't faint like his mother had. He was a military officer, a tough man. I never knew him, but my mother has told me about him. He was very cold, very distant with your father – who'd saved his mother and his daughter from the village and brought them safely to Limassol – because he was a Turk. But he didn't inform on him either.'

'Is this what you mean by the tragedy?'

'Not at all, Melike. You still don't understand?'

'What?'

'I am the *tragodia*.'

'You?'

He nodded. His eyes clouded over. Thinking he was playing a word game, I turned the half-English, half-Greek sentence he had spoken around in my head. *I am the* tragodia. *Tragedia?* Tragedy? No, I didn't get it.

'A week later, just as your father was about to leave

Limassol, they took Mum to the hospital for a check-up. It was there that they realized that she was...'

He swallowed. His eyes stared into mine, begging for help.

'This is harder than I thought it would be... it was there that they realized my mother was pregnant.'

I froze, then sat up straight, wrapped myself in the blanket. My ears were humming.

'From that night? From the night of the rape? Oh, Petro!'

He tried to speak, but no sound came out of his mouth. I filled another glass with water and handed it to him. He drank it down. Putting the glass back on the bedside table, I was angry with myself. What a question I had asked! The boy had said it. 'I am the tragedy.' Ah! My stupid head! My selfish head, busy all the time with its own melodramas. My insensitive antennae that couldn't even pick up on a man's pain.

When he began to speak again, he was unemotional. I understood. He wasn't going to try and work through the trauma of his history with me now; the trauma of being a child born of rape. I was relieved, but at the same time I felt strangely jealous. If he wasn't going to open up to me about this deep, shameful scar, then to whom? I was both his big sister and his sweetheart – even his lover, wasn't I?

'During that time, so many women got pregnant that the Church legalized abortion in Cyprus. Did you know that? But my mother would not consider an abortion. My grandmother was a very religious woman and she supported my mother's decision. But rape, virginity, pregnancy outside marriage, these subjects were off limits in Cyprus, particularly at that time. Even today, they're still taboo subjects in a large portion of the country. It's been thirty years now, and women who were raped then still won't talk about it. Most of the women were immediately married off. People of means sent their daughters to England – though not the pregnant ones, of course.'

'Eleni?'

'Her family also tried to get her married.'

'To my father!'

Anger rose inside me.

'No, to someone else. As I said, my grandfather Akilleas could not accept your father, although he knew that he was technically pure Greek. Anyway... anyway, your father was definitely planning to return to Turkey.'

We were silent. Petro stared into my eyes. He looked tired.

'How did they eventually get married then?'

'They eloped.'

'They eloped? How?'

'The usual way. The way you'll be familiar with. Like running away with a girl from the village.'

My heart tightened. I would probably have preferred that Dad had been forced to marry Eleni. 'But... but you just said that Dad was looking for a way to return to Turkey at that point. Eleni and her family thought he was definitely going to leave.' My silly voice was shaking again.

'That's right. But that same night, when they came back from the hospital, the night Mum learnt that she was pregnant with me, my grandfather had already found a man who would marry his daughter. A friend from the navy, an old man whose wife had recently died. Mum knew the man. He wasn't a bad man, it seems. Probably he was a good man, since he was willing to take Eleni, a rape victim, but Mum didn't want to marry him. She cried and cried. But she couldn't get her father to relent. So—'

'When she couldn't get her own father to relent, she asked my father... and they eloped.'

I turned my face towards the door, not wanting him to see that my eyes were filling with tears. Dad had probably felt sorry for Eleni, which was why he decided to marry her. Add to that his shame at having witnessed her torture, and a conscience that must have been in torment. Okay, those were credible reasons, but still... More than anger, I felt a deep sadness. Was that really sufficient cause for you giving up on your family, Dad? For abandoning me?

'In all the confusion, Orhan was able to continue using Damianos's identity papers. Because of that, they could get married and settle down here. The houses the Turks had abandoned in a great rush of fear were distributed to the new arrivals. My mother and your father moved into this house. They didn't even change the old furniture. In the room downstairs where your dad sleeps, the photograph albums of the Turkish family who used to live in this house are still in the drawers. Mum kept them in case one day someone might come for them. Then I was born.'

'So you're saying that Dad played the role of a knight in shining armour and saved young Eleni.'

I heard the sarcasm in my voice and my cheeks flamed. Petro didn't seem to notice.

'And me. He saved me too, Melike. Your dad – my dad, our dad, Orhan – is a very brave man. *Parapoly.* Very brave indeed.' He sighed. 'That he should be leaving this world so soon is very difficult for me to bear. It's not fair. Not fair at all.'

He turned his head towards the window and looked out. A sweet morning breeze blew in, making goosebumps on my bare, sweaty back. Petro's face had become so sad that I wanted to hug him, to lay his head on my breast. A motorcycle roared past on the street. I bit my lip. I was going to lose my father. We were going to lose him together. I reached out and held his hand. Maybe Dad had called me here not to hear his confession but so that Petro and I would not have to grieve alone. So that Petro wouldn't be on his own. He wanted us to find something else, not just each other, when we lost him. But what? Thinking about it made me more confused.

'What about you? How did you learn this story, Petro? Your father – my father, Orhan – did you always know that he wasn't your real father?'

'No, I didn't know. It came out because of a blood test.'

'A blood test?'

'Yes. It was ten years ago, when he first got leukaemia. I went to the hospital by myself, without telling Mum. I'd told everyone I wanted to be Dad's bone marrow donor, but whenever I brought up the subject, Mum always put me off, even though I knew they were looking for one. The doctor jabbed a needle into my arm and took my blood. After that, everything unravelled like a sock.'

I thought back to that vivid evening when I'd first seen Petro in front of the Bloody Church. Not even a month had passed since then, but it seemed like years ago. It was as if that evening was somebody else's life – a book I'd read or a movie I'd seen. Petro's honey-coloured eyes had glittered in the sun as it painted the Istanbul skies red. He had pulled me into a hug as if we'd been friends for forty years. And we had been, it turned out. There was a forty-year connection between us – maybe even longer. Our fates had been drawn as one.

We were two siblings who had believed in the same father.

When I met Petro, I'd said '*palikari*' to myself, the Greek word for 'young man in his prime', wondering how I knew that term. His lips were as shiny as cherries on the branch.

He was full of life. How could a person born as the fruit of such deep shame have turned into this sparkling young man? I now understood why my father was so important to him. Dad had taken that burden from him. He had cherished him, raised him as his own son. Being Petro's father had lightened the shame my dad had felt at having witnessed such an atrocity. And I had paid the price. So who was going to save me now?

As if he had read my mind, Petro spoke.

'My father – that is Orhan, or rather Damianos, the name I knew him by until ten years ago – did everything he could to ensure that I grew up a healthy child. I am indebted to him.'

The blanket slipped and fell away, leaving me stark naked.

'Damianos – really? Did they tell you your father was called Damianos? You didn't know he was Orhan until ten years ago?'

'Yes – while I was growing up I had a father named Damianos! Adults would whisper when they mentioned him. From time to time we would visit Nana Niki. My grandfather Akilleas died a few months after I was born, and after that my mother began to see the rest of her family again, so occasionally she and I would go to Limassol, but my dad – that's your dad – would never come with us. With a child's intuition I had the feeling that a big secret was being hidden from me. But that same intuition whispered to me that I shouldn't try to delve into it. Kosmas, Damianos, Orhan... those names passed from ear to ear. For example, whenever I asked something about my father's childhood, Orhan would hesitate and Mum would answer for him. Later I realized that they were weaving a past for him based on Damianos's childhood in the village. I think it was more to make themselves believe it than for anyone else. When I found your photograph in the drawer,

I sensed that the truth was different from what they were telling me. But I never imagined it would be so different.'

He smiled.

'You know, your dad and I must have learnt Greek together. When I was saying my first words, he would repeat them after me. We exchanged sentences with each other. Now your dad speaks Greek like the locals, Melike. You can't tell the difference. As for what happened to me... I was deceived twice over. It's like a Greek tragedy, isn't it? I'm not exaggerating, Melike *mou* – I am the *tragodia*.'

For the first time that morning we laughed. He reached out and pushed my hair, which was falling over my shoulders and chest, behind my back. Without taking his eyes from my face, he passed the tips of his fingers over my bare shoulders. How beautiful his eyes were. He opened his mouth to say something, something concerning me, us (us!), then changed his mind. Two rivulets of sweat were rolling down from under my breasts to my stomach. I wiped them away with the blanket. Petro glanced at my belly. I immediately covered it.

'What are you looking at?'

'Nothing.'

'You're looking at my belly.'

'Is that illegal?'

'You shouldn't look at a woman's belly like that.'

He reached out and stroked it. I sucked it in. My bladder sizzled.

'Would you like to have my child, Melike?'

'You must be crazy, Petro!'

'Why should I be crazy?'

I shook my ring finger in front of his eyes.

A cloud of disappointment passed over his face. What? Did Petro think I'd leave Sinan and marry him? Did he imagine I'd settle down here and raise his children, with chickens running around the courtyard? Was that the fantasy that was behind the smile that had spread across his face when he'd seen his mother and me rolling grape-leaf dolma the previous night? I stared at him in bewilderment. His lips were pouting like a child's. I got into his lap and wrapped my bare arms around his neck. He dropped his sulky head onto my shoulder.

'Petro, *agapi mou*, my love—'

A door slammed downstairs. Thank goodness for that, for I had not the slightest notion how I was going to continue that sentence. Eleni's footsteps sounded on the stairs. Petro raised his head, listening with a cat's wariness. Then he removed my arms from his neck, pushed me off his lap and sprang off the bed. The pile of sheets and blankets we'd been sitting among for hours got tangled around his feet and he only just managed to keep his balance. Somehow he gathered up his clothes, which lay scattered in front of the fireplace, and hurled himself out of the room before Eleni reached the top floor.

Alone in the room, I stretched out on the bed. My head felt heavy, the room was very hot and my stomach hurt. Dad was a brave knight, a hero. He had saved Petro. In order to save one of us, he had sacrificed the other, but in the end both of us had lived. He, on the other hand, was dying. We would both lose him together.

I tried to push his death out of my mind. My right hand went to my belly. What a crazy boy that Petro was! Even so, I wondered what it would be like to have a baby with his young sperm. Combining our features in my head, I tried to picture the child we might have. Petro wasn't handsome like Sinan, but he had an interesting face. A nose like a hawk's; close-set, honey-coloured eyes; wide shoulders; a good height.

He could inject life into my already diminishing supply of eggs. All of a sudden, my eyes filled with the pain of a loss I had never mourned. From the very beginning Sinan and I had made the decision not to have a baby. Neither of us was interested in children. We never wavered from that decision, or even questioned it. We used to snigger at the nightmares our friends with children endured. I always used birth control. My hormones respected my decision; my eggs submitted to their fate and caused no problems every month. They were more regular than Safinaz's clocks.

Would you like to have my child, Melike?

Although I'd had sex with a considerable number of men, this was the first time in my life that I'd been asked that question. Was it really? Surprised, I thought back over the men in my life. Take Mert, for example, an engineer; he fell in love with me and begged me to leave Sinan and marry him. He left his wife for me, but even he hadn't asked me that question. He might have thought about it, but he never expressed it. A tear slid down my cheek and plopped onto the sheet. Another one followed. Maybe I'd actually been longing for a man to want to have a child with me? It seemed there was a sensitive scale inside me that judged a woman's essential worth by her aptitude for motherhood. The desire to create a human being together – a little bit from your family, a little from mine. Petro saw me as worthy of this shared relationship. But Sinan... Never once had Sinan wanted to share in the creation of anything with me. Not a project, not a work of art, not a child! It was enough for him that we walked side by side. My husband even preferred to cook by himself and serve me the results on elegantly white-clothed dinner tables.

In front of the window a turtle dove was cooing. Because

her cooing sounded like 'Yusuftsuk' – *dear Yusuf* – in Turkish, the bird was called Yusuftcuk. 'That's Yusuf's wife who is calling,' Safinaz used to tell me when I was a child. The male bird Yusuf flew away one day and since then she's been calling his name over and over. That story affected me. How apt it was, in fact. She was a mother whose husband had abandoned her home and her child. For Yusuf, read Orhan. There was an ache in the middle of my ribcage. I thought about Dad and Eleni, about all that Petro had told me, about the women who'd been raped by soldiers for days, about the war. The island divided by barbed wire. Decisions made and borders drawn without consideration for the human suffering it would cause. Unending deliberations related in a dry manner by the TV newscasters of my childhood. Petro's childhood.

Misery, sorrow, tears.

Why would we want to bring another human being into this world of ours? Blood rushed to my head as I recalled how often Sinan had posed that question, in those exact words, to his friends as they sat around drinking. I sat bolt upright in the middle of the bed, totally naked. Whenever Sinan said that, I would nod my head in a mature fashion. The women would feel sorry for me; the men would grin, dreaming of having sex with a woman who hadn't given birth.

Remembering this, I grabbed a nearby pillow and thumped it on the bed, then threw it onto the floor, stood up and kicked it. It flew into the air and hit the opposite wall, causing feathers to dance through the room. I picked it up and hurled it against the wall with all my might. That still wasn't enough. Again and again! It was as if fire was travelling up my spine, all the way from my coccyx to the crown of my head, setting my whole body alight. Again I kicked the pillow, stamped on it, flung it against the wall. Again and again and again. Finally it burst. Down feathers scattered in the air, falling like snowflakes on my naked body. Panting for breath, I stopped and watched as they fluttered to the floor, twisting and turning. My head was emptied, like after sex. A drop of blood fell onto the pile of white feathers covering my feet and spread where it fell. Then another drop. I leant down to look. From inside my left leg, a red line was flowing down to my ankle.

Quickly, I slipped on my dress, and my underwear, which was balled up beside the fireplace. I found a tampon in my handbag, inserted it, ran downstairs, still sticky, without having washed my face or brushed my teeth or made the bed, and rushed out of the house without anyone seeing me. I started walking through the empty village at top speed. I had to get as far away as I could. Why? From what? From the life I knew. From the Melike I knew. From everything. And everybody. I had slight stomach cramps – the sobs of my grieving uterus after another wasted ovulation. My broken, lost egg mingled with the seeds that Petro had emptied into me.

A breeze from the mountains blew a feather that had got lodged in my hair out in front of me. I followed it.

30

No More Games

It was market day in the village and everyone seemed to be heading for the square. I followed two old women dressed in black who were both carrying a string bag in one hand and dragging a trolley bag behind them with the other. I was very hungry and was hoping there'd be someone selling savoury pancakes in the marketplace. Maybe I could buy a pancake and then sit in the village coffeehouse and have a glass of tea. It had been quite a few days since I'd had time on my own, time to clear my head. Suddenly I missed my calm mornings back home, at Uncle Niko's bakery on Buyukada. Would I ever again enjoy that sense of tranquillity as I sat eating a steaming bread roll under the lightening sky?

I stumbled on a stone and one of the old women turned and stared at me, smacking her toothless mouth, further creasing her already wrinkled face. Here I was again, wandering the streets like a crazy person, my hair and clothes all dishevelled, just like... just like when? Oh, of course! Just like that morning I woke up head over heels in love with Petro and set off along the narrow streets beside Istanbul's ancient city walls. But this time there weren't any children to cry when they saw the matted hair tumbling down my back and the strange light in my eyes. This village was made up entirely of old people. All the women standing behind the stalls in the marketplace selling nothing but tomatoes, peppers and courgettes seemed to be over a hundred years old. Not one of them returned my greeting; not one of them smiled. They all had the hard features of mountain people. They just followed me with their eyes as I walked by in front of them, shaking their heads. Several smacked their mouths.

As I passed the miserable tomatoes and stunted courgettes, the market we used to go to in my childhood came to my mind. It wasn't held in our small village but in the town, on Thursdays. Mum, Mina and I would take up our string bags and baskets, and walk along the path that smelled of sage and thyme. On the path we would meet dark-faced villagers with their goats and donkeys loaded with tall baskets. In the market, women sold herbs they'd gathered from the mountains, vegetables, fruit, detergent, cloth, sacks of dried beans. Mum used to do our shopping there every week, but she never managed to get on with the market sellers. They couldn't believe that she spoke Turkish. She would say perfectly clearly, 'Two kilos of apples,' or 'Let's see if your eggs are fresh,' but the sellers would just stare at her blankly. Sometimes a brave one would step in and try speaking to her in broken German. This went on for months. For months she did our shopping by pointing to the tomatoes or peppers and writing numbers on paper bags with a pen to bargain over a price. If it had been me or Mina doing the talking, we would definitely have been understood, but this had become such a matter of pride for Mum that we were forbidden from opening our mouths at the market. She was seen but not heard. She was not one of them, so she did not exist.

The more her existence was eroded in the unhearing ears of the villagers, the more angry she became, until eventually she couldn't stand it any longer and stopped going to the market altogether. Mina and I took over and did all the shopping. Mina did the bargaining and I kept the accounts.

But the market in the village where Petro had grown up was different. For one thing, it was very quiet. Nobody was loudly hawking their wares, and nobody was bargaining. The women, dressed in black from head to toe, sat in the shade of awnings stretched taut over their stalls, not even talking to each other. They just sat there with their hands clasped in their laps. Shopping consisted of an exchange of money and paper bags. It was as if we were in a hot, soundproofed cocoon. Even the flies and bees, which the old women indifferently swatted, weren't buzzing. At the entrance to the marketplace, trucks stood in the direct sun like hibernating monsters. I felt uneasy, as if water had clogged my ears and I was deaf to the sounds of the world. Maybe the heat had swallowed all noise.

My stomach growled. I had given up on the idea of pancakes with herbs. Almonds? Walnuts? Bread? A bagel? I walked past the vegetable stalls. Nothing there. Figs piled on a stall up ahead caught my eye. I got a stomach ache if I ate fruit in the morning, but I filled a paper bag with figs nonetheless. I handed the bag to the seller to weigh and waited for him to tell me how much I should pay. His stare went right through me, then moved on. Without looking at what I was giving him, I pressed some money into his hand. He dropped it into the pocket of his tattered apron.

On the edge of the market, at the top of the street, an elderly man was selling detergents and cleaning materials with brand names I'd never heard of. A golden-haired dog was sleeping in the shade of a house with tightly closed doors and windows. When he saw me, he stood up, looking at me warily. This was all I needed! The people there had done everything except bite me. If the dog did that, I would run as far as I could from that village. But the dog just stretched his long front legs and yawned. Then he came over to me, wagging his very short tail, and stuck his nose right between my legs. How dogs loved menstrual blood! I took a couple of steps back and he raised his large head and looked at me with his mascara-lined eyes. He was a beautiful dog. His white paws looked like socks against his golden fur, but the funniest part was the stubby black tail at the end of his huge body. Had the rest of it fallen off, or been cut off, or had he just been born like that? I didn't know, but it made him very lovable.

'What's up, big boy? What do you want?'

I petted him, took a fig from the bag and held it out to him. He wasn't interested. He turned his head towards the flat field at the end of the street, which was filled with yellowed weeds. Then he left me and set off in that direction. That had to be the edge of the village. He stopped halfway, turned to see if I was coming and wagged his stubby tail.

'Are you telling me to come? Where are we going?'

Without taking his eyes from my face, he stretched out his front paws, raised his rear end and yawned again. Then he looked up at the sky and gave a short bark.

'Okay, I'm coming. Wait for me, you naughty thing. After all, you're the only living creature in this village who's shown me any warmth.'

My hand went to my mouth. What if they understood Turkish? This had been a Turkish village, after all, and since so many old people lived there, probably all of them had grown up speaking two languages, like Nana Niki. Well, so what? I'd have said the same thing to their faces. Walk on, doggie, let's go.

At the point where the street ended and the flat area began, we turned left onto a street that was separated from the rest of the village by a dry riverbed. On the left side was a row of terraced houses. On the right was a flat, dust-coloured field and then a small wooded area which contained a scattering of trees. The stone houses were solidly built, which was why they were still standing even though it was clear that no one had lived in them for a while – probably at least thirty years. The doors were rotten and broken, the windowpanes shattered, and spiders had created a whole country on the ceilings. Dead. Everything there was dead. The broken plates, torn-up books and beds with holes in them that I could see through the pane-less windows indicated that the houses had been looted at some point. Seeing a bookcase through one of the windows, I approached the door curiously. The dog waited at the threshold, looking doubtfully into my face.

'What? Aren't you going to protect me? Or are you afraid of ghosts?'

He wagged his short tail and lay down in the shade of a shutter hanging by a single hinge. Crossing his front paws elegantly, he sighed. He reminded me of a tour leader who was fed up with people seeing the division of his island as exotic tourist fodder.

I stepped over the shards of glass around the doorway and went in. The interior of the house smelled of mould and was surprisingly cool. I thought I might stay there a while just for the coolness. I went into the front room, where the bookcase was, pieces of glass crackling under my shoes. In the corners weeds had sprouted up through the cement. I passed armchairs without legs. A sofa with its springs hanging out stood in front of the window. Across from it was a table with all four legs intact, on top of which were three empty soft-drink bottles. My foot caught on something and I leant down to have a look. It was a magazine for young people, written in English, and the cover photo was of a female singer in 1970s clothes. The magazine was grimy and mildewed. Seeing it brought back familiar emotions. It was like being transported back to the time of my childhood, to a world that had been frozen at that point. But I couldn't bring myself to pick it up. Everything in that house – the enamel plates in the sideboard with broken glass doors, the television table on wheels, the soft-drink bottles – had remained untouched, waiting there, beneath layers of dust and mould, to be discovered, just like the forgotten feelings inside me.

The inhabitants of the house had obviously left in a hurry, and on the assumption that they'd be coming back. Upon their return, I imagined, they'd return the empty soft-drink bottles to the grocer's to get their deposit money back, sweep the floor, then take a book from the shelf and stretch out on the sofa. As they were fleeing, the little girl would have been crying for the jars of preserved tomatoes she was leaving behind, the boy for his books in the bookcase. The mother would have comforted them, reassuring them that they'd be back. Nobody ever considered, when they left the house, that they might not. Not even Dad.

I sneezed, wrapped my arms around myself in my cotton dress. The possessions left behind by the people forced from their home had a fearful feeling of death about them. Even the summer heat wasn't enough to warm that soulless house. I went over to the bookcase. The books were thick with dust. A shiver passed through me as I read the titles on their faded covers. I recognized some of them. Those same books had been on the shelves in the apartment in Galata, where Dad used to write his articles. I would lie on the deer-patterned rug, swinging my legs in the air and reading out the titles while he was writing. These books' covers, colours and lettering were all so familiar, even though I'd never read them.

I pulled one of the books off the shelf and was suddenly speechless with fright. In the dark, empty space where the book had been were two giant lizards, clamped together. I tried to take a step back with my shaking legs, but I couldn't move. One of the giant lizards raised its head and hissed at me. The other one lunged towards the hand holding the book. It wanted back the screen behind which it had hidden for years. Its long tongue and sharp teeth looked scarier than a cobra's! I hurled the book into a corner of the room. The paper bag of figs which I'd been holding in my other hand fell to the ground, the figs bursting as they rolled along the floor, turning the shards of glass blood red.

I ran out to the street. Seeing me, the dog got to his feet happily. Covering my face with both hands, I collapsed beside him, keeping an eye on the door, in case those giant lizards gave chase and attacked me. Who knew how many years they'd been living there, clamped together in that dim hiding place. I'd been very frightened; very, very frightened. Immeasurably so. My heart was beating like crazy, as if it would never quieten down again. The dog nuzzled my ear and I put a hand on his head. It was warm. I calmed down a bit. Slowly, I righted myself. My tampon had slipped out of place and was about to come out. My clothes were probably stained. Suddenly I felt overwhelmed and began to yell in the middle of the street.

'I've had enough now! I'm going home, dog! I followed you and found this creepy place, but it's too much. I'm going back home. To my own home. Everyone has now said what they wanted to say, so my business here is finished. I'm going back to Istanbul, to the island. Do you understand? I can't bear this heaviness, this heat any longer. I've had enough. I'm going back home, to Sinan.'

As soon as those words were out of my mouth, the naked truth hit me in the face, right there in the middle of the street of terraced, looted houses. I wasn't going to go back to Sinan. I couldn't go back to him. It was impossible now. It was a decision I had unconsciously made long ago, or rather a truth I had always known but had run from. I remembered Mum's words: *There is more to love than the affection you feel for someone. That someone is a vehicle, a way for you to find the door. The secret is hidden somewhere in the story that you'll find beyond that door.* And it wasn't because of Petro – well, maybe partly because of him.

No, even if I hadn't been in love with him—

What? What did you just say, Melike? The dog cocked his head in curiosity and looked into my face. I wasn't in love with Petro… was I?

All at once my heart felt lighter. I took two big strides towards the top of the street. The marketplace awnings came into view. I was in love! Yes, in love. I'd been in love since the first moment I saw him. Since he first pulled me into a hug in front of the Bloody Church. The naughty-little-boy expression on Petro's face came into my mind. The way he'd looked when he'd suggested climbing over the wall into the Red School. Maybe before that, way before that. Maybe I'd loved him since the day he found my photograph. Was that impossible? At a point in time, Melike's photograph and Petro met each other and looked into each other's eyes with a childish love.

With light steps I passed through the marketplace. People's expressions seemed to have softened a little, maybe because the short-tailed dog was following me. I glanced at the eggs on the stalls, the bunches of mountain thyme tied with old twine. Should I go back to the house and make everybody a herb omelette, set an elaborate breakfast table?

Then I stopped. Wait a minute, Melike. Go back to where your chain of thought began. Go back to Sinan – no, I couldn't go back to Sinan. Okay. Go back to your *not* going back to Sinan.

I was distracted again by the old women sitting behind the stalls. This time I saw in their faces not grumpiness but pain. Pain at the island having been broken apart, the sorrow of exile, the longing for reunion. My father's story, Safinaz's secrets, the existence of my uncle, the war, Eleni and the women whose agony had no end. These were not the sufferings of strangers in distant countries that I might hear and feel momentarily sad about before quickly continuing on with my life. No, this was suffering that was worked into my bones, my marrow, my genes. This was the story of my family.

Maybe this was what it meant to have a native land – a large family with a common fate and shared grief. Maybe Dad had stayed because, beyond everything, he felt that this was his suffering, too. As for me, what was I going to do? If I left Sinan, what would become of me? All my life, even though I'd felt lonely, I'd never actually been alone. It hadn't been in my life plan. But if I was going to live my own story, like my mother always told me to, I would have to set out on this road alone. I remembered making love with Petro the previous night, the two sides of the chasm inside me connecting. I couldn't keep playing games, telling lies like I had done all my life. Mum was right. I had used Sinan as a shoulder on which to shed tears over other men, and up to now we'd managed fine. But managing was all we'd been doing. I had never been totally honest with him; I hadn't been able to. Now I had to put an end to this game and set us both free.

He would think it was because of Petro, of course. It would be difficult for me to prove otherwise... but anyway, that wouldn't be necessary.

The dog barked. A single, brief bark. I turned and looked. He was standing at the end of the street, wagging his stubby tail. The black lips around his pink mouth were upturned; he was smiling. Then he went around the corner and disappeared from sight. I followed him. The street was completely empty.

I bought eggs and thyme from an old man. He didn't have a bag so he gave me a basket as a gift. While I slowly walked home, my basket in the shade of the abandoned buildings, the stubby tail of the golden-haired dog wagged in my imagination.

31

The Battlements

The smell of the sea.

Seaweed, iodine, salt.

Putt-putt.

The sound of the fishing boat that had taken Dad away from the village at dawn that morning.

I woke up with a start. It was pitch dark outside and I was lying on my bed beside the window in the village house. I pulled back the curtain. The stars were large. Why had I woken up? Some power had ordered me to open my eyes. It must have been a nightmare – the dwarf, maybe. But no, I was eleven years old now and I no longer dreamt about the dwarf coming out of the wardrobe. Instead, I dreamt about murder. I was the murderer, but I didn't know who I'd murdered. The police were after me and I was running away. Panting. There was no way I was going to turn myself in, so I would have to spend my whole life on the run, guilty and afraid, a fugitive forced to pay my entire life for a moment's mistake.

In my muddled, drowsy state I couldn't seem to think straight. I reached out to the bedside table for some water, but there was no glass. In the chaos of the previous night, Dad had forgotten to leave water beside my bed. Bits and pieces were coming back to me. When Mina fainted, she'd dropped the glass she was holding and it had shattered all over the floor. Cem had caught her before she fell and had laid her on the couch. Dad's bloodshot eyes, Mum with a broom in her hand, sweeping up shards of glass, Mina's prophecy before she fainted... And Safinaz... Safinaz was dead. She had jumped off a cliff. Fishermen had found her. 'Witch!' Mum had called her a witch. I was the only one who'd heard her.

I turned over in bed, shut my eyes. A fat teardrop slid out. If only all of that had been just a nightmare. My heart hurt. But just as I was about to doze off again, a rooster crowed. It was the rooster from the top of the *mukhtar*'s cabin. He perched there all day, crowing nonstop. It was him. I don't know how I knew, but I knew it was him. I drew back the curtain again. A delicate light was breaking the darkness and the stars were fading. Wrapping the thin blanket around me, I turned over in bed again, and it was then that I saw the other bed. My brother was not there. I propped myself up on one elbow and looked carefully in the dim light. I was wide awake now. The room was narrow and Cem slept just an arm's length away from me. He was definitely gone. I could even see the indentation which his head had left on the pillow. Maybe he was in the bathroom. But no, just as I knew that the crowing rooster was the one who perched on the *mukhtar*'s roof, I knew that Cem had gone somewhere other than the bathroom.

Putt-putt.

I jumped out of bed and ran barefoot to the kitchen. Tiny fragments of glass crackled under my bare soles. Maybe a piece of glass had already become lodged in my foot and would go all the way to my heart. I didn't care. I was in a hurry. I pushed open the screen door and went out into the garden. On those hot summer days, you could forget about locking the door to our village house – we didn't even close it. The cool of the morning hit my sweaty neck, and the leaves of the fig tree rustled in the wind. I didn't know our village could get so cool. Behind the castle, the sky was still navy blue, but towards the sea its colour was changing; the world was being painted my favourite shade of blue. In the middle of that blue, Venus had taken her place in all her splendour. I shivered in my thin, pink nightdress. There was nothing to worry about. The sun was coming. Venus was the harbinger of the sun.

I left the garden and began to climb the path in my bare feet. I was going to the castle. The houses came to an end; the tangerine orchards came to an end; the dry weeds began. The village was still in a deep sleep. Both the rooster and the engine I'd just heard were silent; there was only a thin, rattling sound audible in the far distance. Our hill looked like a completely different place in the dark. Frightened, I began to run. Stones and brambles bruised my feet, but I paid no attention. I had to get to the castle as soon as possible. To the top, where the flag was, before it was too late. The police were after me. I had committed a murder. No! That was a dream. I should have saved Safinaz's body from getting tangled up in fishing nets. Safinaz jumping off a cliff.

Night and day, dream and reality, mingling together.

Breathless, I got to the castle. My feet hurt and there were trickles of blood coming from the scratches on my ankles. My brother was there. Of course he was there, under the lightening sky, sitting at the very top, between the battlements, right under the flag. He was looking at the sea through the binoculars he'd received for his fourteenth birthday. He must have seen me running up the hill. When I got near, he put the binoculars in his lap and reached out his hand. I climbed over the wall and we squeezed into the gap between the two battlements together, side by side, our legs dangling down from the castle wall.

The sea was as smooth as a sheet. Behind the uninhabited island the sky was turning red. Venus was rising hurriedly in order to escape from her father, the sun, who was about to swallow her.

'What are you looking at?'

Cem held the binoculars to his eyes again. 'Nothing.'

He wouldn't give his precious binoculars to me. He was afraid I would drop them, or smear them with my greasy fingers, or put them on the wall and scratch the metal. Just a few days earlier I'd left them on the windowsill, forgetting to put them in their leather pouch, and he'd gone mad when he realized that I'd touched the lens with my fingers.

I spoke very sweetly. 'Cem, please give them to me. I promise I'll be very careful. I'll put the strap around my neck. I want to look at the goats over on the uninhabited island.'

'Not now.'

His voice was very gruff. Gruff and broken. I was surprised. My brother was a gentle boy, a real prince, with blond curls and white skin. On the rare occasions he spoke, he never raised his voice. I turned as much as I could on the battlement where we were squashed together and scrutinized him. He had done something I never would have believed if I'd seen it in a dream: he'd come out in his pyjamas. Over them he was wearing a bright green waistcoat that Mina had knitted, and on his feet were his white rubber clogs.

'What are you doing here?'

He didn't answer. All his attention was focused on

something in the distance that I couldn't see. Just then the putt-putt of a fishing boat rose again. Cem's body, leaning against my arm, tensed. The murmurings of morning – the tinkling of bells on goats' necks, the crowing of the rooster perched on the top of the *mukhtar*'s cabin, the beating of my heart – all drowned and disappeared in the sound.

'Give them to me, Cem! What are you staring at like that?'

I grabbed the binoculars from his hand. In an instant his white fingers were empty.

'No, Melike!'

He made a desperate attempt to grab back the binoculars, but I had already looped the leather strap around my neck. He sighed, defeated. He always gave up easily. With a triumphant expression I held the binoculars to my eyes. The sea and the sky merged in hues of purple and pink. At first I saw everything in duplicate: the uninhabited island, the sunken tomb, a motorboat anchored in the distance. I couldn't focus the lenses: my eyelashes got in the way and the sound of the engine distracted me. I turned the binoculars towards the jetty. I was still seeing double. I was doing something wrong, but I couldn't ask Cem for help. He'd retreated into silence anyway.

I was just about to give up and return the binoculars to him when the two lenses matched up and the fishing boat appeared in a single circle. There was only one person on the boat. A man sat cross-legged in the bow, in front of the nets. His black curly hair was too long for a village man's hair. It fell down his neck like a lion's mane, so thick and so tightly curled that the wind couldn't disturb even a single strand. Holding the binoculars with one hand, I touched my own hair with the other. I was trembling. Cem tried to pull the binoculars from my eyes, but I didn't let him.

'Stop looking now, Melike. Those binoculars are too heavy for you.'

'Shh!'

Dad's back was turned away from us. He was looking straight at the uninhabited island in front of him. Venus had risen. Dad wouldn't be able to take his eyes off her. 'When she's there, you can't look anywhere else,' he'd said one morning when we were out fishing. In Greek mythology, Venus's name was Aphrodite, the goddess of love, beauty and pleasure. For a reason I couldn't understand, when Dad talked about her, I would feel jealous. I felt jealous now.

As I stared at Dad's straight back, I tried to imagine how he might look while he sat there in the boat. Were his eyes bloodshot like they'd been last night? I pictured him as he'd been then, his elbows resting on the table, combing his fingers through his hair. The bottle of raki on the table between him and Mum, the two of them both having a drink without hiding it from each other, for once. He'd looked anxious later on, when he was holding Mina's wrist while she lay fainting on the couch. Was he still anxious now?

It's like hell over there, Mr Orhan. If you go, you won't ever come back.

I had just opened my mouth to shout when Cem grabbed the binoculars from my hand. The leather strap was still around my neck. I toppled onto him.

'Stop it, Cem! What are you doing? Are you crazy? I'll fall off.'

My brother then did a completely unexpected thing. He held me by my shoulders, pulled me to him with all his strength, wrapped his long arms around my child's body, in my nightdress, as if protecting me from a storm, and pressed my head to his chest. I could barely breathe. Other big brothers and little sisters in the village would play practical jokes on each other, play games together, sometimes fight, but Cem and I never did any of that. So this was a real surprise, and I knew he wasn't joking around or playing a game. He didn't loosen his grip; he kept squeezing me, as if he was wringing water out of me. I was suddenly frightened. He wasn't acting like Cem.

'Cem, let me go! What are you doing? Stop it! You're suffocating me, Cem!'

I tried to catch sight of the sea between his arms that were holding me like a press. The motorboat looked tiny to the naked eye, a piece of wood floating amid the dozens of islands scattered across the blue-green bay that embraced our village. My brother was squashing my face against his chest, covering my eyes with one hand, cutting out the light. His hand smelled of wild mint. In the darkness there was only the putt-putt of the engine. My whole body was suddenly overwhelmed by a great wave of weariness. Life was too heavy for me to carry. I surrendered myself to my brother's arms and he began to rock me like a baby, back and forth. Could Dad see us from that far away? Two children squeezed between two battlements, one blond, the other dark, in each other's arms. If he wanted to, could he see his two children rocking back and forth?

I tried to gather my thoughts. Dad must have gone out fishing. But why had he gone without me? It had been such a long time since we'd gone fishing together. We still got up very early every morning, but instead of setting out on a motorboat, we would read a book in the coffeehouse. When the sun had risen and Fisherman Ismail had returned, we would buy a bucket of fish from him and take it home. Mum didn't smile when she took the bucket from us in the kitchen any more. And we didn't make up tales for her now either – for example, how we had caught a sea bream that morning, or how a huge rock bass had got away. We used to make up such great stories, and Mum would laugh. It wasn't lying when you made up stories so that someone you loved wouldn't be sad. But in recent months Dad would just hand the bucket to Mum silently and go to his bedroom, take a handful of money from the drawer of the bedside table and put it in his pocket. The next day he'd pay Fisherman Ismail with the money from his pocket, the same money that Mum withdrew from the bank in Antalya every month.

But Dad wasn't in the coffeehouse now; he was on a boat. That meant he sometimes got up before all the fishermen and went out fishing secretly, without telling me. I bit my lip. Cem had loosened his hold a little. My eyes filled with tears, not from sadness but from anger. I'd been betrayed. Dad had tricked me. Cem had closed my eyes so I wouldn't see. I was an incompetent idiot. Not a single fish ever got hooked on my line. Dad definitely wanted to get rid of me. A hot, unpleasant feeling like a slap hit me in the face. With all my might I shook off my brother's arms and leapt to my feet.

'Dad!'

The putt-putt of the engine swallowed my voice, as it did all other sounds. With two steps of my bare feet, which were used to rough surfaces, I climbed up to the top of the castle. Cem called something from below. The noise of the engine swallowed his words too.

The castle had been built on the top of a steep hill. I was standing on the highest point of the castle, high enough to hear the sound of the flag flapping in the wind. If Dad could see the flag, he could see me. He must be able to see me. I straightened up and found my balance, then raised my arms.

The wind blew through my hair, the skirt of my nightdress lifted in the air. My whole body was shivering. He needed to turn his head right now, look round and see how straight I was standing on the top of the castle, perfectly balanced. I cupped my hands around my mouth and screamed with all my strength.

'Dad!'

My voice resounded in waves as far as the sunken tombs, but the noise of the engine didn't let up. I tried again.

'DAD!'

Suddenly I felt dizzy. I stumbled. The goats grazing around the periphery of the steep hill seemed to come nearer and then further away. A hand grabbed my scratched ankle and pulled me down.

'What are you doing, Melike? Are you crazy?'

In the gap between two battlements my brother and I stood looking at each other. Cem's white cheeks were flooded red. His binoculars hung from his neck. I saw pain, not anger, in the blue eyes that were staring into my face. The putt-putt of the engine was receding into the distance. I opened my mouth but no words came. I laid my head on his chest. His skinny arms embraced me. This time he didn't squeeze the life out of me, didn't try to cover my eyes. The sun had poked its red head above the uninhabited island. We turned and quietly watched it rise. Cem's white hand had fallen on my chest like a dead bird. I wanted to hold it, but I couldn't. I let my hair fall across my face and hid behind it.

Venus had been overcome by the sun. She was somewhere in the sky, waiting for evening. The putt-putt of the motorboat Dad was on had gone silent. The fishermen were coming back in, heading for the jetty one by one, two by two, with their buckets and fishing lines. Cem jumped down, reached out his hand to me. Following his shadow, I began to walk down the path, which, now that it was daylight, had transformed back into the familiar route that I trod every day. Down around the *mukhtar*'s cabin, women were wandering about with baskets full of sage and thyme. My brother's head was low, his back bent. He'd grown so much in the past year that he didn't know where to put his arms, which were now swinging on either side of his body in a limping rhythm. I called out from behind him.

'Cem!'

He slowed his steps but didn't turn to look at me. The white rubber clogs that he took such meticulous care of had turned an ugly ochre from the dirt path. Everywhere smelled of dried weeds. I ran and caught up with him, blocked his way in front of the garden gate. Dust billowed all around us. I spoke breathlessly.

'Dad's gone to Istanbul for Safinaz's funeral. I heard him talking to Mum yesterday when you weren't there. They were drinking raki, making plans. Dad will come back next week. He's only gone to the funeral. Look at me, Cem!'

My brother raised his head and looked into my eyes. Then, dragging his feet like a wounded soldier in a retreating army, he walked through the garden gate with the bougainvillea twined over it and was lost from view.

He knew that when the motorboat had disappeared behind the uninhabited island, Dad had left us forever.

32

The Last Piece

Sinan wasn't answering his phone. I hung up, then dialled the number again and let it ring for a really long time. Still no answer. Maybe there was no reception. I looked at the screen. The foreign sim card in my phone showed full bars. Where could Sinan be? Perhaps his brothers had made him go to Bursa for a meeting about the hotel. He hadn't called last night either, though he had said he would. I checked for missed calls. Nothing. Nobody had called me since yesterday. Strange. Very strange. Had something happened to him? Should I call Mum? No, she'd worry unnecessarily. I'd try again in a little while. Maybe he'd call me.

Just as I was putting my phone aside, I paused. There was something else I had to do. It was so obvious – why hadn't I thought of it earlier? There was still one square missing, one last number required in order to complete the puzzle. One action. I sat down on the edge of the bed – which I'd made when I got back from the market – and flipped opened my phone, but then hesitated. What time would it be in Australia now? What time was it in Cyprus? Would I wake them up? A telephone ringing at midnight could only mean bad news.

I imagined my brother, his face anxious, bringing his finger to his lips as a signal to his daughter to be quiet. 'Shh. Your aunt – the one you've never met – is calling from Turkey. It's definitely bad news.' His understanding wife would pick the child up and carry her to her room, or maybe out to the garden. Were Cem's children still small enough to carry? I used to picture my brother grilling meat with his white hands in the green garden of his two-storey house complete with garage. The stereotypical Australian dream. In reality, I knew nothing about his life in Australia. He could as well be living in an old apartment in downtown Adelaide.

Pressing my fingers on the tiny keys, I quickly found his number. Sinan would be so disapproving if he found out. Calling overseas with a foreign sim card was bound to be very expensive. But I didn't care. I pressed the 'call' key without compunction. While the radio waves travelled at the speed of light from that remote village, across oceans and continents, to the other side of the world, I settled myself on the bed and took a deep breath. The phone at the other end began to ring. Maybe they weren't home. Maybe their phone number had changed. Why didn't I have Cem's mobile number? When was the last time we'd talked? It had been when his daughter Sofia was born. At Mum's insistence, I had called. Like actors in a play, we had made appropriate rejoinders and hung up. Was that seven years ago? Or ten? What year was Sofia born? I closed my eyes. How the years sped by. I couldn't distinguish one from the other any more. The phone kept ringing. I was about to give up when I heard my brother's voice at the end of the line.

'Hello.'

'Cem?'

Silence.

'Cem, hey. It's Melike.'

Still silence.

'Cem, forgive me. I might be calling at an inconvenient time. There's nothing to worry about. Mum is fine.'

His breath rustled in my ear. He must have been holding it for a while.

'Cem, I called about something else. Are you available to talk?'

'Wait a minute.'

He muffled the receiver and said something to someone (wife, son, daughter?) nearby. The sound was muted. Then he came back.

'I'm listening.'

For a moment I hesitated. Something inside me felt broken. Was that it, Cem? Just 'I'm listening'? Not 'How are you?' or 'Where are you?' or 'Is everything all right?' Had I done something to upset him; was that why he was punishing me by being so cold? I pulled myself together. Was this not why I hadn't called him in years, for fear of getting a cool reception? My automatic response was to equate being treated coolly with being punished. I needed to reverse that response. I wanted to establish a connection between myself and Cem, a strong, deep, meaningful connection. In my head I saw a brother and sister standing on a battlement, their faces turned towards the sea, their arms holding each other tightly. I leant back on the bed. A golden light was falling on the sheets through the closed shutters.

'Cem, I called you because… I need to tell you some things. About Dad.'

33

The Shrine

When I came down to the kitchen, I found Petro and Dad drinking tea together at the table. Eleni was scattering feed for the chickens in the shady courtyard.

Seeing me, Petro jumped to his feet.

'Melike *mou*! Where did you run off to? We were worried about you.'

I drew up a chair and sat down. I was feeling shy.

'Would you pour me a cup of tea, please, Petro?'

After my call with Cem, I had freshened up, then slept for a while. The angle of the light falling on the marble windowsill had changed; the heat had let up a little. Dad smiled. He looked good; there was a gleam in his eyes. He had got up, dressed, even shaved. The morphine drip was nowhere in sight.

Petro made himself busy at the stove. Dad and I locked eyes. He spoke in Turkish.

'Eleni brewed some tea infused with special herbs and had me drink it. That's what got me out of bed. Petro was brought up on those herbs and now look at him – he's as strong as an ox. I've never even seen him with a runny nose.'

Dad looked lovingly at Petro, who was walking towards the table very slowly so he didn't spill the cup of tea, which he'd filled to the brim. When Petro heard us speaking Turkish, his expression changed. I understood then that, before I'd come down to the kitchen, he'd been telling Dad something of what had happened between us. He was such a child! A child who confessed and expected to be forgiven. And he wanted to be a father!

I blushed when Dad caught my eye.

'Melike, shall you and I go for a walk, now that it's cooled off a bit? Let me show you our humble village.'

God! Now he was going to question me. Good. Bravo, Petro! But... wait a minute. How far could a man who could hardly stand up walk? Petro put my tea on the table, sat down beside me and out of the corner of his eye glanced at the phone beneath my hand. Sinan had finally sent a short message: 'Everything is fine, darling. I'll call you soon, don't worry.' It was as if he was sending a telegram, and paying by the word. I covered the phone with my hand. Petro looked away.

With his head, Dad indicated the wheelchair in the corner of the room.

'This thing is quite bumpy on the cobblestones in the village, but from here to the coffeehouse is flat and easy enough. You could push your dear daddy, couldn't you?'

He smiled shyly. He used to use 'dear daddy' in the past. Like when he was too lazy to get out of the hammock, I would have to make lemonade for my 'dear daddy'. I'd be at the most exciting part in the book I was reading and he would suddenly want to hug and kiss me. If I made a fuss, he would accuse me of not loving my dear daddy, my poor, dear daddy, my dear, helpless daddy. My dear daddy, who would make me feel guilty every time.

Petro intervened, saying something in Greek. He was obviously anxious. Dad turned to me.

'Do you see, Melike? I am entirely in the hands of my children. Our Petro is worried about me going out for a walk with you.'

'Our Petro' lingered on his lips. Had Dad used that pronoun on purpose? Our Petro. Yours and mine. The naive, honey-eyed boy we both loved. Oblivious to what was passing through my mind, Petro turned to me and blinked his long eyelashes.

'Until last month, he used to go out with Mum, Melike, but now... now... it's impossible. Very risky.'

Dad spoke up. 'What is the risk, Petro? I'm dying, as you know. Must I die without having enjoyed a frappé with my daughter in our local coffeehouse?'

It was weird hearing English words coming out of Dad's mouth. When we were children, whenever Mum wanted to prevent us from hearing something, she would say it in English, but I never heard Dad answering her. Feeling squeezed, he would mutter something incomprehensible in a quiet voice. As a graduate of the American High School, Mum mistakenly assumed that everyone understood English. While I was thinking about that, I noticed an expression on Petro's face that I hadn't seen before. His eyes were narrowed, his lips downturned. This was the poisonous look of jealousy. Was that possible? The wives of men with whom I had been having clandestine affairs used to look at me like that. Petro was jealous of me and Dad! I turned to him in surprise. I was probably smiling slightly. (I had smiled like that at the women too.)

Petro avoided my eyes and went and got the wheelchair and helped Dad into it. This was not one of those huge, unwieldly wheelchairs that I'd seen in hospitals. This was a smaller, sportier thing. I tried again to catch Petro's eye, but he wouldn't look at me. I felt like laughing. He'd gone to so much trouble to find me, trick me into coming all the way there, plead with me, and now he was jealous! Did that make sense, Petro? I reached out and patted his cheek.

Dad was buckling his seatbelt, which was similar to the ones on aeroplanes. When the belt clicked into place, he winked at Petro.

'Just in case! Today's chauffeur is a novice, an *acemi*.'

The three of us laughed at the same time, not so much because of what he'd said but because we'd found a word that meant the same thing in both Turkish and Greek. The tension was broken. With one sentence we had become Orhan and his children.

'Melike, my little one, you've woken up now, *kori mou*? Are you hungry? Wait a minute. Get out of the way, Petro.'

Eleni had come into the kitchen, a yellow metal watering can in her hand. This time it was me avoiding her eyes, as if we'd been caught red-handed. With a few short, swift strides of her sturdy legs, Eleni walked to the fridge, took out a plate of grape-leaf dolma and placed them in front of me.

'I hid these from Petro and saved them for you, dear daughter. Enjoy them! You want yogurt?'

I hadn't eaten anything all morning except for a few of the figs I'd bought in the market. At the first bite, I realized how hungry I was. The salty, bitter, sweet and spicy tastes of the dolma melted in my mouth. I moaned in pleasure.

'The ones you rolled were more beautiful. Weren't they, Petro?'

Petro responded with a blank stare to his mother's question, which she'd posed in Turkish.

'We never managed to teach Turkish to this Petro!'

After I'd finished the last dolma on my plate, we all went out onto the street together. Petro helped me lower the wheelchair down the two steps at the front door.

'There's a walking stick tied to the back. Use it if he needs to stand up. Raise the front wheels slightly if you need to go over a low step or if you encounter a biggish stone. The front wheels can get stuck because they're small. At the entrance to the coffeehouse—'

'*Asto*, Petro! Leave it! Melike and I will manage. Don't you worry, Melike is strong.' Dad gestured dismissively, looking very much like a bad-tempered old villager.

Petro had stopped on the front doorstep and was staring anxiously at my grip on the handles of the wheelchair. Eleni lovingly put her arm around her son's waist and pulled him inside. As soon as his mother was out of sight, I blew him a secret kiss, but that wasn't enough to wipe the concern off his face.

The sun was slowly setting behind the mountains, decorating the sky in reds and pinks. A sweet breeze had picked up and even the dun-brown mountainsides had come to life in the evening light. In springtime, when all the trees and hills were green, it might well be a quite delightful village. I began to push the wheelchair over the cobblestones.

'Look at how the Lord works, Melike, my angel,' Dad murmured. 'It seems like only yesterday that I was pushing your pram up and down the cobblestones of Galata to get you to sleep, and now it's you who's pushing your dear old daddy. I could never get you to fall asleep when I pushed you along our street or over by the tower, but you'd always doze off once we were on Camekan Street. The stones must have rattled the pram in a different way.'

I bent down to hear what he was saying. Pushing the wheelchair was harder than I'd expected, and my underused arm muscles were rebelling. This wasn't a baby in a pram, after all, but a grown man. Whenever the small front wheels hit a stone, Dad's body was thrown one way, his head the other. My palms were sweating; I gripped the handles tightly.

'Are you getting tired? We're almost there. Once we're past the coffeehouse, we'll take the road across from it. Just over there—'

'Are we not going to the coffeehouse?'

'No. I just told Petro that so he wouldn't worry. He was upset enough about that as it was – as you heard. There's somewhere else I want to show you.'

The marketplace stalls had been collected up and stacked in a corner under an awning. When we passed the coffeehouse, Dad nodded greetings at the men sitting at the old, Formica-topped tables set out under the grapevines. They greeted Dad silently in return. Some were reading newspapers, a couple were playing backgammon. It seemed they were used to seeing Dad in his wheelchair, for no one got up to ask how he was. They didn't even look at me for any length of time. Again, I had the feeling that people in that village didn't see me. Knowing perfectly well how silly I looked, I waved to them. No one waved back. This time I didn't care.

'There's only a handful of people left here now,' Dad said quietly. 'Nobody on this island encircled by sea wants to live in a remote village like this any more. All the young people have gone, and who can blame them? Two years ago they took a census and do you know how many people they counted here? Thirty-nine! Every one of them over fifty years old. Who would stay here, and for what?'

We'd left the village now and were on a narrow path,

which was easier than pushing the wheelchair over the cobblestones. On all sides there were bushes and cactuses and thorny weeds as tall as me. In the distance I could hear the jingle of cow bells. Two crows flew up out of the bushes as we passed, squawking.

Dad gestured towards the mountains surrounding us. 'There are villages scattered all through these mountains, but in some of them the population is down to just twenty or even fourteen. Once we're dead and gone, life in these parts will be finished, and maybe that's for the best. People around here haven't been able to get past the trauma of the war. The ghosts of those who've gone plague every aspect of life, which is why so many mountain people are so dour. In the cities, people have started afresh, and once they make it easier to cross the Green Line... Stop! Stop, stop! Oof! My head!'

He buried his head in his hands and moaned as he drew breath. I walked round to the front of the wheelchair and knelt down on the dirt path so that I could see his face. Bushes as high as my head were rustling in the wind. Rocks jabbed into my knees through the trousers I'd put on after my shower. Dad had closed his eyes. I didn't know what to do. I locked the brakes on the wheelchair. He began to rub his temples.

'Ah, this morphine – you've no idea how it entraps you. I told myself that I wouldn't take any today, so that my head would stay clear while I was talking to you, but now see what's happened. Oof! I've heard there are places in India where they tranquillize terminally ill cancer patients like me with heroin. Believe me, I dream of being there. Would it be so bad to bow out with a golden shot at the age of sixty-five?'

'Dad! Don't talk like that!'

'No, Melike,' he said gently, taking his hands from his face, his cheeks now even more sunken, 'I'm very close to the end now, which is why I brought you all the way here. I want to talk to you about that. But first, turn around and take a look at that.'

Hoping his pain had lessened, I raised my head and looked in the direction he'd indicated. The last rays of the sun as it set behind the hill were dazzling. I put my hand to my forehead to shield my eyes. When I realized what I was looking at, I was stunned. Amid the cactuses and olive trees were the ruins of an ancient castle wall, and right in the middle, glowing red in the setting sun, was a medieval gatehouse.

'Ahh!'

Leaving Dad right there, I walked over to it. Was this a dream? I touched the stones and a welcoming cool spread to my hands. It wasn't tall, but it was very old, built before the Ottomans, before the Venetians, most probably by the Lusignans, back in the thirteenth or fourteenth century. I stood inside the arched gatehouse and raised my arms. The heat and noise of the day faded. There was the flap of birds' wings up in the roof, and my nose detected a slight whiff of incense. The gatehouse was broader than it appeared from the outside, more like a cave than a rampart gate. Perhaps there had been passages here that led to tunnels under the ramparts at one time. Candles of varying sizes, some big, some little, had been set in niches carved out of the wall. There were a few glass bell jars with pictures of the Virgin Mary on them and many yellow and white candles, burnt down, melted, standing in their hardened wax. The place was obviously used as a shrine. Once my eyes had become accustomed to the dim light, I saw that someone had fashioned somewhere to sit, about the width of a bench, from fallen chunks of stone. On top of it was spread an old kilim.

Outside, Dad had got up from his wheelchair and, with the aid of his stick, was taking slow, cautious steps towards me. I leant against the cool walls of the ancient gatehouse and looked at him, a little old man in the shadow of purple mountains, one of the billions of people on earth who were born, lived their lives, then died; a man who'd made a few strides in life, had wanted to be loved, had erred, had experienced regret, pride, happiness – one of us, in fact. He would die soon. He would die and the world would keep on turning. Was the life of one person out of so many billions of any real significance? A swell of protest rose within me, became a knot that lodged in my throat. Yes! It was! For those few lives that he had touched, there was all the significance in the world. A person's existence had meaning, not in itself but in the connections they forged. My father and I had a connection, and that connection was valuable to me. I had spent my life denying its value, but now I was reunited with him, had accepted him and found consolation. My eyes filled with sudden tears. Oh, Dad, why had it taken us so many years?

When Dad reached me, he leant his back against the wall and caught his breath. One side of the ramparts was in shadow. On the other side the stones which the setting sun had painted red were blinking. Arm in arm we went into the gatehouse and sat down next to each other on the bench. My feet barely touched the ground. Dad rested his head against the stones.

'Isn't this a beautiful spot? It's cool even on the hottest day – did you notice how thick the walls are? It's been here since the time of the Crusades. I discovered it when I first came to the village, and although other people clearly know about it too' – he gestured towards the candles set around the walls, and the icons of the Virgin Mary – 'no one ever disturbed me when I was here. I would always come by myself, and I'd sit here and think, withdraw into my own head.'

He was silent. He was probably waiting for me to say, 'What were you thinking about, Dad? About me? About whether or not it was all right to have abandoned us? About whether or not you were living the right life?' I held his hand. So dry! Bones without flesh – truly 'just skin and bone'. I gazed up at the arched ceiling of the gatehouse.

Dad coughed. 'Melike, I... When I die, I want my body to be cremated.'

'What?' My voice echoed off the dim, eight-hundred-year-old walls.

'I want my body cremated. And the ashes—'

'Dad, please, let's not talk about that now.'

'No, on the contrary, now is exactly the time to talk about this. Because if we don't...' He coughed for a long time. 'Have you thought about where you'll bury me? In a Christian cemetery? Under which name? Damianos? Kosmas? In a Muslim cemetery, as Orhan Kutsi? In Turkey, where I haven't set foot for almost thirty years? In Cyprus? Cremation will solve all those issues.'

Safinaz's grave came to my mind. Her single, tiny, narrow grave beside the city wall. The morning I'd found her grave seemed like centuries ago now.

'Listen well, Melike, my angel. There's no cremation in Cyprus, for religious reasons. There's none in Turkey or Greece either. You can't own your own body, even after death. But Petro spoke with Zeyno when they met in Athens. Zeyno will arrange everything in Germany, then send the ashes to all of you.'

I felt a pang of the old anger in my heart. So Petro and my

aunt had solved this problem without consulting me. Maybe my father's cremation was what they'd been whispering about when I'd been lying there with a fever. I let go of Dad's hand.

'Eleni isn't very keen, but she'll come round. You can either keep my ashes or scatter them in some beautiful place. That's up to all of you. You know I don't believe in the hereafter, but the idea of being buried under the earth makes me uncomfortable.'

I bowed my head.

'Are we agreed, Melike? Lift your head and look at me. Okay? Are we agreed?'

I nodded, almost imperceptibly.

'We are agreed.' My voice came out in a whisper.

'Good.' He reached under the wool kilim on the stone bench and took out a lighter. 'Would you light the candles, my beautiful daughter? Darkness falls quickly here. Let us not be food for bats!'

When he tried to laugh, another coughing fit overcame him. I got up and, one by one, lit the candles stuck in the niches carved into the stone wall. The dark gatehouse transformed into an amber-walled shrine. The shadows cast by my hair in the light of the flames were like a giant Medusa.

Dad pressed his handkerchief to his mouth and spoke in a hoarse voice. 'Petro told you the rest of the story?'

I nodded.

'I... I thought I would have enough strength to tell you everything, but I didn't. Melike, my angel, I didn't mean to hurt you.'

Maybe it was the light, but the expression that appeared on his face reminded me of Safinaz's the last time I saw her. Waves of emotion surged through me. What did he mean? When had he not meant to hurt me? I couldn't even ask him. I was afraid to, and I didn't even know why. I never came right out and said what I was feeling; I always told myself that I needed to be strong, so I hid my feelings and dissembled, did things behind people's backs. I didn't know any other way of conducting relationships. I had never learnt.

'But... but I was hurt, Dad.'

I stared down at my feet, dangling in the air.

'I'm sure you were, my Melike.'

I turned towards him. His face was wavering in the flickering candlelight. My eyes were brimming with tears, and I was desperately trying to hold them back.

'You might have stayed on here for very noble reasons. I know what you did. You saved Eleni's life. You were a father to Petro. But... but...'

I stopped. I couldn't say any more without making him feel bad. I searched for sentences that began with 'I'. Do you know what happened to me, Dad? I was destroyed, shattered, smashed into pieces. I never got over it, was never able to mend. None of us could heal. Not one of us. Not me, not Mum, not Cem. Was it worth it, Dad? Was it worth it, your sacrificing of us?

He reached out and stroked my cheek with his calloused hand. With my words came the tears. I surrendered to them.

'Why, Dad? Why? After you'd delivered Eleni safely to her family, why didn't you come back to us? She was with her family. She could have married that man and raised her son. Why did you have to commit to doing all of that, when you'd already done what you needed to.'

I swiped at my tears with the back of my hand. I hated myself. I was such a mean-spirited person. A good person would never have had such thoughts. A good person would have been proud of her hero of a father, would forgive him.

But my heart was dark. The people who committed murder, who tortured their children, were people like me. Evil people. Dad would be within his rights to get up and leave. But he couldn't get up and leave because he couldn't walk. I drew my knees up under my chin, wrapped my arms around them, and hid my face. Dad touched my hair. Don't caress me! I was not a woman who deserved to be loved.

'You are right, my Melike. I did not have to marry Eleni. And I wasn't going to marry her. I was married to your mother, don't forget.'

Sniffing, I straightened up and leant back against the hard, slightly damp stones, shivering inside.

'But she wanted to divorce you. Didn't she tell you to find a lawyer when you went to Istanbul? When you talked with her on the phone in the *mukhtar*'s cabin?'

He sighed, scratched his bald head.

'Yes, you're right. How do you know about that?'

'Mum told me.'

'Really?'

He sounded surprised, even happy. He was obviously pleased that Gulbahar had mentioned him after all that time, even if it was about something unpleasant. Oh, we humans! No matter our stage of life, we still need to be loved.

'Yes, your mother did say words to that effect, but I didn't take her seriously. Until…' He stopped, as if weighing up how much to tell me. 'Until I called again.'

'What? When? Who did you call?'

I sat bolt upright and turned towards him. It seemed there was a part of the story I still didn't know.

'I called your mother, of course. It was the 14th of August. I'd been wandering around the docks in Limassol, trying to find a way to make a phone call to you all. The country was war-exhausted – confused, angry, in disarray, wounded. Turkey had placed an embargo on Greek ships, the airport was closed, and phone and telegram lines were disconnected. I couldn't cross to the north part of the island because Nana Niki had burnt all the documents which proved my Turkish citizenship at the hospital in Nicosia, before we set out for Limassol. It was a good thing she did, or I would have been captured as a prisoner of war. They were rounding up all Turkish men at that time. I had no ID card and no passport, only my dead twin brother's student ID. I found a ship's captain, who said he could take me to Beirut in the cargo hold of his tobacco ship. I spoke English with him and we made an agreement. Buoyed up by that, I put aside my fears and doubts and begged my way onto an English army base – of all the telephones on Cyprus, the only ones with connections to Turkey were on their bases. I don't know whether they took pity on my situation, or if it was a twist of fate. I still wonder. My hands were shaking as the operator dialled the number and I dropped the receiver several times, but finally the line was connected. I had to continually scan my surroundings – if a spy had heard me speaking Turkish, I would have been reported – and I wasn't about to waste time chitchatting with the *mukhtar*, so I immediately asked to speak to your mother.'

He stopped talking. Sitting side by side as we were, I could feel the weariness coming off him in waves.

'Wait a second, my Melike. Let me lie down here. I don't have the strength to sit up any more.'

I shifted to the end of the bench and he stretched out on the kilim, with his head on my knees. I didn't know what to do with my hands. He didn't have any hair left to stroke. I looked down at the small face on my lap. His eyes were closed and his murmurings, which seemed to be coming from a distant dream, echoed around the dim walls that smelled of candlewax.

'"They've gone," said the *mukhtar*. "What do you mean, 'They've gone.'?" I'd had no way of calling the village for three weeks. Your mother knew I'd gone to Cyprus. She must have been terrified, I thought. But the *mukhtar* said, in his rudest, most familiar tone, "Orhan Bey, did you forget what your wife said to you when you talked last time – that you should find a lawyer?" No, I hadn't forgotten. Quite the contrary. When I was in Istanbul for Mother's funeral, I'd given the lawyer who was handling the inheritance business my power of attorney for a divorce, but... but that seemed like a different time. I'd become a different person since then.'

I put my hand on his forehead. He was burning up. He opened his eyes and smiled tiredly. I understood. He was using the very last breaths of his life to tell me this story.

'The *mukhtar* said, "That wife of yours got on the morning boat and ran off to Mr Ibrahim." Do you know what went through my mind when he said that, Melike? I wasn't thinking about Gulbahar or the teacher, Ibrahim. No. Not about them. The *mukhtar* said something about telegrams, the postman, writing in code, Antalya, but I didn't even hear him. I was thinking that the *mukhtar* hadn't liked me from the beginning. He'd laughed with me, he'd let me use his boat, but he'd never warmed to me. And it wasn't only him. Nobody in the village had warmed to me, to us. Taking you there had been a mistake. A big mistake. And now I was being punished for that mistake.'

He raised his head with difficulty and looked into my face. The quivering flames of the candles trembled in his black eyes.

'I apologize, Melike, my angel.'

My brain was roaring. Had I heard correctly? Had he said

sorry? In my heart a single note reverberated repeatedly. 'I apologize. I apologize. I apologize.' I leant my head against the stone wall and took a deep breath. There were wounds in my heart that had never scabbed over but had stayed hidden, untouched, and now a lone word had lit the touchpaper and those wounds were burning once again, as fiercely as when they were first inflicted. I looked at Dad. As the candlelight intensified, so the light in his eyes was dimming.

'When I got home, I was exhausted. Eleni was crying. They had gone to the hospital and learnt that she was pregnant. Her father was going to marry her off to an old man. I was dazed. Was this fate? As one door closed, was another one opening? If I started again, from scratch, I could leave my mistakes behind, I thought, the mistakes that were weighing me down like a nightmare. I would have a new identity. I remembered those thugs on top of Eleni, that moment of cruelty when she raised her head and looked at me. Her scream – "Save me, Orhan!" – echoed in my ear, together with the screams of all the young girls they had filled the churches with. I felt the knife at my throat. My helplessness. I would leave my Orhanness behind. I would become a new person. I would begin a good life.'

He stopped. Watching the flames dancing on the gatehouse walls took me out of the present. I thought of Safinaz's house; there, too, in spite of the dozens of clocks, I used to lose all concept of time. The dusty, rose-scented smell that permeated the furniture would transport my child's spirit into past histories that I had never experienced but remembered like a dream. I understood the longing Dad had felt, his sense of incompleteness. Throughout my life I'd felt that exact same way. He'd wanted to find completeness in Cyprus.

'That night, I carried Eleni in my arms and put her in the

car. Towards morning, Turkey landed soldiers on Cyprus for the second time. That attack was worse than the first. We drove around in the car for days looking for a safe place. Wild animals were roaming loose over the mined fields, starving. Somewhere we came across an old Greek woman sitting, with blank eyes, on the steps of a house peppered with bullet holes. We tried to get her to come in our car with us. "No. I'm waiting. They will return," she insisted.'

My brain was still howling. That night… while Mum was on the bus weeping over Mr Ibrahim's death, Dad and Eleni were enduring this utter savagery together. Were our destinies always to be forged like that, on dark nights and without our knowledge?

'By the time we finally arrived at this remote village, I knew I would never return to you all, my Melike. It was too late by then, much too late. That old Orhan had died somewhere on this island divided by bloody tears. I thought of myself as one of those men who had been executed by the side of the road, whose bodies have to this day still not been found. I cut all ties with Turkey, with all of you, with Zeyno. I was a person of this island now. Maybe that's what I had been from the beginning.'

With difficulty, Dad sat up beside me. Resting his elbows on his legs, he clasped his head with his hands. His breathing was shallow and rapid. He was groaning as he coughed, and muttering something.

'Okay, Dad, that's enough. Let's go home.'

I stood up. I was going to bring the wheelchair. He spoke from between his palms.

'There was nothing you could have done, Melike.'

I was standing in front of him. He was still bent over on his legs. It had got dark outside.

'I know, Dad. Come on, let me get the wheelchair and let's go. You've exhausted yourself.'

He lifted his head and looked at me. Flames were playing on his face. I was frightened. This, then, was death, slowly rising in Dad's face, sucking out the moisture, absorbing and extinguishing the light of his soul. The dark of Dad's eyes was fading fast. I saw the flesh of his face melting, his bones protruding.

'There was nothing you could have done. Do you understand that?'

'I know, Dad. I understand, of course.'

Impatient now, I glanced outside. The first stars had appeared in the sky. The wheelchair was where I had left it, under an olive tree. Dad reached out and grabbed my wrist, pulling me towards him with a strength I wouldn't have expected from his frail body. I stumbled. As I steadied myself with a hand on the stone wall and regained my balance, our faces were close enough to touch each other.

Without releasing my wrist, he whispered, 'You were a child. There was nothing you could have done.'

My head was spinning, my shoulders shaking. I wanted to be free of his grip. He squeezed harder.

'None of it was your fault, Melike. You couldn't have changed fate. Look at me. Look into my eyes.' The gatehouse had become a shrine, and all of a sudden the candles blazing in its niches flared simultaneously. In his sunken eyes I saw a deep, dark well. 'The game being played was larger than you, than me, than the two of us, than all of us. We played the roles assigned to us. That's all. It was no fault of yours, my beautiful daughter. I have always loved you very much. Do you hear me? I have always loved you so very much.'

When he squeezed my wrist a little harder, a sob escaped

from my throat. My whole body was shaking. My legs gave way and I collapsed onto the ground. Stones pricked my knees. My head fell into Dad's lap, my hair spread out over his skinny legs, and tears streamed down my cheeks and onto his trouser legs. Dad was stroking my hair, whispering the same words over and over in my ear, calming the lifelong rebellion inside me. I was a child. There was nothing I could have done. Those words turned into a prayer, a prayer which gained strength in repetition as the meaning penetrated my heart. The ancient gatehouse, as old as history, was a shrine and as we sat within it the world and time as we knew them were erased.

In that moment only the two of us existed.

Orhan and Melike.

Beyond all time.

A father and his daughter.

The candles flickered in the gentle wind blowing down from the mountains. I reached up to my hair and found Dad's hand. Our fingers locked together. The image of our united hands filled an empty square in the puzzle called time. A delicate gauze curtain was pulled across them.

34

The Accessories of Death

Cem didn't make it on time.

Dad took his last breath in the early hours, and Cem's taxi from Larnaca Airport reached the village very late that night. I greeted him at the door. His face was pale and his hair was sparser than it had been, but he was still stick-thin. We embraced wordlessly. I leant my head on his chest and he passed a tense hand over my back. I was exhausted. Eleni, Petro and I had taken turns at Dad's side through the night. Dad had thrashed about in an uneasy sleep, talked deliriously and moaned until morning. Then, as first light crept through the shutters, he breathed his last. The doctor Petro had brought to the house said that my father's heart had been unable to withstand the morphine.

Cem and I went into the dim room, me in front, him behind. Petro and Eleni were sitting together beside the bed where Dad lay. My nose was again filled with the smell of pine resin and pharmacies. Mother and son raised their heads at the same time and looked at Cem. They both had bloodshot eyes. In that sorrowful state they looked so much alike, they could have been big sister and little brother. Cem greeted them with a nod and remained standing. With the cloth Eleni had wrapped around Dad's jaw to hold his chin, Dad looked like a patient who'd just had his tooth extracted. We had also placed a knife on his stomach, right under his navel. The accessories of death: a cloth band for his chin, a metal knife to prevent the body from swelling. We had no idea whether they served any real purpose or not, but we'd followed tradition. A kind of ritual.

Without saying anything, Petro and Eleni left the room. Cem and I sat side by side at the foot of the bed. My brother couldn't look at Dad. I wondered if he'd have preferred not to have seen him like that. But after our phone conversation he'd got on the first plane over. When I'd first come into that room, just three days ago, hadn't I had trouble believing that this man, whom age and illness had ravaged, was my father? The most unbelievable thing now was that that moment had been only three days ago. It was as if three years had passed.

Without taking his eyes off the stripes of light on the floor, coming in through the closed shutters, Cem cleared his throat.

'Do you know, my daughter looks just like you, Melike. Her mother's blond, but Sofia has curly black hair. This genetics business is mysterious.'

He took his wallet from the back pocket of his trousers, pulled out a photo from among the cards, and handed it to me. I got nearer. The thin, pale face of the little girl in the photo was surrounded by a huge bush of curly black hair.

'If she likes, I can teach her how to manage this hair.'

'She would love that. She knows she looks like you, and I think she's even proud of it. I showed her a photo, which she liked very much. Now she puts on airs with her friends, saying she takes after her Turkish aunt. It seems exotic to her, I suppose.'

I took another look at the little face in the photo I was holding in my fingers. She had enormous brown eyes, very familiar eyes – sad, watery eyes, that looked as if they were about to cry. The iris, heredity's representative. Iris, the goddess of good news.

'May I keep this photo?'

'With pleasure.' My brother's eyes shone. He turned and looked at Dad for the first time. 'He lost so much weight.'

I nodded. We looked at the lifeless body on the bed for a while without speaking. Dad's hands were clasped on his stomach. He looked as if he had fallen into a deep and peaceful sleep.

'Do you remember how he used to snore?'

'How could I not remember? The windows would rattle.'

He smiled. 'I'm glad you called me, Melike.'

'Really?'

'Really. And you know what, if it had been him that had called and not you, I wouldn't have come. I would normally have fobbed you off too, given you some excuses about workload, and about Adelaide being a not insignificant distance from here – a thirty-hour flight to see a father I hadn't seen for thirty years was a big ask. But, I don't know, I heard something in your voice that day you called. How can I say – it was like…'

My brother thought for a bit. His brain hadn't been able to switch to Turkish yet. I helped him.

'… like a reuniting?'

He looked down and scanned my face. In the dim light of the room his blue eyes had deepened to navy.

'Yes, that's exactly it. I was going to say "connection". Tying together something inside me that's been broken apart. Even my wife could see the difference in me after I hung up the phone. When I said, "I have to go," she was very supportive, whereas usually she sulks when I have to go on a business trip. So, tell me, how did Dad persuade you? You're even more stubborn than I am. When that telegram came – you remember, the telegram where Dad said goodbye to Mum – you attacked me! You jumped on my chest like a… what do you call it?'

'Like a hellhound?'

'Exactly! You sat on me like a hellhound. Do you remember? In the basement of the house on Buyukada. You were about to strangle me, and Nanny Fati saved me.'

'I'm sorry, Cem. I was so angry.'

When he waved his hand, he looked exactly like Mum. 'Forget it! But I'm curious – what persuaded that furious daughter to come all the way over here?'

I looked over at the door and smiled.

'It's a long story, Cem. Let's go to the kitchen. I'll make you some tea and fill you in while you're drinking it.'

Just as we were leaving the room, my phone rang. Motioning for Cem to go on to the kitchen, I returned to the room, to Dad's bedside. Sinan was calling. Finally!

'Melike?'

'My father died this morning, Sinan.'

A long silence. My eyes filled with tears. I sniffled.

'Sinan?'

'I'm so sorry, darling. I don't know what to say. I thought he still had some more time.'

In the background there was again the clatter of plates and dishes. I bit my lip.

'What would you like me to do now? Shall I come over there?'

I pressed the phone to my ear and closed my eyes. A tear rolled down my cheek. I'd rather you didn't have to ask that, Sinan. I'd rather you just jumped on the first plane and came... But then I remembered the visa business. And there was Petro, too.

'Don't come, Sinan, dear. You can only get a visa in Greece, and to get into Greece you need a Schengen visa, and you'd have to wait in Athens for the visa for Cyprus. By the time you've done all that, I'll be back home. Cem came.'

'Cem, eh? Your brother Cem? From Australia?'

'Yeah. He just arrived. It was a thirty-hour flight.'

Silence. Sinan was probably thinking that if Cem had travelled all that way, he should too. I didn't say anything.

'I had a surprise for you, Melike, but given the circumstances...'

'What surprise?'

'Do you remember Shefik's restaurant in Istanbul? The one in Nisantasi, where he wanted to sell my pickles? I took him a few jars of the cabbage and beetroots as testers.'

'Yeah...'

With the phone to my ear, I walked over to Dad's bedside, to the chair I'd sat in that first day, and reached out to straighten the edge of the blue blanket. Up close, I could detect a slight odour. How quickly flesh decayed, especially in that heat. Although we'd closed all the windows and shutters, we couldn't keep the heat out. Just last night he'd been lying there asleep, alive. Now he was dead. As soon as life left the body, it began to rot, like meat left in a fridge after the plug had been pulled out. A lifeless body was not a person any more. It was a thing. No, a corpse. A flat line. That was all. Where are you, Dad? Where have you gone? Familiar questions that had troubled me all my life. I bit my lip to keep from crying.

Sinan was still talking in my ear.

'Everything developed so quickly after you left – actually,

I was considering it as a project while you were here, but I didn't have the chance to tell you about it. First there was your documentary job, then your father, then this trip...'

'What do you mean, Sinan? What project?'

'I've taken over Shefik's restaurant, darling.'

'What?'

He'd forgotten me and was speaking excitedly. 'He doesn't want to bother with it any more. He's got it into his head that he'll spend the winters on Buyukada. A while ago, when we were talking, I threw out some ideas as to how he could improve the menu, be more creative and so on. I told him about what they'd done in similar restaurants that you and I have been to in New York and London. Then – I don't know how the subject came up – he said, "My friend, you're so enthusiastic and full of ideas, why don't I turn it over to you?" After that, everything just took off so fast. These last couple of days, I've been running around like crazy. We've had to recruit a whole new team of staff; the chefs were too old-fashioned, but I found a good replacement – he studied in Berlin and everything – and now I'm training the staff for him. I'll be in the kitchen too, of course. Maybe I'll be a sous-chef, ha, ha.'

He came to an abrupt stop.

'Oh, my God, Melike, listen to me! Please forgive me, darling. This new project has just been so all-consuming that...'

'... that you forgot about me.'

'No, that's absurd. I mean...'

'It's not important, Sinan. It's perfectly natural that you forgot about me. I've often forgotten about you when I've been caught up in something. Don't feel guilty. When I get back, we'll sit down and talk. Anyway... anyway, there are other things. I mean, things we should talk about.'

I got up from the chair, opened the door, and glanced

out into the corridor. In the kitchen, Petro and Eleni were chatting with Cem in low voices. The smell of roasting pine nuts wafted over. Eleni was cooking *koliva*, a kind of semolina dessert with cinnamon and cloves that it was traditional to serve to neighbours following a death in the family. Earlier, Petro had gone out with the doctor to organize a group of old village women to come to the house to lament at Dad's bedside. They would be arriving soon, and other villagers would follow. Eleni had agreed to the cremation of Dad's body only if this very old lamentation tradition was upheld. Under no circumstances would the church allow Dad's funeral service to be held under its roof. The old women would sit wailing beside Dad until evening, so that his soul could find peace.

'Okay, Melike, my dear, my sultana. Just forget about all that now. Are you sure you don't want me to come? I can leave everything, get on a plane. Melike?'

Someone was shouting behind him and there was a clattering of forks, plates and frying pans. Sinan was meant to be overseeing the staff he was training.

'That's fine, Sinan, you don't need to come, thank you. I'll call you again. I have to hang up now.'

'May his soul rest in peace. Are you going to call your mother or should I tell her?'

'I'll call her now.'

'Please forgive me, darling. I haven't been as involved as much as I should have been. I'll call you this evening when things are quiet. Okay? I love you very much. Don't ever forget that.'

I paused, contemplating the weight of his words. 'I won't forget, Sinan.'

He had already hung up.

35

Dad's Ashes

We divided Dad's ashes in half.

Petro and Eleni took one half.

Petro wanted to scatter the ashes on the Green Line that divided Cyprus into two separate parts. Taking Eleni and Cem, the four of us went to Nicosia, the divided capital. We walked around, searching in vain for a place among the barbed wire, the oil-drum barricades, the ruins of former shops, the soldiers on guard duty. The buffer zone between the two sides, with trees lifting their branches towards the sky and dilapidated buildings untouched by human hands for thirty years, kept the two sides apart. Yes, a border crossing had been opened the previous spring, and if Petro and Eleni had wanted to, they could have stood in the middle of that crossing and poured his ashes into the buffer zone. But, quite rightly, they didn't want to say farewell to my father under the gaze of dozens of police and rifle-toting soldiers.

After walking for hours among war-weary buildings on the dark-faced streets, we were about to give up, when a Catholic church appeared in front of us, squeezed into a corner where the buffer zone thins out into a barbed wire border. Its front door was in the southern – Greek – part of Nicosia, and its back door (which, after the war and the hasty drawing of the border, had been officially sealed shut) was in the north, in the Turkish part. Fortunately for us, the priest was either an understanding man, or he simply felt sorry for the sad, strange people waiting at his door with an urn in their hands. He gave us permission to climb the bell tower.

From the church bell tower, the two parts of the island looked like two brothers who had turned their backs on each other. In the buffer zone around the tower were the abandoned buildings of the walled Old City, half of them within the north, half of them in the south, the sun playing on the shattered glass of the derelict, ownerless properties. Here, the capital city was still mourning its old loss.

'If you carry on down that road for half an hour, you'll come to our old village,' said Eleni, gesturing towards the Kyrenia Mountains in the northern part of the island. Cem put his hand on her shoulder. He had warmed to his stepmother immediately, and he sensed the significance this view held for her. Paradise lost. When the prospect of the two Cypruses being reunited had come up, Petro and Alex had rejoiced, and apparently Dad had been hopeful, but Eleni didn't much care about the opening of the border gates between the Turkish and Greek parts of the island. 'It's not even a real border,' she said. The possibility of the two peoples coming together again did not excite her. The dead were gone, and even if she were able to get back to her village, she could not change what had happened there.

I looked over at Petro. In the light of the setting sun, his eyes were the colour of honey, his lips dark pink. Our eyes met. The copper urn that Aunt Zeyno had sent from Germany was shining brightly. It looked like a tiny samovar, or Aladdin's magic lamp. It was as if Dad might come swaying out of its narrow mouth if we rubbed its copper surface hard enough. Maybe it was wrong to have divided the ashes. If he came back, how would he come? In parts – body, mind and soul? Which part would I want to be mine? I stopped myself. You're being ridiculous, Melike!

Petro closed his eyes. His lips appeared to be moving in prayer. He wouldn't have questions like mine in his head. He believed in the eternal soul, and it was Dad's soul he was saying goodbye to. That day we met in the Bloody Church, he'd unselfconsciously kissed the icon of the Virgin Mary and crossed himself in the presence of Christ. Now he was praying for my father's soul.

Father, Son and Holy Spirit.

I leant my arm against his. His hair was tousled over his forehead and temples. He looked like a little boy who'd come home for supper at the end of a summer's day spent on the beach in the sun, sea and salt. Our child would be like that – a child of the wind, of the sea, of salt. An island baby. It was impossible at the top of a church bell tower in the middle of Nicosia to smell fishing nets thrown off a jetty, but the scent of seaweed came to my nose. I glanced sideways at Cem. His delicate face was turned towards the sky and he too was sniffing the air. Now that he was older, the sharp, pronounced chin and long, thin nose made him look so much like Mum.

Petro finished his farewell prayer, opened the urn and raised it in the air. As if he were offering a libation to the gods, he stood motionless for a time. In the distance, the bell of a different church struck five times. I held my breath. He did too. Then he turned the urn upside down and emptied the ashes from the tower. Eleni closed her eyes. Cem put his arm around her shoulders. My father's last remains, a handful of grey ashes, drifted down onto the city like snow, falling to the ground and mixing with the earth on both sides of the line that had torn people from their homes, their villages, their neighbours.

The sun disappeared behind the mountains. The copper urn, which had shone so brightly in Petro's hand just a short while before, had now become a lifeless metal container. I turned to Petro. Tears glinted like diamonds in his eyes. We hugged each other, not like man and woman but like a father's two children. I rested my head on his broad chest. Could the ear detect pain in the beating of a heart? That evening, in a city divided by barbed wire, I discovered for the first time that you could feel in the centre of your own heart the ache of another heart.

Just as we were leaving Nicosia, Eleni held my hand.

'I want to tell you something, Melike. The real grave of Damianos and Kosmas is in Istanbul. According to legend, there is a monastery beside the ancient city walls. I forget the name of the gate. Your Dad, he read about it and found it – it was called something like Porta Kaligaria. When they died, they were buried there. Maybe you can bury his ashes at that place.'

Of course I knew that the old name of Egrikapi was Porta Kaligaria, and I wasn't at all surprised at this coincidence. I had been keeping this knowledge in my soul anyway. But now all the squares had been filled, the puzzle of my life had been solved, and the miraculous layers of time were spread out in the open. The feelings I'd experienced at Safinaz's grave, where that strange ray of magical light had shown me the way, had resurfaced within me. I was part of a gigantic consciousness, a perfect particle in a magnificent universe.

Eleni thought my pensiveness was caused by my sadness.

'Next time you come over, you can fly direct from Turkey to the northern part, and Petro can cross the border here in Nicosia, and you can meet each other in Safinaz's village. Then you can visit the grave of your uncle Damianos. Maybe you can save a pinch of the ashes to leave there too?'

Petro, who was driving the jeep, caught my eye and we smiled at each other. Even if that never happened, we could hold it as a dream in our hearts. Didn't the most beautiful romances always leave something to chance?

Cem had left Dad's ashes with me. For weeks I was unable to decide what to do with them. I wrapped the copper urn in a silk scarf and began carrying it around in my handbag. I thought about doing as Eleni had suggested and scattering the ashes in the ancient cemetery at the edge of Egrikapi. There was apparently some data concerning a monastery near Egrikapi that was dedicated to Kosmas and Damianos – the healing twins – and it would be nice to have a grave that I could visit when I missed him. Also, I wasn't completely on board with him being dispersed in the air or in water rather than into the earth. But then I gave up on that idea – Dad had expressly said he didn't want to go under the earth.

With that thought in mind, I decided to scatter the ashes into the firmament in the neighbourhood where Dad had spent his childhood. I would do so from the tower of the Red School. This time, rather than surreptitiously jumping over the wall, I made a polite request to the principal. When she heard that Safinaz had been an art teacher at the school for many years, she relented. On that day, following behind the school caretaker, I climbed up to the tower, which was being used as the physics laboratory. With its wooden desks, high ceiling, nineteenth-century instruments, models of celestial bodies and geometric figures, it was still as magical a place as I remembered from my childhood. True, the school caretaker was not Pavli, but, like Pavli, he was a little fellow with deep-set eyes.

I went across to the window that looked out over the Golden Horn. The places where all the memories I had accumulated during the short time Dad and I had lived together in Istanbul lay at my feet. Directly below were the stone steps we had climbed hand in hand every Saturday, the church, the house where Safinaz had lived accompanied by the ticking of clocks. Opposite was the Galata Tower and our apartment with its bright kitchen where we had eaten family breakfasts. There could be no better place than this to say farewell to Dad. But still I questioned myself. Hoping the answer would come to me, I opened the lid of the copper urn. I smelled the ashes settled in the bottom. It wasn't a smell that reminded me of Dad, and besides, my share of the ashes had left me with just a handful at the bottom of the urn. Dad's body. His mind. Or his soul. I closed the lid. It wasn't right. Putting the magic lamp back into my handbag, I followed the caretaker down the steps and exited onto Red Square.

I wandered those streets for several more weeks. Inside me, a mixture of happiness, sadness and longing was simmering. I held tight to those feelings, just as I held tight to the copper urn that I carried around in my bag. The mixture settled inside me like red-hot magma; it woke with me in the mornings, disappeared for hours while I was distracted by daily routines, then spread through me the moment I was alone. But some things had changed. Now, instead of avoiding it, I owned this feeling inside me. I didn't know exactly who it was I was longing for, and I wasn't trying to find out. Nor did

I revert to the strategies I used to employ to divert me from that yearning. Instead of summoning old lovers for a brief afternoon fling, I walked the streets alone, trying to find a suitable place for Dad's ashes.

The fire in my heart was mine. No, it was not mine; it was a legacy handed down to me from Safinaz, from Orhan, from Damianos. Maybe it was an ember from our intermingled chemistry and it was now me who must carry it. And I wouldn't just carry it. It would become a flame that I would pass on like the Olympic torch. Now I understood why Dad had called me and not Cem to his side. Only a woman, a female voice, female words, could fill the familiar burning emptiness where silence sheltered. Stories were female. I would mourn past losses that had remained unmourned; I would become the voice of silent souls. Whenever these thoughts came into my head, I would take out of my handbag the photograph of Cem's daughter Sofia. As I looked at the black curls surrounding her dark eyes, I was surprised at how impatient I was to meet her.

Sinan was very busy. The restaurant was a huge success. Newspapers and magazines were following him around. I had no idea that so many people in Istanbul were interested in healthy, organic food. Every evening, jostling crowds gathered outside the restaurant, with queues of people keen to try dishes made from grains and vegetables they'd never heard of before. Food critics praised Chef Sinan to the skies. Sinan tried to put the record straight in every interview, telling them that he was simply the sous-chef, but none of them were interested in kitchen hierarchy; to them, Sinan was a gourmet genius. A German firm was about to sign a contract for his homemade pickles.

When I returned from Cyprus and told him I thought it would be best if we lived separately for a while, his handsome face winced with pain. For the first time in the fifteen years of our marriage, he asked, 'Is there someone else?' Confronted by the silence that followed his question, his beautiful eyes filled with tears. That night, he left our house in Galata and moved into a flat of Shefik's in Nisantasi. He never called after that – he was waiting for me to call him.

I had left Petro in Nicosia at the newly opened Ledra Palace Hotel, which stood right at the border gate, on the south side. Cem and I had taken a plane from the Turkish side of Nicosia and returned to Turkey. Petro was going to stay with his mother a while longer. When we parted, he'd kissed the inside of my left wrist, and the place he had touched with his cherry-pink lips still burnt. I didn't call him either. I did nothing except wander the seven hills of Istanbul with my father's ashes in my handbag.

It was on one of those days that I entered my fortieth year. Mum called and invited me to dinner that evening. They were still on Buyukada and it was Cem's last night in Turkey. Without a second thought, I went down to Sirkeci and jumped on a ferry to the island. In Sinan's absence, Mina and Mum had prepared a modest meal of pasta with mushroom sauce, salad and, for dessert, lemon ice cream bought from the ice cream truck in front of the club. Cem and I heated up potato puffs I'd bought from the boat landing and poured melted butter over them.

My mother had found new life with Cem's visit. She was all dressed up and was wearing a sapphire necklace and earrings that I hadn't seen on her since my childhood. She looked very pretty. The whole evening she told stories that I hadn't heard before about her university years, about Dad and Aunt Zeyno. When she acted out the story of Dad putting a candle on the back of Ugur the tortoise and letting him loose in his mother's garden, so that Safinaz, thinking that djinns had come for her, roused the whole neighbourhood, Cem and I laughed so hard that tears rolled down our cheeks; we had to hold onto each other so we didn't fall off our chairs. Maybe the story wasn't all that funny; maybe if we'd heard the story at a different time, in a different place, we wouldn't have laughed at all. But that night, at the dinner table out on the balcony, when Mum presented us with things from the past that we had forgotten or had never even known, Dad's death, as well as the thirty years of his absence, were forgotten.

Which meant we could also mourn like that, by laughing until tears came to our eyes; by a mother, a big brother and a little sister holding onto each other like carousing youngsters trying to stay upright as they walked; by seating the deceased in an empty chair, even if he was in a copper urn, and laughing with him.

By forgiving.

After our meal, Cem, Mina, Mum and I went down into the mansion's jasmine-scented garden to drink cherry liqueur. The tortoise Ugur, who had once frightened Safinaz with the candle on his back, came rustling through the grass and settled himself by Mum's feet like a faithful dog. In the light of the candles in the candleholders Cem had stuck into the ground, I thought I had never seen my mother so beautiful. The wrinkles on her skin were erased and her deep blue eyes shone like the sapphires on her necklace. Our reuniting had been good for her. She was happy. Naturally, it was she who told me where I should take Dad's ashes.

36

Farewell

As the boat approached the shore, I realized with surprise that the village hadn't changed at all in thirty years.

'It's a protected area. You can't even hammer in a nail,' explained the captain, Emre. From the pride in his voice you could tell he was a native of the village. He was a young boy. With strong shoulders bulging out of his black vest, suntanned arms and an arched nose, he reminded me of Petro. I chatted idly with him, though that wasn't something I would usually do.

'You know, I used to live in this village.'

'When was that then, big sister?'

With some expert manoeuvring, he motored around the ancient sunken tomb and approached the dock. I decided not to make an issue of the 'big sister' appellation. He could have called me 'auntie', which would have better suited my age.

'Long before your time. There wasn't any electricity here then. We lived here for three years, winter and summer.'

Now I'd got his attention. He tilted his cap and looked me over.

'Do you have a place to stay, sister? I can take you to our

guesthouse. My granddad used to be the *mukhtar* of this village.'

Hearing that, I regretted having opened my mouth. Who knew what gossip had been spread about us after we left? If the postman and the *mukhtar* knew that Gulbahar had run off with Teacher Ibrahim, then the whole village would have known that too. What happened later would have been irrelevant, for the news of Mr Ibrahim's death wouldn't have reached there. In village lore, it would be all about that city woman, Gulbahar, taking up with the communist teacher, and Orhan as the cuckolded fool of a husband.

'No need to trouble yourself, Captain Emre. I'll walk around and find somewhere.'

'You won't find anywhere like our guesthouse, sister. And anyway, there are only three places to stay, and they're all full at the moment. It's high season. But since you're one of us, my ma will make space for you.'

I sighed as I got out of the boat. I would pay the price for having talked too much. My nostrils filled with the smell of seaweed. At the end of the dock a fisherman was repairing his nets. A cigarette between his lips, his dark hands skilled, his movements calm and steady – a square that wasn't bound by time. The fisherman's eyes caught mine and he gave a slight nod. Was it Ismail? No, Ismail would be over seventy by now. His son? Could a man with such a lived-in face be the same age as me? Why not? I was forty now. Middle-aged.

Emre was waiting for me at the place where the *mukhtar*'s cabin used to be. I walked slowly over to him. We crossed a stone threshold and entered a shaded courtyard. At the back, under a fig tree, three women were cooking pancakes.

'Ma, this sister wants a room. She used to live here, a long time ago. When was it, sister?'

I waved my hand as if to say 'forget it'. The woman who was filling the pancakes came over, wiping her palms on her apron. She was pink-cheeked and chubby, and as I looked closely, I recognized her. It was Fatosh, the middle daughter of Naciye and the *mukhtar*.

'Welcome. Come on in.'

I breathed a sigh of relief. She hadn't recognized me. Did I think we were legendary or something? Why should anyone remember us? We'd been there for three years, at a time when there was just the one television – which ran off the village generator – and just one telephone line. Then we left. Who was to say how many people had come after us, what had gone on?

'Captain Emre said you might have an empty room.'

Fatosh glanced crossly at her son. She'd clearly been expecting him to bring a foreign tourist. Emre grabbed my bag and we went in. Fatosh opened the door of a room on the top floor overlooking the sea. It smelled clean and fresh. The floor had just been scrubbed with soap, the sheets washed with pine resin. The image of Mum and Mina in our garden, treading clothes with their bare feet in a huge blue basin, came into my head They would pull their baggy trousers up to their knees and, laughing, would stamp on Dad's shirts, pine-resin soap splashing up their legs. How old would Mum have been then? Thirty at most. A child!

'You've been to our village before, so my boy says.'

I turned and looked at Fatosh. We'd been in the same class at school, and now she was a plump, pink-cheeked village woman. She never managed to get past Year 6, and I'd been surprised that she couldn't even read the Year 2 books.

'Yes, I came a few years ago to do some archaeological research.'

When Fatosh smiled, she looked like her childhood self. 'Oh, yeah. We have a sunken city near here and tourists come to see it. My big brother has a boat, the first motorboat in the village. He's made the bottom all glass now. You can hire it for the day, go out and see it.'

When I heard that, I felt like laughing. The *mukhtar*'s sons and their tourist motorboat. How Dad had made fun of it! *The mukhtar's tourists come from Castellorizo, Melike. Those trips are money-makers all right, and they do transport Johnnies and Jims, it's true, but they're not the sort of tourists you're familiar with. This lot make the trip in strongboxes.* Mum was right. There could be no better place than the village to say farewell to Dad. First I had to dig through my memories and lay Dad there, for a person was not buried in the earth but in the memory. I hugged my handbag. The copper urn was warm. I imagined Dad purring with pleasure, like a cat, inside Aladdin's magic lamp.

After Fatosh left the room, I walked over to the window and looked out at the sea. Facing the village, the uninhabited island sat in the middle of sea like a silent green whale. The village bay was full of boats bringing day-trippers in. Red-faced Europeans were sitting at the long tables at the only restaurant on the shore, eating fish and drinking beer. As far as I could tell, the restaurant was the one thing that had changed in the village, along with the houses that had been turned into guesthouses, like Fatosh's, of course. I wondered what I would see if I walked up to our house.

I went into the bathroom, washed my face and changed my clothes. Emptying out my handbag, I unwrapped the blue silk scarf, took the copper urn in my arms and left the room. Just as I was about to step into the courtyard, I got a cold shiver down my spine, as if someone had blown on the nape of my neck. I stopped in the doorway and turned around. An old woman was sitting cross-legged on a white settee in a dim corner, smoking a cigarette. Naciye! Mum's cigarette friend. They used to smoke black-market Marlboros from Castellorizo together. How she had aged; she looked a hundred years old. But it was Naciye, the *muhtar*'s wife all right. I could tell by the way she sat, the look in her eye, something. The effect some people had on us never changed. I felt as if a fish bone had got stuck in my throat.

Squinting her eyes, which were lost in the middle of her wrinkled face, Naciye looked at me and mumbled something under her breath. I didn't know what to do. Anxiously, I took a step towards the courtyard. At the marble threshold, I stumbled. She called out behind me.

'Where you running away to, girl? How's your ma? Is she good?'

I stepped backwards into the guesthouse and went over to the settee. Naciye stuck her hand out through the smoke. I kissed it and touched it to my forehead.

'She's fine, thank you. She sends her greetings.'

She nodded. She looked like an old witch. I began to cringe with embarrassment in front of her.

'What did ya come for?'

Her eyes were fixed on the urn under my arm.

'Nothing. Just to relax a bit.'

'Your husband?'

'In Istanbul.'

Why was I squirming in the presence of this village woman, like a schoolchild called upon to recite something?

'Children?'

'I have no children.'

A charged silence hung between us, like the blue smoke of Naciye's cigarette.

A woman who seals her womb of her own free will is the most dangerous creature in the universe.

'You need children. Make one.'

I swayed uncomfortably on the spot. What could I say to get me out of there right away?

'Your pa loved you very much.'

'I beg your pardon?'

'Your pa, I said, he loved you very much.'

I had perched on the edge of the settee, I realized later. Naciye took a huge puff of her cigarette. The television in front of her was on, the sound turned down low. She spoke without taking her eyes off the women's programme.

'Some days I went down to the landing to take my boys their lunch. All you children be there, playin' by that old tomb. Your pa, he would stand on the landing and look at you. When he saw me, he said, "Naciye, I love that child differently. I look at her and my heart expands." Then he held his heart like this, to show what he meant.'

The fishbone pierced my throat and I could not speak. I tried to cough. Naciye stubbed out her cigarette in the metal ashtray that lay between us. She was sitting inside a grey-blue cloud, like a ghost.

'You can start from there, see.'

She turned towards me. Her eyes glittered in her face, which had forgotten how to smile.

'What?'

She didn't answer. Taking another packet from the pocket of her baggy trousers, she lit a new cigarette. From inside the smoke she murmured, 'God is great.'

I left the guesthouse and took the path up to the castle.

A vein in my neck was throbbing. I held tight to the copper urn. Groups of camera-toting tourists in colourful shorts and hats were walking down the path, and their guide, a skinny woman, called out 'The castle's closed!' to me as I went by. I paid no attention. No one could stop me. I continued climbing the hill, full speed ahead. The houses were in better shape than I remembered, the trees taller, and the bougainvillea twined around our garden gate had spread out joyously, covering the whole wall as far as the path. I passed the red, pink and purple flowers at a run. I came to the tangerine orchards. The sun had gone down behind the castle and a sweet evening breeze had picked up. There were goosebumps on the sweaty nape of my neck. The guard at the ticket booth beside the entrance to the castle, another new addition, stood up when he saw me.

'Closed! Closed!'

It was Ali, one of the classmates that our teacher, Mr Ibrahim, had never been able to get to sit beside me. In Year 5, while the teacher was writing things on the blackboard, he used to sail paper aeroplanes. Now he was an elderly castle guard.

'I have a very quick job I need to do, Ali. Please let me go in.'

He looked doubtfully at my face. He didn't recognize me, but he stood aside as if enchanted. He must have thought I was the goddess of something.

I began to jump up the steps like a cricket. The hot smell of dry weeds rose from my feet to my nose. One morning at dawn I had climbed these steps barefoot, my child's feet bruised and sore. I had been afraid. Raising my head, I looked at the crooked steps extending before me.

Dad's smile under his black moustache came into my head.

My shrieks of joy when he threw me into the air in a monkey swing.

One more step.

The putt-putt fading away. The tinkle of goat bells. My sad grandma's white hands lighting a candle. My mother's dimple that appeared when she laughed.

Two more steps.

The wind had got stronger, heavy now with the scent of sage and thyme.

Down below, Ali was standing at the door of the castle, peering up at me.

Love is a door, Melike.

Barish's lips moving over my neck under Egrikapi. Sinan's grape-like eyes staring into my face. I ran up five steps. I was breathless, almost at the top. I didn't stop. Down below, the leaves in the tangerine orchard were rustling. Petro in front of the Bloody Church pulling me into a hug when I'd held out my hand for a shake. Thousand-year-old tombs under the sea. Orhan watching the children playing around the tomb. *I love that child differently. I look at her and my heart expands.*

Yes, this was the battlement. This was where Cem and I had hugged each other as we watched the boat that was taking Dad away disappear from sight.

Dad.

His body like a hazelnut shell under the blue cotton blanket.

Dad.

Inside a different castle gatehouse.

Dad.

My head on his lap, his hands in my hair, his fingers interlaced with my fingers.

By the time I reached the flagpole at the very top, my

cheeks were wet with tears. I turned my face towards the sea. My ears were filled with the flapping of cloth in the wind. The sea had turned navy blue, and shadowed scrub covered the uninhabited island like a dark green blanket. I opened the lid of the urn, raised it in the air. The light from the sun as it sank behind the castle struck the urn and sent pink rays shooting down my hands and arms to my shoulders. Down below, at the dock, Captain Emre was starting the engine for the last boat of the day.

Putt-putt.

It was here that you and I parted, Dad. Our farewell was incomplete.

In a single movement I flung the ashes into the air.

A soft grey cloud enveloped me for a moment. I closed my eyes.

Dad had loved me with all his heart!

I could begin from there.

By the time I opened my eyes, the wind had already whisked away the ashes. I closed the lid of the urn. A peace I had never known spread through me.

Captain Emre's boat had set out on the dark blue sea and was disappearing behind the uninhabited island.

I turned my left wrist over and kissed the inside.

There was another island somewhere beyond the blue, waiting for a reunion.

Glossary

agapi (mou)	*Gk*	(my) love
ayran	*Tur.*	savoury yogurt drink
Bey	*Tur.*	Mr
canim	*Tur.*	my dear
ela	*Gk*	come on
ellinikos	*Gk*	Turkish/Greek coffee
Hanim	*Tur.*	Mrs
hodja		spiritual teacher, muslim priest
kori mou	*Gk*	my daughter
merhaba	*Tur.*	hello
mou	*Gk*	my
mukhtar	*Tur.*	elected village chief
ohi	*Gk*	no
palikari	*Gk*	young man in his prime
Panagia	*Gk*	Mary, Mother of God
parapoly	*Gk*	very much
pasha	*Tur.*	title given to a high-ranking Turkish officer
raki	*Tur.*	sweetened alcoholic drink, often anise flavoured
se parakalo	*Gk*	please
tavli/tavla	*Tur./Gk*	Greek backgammon
telos pandon	*Gk*	never mind, anyway

Thee mou	*Gk*	my God
Turkos	*Gk*	Turkish man
Usta	*Tur.*	Master
vre	*Gk*	you
yavri mou	*Gk*	my child
yiayia	*Gk*	grandmother

About the Author

DEFNE SUMAN was born in Istanbul and grew up on Buyukada. She gained a master's in Sociology from the Bosphorus University, then worked as a teacher in Thailand and Laos, where she studied East Asian philosophy and mystic disciplines. She later continued her studies in Oregon, USA and now lives in Athens with her husband. Her English-language debut, *The Silence of Scheherazade*, was published by Head of Zeus in 2021, followed by *At the Breakfast Table* in 2022.

Find out more:
defnesuman.com
@defnesuman

About the Translator

BETSY GÖKSEL is an American teacher and translator who has lived in Turkey since the 1960s. Her translations include *The Hate Trap* by Haluk Sahin and *The Silence of Scheherazade* and *At the Breakfast Table* by Defne Suman, as well as several books on art and architecture for the Istanbul Municipality.